I0557836

ACCESS RESTRICTED

ACCESS RESTRICTED

BOOK 2 OF THE ACCESS SERIES

ALICE SEVERIN

OWN ROOM PUBLISHING

NEW YORK

Copyright © Alice Severin 2013

Cover photo copyright © Alice Severin

ISBN: 978-0-9882520-0-4

This novel is entirely a work of fiction.
The names, characters, places, and incidents portrayed in it are the work
of the author's imagination or used in a fictitious manner. Any resem-
blance to actual persons, living or dead, or events is purely coincidental.

To J with love

To S for listening

To S for being there

To A for sticking around

To RP for restoring faith

And to all the musicians who inspire us.

Chapter 1

The day before you fly transatlantic, the day before you leave a country, is always somewhat difficult. What to bring, what to leave behind. You begin thinking of who and what you will miss, and what would happen if you never came back. You realize you do feel at home, and you suddenly don't want to leave. Then there are those moments where you want to go right away, stop waiting and fearing and anticipating and just get the fuck on with it.

This wasn't just a holiday though. I was flying out to work. Lily Taylor, the rock writer. I wasn't at the point where the hotel reservation needed to be under a different name, but the printout I'd been given by the office did say VIP. Flying out to cover a concert that would kick off a tour. To do interviews for the possible documentary and book. And then there was Tristan—the reason that all this was happening. Tristan Hunter, the legend in his own time, as much for his inescapable talent as for the stories that followed him. The first band, the worldwide success, the corrosive break up. His disappearance, and now his return to the stage. He had played with some of the most respected names in the business, and in a few short years had written some songs that were already considered classics, reinventing a style that everyone tried to copy. Now the music business would be watching to see if he could stay at the top, or if he stumbled. And then there was the man himself. 6'2", dark hair, long legs, a rock legend in leather, with a stare that could make you want, hard, or make you back out of the room, nervously, sorry to have bothered him. Tristan in charge. Tristan organizing the first part of his tour. Tristan, the rock star, the enigma, the man I had been warned about and who I had tried to resist—with little success. The tall, darkly powerful presence who I had given myself over to, against my own better judgment. And now he held the key to my professional future. Too bad I was falling in love with him. Nothing professional about that.

I'd followed him and his music for years now. I'd met him, briefly, drunkenly, at an awards show. That moment had turned out to be the turning point in my career—the moment when blogging and turning up had paid off, and suddenly what I loved doing I could do full time. But the big adventure had started with me falling over on my face right in front of two of my musical heroes. Tristan had picked me up and looked at me, and I'd felt something—a force, some kind of power that swept right through, filling me with an energy that made everything seem possible.

The next time I'd met him, five years later, was different. I was sent to interview him. I was nervous, but I'd done this before. I was a professional. I was used to being up close and personal with the rock world and its big, egotistical stars. "Laughing, joking, drinking, smoking," just like the old Yardbirds song.

Except Tristan was different. He didn't just play with his power, he controlled it. And I wasn't prepared for the effect proximity to his complicated beauty had on me. I wasn't prepared for the look in his eyes, curious and gentle and hard all at once. I wasn't ready for the way his lips brushed my ear telling me it would all be all right. I tried to fight back but struggling only made it worse. And by the time he started playing his new music for me, all my guards were down. I'd like to think he wasn't really prepared for the effect I had on him either. There was something there. There must have been. Because Tristan and I met up, privately, a few days later, and the rest, as they say, is history.

And now here we were, trying to negotiate our way through our careers and nasty gossip, trying to figure out just how casual we wanted to keep all this. Initially, Tristan wanted us at a distance, possibly to protect us both. But apparently that was all changing. The text, that simple text he had sent me. We were going to know each other publicly. He was going to send a car for me at the airport, to meet me when I landed in London. My old hometown. My old stomping grounds, where everything of significance in my life had happened—except for this. What would it all mean? I had no idea. This was his big chance at a comeback. But this was also my lucky break for the big career path. I was going to interview the people from his past—people over there who had been instrumental in breaking his first band, Devised. People he'd been close to. People who knew his secrets. Except no one knew about me. I was still a dirty little secret, and likely to remain that way. It was probably for the best, I thought, thinking of the warnings my extremely powerful boss had given me.

The boss. Dave, David Fanning. The impeccably dressed, educated, slightly cold, very wealthy man, who could have been anything, but chose to be the editor and publisher of the most influential music magazine out there, *The Core*. He was the Anna Wintour of the music world—if he ran something, if he put you on the cover, you were made. That was it. You'd gotten the nod. And not only was I writing the article about the musician he now wanted the world to notice, he seemed to be taking notice of me as well. Our dinner together was tonight, and his words to me made it clear that he wasn't thinking of me solely as a writer. No one says they want to take you to dinner in that way because they think you'd make a great friend. I felt like a confused teenager. I had two invitations to the same party, and I was in danger of losing both. If I were smart, I'd follow the money. Too bad I'd never been that smart.

Still, I seemed to be clever enough to have said yes to dinner. And it would be a nice dinner. Expensive, elegant, cool. There wasn't that same spark between us, not like the insane burning I felt when I was anywhere near Tristan. Nowhere near. But curiosity could and would have to make up the difference, if it came to that. If. I tried to ignore the sudden twist in my stomach that came when I thought of Tristan pushing me out of his life. Don't predict the worst, I thought. I hated wanting something that much. I really hated it. All that desire left you vulnerable and easily damaged. And I wasn't sure I could take any more damage. In that at least, I suspected Tristan and I were more alike than either of us realized. But we were both trapped in our own game, our own way of viewing the world, and our own ways of coping with it. The risks of really opening the door were so high. Still, there was something there. He had searched me out, worried about me, taken the time to make sure his plans and mine coincided. I had a vision of him at that concert, steady on his long legs, standing on the stage, covered in smooth leather that seemed to move on him like a second skin, revealing more of what lay underneath in quick flashes, as his muscles flexed with the music. And then the reality of his bare skin, pale, hard, soft, shockingly real, as he stood over me...

I shoved that thought away, adding the slow burn I felt to the last hundred times I'd thought of him and what we had done together, and let the feeling melt through my body. I leaned on the dresser and closed my eyes. Too late now. All the images were rushing back at me. Tristan in the bath, dripping wet and hard, the veins in his body standing out from the heat of the water. Tristan standing over me, his big hands undoing his jeans slowly, pulling himself free, teasing my mouth with just the tip. His face, closed off and hard, when I ran from him. His arms wrapped around me, soothing me with little touches, whispering in my ear, how well I'd done, how sweet I was, little words that could mean nothing but that he filled with sound and tone, that voice wrapping around each syllable, his heartbeat strong against mine.

I shut my eyes. It seemed like a dream. It was a dream. Except there was the bruise just below my neck where he'd licked and teased me, running a path from breast to ear until I no longer recognized my voice. There was the number in my phone, under "control," of which I had none, clearly, where he was concerned. And there was the car, thoughtfully sent by Dave, my boss, the head of the *Core* empire, which was going to take me out to the airport tomorrow evening. The e-ticket was printed out and in my bag. Business class, JFK to London Heathrow. Seven, nearly eight hours in the sky, drinking champagne, keeping my cool, staring at the stars. Then, on the other side, another car, this one sent by Tristan.

And then the fun would begin.

Chapter 2

8:00 p.m. came around, much more quickly than usual, mostly because I wasn't counting the hours down. And at this point, I was exhausted, really exhausted. All the thinking, all the figuring out, the hours of intense sex. Yes, that might have had something to do with it. But I was trying to push all that to the back of my mind. Now I was looking forward to what could turn out to be a pleasant enough evening. Dave was an interesting person, obviously. I'd always known that. Still, I wondered what we'd talk about and if I was allowed to ask the boss questions. I laughed, as I screwed the top of the mascara back on, and appraised myself in the mirror. After last night, was there anything I wasn't allowed to do? Only the things he tells you not to do, a familiar voice echoed in my head.

I bent down and stretching out my hands on the floor, I felt the burn in my muscles and on my skin. One minute of memory, that's it. Then all business. Thinking about his instructions, his huge hands on me, his tongue playing with me...oh god. Ok. Enough. I ran my fingers through my hair, and rolled up to a standing position, feeling slightly dizzy. Even the smallest thought of him acted on me like a drug. I held on to the edge of the old pine dresser, and clung to the soft wood until the feeling passed. The rush faded away, leaving that ache that I knew I'd see mirrored in my eyes, if I bothered to look. I watched my chest rise and fall with my breathing and tried to slow it all down. Better. I was ready.

I pulled on my jacket, and grabbed my bag. I didn't leave Alice, my roommate, a note. I'd decided there was no point in leaving her with written evidence of what I was doing. In fact, this was a perfect opportunity to cover my tracks. I could always say I had been out with Dave, and I wouldn't be lying. Besides, when did it become any of her business? Alice had drifted to the periphery of my worried mind, especially now that I knew I was about to have a lot more people looking at what I was doing. Rumors, though. I wondered if Alice was out in the bars, adding me to Tristan's history. I really needed more information. It would be safer to know more of what was going on out there, before some slinky blond chick in London spelled it out for me, while I tried to hide my surprise, or worse, my jealousy. Dave alluding to the gossip around Tristan made me curious. Even if I was sure I'd regret knowing.

I walked downstairs, and waited outside. I couldn't sit still anyway. As I saw the town car turn the corner and make its way to the front of the building, it occurred to me that Dave didn't mind picking me up in front of my building. No hiding there. Of course, darling, I thought, it's unlikely you'd be rubbing yourself on him like a cat in the back of the limo, either. He didn't strike me as the type. Most guys didn't really like the kink. They said they did, but what they really wanted, it seemed to me, was someone who would make them believe they were up for anything, while actually having orgasms, faked were fine, on cue was what counted, and most importantly, providing eye candy, meals, and organization.

I remembered a conversation I had once with an old friend and part time lover, who claimed that no woman had ever faked it with him. I had laughed out loud, in the middle of the restaurant. I had been quite innocently insensitive—then. But I really couldn't believe he thought that. I had the proof, having just given an Oscar-winning performance the other night. He was distracted, I was tired, he was ready, I wasn't. Why rock the boat? I didn't reveal my secret either; I had just laughed. He had been annoyed at me the rest of the evening. Yeah, well reality's a bitch, isn't it, I'd said to him. Little had I realized. And I'd never understood, until now, how much it meant to be with someone who understood what was real. Who liked sex. Who saw through all the crap about how to act, how to be. Composing the touches, like music. Tearing down the walls.

As I climbed into the car, I found it blissfully empty. I didn't have to make too many awkward comparisons in my head, between Tristan leaning back, hooded eyes and long legs, and Dave, who would be dressed impeccably, if a bit preppy, looking big, warm and comforting. I said hello to the driver, who started heading downtown. Of course. Did anything happen uptown anymore? I hadn't even asked where we were going. I sat back against the seats, cracked the window for a bit of fresh air, and closed my eyes. I still felt a bit disoriented. I had made myself eat some toast when I got home from the meeting. Sorting out London, and my place in it. Did we just meet this morning? Incredible. But once away from the adrenaline, I'd thought I was going to faint. And I was still slightly lightheaded from not eating, the tension. Things were speeding up, so quickly. Racing against time and logic. I opened my eyes at the red light, and looked out the window. 8:00 p.m. Was Tristan on the plane? Was he thinking of me? I closed my eyes again. I didn't want this. I'd sent a one word reply to his text that told me he'd send a car to meet me in London, deciding on "yes" again. "Yes" had worked before, all too well. And I thought it seemed cautiously hopeful. Cautious was all I wanted to be, even if it was too late for that. But I couldn't let go of the hope, stupid as it seemed.

I checked my lipstick and hair as the car slowed down. We turned down East Fifth Street, and stopped in front of the plain storefront, name printed in modern font down the side of the door, like a book. Jewel Bako. Well, it wasn't new, but it was supposed to be good. I wondered what happened to the other place. This one was a see and be seen night out, with excellent food. I reminded myself to be grateful. This was a perk, not a punishment.

I got out, thanked the driver, and walked towards the door. Thresholds. I presumed Dave would be waiting inside, and I gave his name to the hostess, who immediately became much more welcoming. She led me through the tunnel-like restaurant. The walls were covered in a kind of bleached bamboo, like a glowing cave, and the whole thing made me slightly claustrophobic. I thought of airplane fuselages, and seats, and people taking off, and dark eyes looking out on to darkening skies. I brushed the image aside in favor of a smile and the thought of hot sake awaiting me. That cheered me up somewhat. The restaurant was already filled with diners, mostly expensively dressed couples, and the noise level was loud, but toned down, unlike some of the New York restaurants I'd been in, where the volume seemed in proportion to the buzz they were trying to create. I really didn't like places like that.

I was pleasantly surprised to see Dave sitting at the sushi bar, chatting to the chef, and a flask of hot sake in front of him. Excellent. No angst, just conversation. Some drinks. Great food. An early night.

The hostess led me right to the chair, and smiled and bowed to Dave. He slipped her a tip, and she bowed again, and pulled out my chair. He leapt up, and took over, but not before kissing me on each cheek. I closed my eyes, then opened them again quickly, just in time to see his perfectly trimmed short sideburns and immaculately shaved and moisturized skin up close. He was the visual definition of a high powered media exec. The leather jacket, buttery and expensive. Probably Burberry. The perfectly fitted jeans, fashionable without being sexy. The bespoke shirt. The hint of woody and exotic scent. If they distilled money, that's what he smelled like. A leather wallet and new bills. No want. No emptiness. I kissed the air next to him. When did we all become so Parisian?

"Lily, so glad you could make it. Here, let me take your coat." And he swept it off my shoulders, and handed it to a server who had miraculously appeared out of nowhere. "Would you like some sake?"

"Yes, please, Dave. Thank you for inviting me." I sank down into the chair, and watched him pour out a small cup for me, and refill his own. Ah, so it was going to be like that, was it? I looked into his eyes for a moment. Game on.

"No, pleasure. I'm glad this has given us the opportunity to get to know each other better." He smiled, and he raised his cup. "To our mutual success." He winked at me, and drank off half of it. I buried my nose in the cup and breathed in. Ah, sweet oblivion. I kept myself from downing it in one go, and tried to be ladylike about it.

"I've ordered the Omakase dinner for us. Is there anything you don't particularly like, so I can inform the chef?" He looked concerned again. Could he really be trying to impress me? Yes, and doing a good job of it—mostly by not insulting my intelligence by asking if I knew what it meant.

"No, I do like most things." I paused and thought. Demands are good. "Actually, now that you mention it," I tried to sound as though I had just remembered, "I'm not a big fan of sea urchin, sadly. I've tried to like it, but it just doesn't do it for me." I smiled, hoping for a mix of apologetic and imperious.

"Of course." He turned to the chef, who was instantly there, attentive. He spoke a few words in Japanese, and nodded at me. I nodded back, impressed in spite of myself. Just because it was a music magazine he headed up, didn't mean he wasn't a CEO in every sense of the word. I tried to remember what I knew about him. Harvard, wasn't it? Rhodes Scholar? Peace Corps stint? Some heroic moment, followed by a year following the Dead. Writing. Management. Meteoric rise due to obvious talent, background and his adept handling of situations.

And now he was here in front of me. Trying to impress me.

I drank some more sake, and he refilled my cup. He turned his upper body towards me, and I pulled my gaze away from the beautiful fabric of his very light pink shirt, the Italian collar open, revealing a strong neck, and back to his eyes. He had a kindly expression on his face, and I could tell he was trying to put me at ease. He took another sip of sake, and smiled again.

"This is a great place—their food is just fantastic. I thought you'd like it here better—more suited to your tastes."

I wondered what he meant. "It's very lovely. I've heard very good things about it." Damn, now I'd shown I hadn't been here before. Well, my life hadn't taken the same path his had, even if they had started out in similar places. I took another sip. Time to go on the offensive. But he was speaking again.

"Of course I know about your background, your education, experience. Like me, your entry into writing about music might seem unexpected to some. But I think I understand it." He looked thoughtful. "The usual paths set out for us don't always provide a challenge, do they? Yet we still feel compelled to succeed, even while craving experience that throws us in at the deep end." He refilled our cups, and nodded to the server to bring another flask. He spoke slowly and quietly, as though we were discussing some spiritual quest. I stared at him. Yes, it was true, but did he realize how much of what he was saying applied to my more recent and secret activities? Still, I found myself drawn to what he was saying.

"Yes, I think that's accurate." I tried to find my voice and pull myself away from my other thoughts. "Were you groomed to be in finance? Or the Foreign Service?"

"Very close. Politics, actually. My older brother managed it; he's the state senator for Duchess County." Now it was my turn to look surprised. "Well, the two worlds don't always go together, although I've helped supply some bands to perform at fundraisers." He looked at me. "The rest of it—the usual rock and roll lifestyle issues—he doesn't ask, and I don't tell. Not that I really get involved. But I see and hear a lot, as you might imagine."

"That's why you warned me about Tristan."

He shrugged his shoulders. "Not so much a warning, as perhaps a very strange way of telling you I am looking out for your wellbeing." He looked at me, settled and calm. "We come from a world of certain standards. One, not everyone shares them. And two, some people are so eager to get away from those standards, break the taboos, find the chaos. 'Mon innocence me ferait pleurer.' My innocence would make me cry—it's..."

"Rimbaud," I finished for him.

He nodded, smiling. "Just so, just so."

I felt torn. I liked him. In fact, he was everything I had been brought up to like, in many ways. Intelligence, stability, understanding. Money. Ambition. And was he kind? What were his motives?

I felt restless before him, impulsive. No. Slowly. Carefully. I pushed down my impulse to demand what he knew, about everything. "Please don't think I don't appreciate your efforts on my behalf." I tried to soften my features. "I do. It's just that I'm, well, a little confused." I stopped, and then stopped myself from drinking more before I spoke. "I think we both know James, Tristan's manager, is not to be trusted. But Tristan?" I tried to think of something that would make me sound indifferent. "He seems...typical. Driven. Tortured. Un peu égoïste." I grinned. Maybe the French would get him.

His eyes lit up. "Mais oui, chérie, comme ils les sont tous. Après moi, le déluge. Mais moi aussi, peut-être je suis un peu comme ça?" He winked at me again. Oh, it did sound both better and so much more obvious in French. "*Of course, my dear, they are all like that. No one else matters. But maybe I'm a little like that as well?*"

Maybe he was a little like them. Certainly he had an ego. He spoke French beautifully. Of course he did. I could get used to this, expensive meals, expensive clothes, and discussing French poets. Yes. Luckily, at that moment, the first fresh morsels of sushi were placed in front of us, the small grey and white shrimp that the chef had just plucked from the tank behind him and had quickly filleted and placed over the shining white sculptural piece of rice covered with bright green wasabi. We each picked up a piece, and with a glance, bit down at the same time. It was divine, and the strange energy that you could feel on your tongue from eating something practically still alive was oddly erotic. Cheating death somehow. It tasted of brine, the blood of the earth. I closed my eyes for a moment. It felt strangely healing.

I opened my eyes to find him looking at me, his pupils dark, his face normal in contrast. He said nothing. I looked back at him. Silence was power. I wasn't going to break the moment, but let him feel what he was feeling. Clearly.

He returned to himself a moment later, with studied poise. These people never lost control. Or did they? I wondered what it would be like to see him, losing it. Would he resent me? I recalled the quote I had once heard a society girl in London mutter over her champagne, sitting at the next table to me, at Prince Charles' favorite wine bar, if such a thing could be believed. Certainly it had been filled with the braying long range voices of London's favored classes. And what had she said? "Sex is a great leveler."

I wondered what he would say if I repeated it. I wondered why I was wrestling with the urge to shock him out of his cultivated demeanor.

His voice was calm and soothing, and I felt guilty for my

thoughts. "It's delicious, isn't it? Their food is so...I don't know. Healing."

Startled, I exchanged a look with him. "I was just thinking that. How strange."

"I told you, I think we have a lot in common. Here, let me pour you some more sake, and tell you about my ideas for the tour." He looked around, and within moments, our plates were whisked away, and the server was pouring freshly warmed sake into our cups.

"That sounds good." I wanted to trust him. I felt like I was going to need an ally in the weeks to come. I was entering potentially dangerous territory. Maybe it wasn't such a bad idea after all, Tristan and I not knowing each other. I was beginning to see Tristan's stance as self-preservation. Now that I had more to lose, it made more sense.

Our next course had arrived, and over delicate nibbles of sashimi and ginger, I listened as he outlined his plans. He knew that James intended to embarrass Tristan in some way, but he wasn't sure why. He looked at me quizzically as he said it, but I tried to involve myself in dipping some black cod into the bowl of seasoned miso broth to avoid looking at him. When I was certain my face was calm, I took a bite, and turned towards him again.

"No, it seems odd." Offense. "I think he feels protective of him, in some way. And perhaps he feels I might be a danger, although I can't think why. Perhaps it's all journalists he doesn't trust."

"Maybe." He watched the chef for a minute. "I want all interviews to be vetted through me first. Prevention being better than cure, as they say. I think he..." Dave stopped and wiped his mouth with his napkin, delicately. "Perhaps you will uncover his motives. But keep your eyes open. A bit of a detective game for you."

I nodded. What did he know? I tried to pretend I wasn't concerned. We set up the meet with the Australian band with the girl singer. "Flash in the pan, but the latest eye candy for this week." He stopped and considered something. "No, she's not important enough, otherwise I'd suggest taking her to the after party for Tristan's concert. But she doesn't belong there, however much it might add to your story, watching him and the girls."

The girls. God, there was that phrase again. "The girls?" This seemed a neutral ground to begin interrogation on.

"Oh, yes. You don't know the rumors then. Or the facts. Well, I won't go into huge detail, but obviously," and here he paused again and gave me a pointed look, "his fan base does consist in part of, how shall I put it—excited females. No, I jest. But he does give off quite a, let's call it a blatantly physical, sexual aura?" He gave a half laugh. "That's what makes a good front man. But some people, if you give them the candy box, they're flattered. They pick. They choose. Others eat the entire thing. And some," he continued, "think of new ways to use sugar. Seeing as it's running hot and cold all the time, if you'll forgive that revolting mixed metaphor." Now he did laugh.

I tried to laugh. This time I did drain the small cup. I hoped Dave would see it as a sign of my offended sensibilities. He refilled my cup, and was silent for a moment.

"I hope I haven't shocked you. But you are going on the road with them. And James wants you to interview some of the groupies, although that's not what anyone calls them anymore."

I felt sick again. I focused on the elegant crispness of his appearance. That was what I wanted. Safety. Elegance.

I took a deep breath, and tried to swallow down some of the tofu. It was delicious. It felt like Styrofoam in my mouth. I hoped it wasn't obvious that I felt like I was chewing pellets. I glanced at him. He looked happy. Smug, even.

I regained my composure. "Let me ask you—what is the angle the magazine wants on this? Presumably not a hatchet piece."

He laughed. "No, no, of course not. But in the same way that all the stories about Led Zeppelin created this aura of mystery and sexual excitement around the band that lasted for years, to this day even, some might say, I think we can take what James hopes for, which is to shock you and threaten Tristan with blackmail, and turn it into a marketing dream, both for us and for Tristan." He looked excited now. "That circulation increases the minute fantasy and sex are placed into the equation is nothing new. But the curiosity around him, the failed marriage, the rumors—pure sex, drugs and rock and roll. Nothing's changed." He glanced at me, and the look on my face. "And we will sell more records for him that way. The music is unique, inspiring, monumental." He nodded to the server, who cleared away our plates again. "I'm a big fan, always have been. And AC, who's a family friend, could use the boost, quite frankly. Which is why he will be joining the tour," he lowered his voice, "unexpectedly, for a few dates. Surprise guest. His music is not as commercial, or as inventive. But it's solid, and he's a good person." He paused, and raised his cup. "So that's our job. Reminding everyone of the history, while steering them to the present. Teasing them with tales of debauchery, while proving nothing. Making them feel like they are there, and that it could happen to them."

"And I'm the right person to do this?" I couldn't help it. "Why?"

Dave looked at me. "You're beautiful and talented and honest. You will do a fantastic job, because you have a gift for detail and atmosphere. And—Tristan wants you. So he'll be more open." He watched the chef again. "Now why do you think that might be?"

I quailed, inwardly. Discreet. Discreet.

"You don't know? That's good. But I'll give you my take on it. He sees your talent, that's been proven by the last interview. He wants the approval only an established enterprise, as the magazine is, can bestow. And," he turned and took my hand in his, leaving me staring at his fingers on mine, "you're a challenge for him. The unattainable, intellectual woman. What he's never had, what he can't have."

I followed his hand still joined to mine as he raised it to his lips and our eyes met.

"Je ne suis pas prisonnier de ma raison."

I couldn't help it. I looked up at him from under my lashes, playfully. "Evidemment." He was still holding my hand. "What should I say?"

"Say you will come out with me again when you get back from London. And not talk business." He suddenly looked tall and imposing, yet the expression on his face was boyish and pleading. God it could be so simple. An elegant, comfortable relationship, the lid closed on the Pandora's Box of curiosity and risk I'd kicked open. It made so much sense.

"I'd love to." I smiled at him, as he kissed my hand again, and placed it carefully back in my lap.

"I'm delighted," he answered. And he did look happy. He

called the chef over and introduced me and watched as the chef bowed and smiled at both of us, as though something had been settled. The server came over and poured us some green tea, which I drank as Dave pulled out a black card to pay for our dinner. My jacket appeared. We walked out of the restaurant, his hand guiding me lightly on my back, the other diners watching. There was nothing discreet about this; it was going to be a piece of news passed along. I glanced over. There was frank interest on the faces of the women, a strange acknowledgment on the faces of the men, who returned more quickly to what they were doing. The tunnel seemed endless, but at last we were out, leaving behind the echoes of the hostess wishing us well again, out on the streets, the cold dirty air clearing away the haze of the sake.

He looked at me. "Let's walk a little bit, get some air. The car will follow us." And he pulled out his phone, gave instructions, and put his arm around my waist, carefully. "Did you enjoy that?" He was all solicitude.

"I did, thank you." Ah this felt good, crossing the avenue, heading east, the car somewhere nearby, this tall elegant man holding me protectively. "It was a lovely evening, I really enjoyed it."

"I'm glad. I did as well. I'm glad you said yes."

"Are you?" I looked up at him. He was tall and handsome, the light and shadow of the night giving his face depth. There were no passions etched there, no torments, aside from a certain set to the jaw and the brow which made his face seem immobile and solid, somewhat like his presence. It was comforting, rather than exciting. But not boring.

No, not boring.

We walked over to Second Avenue, while he told me funny

stories about meetings he had had with different musicians, their demands, their quirks. He asked me about my French, and we began a reminiscence of moments we had spent in Paris. It turned out we had both lived there for a time. It was his friend, whose father was the head of Publicis, the largest advertising agency in France, with offices all over the world, who had given him the idea to go into media.

"We must be there together sometime," he said, his face serious and still.

I looked at him, surprised. He shrugged, a very Gallic gesture, and smiled. "You would be fun to go out with in Paris."

"It's a beautiful city." I tried to think of something light to say. "It's a place one is never sorry to visit."

"Soon," he said, as though we were discussing something else entirely. "But New York is beautiful as well."

I looked around, from the cars racing past, heading downtown, to the broken awnings, the neon lights, the corner market and the white plastic tubs of flowers, the twenty different varieties of people walking past, and up to the silver white lights of the Chrysler Building. "It is," I sighed. "It really is. Strange and beautiful."

His phone buzzed and he answered it. "Yes. Second and Twenty-Third. Yes. Five minutes." He closed his phone, and placed it carefully back in his inside pocket. "Lily, the car is going to meet up with us. I've got an early appointment, and you—well, you're flying out to London."

I sighed. Yes I was. Ready or not.

He took my sigh for something else. "Lil, I've had a wonderful time tonight. Brilliant." He held me at arms' length and looked at me closely, then held me to him for a brief moment, and kissed me on the cheek. "Soon," he whispered, "I don't like to rush."

Then he stepped away, and took my hand again. "If you need anything, anything at all, do not hesitate to call. Even if it's just to hear a normal voice." He laughed. "Here's the car."

I protested.

"No, I'm walking. The driver will take you home. At least then I know you're safe for part of the journey. And he will personally pick you up tomorrow for the trip to the airport."

"You don't have..." He interrupted me.

"Yes, I do." He kissed both cheeks again. "Be good chérie. And good luck." I got into the car and looked up at him as he shut the door. He smiled down at me.

I started to give the driver the address.

"No, ma'am, I know it already. Just relax. Mr. Fanning told me to take very good care of you. Precious cargo." And he turned around and gave me a happy, toothy smile. He seemed genuine, but I wondered how big a tip had gone into that smile.

And as I sank into the leather seats, I wondered, yet again, what the hell I'd gotten myself into.

I checked my phone, involuntarily. Of course no messages. He was in the air. Away from it all.

Yes.

Chapter 3

The ride to JFK was smooth and problem free, and I thanked Dave inwardly for the chance to relax. I'd spent the day running around like mad. I had the tickets, the schedule, the hotel information, a list of contact numbers, the password for sending updates, the contact at the record company, and a list of times when I'd be interviewing various people. The one I was actually looking forward to was the head of Working Class Records, Trevor Sears, the first person to sign Devised, back when they were just fresh faced kids with a lot of drive and a knack of being in the right place at the right time. He was famous in his own right, a track record and history that made him one of the major players in the game over what was now a long period of time. He had the gift—knowing what was important—and maybe more crucially, trusting in his own judgment. He had been behind Devised and the early breakthrough. They were just another band to him though, however good they were. He'd been responsible for getting some of the most revolutionary and subversive acts out there, and turning them into mainstream success stories. I really wanted to ask him what he had seen in them that made him think of some of the great bands of the past, because that's why he always said he had signed them. If I could pin him down on a chord progression, or a lyric, or even a vibe, that could be the hook for the rest of the story. I had made notes—I had the entire flight to write things down. I looked out the window. I was thinking too fast. I needed to calm down.

It had been a bit tricky telling Dave I didn't need a car at Heathrow. "Friends, Dave, friends, waiting to see me," was what I said to him. It wasn't a lie. Not really. What it was—sheer juggling. It struck me how casual I was trying to be about it. Trying. Denial. All those things. After the dinner with him, it seemed easy. I could almost hear my family shouting approval from the roof tops. Rich, connected, sensible. As opposed to what? Rich, connected, outrageous? I felt my heart constrict at the idea of even making the comparison. There was more to it than that, even if knew I couldn't go there. Those feelings were safely hidden. I'd gone to bed early, trying to be sensible, pleased with my decision to be self-protecting.

But I'd been woken up by a text in the middle of the night.

> Yes is a good word coming from your sweet mouth. But it's so small. And lonely. Don't forget your pick up at Heathrow.

I sank back down into the pillows. Cute. Bossy. And pick up. What did that mean? I couldn't think what to text back. Everything I thought of made me seem either desperate or uninterested. Finally I decided.

> Haven't forgotten. Thanks for the ride.

The reply came back in a flash.

Don't thank me until you've ridden.

That answered everything and nothing. My heart started racing. Oh god. What happened to discreet? "Work first, then games"? I shut my eyes. I'd been working so hard on shutting him out. And the minefield ahead of us, me, whoever, fuck it. I resisted the urge to throw the phone against the wall. The truth was, I had no idea how I was going to react to him when I saw him. Would I stay under control? Keep it all cool and professional? Or was I just scared of what I wanted? I turned over in the bed and flipped my pillow over, trying to cool my overheated brain.

When had I become so crazy?

• • •

Business class on the plane was good, and the stewards and stewardesses were a lot less stressed and a lot more friendly, than in economy class. I got to have my glass of champagne before take-off—civilized—and I could actually sit cross-legged in the seat, the way you used to be able to do. As the plane made its last turn to point its nose straight down the take-off runway, I felt that odd emotion of pain and excitement. The Earth, New York, everything suddenly seemed much more precious, even as the engines roared into life and the pulse of the sudden acceleration made action an imperative, a sharp want. It was what lay beyond the fear—the thrill of the unknown, the need for speed like in the comic books, the sheer power involved in getting something this massive off the ground. I watched the ground speed by faster and faster, the lights of Jamaica Bay and the Rockaways, flat and like part of the ocean go past, then tilt, as the plane lurched into the sky, jerk with the wheels being pulled in, and disappear as the plane banked to the North to follow the coast up to Canada. I closed my eyes. This part did always frighten me, and I drank down the rest of the champagne to try and dull the feeling. I wished I could be excited about seeing Tristan, but at the moment, it all seemed detail. Interviews to conduct, players to meet, speech to control and use to manipulate. I started to cry. The pressure, fuck, why couldn't I just push it away? The plane began to ascend, then dropped for a moment, the way they always do. If I knew all this, why did it still get to me? Shit. The fear. I liked people. I was thrilled to meet some of these people. It would be great to get these insights into who and how. It was just that what I said would decide what they told me. And I didn't always get it right.

And then there was Tristan. The girls. The rabid fan girls. His own interesting tastes. I stopped a steward and asked for another glass of champagne. He came back, and placed the glass down on my tiny table, and his hand on my arm. "Are you ok? Can I get you anything else?" He looked concerned. I wondered why I felt guilty at the attention.

"No, not right now, but thank you. Just having a bit of a moment."

"It's a hard place to leave, and a hard place to return to." He looked serious for a moment. "Let me know if I can get you anything." His face returned to its professional mask, as he moved away to another paying customer.

I looked out at the darkness, and tried to spot some stars in the sky, which was my home for the next seven hours. The constellations changed depending on where you were—in London I remembered being surprised to look up and see the Big Dipper—at completely the wrong angle and almost directly in front of my door. You didn't usually see stars in the Big Smoke, that name for London that stuck, despite coal fires being made illegal—chimneys boarded up—it still didn't make the thick mix of wet air and pollution clean.

Seeing the stars directly overhead had made me feel strange. Something so eternal and fixed, yet altered in a significant way. There had been a time when every summer had meant knowing where I could find my handful of constellations, looking at the sky, imagining what lay out there, what lay ahead for me in my future, which would naturally be well cared for and warm and fed. There were the sounds of the summer; the crickets, the mooing of a cow waking up in the middle of the night, a car going by every so often on gravel and dirt roads. And the smells—the fresh green warmth of clean air and summer breezes. And then September would come, and the return to the big bad city, hot and dirty and exciting. And the steward was right. It was hard to leave and hard to come back—no matter where you were. But I always wanted both—the adventure and the caring. The fields and the streets. Well, you managed one of them, anyway, I thought to myself. Don't complain. Don't remember.

I looked at my bag and thought about making some more notes. Going over my list of questions. I put down the glass and massaged my forehead. And don't think about what you want, besides another glass of this when this one's done. But there was another voice underneath it all, wet and dark and angry. Tell me what you want, it said. Don't lie.

But I pushed it aside, and stared out the window, resolute.

They came around with some nibbles and refills of champagne. I took both, but ignored the roll filled with whatever it was filled with. Eating. Meant comfort. And there was none. Nor was there likely to be any for the next few weeks. Years. Ever. I sighed and closed my eyes. Focus on drinking some more, and sleeping. He may be there. In the car. Maybe not.

And will he play you like an instrument? I felt like I knew the answer to that one. The real question was whether I'd let him. And whether I'd like it.

The answering voice inside my head came up too quickly. You will.

I pushed around the food, drank two of the little bottles of wine, and put on my headphones and covered myself with the blanket. Them Crooked Vultures. That would erase thinking. I could fall asleep to any music—the fact that it was loud was a positive in my book. The drums alone would remove the buzzing from my head. I put it on repeat, and pulled the blanket so it was forming a hood over my face. I didn't want to see, didn't want to think, didn't want to feel.

I dropped into a kind of fitful sleep, where pink shirts hung dully in beautifully neat closets, and leather jackets were removed and sent away. I was running around, shouting, but when I woke up, I couldn't remember what I was saying. I was upset, that was all.

The lights were being turned on, and the breakfast was being handed out—even in business class, it wasn't a lot more than a packaged muffin and fake juice. I chose the coffee, as it drowned out the taste of the water more than the tea, and nibbled at a piece of the muffin. I was starting to feel a little bit excited. London. Again. Once, my favorite place in the entire world. Now? Landscape for confusion, I thought. And scribbled the phrase down, along with some fragments of the dream. A few questions for my interviewees.

I pulled together my makeup bag, and went to the toilet to work on myself. At least up here, there were really no lines. I waited for a moment, then went in. Yup, I looked like I'd been drinking and up all night on a plane. Shit. Oh well. The rock and roll lifestyle. Here it was. I brushed my teeth and cleaned my skin, threw on some foundation and eyeliner. A little better. More rocking than homeless. I fixed up my hair, and tried not to feel my heart beating. Would he be there? Was I ready? Did I have a choice? That last thought, funnily enough, calmed me down. I had agreed. Therefore there was no choice, I'd already made it. And I was stepping further into the unknown. As far as Dave and I were concerned, there was nothing. I wasn't cheating. I wasn't doing anything that anyone needed to know about.

I sprayed some Jo Malone, everywhere, and reapplied the lipstick. Yup. Ready for battle. And hopefully too tired to fight. I made my way back to my seat, swaying with the turbulence in the plane, and tried to read a magazine for the next half hour, before the real descent happened.

Chapter 4

"Ladies and Gentlemen, Welcome to London's Heathrow Airport. Please remain in your seats until we have safely reached the gate and the seat belt sign has been switched off."

We bumped along the runways, heading for the gate, and I could feel my heartbeat start to skyrocket. Here. All that. Him. Would he be in the car? I suddenly wished I had taken this more seriously, drank less, stayed focused. I shut my eyes, and heard the engines power down, immediately followed by the metallic click of 300 people unbuckling their seat belts. A part of me wanted to jump out of my seat, grab my bag, and push past everyone and everything just to get to him. Instead I sat there, trying to stretch, watching everyone else drop things and wait in line. Deep breath. There was a song running through my head, but I couldn't place it. All I could remember was just the beat of the drums, over and over. Shit. Enough. Now. I felt like I'd been pricked with a needle. I needed to know. And I rose up out of my seat, and reached for my bag out of the overhead locker. In a moment, the steward was there, helping me get it down. I looked at him, and nodded my thanks.

"No problem. Enjoy your stay in London." His voice was gentle, his eyes full of compassion. I wondered why, and who he was, and what he saw in me that made him look that way.

"Thank you. I hope I will." And I turned, knowing that I would never lay eyes on him again, and walked through the spaceship-like hatch to the plane and away, onto the gently uphill carpet of the gateway.

Long. Very long. The walk to immigration. The wait. The turbaned man examining me and my credentials. His brief question—you've lived here before, are you intending to stay this time? My curt answer. The stamp. Passing through the small space between his lectern-like desk and the one next to it. Forward, and left. Everything seeming yellow and beige. Down the stairs. Which carousel was mine? 8. Fine. Walking straight ahead. Carts. Families. Voices. The black rubber of the belt, going around, empty. Boxes coming out first, wrapped in plastic and the colored tape of the airline, bringing color to the monotony of the black circuit. The silver edge. Suitcases dropping down the slide, around. Once, twice. More suitcases. I struggled to remember what color my bag was. Right. Purple. That one. Where was I? It felt like a hundred years ago, and it reminded me of when I had first moved back here. Stepping through time, in and out of memories, of standing exactly here, waiting for my bags. Excitement. Fear. I moved closer to the edge, someone bumped into me. I didn't even look up. Just staring, watching the bags go around. Breathing. In. Out. Not thinking. No. Not yet.

Finally, my bag slid down, and I pushed my way through to the edge. People didn't move, I nudged them, excuse me please, nothing, and pushed harder. Grabbed my bag. Go. Wheeling through customs. Nothing. No snakes. No food. No drugs, even though I felt stoned. I felt the eyes of the officials on me as I walked through the crowd. The air around me felt shimmering and unreal, and old and recycled. It was like being on speed. All there was—my heartbeat, reminding me to breathe.

I walked through the doors, and was instantly overwhelmed by the noise, and the number of people waiting. And there we were, the arrivals, on show as we walked through the gated off crowd, craning our necks to look for people who were hopefully glad to see us. I headed towards the line of drivers, holding up cards with names. My name, the magazine's name, his name, they all blurred together. I stopped and ran my fingers through my hair. Breathe. He said he would send a car. It will be here. Or you will get a taxi, calm down. I looked around again. I felt so out of it, like I couldn't connect with my surroundings. I retraced my last few steps, and began the search again. There. Right there, Lily. Jesus.

I went up to the driver, who looked at me, and smiled. "Right this way, love."

Ah, it still made me smile. Old customs, old habits. I always liked being called love, missed it when people stopped saying it as much. Sexist? Yeah, like being called beautiful is an insult. Oh god. Beautiful. Should I ask the driver? Or be surprised. We weren't walking to the car park. Oh. That would mean that... someone was in the car.

We went outside and there was a policeman by a limo, with a tall, dark haired man next to him, chatting amicably. We walked up to them, and I watched the unlikely couple, one short haired and in uniform, one with hair brushing the back of his neck, and in leather, shaking hands, the cop smiling. "Thanks for the passes, mate. Brilliant. Have a good trip over here." And he nodded to me and walked off.

I looked at Tristan, and my heart stopped. He smiled, a big happy smile. And then we were hugging. His arms around me. My head on his chest. That liquid feeling of warmth and safety ran through me. He smelled good. He held me more tightly. Then he kissed the top of my head, and let go. He looked down at me, smiling. There was no guile, no worry. He looked amazingly young actually, and fresh, and had a sort of brightness around his eyes, that hadn't been there before. God he was beautiful. I beamed back at him, blissfully unconscious of everything around me.

"Come on, babe, let's get in the car. Otherwise I'll have to give away more tickets. I told John here that I'd watch the car—didn't realize how lucky I was to find a fan. Thought they were going to arrest me." The driver—John—went to open the door, and Tristan waved him off. "I'm good," he said, and held the door open for me. I quickly scooted in, and he followed, shutting the big door briskly behind him. The driver pulled off, and I didn't ask where we were going. I didn't really care.

He was pulling me close, and I leaned against his shoulder, filled with a sense of wonder at all this. I looked up at him, and before I could say anything, his mouth was on mine, a sweet kiss, as soft and tender as he had been passionate before. I opened my eyes to find his were already open, looking at me. I pulled away so I could see him better. I wanted to see him. I needed to talk.

"I'm glad to see you." I smiled at him. "I didn't know what to expect."

I was instantly sorry I'd said it, because his eyes became instantly less glowing, and more suspicious. I tried to say more. "I wasn't sure if you'd be here, or..."

"Or what I'd want?"

I nodded. Fuck fuck fuck. Why had I said anything? I wanted sweet Tristan back, happy, soft, smiling.

"What did you think, I'd meet you with a pair of handcuffs, and a list of demands?" He pulled away and rubbed his eyes with his hands. "Is it the stories you've heard about me already? Or just that you think I'm a monster all by yourself?" His eyes were black and he was biting his lip. The expression was menacing and defiant. My brain was warring between finding him incredibly sexy, and wanting to pet and cuddle him, go back to what it was, or could be, two lovers meeting up and being happy.

I burst out with my thought before I realized what I was doing. "Can't we find a way to be happy?" He said nothing. I swallowed. Now I was in it. I blustered on. "Yes, I wondered. Yes, I was nervous. Did I expect you to look so happy? No, but it felt good while it lasted."

His face twisted into a smirk and I shut my eyes. "So, I'm not a monster?" His voice was teasing and dark.

I breathed in again. Every moment felt like the edge of a precipice. Somewhere between fear, and annoyance, and jet lag, and delirium, and my own sense of pride, I tried to find something to say that would show I was ready to fight back. Fucking with my moment of happiness. Fuck.

I stared at him. "No, Tristan. Not a monster. Despite everything I've heard. I've been warned off you."

He laughed again, that bitter bark. "Have you now? I suppose Dave whispered in your ear while you were having sushi?"

My face said everything.

He took my hand. And stroked it, gently. "Just tell me, and I'll believe you. Did you fuck him? Or did you just want to?"

"Fucking hell, Tristan. No. Absolutely not. It's not like that. He's not..."

Here he cut me off. "But you are? And you were worried about acting like a whore with me? Interesting."

It was a low blow. I felt my face going red and my fists were clenched up. "Oh fuck you, seriously. You're the one stalking me, and you're judging me. But you know the worst thing—I don't think you even care." I paused, looking at the reaction my words were having. I carried on. I didn't think he was getting it. "You don't trust me."

"Give me a reason to trust you."

"Ha. I know what this is about. While I'm being told stories that imply you fuck groups of women in strange positions like some people buy assortments of chocolate," I laughed at my own joke, "your manager has been telling you I'm another creepy soul-sucking witch journalist à la Jim Morrison, and I'm going to bring you down. Nice."

He looked out the window. Direct hit, I've sunk your battleship. "It's true, isn't it?"

He was silent, his lips a thin line of distaste. The car was entering London, and the traffic had brought us nearly to a standstill. The Great West Road. Not so great.

He finally turned to me. "Maybe you're right. Maybe this is a bad idea."

I felt all the blood rush to my feet. There were black spots in front of my eyes. Shit. I couldn't handle this. "I didn't say that!" I grabbed his arms and made him face me. "Why were you so happy to see me this morning then? Why?"

He just stared at me. His eyes were dark and intense, almost hypnotic. I felt as though he was examining me, searching through my mind and finding all my secrets. All the events of the past few days came rushing up at me, the dinner, Dave, my determination to avoid thinking about Tristan, my blind panic and fear at the airport, the warm bliss I felt when I saw him smile. The last thought made me smile.

His eyes lightened when he saw me smile. "You've got a secret," he murmured. "I can tell."

I regarded him steadily. He could be so intimidating, so quickly, grabbing all the power out of the air and wrapping it all around himself. But I wasn't going to let him. This wasn't the disengaged rock star; this was the beautiful man, the complicated artist, the demanding lover, and...I needed him. But to be with him, I was going to have to take risks. Big ones. What to say? Where to begin? It annoyed me that I still didn't know what to do, getting in my own way.

"Yeah, a big secret. And it has to do with you. All the rest of it, my dinner with Dave, what he wanted, what kind of sushi I ordered, the strange stories about the groupies and your weird sex life—that part," here, I paused for effect, "I'm happy to share. What do you want to know?" I smiled, winningly, I hoped.

His face changed, and it wasn't an expression I recognized. Not from the pictures, not from our times together, it was something new—all of those, but different. His eyes looked bigger, more brown and grey, and was there—sadness—in them? He shook his head, his hair in his eyes. Then he raised his hand to my face and ran his long fingers over my skin. Then he was running them down my neck, into my cleavage, over my breasts, and descending to the heat between my legs. I gasped, but he only stopped there for a moment, then carried down across the top of my thigh, and made a line along the outside of my leg, past my knee, tracing my calf, right to the tip of my booted foot. The whole movement couldn't have taken more than a minute. It woke up my body like the splash of cold stream water in the middle of winter. I was shivering.

"You're mine. Ah, you forgot. But now," and here he took both his hands and placed them on the inside of my knees, and started to spread my legs apart, slowly, "now you remember. And we both have a new reason why that's so." He stared at me. "Get on me."

He pulled my leg over him, and suddenly it was like the limo in New York, that first time, all over again. The rush of heat that sped through me was an unexpected sensation, and the strange ache, almost painful, sending electricity running down my legs, was getting stronger. He sat me down on him, and I could feel him, hard, gratifyingly so, close to where it hurt. I shifted my hips and pressed against him, and we both groaned.

"Shit, girl, you drive me crazy. Why do you want to hurt me? No, don't answer..." And he thrust up against me hard, while his huge hands dug into my ass and held me against him. He got bigger if that were possible, and I could feel him pulsing against me.

"Hold on," and he bit my neck and he pressed the intercom button to the front of the long black car. "John,"—I was amazed he could remember the driver's name, I could barely remember my own, and he was tickling my nipples with one of his fingers while he spoke. "Look, slight change of plans, could you just drive around for a while, then we'll go to the hotel. Ok?" There was a mumbled assent. "Great. Thanks."

He turned his face back to me. "Now," he muttered, "as they say, where were we?" He began moving against me, in a slow almost off time swaying back and forth, every roll of his hard cock and his hips, going over my clit and making me jump.

I hissed out a curse.

He licked a trail from my breast to my ear, and bit down on the nape of my neck, making me shudder against him and moan. He whispered in my ear. "Why would I need all those stories, if this is so good like it is? More importantly, why would you want anyone else? No, I'm not going to ask. For now, we'll do this the way it plays."

And he pulled me to him suddenly, forcefully, and licked my mouth, his tongue wet and slow. He was almost muttering to himself now. "I can't help it, I want to fuck you, just like this." His voice was almost pleading, and his eyes looked deep set and lost. He licked my mouth again, and bit gently on my lower lip. "Say yes. Little words." Then he moved me slowly away from him, and started to unbuckle his belt.

I moved off him, and he looked confused for a moment. But I was all business. I couldn't wait to give him what he wanted. I needed him and his eyes on me. I sat on the seat and quickly took off my boots, and started pulling off my jeans.

His voice was dark again. "That's it, darling. Strip for me."

The sound rolled through me like a wave. I wanted to make him want me. If teasing him did that, then I could tease. I left my panties on and pulled off my shirt, slowly, and dropped it behind me. I rolled down the straps of my bra over my shoulders, one at a time, and ran my hands over my breasts, pinching my nipples until it hurt, first through the satin, then pulling the cups down, exposing them to his view.

He sucked in his cheeks and whistled. His hands went instantly to the zip on his jeans.

"No." I barely recognized my voice. He looked up. "No, not yet—when I tell you."

His mouth opened into a slow, slightly dangerous smile. But his hands stopped. I carried on. "I want to see you naked."

He twitched in his seat, then almost as though he couldn't help it, he opened his mouth, and ran his tongue carefully over his upper lip, leaning forward, his eyes black. "You? You're telling me what to do? What is it, the English air? Or did they feed you something on the plane?"

I laughed. Out on the edge for my whole life. I was going to tell him what I wanted.

"Shut up, Tristan. Skin."

He licked his lips again, and gave me a look that made me wonder if he wasn't just going to leap on me from the seat there and then. But he kept his eyes locked with mine, and breathed out.

"I like it," he muttered, as he bent down, his huge hands skimming over his body to his feet.

He started with his black leather boots, then removed his jacket. He pulled off his vintage t-shirt and then his chest was bare, pale and creamy, his skin begging to be touched. He pulled open his belt and leaned over, pulling his jeans down over his ass. He stopped to peel them over his calves, they were that tight, and finally pulling them over his long, elegant feet. He sat there in his underwear, hip hugging and silky, wide purple and white stripes, his cock at an angle under the fabric, waiting to be released. He looked like sex. He sat back, his body on display, his legs slightly spread.

"You first," was all he said.

With that I unclasped my bra and threw it with my jeans. Then I slowly took down my panties until I was sitting there bare assed on the leather upholstery of the car. Looking at him. Waiting. Now it was his turn.

He tilted his head slightly and grinned. "You take them off," as he reached for a condom out of the pocket of his jeans. "And while you're down there, put this on." He flipped it to me. I glanced up at his face after I caught it, but he only looked amused. I frowned for a moment, and his expression changed, and just for a second, there was something else there, almost tenderness, but it was gone before I could tell.

I knelt in front of him on the scratchy limo carpet and pulled off his underwear. "I love these. Purple stripes, crazy." I ran my hands over his legs. My voice was still coming from a long way away. "You're sexy as fuck, you know it?"

"Yup." He smiled. "Get on with it, I can't hold out much longer." I ran my hands over his cock. It was hot, against the cool pale skin of his legs, throbbing, the veins sticking out. I breathed out, the idea of him about to explode making me throb. I couldn't help it; I leaned over him and licked the wetness off the top, slowly. God, the taste of him went right to me. I licked again.

He groaned and grabbed my head. "Fuck I told you, no." My only response was to place my hands over his and make him push my head all the way down on him. I took the whole length down my throat and he let out a ragged moan. "Oh my, clever, but oh no, fuck, not yet."

And he pulled me off him, grabbed the condom out of my

hand and put it over himself with an incredible speed. He leaned over and pulled me towards him, but stopped.

"Turn around." And he held me on his legs, carefully. "Now listen to me."

And he opened the window, just an inch or two. "We'll both look out the window, and try and concentrate on other things, and then maybe I'll last long enough to make you scream my name. And while you're doing it, I want you to look out the window. Don't even think about looking away."

I started to protest. "We're in traffic, someone will hear us. See me."

He pulled me back against him and placed his hands on my breasts and started slowly circling my nipples. It was a direct current to where I wanted him, and I wriggled against him with a sigh. He laughed. "That's the idea. But only if you catch their eyes. And I want you to. Somebody. Make them watch you losing it, on me."

I still wasn't sure. "They won't want to. They won't do that."

He ran his hands delicately up and down my sides, making me shiver under his touch, humming gently. He brushed against my ear with his tongue, and spoke very softly. "Darling, there isn't a man in the world who isn't willing to watch a beautiful woman have an orgasm. I'll prove it to you." He turned my head and kissed me, the heat of him, the softness of his lips making the hurt worse.

And with that, he held me up over his lap and lowered me down onto his cock, slowly, so slowly, slower than I thought possible. His fingers were pressed into my hips so hard, I knew there would be marks. Tomorrow, later, I didn't care. I could feel the tip of his cock just teasing my lips apart, and then he was there, and I was sinking into him, lower and deeper, opening me up, almost too tight, then pushing all the way through.

And at last he was in me, completely in me, and I squeezed around him. "Oh fuck, darling, there you go again. I want to come all over you, in you. Fuck—do that again." His hand moved to my clit, and began teasing it, then his hand sank lower to caress his balls, heavy and tight between his strong thighs. I tried to look down to watch, to see him in me, playing with the two of us, joined that closely, but he hissed out a command.

"Look out the window. I told you—find someone to watch you come—or you won't." He began circling my clit with his long, practiced fingers, and at that moment I didn't care what he had done before, as long as he didn't stop what he was doing now. I couldn't control the moans coming out of my throat –loud, and I didn't care. About anything. I just wanted to thank the universe for letting him be this good. For me.

"Tristan, you're too fucking hot, it's too much." He slowed down his movements. But the thrusting became more out of time, and I could feel it both creeping up on us. Oh god. The feeling was overwhelming—his hands on me, everywhere, his cock filling me up, his dark tone.

He stopped. And his voice held my attention. "Find someone. Now."

"You know all my secrets. And I don't want anyone else to watch me come—except you."

He wasn't moving and I could feel him, huge and still in me. I squeezed against him and he moaned. "I know, that's what you think. But you're wrong." I clenched against him and tried to move, my eyes shut, feeling him deep inside me. And he moved just a little and I pulled in against him again. He stopped again. "Do me again like that, yeah, oh god, that's it, shit, babe, trust me, you'll like it." And he began thrusting into me, faster, over and over, teasing my clit and hitting that spot inside me at just the same moment and I cried out. Loud. So close.

His voice in my ear. "Look over there, darling. He likes it loud."

I looked out the window. Oh, I had gotten someone's attention.

And the man was riding in the back of a large black BMW, not a limo, but being driven, and he still held the paper that he had been reading. I could see his elegant suit, his well-groomed greying hair. And I knew he could see just enough of my face, so close to orgasm.

Tristan began thrusting up in me more, pulling my body against him. I moaned his name, and I shut my eyes for a moment.

"So close baby, so fucking close."

Tristan's voice was a low rumble against my neck. "Open your eyes. I can see him too. Rich businessman. Could be the English Dave. Let him watch what I'm doing to you. What he can't."

Oh that's it. I got it. But I didn't care anymore.

And he continued, his slow sweet fucking, his long fingers teasing my clit and the base of his cock, and we were just in time and I was gasping. The man was turned towards me, the traffic moving slowly enough that the cars stayed together. He looked guilty but he wasn't looking away, either.

Then there was Tristan's deep drawl in my ear again, dripping into me. "I'm going to come baby, I want to hear you, hear you fucking scream my name."

He was moving me up and down with more fury, each word he spoke punctuated with the effort he was making not to come, his breathing coming in hard. "Let him watch. He can't do this to you. But I can. Let him see you." With that he buried himself in me so deep it nearly hurt and he cried out with me and I knew he was nearly there. I started to close my eyes and let go, breathing into him.

"Keep your fucking eyes open now." His voice nothing but dark commands, his cock filling me in waves, "do it, now."

And I could feel him take me under, his fingers on me, slick and hot, his cock burning in me and the stranger, his eyes on me. I let all my fears fly off and focused on making everything I was feeling show through my face, knowing Tristan was watching me too. I felt like I was losing my mind. Too intense. "Baby, I'm coming, help me, help."

"Yes, darling, yes, that's it...keep your eyes open fuck feel that oh god yes, fuck, at last," and he gasped, his voice strained and breathless as he pushed himself into me. I could see the eyes of the man in the car widen as though he couldn't believe what he was seeing. But I knew he was excited, the fascination on his face evident.

Suddenly, pleasing two men, it felt so easy to be crazy. No holding back. No quiet. No restraint. His body, in me, now. I cried out for him, knowing what he liked. And I found I couldn't hold it in anymore. "Tristan, don't stop, please, fuck me, please." Moaning, out of control. He was getting harder, burning up inside me.

His voice was raw and loud, so loud. "That's it, take it, show him...show him...you're mine...mine, so fucking good." And suddenly he stopped, clutching me to him, then he was thrusting into me, calling out my name, his endless after-shocks coming in waves, making me come, again, again. The suited man couldn't turn away, watching me riding Tristan's wildness, pouring into me. My body pushed against him, out of control, writhing like a pulse, until finally exhausted, I fell back against his chest. I could feel the sweat on my back, on his legs, superheated against me. My chest rose and fell as I tried to catch my breath. Fuck.

I started to close my eyes and lean into him, but he suddenly leaned me forward, and sat up.

"You can rest in a minute," he said, kissing me, "just one more thing to do." I watched as he opened the window another inch and stuck his head out partway, so the man in the suit could see clearly who I had been sitting on. Tristan stuck his hand out the window and gave the man in the BMW a thumbs up. Mr. Expensive Suit's mouth dropped open, shocked. Tristan started laughing, and shut the window, shutting him and the rest of the world out.

I didn't know what to think. But my body did, wet and sticky and rocking gently with his laughter. Oh yeah.

Tristan was still giggling. "Sweetheart, you are so perfect. Fuck, you gave him an image hell won't burn away. He's going to have your face on his mind for months to come. Years. How does that feel? Good? Weird?" And he pulled me down to his shoulder and kissed me. "You felt weird, didn't you? But you've fucked me senseless, again, and given your audience a performance that we'll all remember." He kissed me again. "And come like a banshee yourself, darling."

His eyes were bright again. He closed them, a satisfied smile on his lips, and pulled me tight to his chest.

"Now you understand what it's like to be a star. What you need to do. Don't forget it. Your biggest lesson so far."

I leaned against him, confused, but feeling so good, but so tripped out. But I thought I knew what he meant. That power, electric. Displayed, open, focused. Amazing. There was really nothing else I could say about it. Not yet.

He kissed my head and his arms went around me, warm and strong. "And you're mine, darling. Don't forget that either."

Chapter 5

The car continued its way through the traffic. I was barely aware of the movement, or the passage of time, lying against his smooth skin, both of us breathing in time, the sweat gently cooling on our bodies, so close. If I could just lie like this forever, if there was going to be just one moment to hold on to, this was it. It was strange, how such a random, unexpected thing like what we'd just done felt as though we had created this durable bond between us, tender and strange, human and fragile. Would it be enough to sustain us, to sustain me anyway, over the next few days, which were bound to be difficult? Tough to say. I sighed.

He kissed my head, where it was nestled against his shoulder. His voice, soft and slow, broke the silence. "We've got to move, darling. Here, let me lift you up." And he helped me roll off him. I sat on the seat, and watched him strip off the condom. I still felt shaky, filled with the mystery of how such small things could be so important. Touch, windows, even little packets. Then I thought about how I'd like to feel him come in me, and I smiled as the idea took shape in my mind, crossing from one side to the other.

"You've got that look again. Your secret face." He looked happy, his eyes tired but content, focused on me. I could have him look at me like that forever, I thought. And we stayed like that for a minute, not speaking, just watching the other, no longer wary, but as though something had finally been resolved.

He closed his eyes, and held out his arms. "One more cuddle, and then we've got to face the world. Ok?" And he held me close again. He was warm, and solid, and he was giving me his strength, making me feel able to do everything I needed to. Placing his smile, his clever and intense gaze, inside me, like an energy field. Like a reaction—I couldn't help it—and filled with a sudden burst, like a bubble inside me, I looked up at him, nestled his sweet face in my hands, and kissed him, gently, slowly. I couldn't say it. Not yet, maybe not ever. But I wanted him to understand.

When I pulled back to look at him, his eyes were bright and shiny, sparkling. "Yes," he whispered. "Little words."

A long moment passed, his eyes locked with mine. But finally, he turned away and leaned over for his underwear. "Come on darling, we've got to get dressed." We busied ourselves for a few minutes, putting, or trying to put everything back on, so it didn't look too much like we'd just been naked in the back of a moving car. I entertained myself watching him peel his jeans back on, so tight, he almost had to put them on like stockings.

He looked over at me, amused. "There's a method to this, you know. Years of practice. Not sure I should let you watch. Trade secret." I snorted, and we both started giggling.

"Poser."

"Fan girl."

"Satyr."

"Nice vocabulary. But I know that word too. Stop it, or I'll have to fuck you again." And he winked at me.

When we were finally dressed, and had made sure the back was cleaned up, Tristan buzzed the driver. "We can head to the hotel, now, thanks." There was a mumble, and he switched the communicator off.

He reached for my hand. "Lily—look at me." His eyes were dark and serious now, and I felt my heart spike again. My name in his mouth. I hoped it meant something good. My thoughts were racing. Had he said it before? He must have. "No, really, stop thinking." His words got through to me, and I looked into his eyes. I was trying to analyze what his look meant. "No, stop. Listen. Really." He started stroking my hand. "Don't talk. Let me just say this."

I nodded, terrified. I had no idea what was coming next. His face was giving nothing away.

"I wanted to say I'm sorry."

My heart rushed into my mouth. "What? Why are you sorry? For what?"

His mouth was a thin line. "Listen. Just listen. I don't apologize that often or that well, so give me a chance." He continued stroking my hand. "What I mean to say, is, everything I said about us not knowing each other..." He turned towards the window, and opened it a tiny bit, letting in some fresh air. "That was crass. And uncalled for. And stupid. You're not like, well..., how can I..." He stopped again. "You're going to meet some people from my past, and maybe, well, maybe you'll see some things you won't like."

He sat back and opened the window another inch, and turned towards it, as though he were clearing his head. We were on the

Cromwell Road now, headed into Central London. But any residual excitement I felt about being back here, seeing the grimy buildings, the London smell coming through the window, was discarded, at the back of my mind.

I made him look at me. "Tristan. Just say it. I understand. I think, anyway. You're just trying to warn me. Right?"

He blew out a long breath. "No, well, yes, not exactly. I don't know what some of these people are going to say. At a chance to get into print, and spin it into some boost to their non-existent careers, some of them might say anything. But I figure you know that." I nodded. "But us." He ran his fingers through his messy hair. "You're a professional. You want to do a good job. I want you to do a good job. But…if people think we are together—ah, shit. I don't know."

He shook his head. "I don't know what is better or worse. I just want to protect you, and I'm not sure if that's better done at a distance, or close up, right?" He looked frustrated. "Look, let's play it by ear. How's this? You've got my number. You need me, for anything, call me. If someone says something you don't like, then call me. We'll work this out. And for the world at large, at the moment, we're friends. Good friends. And if I need to put up some warning flags and make it clear we're more than that, I will. Ok?"

I didn't know what to say. I nodded. Protecting me. Letting people know. But I was starting to feel as though I was entering a viper's nest. I looked at him, his face was dark and serious, slightly unhappy. I needed to process all this. None of it was bad, just…surprising? "Tristan, I'm…I don't know what to say. Thank you?" I raised my hand and ran my fingers over his face. "I want to trust you. Oh hell, I do trust you." I took my hand back and touched it to my own face, I didn't know why. "Ok, let's play this game. Ok? I'll call. If something comes up. Promise. And let you decide how to handle this. Just," I thought about what we were saying did not cover what I felt, "please just let me know what's going on? Ok? How you're feeling. And I will call."

He looked relieved. "I'm glad you trust me." His mouth went up at the corner, a teasing half smile. "About time. And I'll see you on Saturday at the show, anyway. Up front please, with the rest of the media hacks, so I can see you." He smirked. "And the party."

"And the party." I echoed him.

"You know London well."

"I do."

"So we can get the hell out of there, if we need to." His grin was back. It was infectious.

"I think we can do that. Maybe bring a hat."

"And a mask for my face?" He laughed again.

I had a thought. "What about your manager? He hates me."

Tristan shrugged. "He hates everyone he thinks might be a threat to his bank balance."

"That's a harsh thing to say."

"It's a true thing to say. I'm watching him, don't worry."

"Good, Dave was concerned." I knew instantly it was the wrong thing to come up with, but it was too late.

His voice was dripping sarcasm. "How thoughtful. Well let's try to sell him some more magazines, shall we, so he can keep the lifestyle." I winced. "I think I've got it covered, thanks."

I was quiet. "Ok. Ok, fine."

He sighed. "No, doll, I'm sorry. Let's not fight." I stared at him. He took my hand. I looked out the window. We were driving down a small street, nearly to my hotel.

"No, please, please—no fighting." I didn't mean for my voice to come out that way, plaintive, needy, but it did. His eyes widened. And he pulled me to him again, and I curled up against him, breathing in the warmth and scent of him, in the dark cocoon of the car. He rubbed his nose against my hair, nuzzling me, whispering softly.

The car stopped. We could hear the driver open his door. The bubble was broken.

"All right, showtime, darling. I'm just going to drop you off, not get out. But that's the world we live in, not you." He took my hands in his. "Look, we're a united front this weekend, don't forget. If you need me, call me." The mischievous look returned to his face. "Consider it a command." He winked at me.

I giggled. "Is that so, master?" I was surprised to see his eyes darken instantly.

"Ah, dangerous ground. Don't play with fire unless you've got the intention of using it." And his mouth was on mine, warm, strong, faintly possessive, and making me ache again. We pulled apart, slightly out of breath.

There was a knock at the window. He pulled me to him and hugged me. "Call me. No matter what for, or when."

I kissed his cheek, feeling the tiny bits of stubble around the moles by his ear. The things I knew about his body. Already. That I needed to memorize, right now. "I will, love," I said in my best London accent. I pulled away from him, to see him looking slightly shocked, but happy.

"Ok—love." He swatted me on the ass as I opened the door. I turned to look at him, but he was looking over my shoulder, mouthing, "go, photographers." I nodded to him, quickly shutting the door, as he sunk back into the darkness, away from the window. As I stood there, slightly dazed, the driver handed me my bags, and I thanked him, watching him get in and the car pull away, turning the corner.

The doorman came over to me, said "checking in?" and I smiled and mumbled something, as I surreptitiously tried to look around for the paps. Yes, Tristan wasn't kidding, there they were, over on the other side of the potted plants lining the staircase to the door, trying to look like they didn't care, while, rat-like, they watched with beady eyes out the sides of their heads.

I followed the doorman with my bags up the stairs, attempting to steady my features into an indifferent mask, trying for an "I'm important, but I don't care" attitude. It wasn't me they wanted, anyway, right? I wouldn't look at them. So I blinked hard at the flash when it came, unexpected, catching me off guard. I hoped it was on spec, and not because they knew something. Britain—the land of the press stalker. I wondered if my friends would see me in the gossip columns before they saw me in person. And I started to laugh, as the doorman opened the door for me. It was going to be an interesting weekend.

Chapter 6

I sat on the bed, suddenly exhausted. It was a big room, all pink and green and gold, a sort of tasteful cross between French Rococo and English Country. Big windows, big curtains, a large reproduction oak armoire against the wall next to the window, a desk next to the bathroom door, which revealed white tile, white towels, and little bottles of Molton Brown product in white painted baskets. A TV near the end of the bed, which faced one of the windows, which looked out on the square. One of the windows had the curtains drawn shut, which left that side of the room in a sort of shadow. It was fine. For London, it was actually very nice. But I didn't really care. It was more than I was expecting, and I figured that was Dave's fault. I'd been struck by how solicitous they had seemed during check-in as well, happy to accept me, room ready although it was too early for the regular arrival time, would I like it if they sent up some tea, was I expecting any calls. That last one made me stop and take a closer look at the receptionist. Yes, I could certainly see her supporting her income with a few tips passed along to the paparazzi. Sure. And I made a mental note to tell Tristan not to call me at

the hotel, not that I thought he would. So any meetups probably wouldn't happen here. Well, I didn't expect them anyway.
I thought of the driver, and hoped he was either honest or well-
paid, because there was no way he hadn't known exactly what
was happening. I wondered how much you could hear up front.
I'd have to check it out some time. Or not.

So I said no to the messages, yes to the tea, and no to the
porter. I just wanted to get away and lie down for a minute. A
moment of quiet, all alone, before I needed to start making
phone calls. I had two interviews lined up for today—the band
from Australia with the pin-up girl singer, and the first of the
old band entourage—I'd figured I might as well dive right in.
Then dinner with my friends, maybe a walk around some old
haunts, and an early night. First thing tomorrow was the meeting with Trevor, which I hoped I wouldn't be disappointed with,
seeing as I was looking forward to it so much. That was for just
after noon. Now. Shower and nap? Nothing? I looked at myself
in the mirror. Ah, what an improvement from a just a few weeks
before. Well fucked really did suit me, I sniggered at my reflection. And it felt better than a facial. But some of it did wind up
on your face. Ok, delirious and jet-lagged. Not funny.

I was interrupted by a knock at the door. Tea. Of course.
I went over to the door to answer it, and was greeted by an
older man carrying a tray. I instantly felt suspicious, and yet I
couldn't say why. I gestured to him to put the tray down on the
desk, and went to get my bag, walking backwards as I did so,
keeping an eye on him. Stupid, maybe. But I just didn't want
any hastily snapped phone pictures of my bedroom used. I
wasn't anyone, not really, but if they wanted to turn this into
something, they could. I knew the tricks. I fished around for

some pound coins and dropped them into his hand, after I herded him back out the door. Hmm. I might have to switch hotels. Then I suddenly had the thought that maybe this wasn't the paps, but Dave. Dave wondering who I was meeting, wondering if they had come up with me, Dave keeping an eye on me. Ok, I needed to slow down.

I poured myself some tea. Fancy hotel, fancy tea—no muddy thick builder's tea here. That meant I wouldn't have to add milk, the traditional English way. I'd never really liked milk in tea. After all that time here, I tolerated it. And as I stirred in one of the brown sugar lumps, I thought about my paranoia about the hotel and the staff. Just because you were paranoid, didn't mean they weren't out to get you, right? I sat on the bed and finished the tea, trying to clear my thoughts. Tired. I was just tired. I was in London, about to do the piece of my career, and I was worried about the guy with the tea tray. Wow. I put the cup down, a little too hard, and went to wash my face. And changed my mind. I'd decided against washing off Tristan. I needed his scent on me, like a protective mark, for me to know, no one else. No one else would know.

Oh fuck, I was so screwed. I knew how I felt. I knew. I knew all this went against everything I'd ever learned, or been told. I should be the hardass, devoted to my career above all else, except for my primitive search for a mate, looking for the perfect man, who in this scenario, was Dave. Money, respect, above judgment. The right choice.

The thing was, I'd never cared less in my life. About any of the shoulds. Instead, with Tristan, every transgression, every moment when he called me on something thrilled me, woke me up in a way I'd never expected. This morning, those moments, the way things seemed...altered, somehow. Tristan. His eyes, the way they had looked when I kissed him, his hands holding mine, the way he laughed at his thumbs up to the man in the car. He was a little crazy, of course. And sharp, witty, and fucking sexual dynamite. And this connection...and I wasn't going to go there. Stop thinking. It was going to be my little secret. But I lay there on the bed for a moment, remembering his hands all over me, feeling the ache as I stretched out, and wished he was there, over me, reminding me who was in charge, and why.

And as I finally sat down at the desk, and flipped open my laptop to send a few confirmation emails, and get some phone numbers, I tried not to smile, thinking of him, pushing the feeling away, to keep it safe. I called Dave's number at the office and left a message on the machine, to let him know I'd arrived safely, thanking him for the upgrade on the flight, and saying I would update him once I'd had some meetings. I might have been crazy, but I wasn't stupid. I wasn't going to fuck this job up, not if I could help it. And if playing by some of the rules got a result, then this was one little test I intended to pass. High marks. I poured out some more tea, and phoned the agent for "Tits from Oz" as I was calling them in my head. I wouldn't be using that in the article, but I wished I could. Maybe I could. Easy laugh, too easy, but not wrong. We'd see.

I listened to the foreign ring tone and reflected on how not so long ago, it was the American trilling that had sounded strange to me. A man picked up, saying hello with a strong Australian accent. I put on my best "I care but not really" journo voice, and stifled the impulse to ask for Tits from Oz. "Hello, may I speak to Rod Seger please?"

"Speaking."

"Hi there, this is Lily Taylor from *The Core*. I'm calling to confirm our interview this afternoon."

"Oh hello there. God, it's today is it? Oh right you are, it's Thursday, isn't it." He paused for a moment. "I hope you understand. They've been touring. And they've had a night off, you know how the kids are."

That wasn't the answer I was expecting. "Right, of course. Ok, but where are they now? Can we round them up? The magazine is holding space for them, but it won't last forever."

"Sure, sure." He cleared his throat. "Are you the secretary? Hey, we were expecting Dave to talk to us directly about a cover shoot. I thought he was coming out with Matt to do the interview."

Oh, nice, I thought. In your dreams, mate. Cover shot. And Matt Black. Numero uno. Almost as famous as the people he interviewed. Matt talked to Bono, not a bunch of drunks on a rider, with one single released. God, why was the world filled with assholes? I smiled at the phone. Reminding myself to be pleasant. It was their future after all. "Really? Who told you that? Well, Dave sent me personally. I am sure he'll be very disappointed to hear that the band didn't want the interview. Not a problem," here I was counting in my head to see how long it would take before he backtracked. "I'll just move on to my next appointment then…" He spluttered. There we go. What was he, drunk or stupid? That took more time than he had.

But his attitude had altered somewhat. "No, no, of course we want the interview. The band's been really looking forward to it, um…what did you say your name was again?"

My voice was crisper this time. "Lily. Lily Taylor. I'll need them in an hour; I've got a very full schedule on today." I pronounced schedule the British way. I didn't think he'd notice, but any chance to wind him up a little, make him realize his huge, huge mistake thinking he was dealing with some newbie girl.

"Uh, they're having breakfast in the pub...I'm just going to meet them there now."

"Fine. Get a table for all of them, and I'll meet you there. Where are you going to be?" I felt like I was talking to a complete idiot. Tell me the right answer. Slowly.

"The Good Mixer, in Camden. Do you know it?"

I laughed. "Yeah, I know it. I'll see you there," and pressed the red button, cutting him off in mid goodbye. The Good Mixer. God. The place used to be a hangout for musicians, now it was a meeting place for old smack heads and Japanese tourists, taking pictures of each other where Oasis had once stood, hoping for a glimpse of someone, anyone. It was a dive. Especially at lunch. I knew that first hand. Great. Fine, it'd be quick. Get the pics taken at their show tomorrow. I looked at my phone. 12:00 p.m. And they were already there. Well, they'd be worse for wear. Maybe they'd say something sound bite worthy. Or outrageous. Either one would do.

"On, on, on to the next one." I sang the snippet of Foo Fighters to myself. Next I had to call the woman who had started and been head of the fan club over here when Devised first came out. This, I was not looking forward to. I figured this was the real beginning—where all the stories were finally going to come out. Had he slept with her? I drew in a breath. Ouch. The thought actually hurt. But I wasn't going to let my weakness fuck this up for me. I stiffened up. Ok bitches. He was with me now. At least for now. And it was fucking brilliant. And that was that. End of thinking. A little voice in my head said, yeah for now. And he'll still be pulling the girls when you're telling the story drunkenly to your flat mates as they creep out, leaving you passed out in your own aging memories. I shook my head. No. I wasn't having it. Any of it. But the music business had its own little secrets. For instance, that for all its supposed cutting edge, change society and feed the world, did you say you wanted a revolution bullshit, the business was as traditional as a fairy tale. Macho intimidation and sex-as-a-weapon girls with an early sell-by date. Very few managed to get out of that little tradition unharmed. I was not going to be my worst enemy on this one. Fuck them, fuck all of them. I wasn't dead yet.

I sat on the edge of the bed, crossed one leg over the other, and stared towards the street through the gap left by the curtains. The usual street clatter, another day already heading past its apogee. A few black cabs went by. I punched in the number and pressed the button with the green phone receiver on it. Ringing. What to expect. Answerphone. Light, breathy voice. Cultured accent, but not too much. Sounded a bit tired. "You've reached Poppy. You know what to say." Do I now, I thought. I left a brief message with my phone number. We were due to meet around five, where she lived in Notting Hill. I wondered if she was money Notting Hill, or holdover Notting Hill, from when it was street, and Reggae and Rasta and Rock and Roll, so different from now. Another mystery. I wondered if she was pretty.

Tossing aside that thought, I marched into the bathroom, rinsed out my mouth, put on some fresh lipstick and touched up the eyeliner. I looked rough, but a kind of sexy, dirty around the edges rough. Perfect. I came out, zipped my suitcase up and put it on the rack next to the oak wardrobe, and zipped a tiny bit of toilet paper into it, by the corner. A little James Bond, but better safe than sorry. I'd like to know if someone was sniffing around. Laptop back in case, planner back in case, and I was ready to go, the recorder was already in there, all charged.

I picked it all up, and looked around the room one last time. Fine. But empty. And for a minute, the loneliness of London hotel rooms swept over me, a vast parade of people who didn't care catering to other people who didn't care. The sunshine was already past the point where it could come through the windows into the room, a sort of eternal afternoon shadow falling over the plush pink carpet. Empty. Waiting. Alone. And possibly forever, moving on from floor to grave.

Thinking like that, thinking of what could go wrong, the isolation of sitting in some perpetual shade, made me want a drink. Lots of them. Well, the idiocy of the band I was about to interview would probably put me off, along with the dirty glasses at the pub. What I needed to do was keep it together, not fall into bad old ways, partying it up with a collection of strangers.

I shut the door a lot harder than was necessary, and went to have the doorman get me a taxi. Hooray for expense accounts. No fucking Tube. And moments later, as I sat back in the taxi, being driven around for the second time that day, but not so memorably, I thought, I looked out the window at the London I used to vaguely inhabit. I almost believed we would turn a corner, and I'd see myself, coming out of a pub, or a charity shop, or my latest tutoring job, looking wistfully at the taxi, before setting off to walk home. I'd always hated the Tube. It made me claustrophobic, and slightly paranoid. And of course it was a well-known fact that when you blew your nose after taking the Northern Line, you would see the residue from the smoky, soot encrusted air you breathed in while waiting on the platform.

They don't show that in the TV shows. So, back in the day, I'd done a lot of walking, and a lot of thinking.

And now I was in my own black cab, paid for by Dave, and thinking about the band. I could complain, but I wasn't going to. And there was Tristan. I closed my eyes when I thought back to just…this morning? Now it seemed a hundred years ago. I wondered what he was up to. I didn't even want to think about him too much. I couldn't afford to get all dreamy and misty eyed now. It was enough to feel the ache between my legs, and smile at how it got there. A united front, he'd said. God, I hoped so.

Right now, I needed to be hard. Or else these people would tear me apart, and I'd wind up letting them, too bemused and lovesick to do anything else. No. I'd make him proud of me. Hell, I'd make me proud of me. It had been a long fucking road, after all.

Chapter 7

I had the cab drop me off on Camden High Street, just past the corner. It all looked about the same, grotty, busy, a bunch of kids sporting punk pink Mohicans hanging out by the Tube station, private school kids with their skirts hiked up as high as they dared trying on sunglasses and buying the little transgressive bits of paraphernalia that would make them feel like they were breaking out. Nothing changes, I thought. And the tourists with maps and cameras, and the older women dragging behind their shopping trolleys, going home from a trip to the frozen food store, Iceland, after getting their pension cheques. Two frozen fish fillets, a packet of biscuits, tea, and a pint of milk. The mini gangs dealing drugs, some actually dangerous, and the police hardly ever moved them on. The metal lovers, so pierced up and tattooed that they couldn't get any other job besides handing out flyers, killing time and making a few quid until the next gig. Yeah. Plus ça change, and all that.

I walked down the pedestrianized street, by the few stragglers selling junk from their hastily put up stalls, with the red striped tarps overhead, and the two homeless guys sitting in a doorway, drinking from a huge bottle of cider. The pub was right on the corner, white paint, some graffiti here and there (Liam rules!). I went in and the smell of old beer soaked carpets made me gag. Jesus. It was even worse than the last time I'd been in here. I nodded to the guy at the bar, and went to the other side. There they were. Three guys, one with a beard, fairly average and nondescript, dressed in jeans and flannel and t-shirts. One guy, a bit older, already losing his hair. That must be Rod, who I'd spoken to on the phone. And then the girl. They hadn't even noticed me. They probably hadn't noticed anyone else since the day she came into their little orbit. Super blond, big blue eyes, hard mouth prettified under a dollop of shiny red lipstick. She was wearing a dress that reminded me of what Julia Roberts wore at the beginning of *Pretty Woman*. Total hooker clothing. No bra, big tits. Yeah, no wonder no one really cared if she could sing. Their ears had no blood supply, it was all down in their cocks. Man. What a set-up for these guys. They needed a hook, because they weren't star quality, and she needed some safety, and most importantly, some guys who would tell her she was great. All the time.

Of course, she noticed me first. Her eyes narrowed. This was the type that didn't pray at night before bed for good things and world peace, but practiced her cutting put-downs. I quailed a bit inside, and crushed it. Turn it around. Let's see what you got bitch. I'm writing your future.

I grimaced, and walked over to the table. I smiled at all of them and looked at the manager, holding out my hand, waiting for him to stand up. No. He didn't. Idiot.

"I'm Lily Taylor, you must be Rod, nice to meet you."

"Oh right, Lily, Rod, we talked on the phone." He finally extended his hand, and I took it. It was clammy, and spongy. I was thrilled when he dropped it to point out the members of the band. "That's Jim," he said, indicating the guy with the beard, and the big eyes. He probably wrote the songs, we'd see. "This one's Andy," pointing out the big blond with the glasses. He, at least, stood up to shake my hand. Something to go on. Maybe we can get a few sentences strung together out of him. "And Joe," stretching out his moist hand towards the guy with the curly ginger hair. "And of course," he said, his smile oozing across his face, "our star, Fee." I smiled at her and watched her stare at me evilly, then suddenly burst into a big smile.

"Oh Rod told me we were being interviewed by *The Core* magazine! I'm so excited. Really." Her accent was incredibly thick, bouncing up and down as much as her boobs, which seemed to have a life of their own. "You're not who we expected though."

Oh here it comes. Let's see if those nights practicing have paid off, I thought.

She carried on. "We thought we were getting the big boss. Are you sure you're good enough for us? We're the next big thing you know!" And she squealed and high fived each of her band mates.

The looks on their faces were priceless. I smiled at her. "Oh, I'll try my hardest," I said, looking around at her band mates, "to make sure you have the write-up you deserve." I sat down, and put my best "I'm really boring" face on. It worked like a charm.

"Oh this is probably so exciting for you, this job, isn't it? Getting to meet all these cool people you wouldn't ordinarily meet." She hissed and gurgled. The boys in the band all laughed. She was one of those. Warming to her theme, and sticking to it. Well, if you've got only one theme, use it, I thought.

"Yes, I'm so lucky," I replied drily, getting out the recorder. This was going to be captured for all time. We were all so lucky. "Hang on just a sec while I set up the mic. I'm going to record it, hope that's ok."

She spoke again. Didn't the rest of them have balls? Or had she eaten them already? "Oh that's fine. We're so used to it now, aren't we guys?" They all beamed. "We just love it here, so exciting."

"Ok, hang on. All right, good to go," I said, pressing the button that would render her squeak to an electronic eternity. "Why don't you tell me how you met these," I paused, "talented gentlemen? You must have done something out of your usual circuit, to come across them." I smiled. She looked up at me. Yes, dear, I thought. Well done. You noticed. She hesitated. "Maybe one of them was a high school sweetheart? Or a friend of your brother? Do you come from a big family?"

She giggled, and put her arm around the guy with the beard. "Oh, you're so right! How did you know? Jim here was my older brother's best friend. They had a little band together in my parents' garage. And when I was thirteen, you know, just starting to...develop," here she dissolved in giggles again, "I was interested in music, you know. They played like, AC/DC, real Aussie boy stuff, but I got them to learn a Spice Girls song for me."

I nodded, and looked encouragingly at Jim. Maybe he would say something. "Jim, how did she convince you?" He started blushing. I followed it up. "This sounds like a great story, how it all begins..." She interrupted me.

"It was the funniest thing! They were down there, all serious." Fee was loving the spotlight now. Some of the other punters had moved a little closer. A little bit of sex and rock and roll to break up the monotony of getting wasted. "So, first," her accent actually got thicker, "I threatened them. I told them I'd tell my parents what they were up to, um, smoking and all. And they said they didn't care. But I kept bothering them, you know? And I'd be down there, listening. Then I said I'd show them my bra! That worked! But I had to take it off to get them to let me sing.' She sighed happily. "But it was worth it. Because here we all are."

Nice. Lovely. I tried to act like I'd just heard a heart-warming tale. "That's great. What a story. And you two," I said, looking at Andy and Joe, who hadn't said a word, "how did you get involved?"

Rod spoke up. "They met up at school, you know, the usual thing."

Interesting. They don't speak. "So how old are you all now?"

Jim spoke up. "I'm twenty-two, and Andy and Joe are both twenty-three."

I turned my attention to him. "Do you write the songs?" Let's see if my guess was right, I thought.

"Yeah, I do mainly. The other guys come in with ideas, and Fee, she'll change a lyric if she thinks it goes better with the song."

"Is there a particular genre of music you feel you fit into? You've got a lot of influences here—surf music, hard rock, pop— are you drawn to one of those in particular?"

"I've always been a big fan of hard guitar sounds, so we try to put those in and mix up some keyboards. Electronica as well." He looked nervous. "I put things together, and then we adapt them to Fee's style of singing, and..." he stopped, interrupted by Fee.

"You see, we all just work so well as a team! We're really sensitive, at least when we're not in the mosh pit, or like when we used to push our way into clubs. We all love each other, don't we boys?" They all nodded. She was bouncing up and down in her seat. They were riveted again. It was quite something to watch. "We're all about the fans, trying to give them a good time, a good party, like we've got back home, right? If they get a bit drunk and wild, that's good, then we know they're getting it, having fun."

I tried to turn the direction slightly. "What are your audiences like? Do you think there's a certain type you see in the crowd?"

She giggled again. It was getting irritating. "Of course, we get a lot of guys. Really cute guys." The boys in the band all sagged at bit at this. They'd be sloughed off soon enough, it was obvious. Jim might survive, with his quasi-schizoid appeal. I hoped his songs were developing. I felt kind of sorry for him, strangely enough. I turned to him.

"And Jim, of course you get a lot of girls." He actually smiled. Bless. "Have you gotten to meet some other songwriters, people you admire?"

"I met the guys from Death Cab, they were really great. And Modest Mouse. Great band, love them." He actually seemed animated. I glanced over at Tits. She was sulking, waiting for her moment. "But I'd love to meet some of the classic heroes, like Angus," he added. "Love you Angus! If I could get to meet him, I'd die a happy man." Ah, a real fan. It made me like him more.

But Fee was shouting. "Off off off! Angus showing his ass, but everyone strips down! I love their shows, they're just brill. And they are still going, even though they're what, like a hundred now! Yeah!" She stood up and started singing, with fervor, if a little off key, "she was a fast machine, she kept her motor clean, she was the best damn woman that I'd ever seen" to general applause from the half empty pub. She then took a bow, bending over so low I thought I got a glimpse of her belly button piercing. More general cheering. I wished I wasn't sitting directly in front of her. I was sure most of the people behind me felt the same way.

As the cheers died down, I thought maybe I'd had enough. A couple of more questions about the album, and I could get the hell out of there.

"So guys, the album. There's a lot of buzz around you, and your show at South by Southwest really got a lot of interest. You've got a label now, when can we expect the album?"

Rod stepped up for this one, as I figured he would. "Yeah, it's been great, the label's so behind us." And then he added, as though he couldn't resist, "I think Dave's going to wish he got us for our first cover, it's going to be historic!" They all cheered again.

I wouldn't be deflected though. "Have you got tracks ready? You must be hoping to go into the studio very soon."

"Yeah, we'll be in there next month. Jim's just finishing up the last few songs." He looked over at him, and Jim shook his head, his smile a bit more of a grimace than an actual smile. No wonder he was nervous. "We're going to be doing it in LA—all sunshine! We're ready to put down the tracks."

Man, I hoped so, for Jim's sake. They wouldn't get another shot at this. One more quote. Maybe I could get the whole band to talk. "So, to wrap up, maybe each of you could send a shout out to your fans. Jim, let's start with you." I looked at him.

"Uh, yeah, thanks for coming to the shows and being there." Great.

"Joe?"

He took a big swig of beer before he answered. "It's a party, it's all good." Ok, that was a bit more promising, if unsurprising.

"Andy?"

"Love you, all the fans, just keep on coming." Fair enough.

"And last but not least," I simpered, "Fee."

"All you guys, you're the best, I wanna see more of you, and you'll see more of me! Yeah!"

God.

I thanked them, told the manager I'd be in touch about the photographer for tomorrow's show, and packed up as fast as I could. Even the air in the fetid little side street felt like sweet nectar after the fermented beer and smoke smell in the pub. I took a couple of deep breaths, which made me dizzy, and headed over towards Primrose Hill. I checked my phone. 3:30 p.m. No messages. Ok. I'd sit in the park for twenty minutes, then get a cab over to Notting Hill. I messaged Dave:

> New band done. They thought they'd get to meet
> you. I sent your regards.

I thought about sending a message to Tristan. No. I'd sit first and clear my mind. Make some notes. Walking through the pastel colored stucco houses, and the curved road leading to the park, it occurred to me, not for the first time, what a city of contrasts London was. That all the tea and gardens, pretti-fied urbanity, was just the organized surface, minutes away from dirt and disorder. And the Queen and country image only a very small part of what was out there. Maybe that was true anywhere. You could always be surprised by what lay underneath.

The interview had been strange, but ultimately, safe. Not so for the next one. I wondered what would happen. This time, I couldn't predict what she was going to say.

Or how I was going to feel.

Chapter 8

Poppy, for that was her name, really, called me back to confirm while I was sitting in the park, fighting jet lag and looking around at the people walking by. Dog walkers, nannies with children, some German tourists, a few hipsters wandering around, their pork pie hats and brightly colored sunglasses looking weirdly over lit in the bright sunshine. I had almost not heard the phone ringing, lost in my own thoughts. But I managed to get the call just in time, and I must have sounded a bit breathless when I answered. Poppy was all kindness, thrilled to do this, about time someone started writing about the crazy scene that sprung up around the band. She sounded...wistful. I got the address, and arranged to meet her at her house around five. Fine. That gave me a little more time afterwards.

I walked up the hill and looked out over the skyline, completely altered in a very short space of time. Not that long ago, there were certain landmarks that stood out, being the tallest structures amidst the medium sized buildings of modern and old London. The BT, or Post Office Tower, London's example of the 1960s craze to build towers that looked like communication posts with satellites, missiles, aliens. There were many of them scattered through the world. NY, Moscow, Berlin—each had an example. And then there was the icon, St. Paul's Cathedral, its sturdy white dome a landmark, the sightlines to it still unobstructed. The Nat West building in the city, brown and black, striped, ugly modern. Then in the 1990s everything started to change. Canary Wharf, the mini version of New York, built in the Docklands. The London Eye, a weird, white Ferris wheel directly across from the Houses of Parliament. The 1970s modernist buildings around St. Paul's torn down, replaced with newer, shiny structures. The Egg, or the Gherkin, the strange spaceship-like building in the city in tones of black and grey. Now, the odd pyramid of the Shard. And all the old buildings were fading into the background, and London was becoming an uneven line, bounded by Canary Wharf to the east, and the Eye to the West. Strange little flood plain, I thought. Not even beautiful, like Paris, or startling, like New York, but there was still something to it. What? I wasn't sure. Maybe the visible signs of change, all fighting each other for space, waiting to grow and have their moment. I didn't know.

I sat there for a bit, lost in my thoughts and the residue of jet lag, trying to feel the Druidic energy of the place. Finally, I walked back down Primrose Hill and got a taxi down near the Zoo. I gave the driver the address, and leaned back, exhausted. I'd keep an eye on him, but at least I knew he'd know exactly where he was going. All the cabbies, for black cabs anyway, had to do the training called The Knowledge, where they'd spend all their free time whizzing around on little mopeds, their maps in front of them, learning every one of the 25,000 streets and over 300 routes that were required in order to pass the test. Some of the cabbies had to retake the test ten times to finally master it. Now all I had to worry about was if he'd be taking the long way around. But I was so tired, it hardly seemed to matter. Dave was paying, after all.

Tiredness was also helping me not think too much about this meeting with—the woman. Yes, she sounded fine. I just wondered what she was going to come up with. She'd obviously met the whole band. I wondered if she still talked to any of them, Tristan included. What did she think about the break up? I could deflect her a little bit, but the focus of the article was supposed to be Tristan, so we would have to discuss him directly. Oh hell, I couldn't avoid it. And did I even want to? There was a kind of morbid curiosity, to know exactly what he had gotten up to. The jealousy that would arise would be a kind of burn, maybe. Cleansing. Or maybe it was going to be like meeting the family; slightly embarrassing, horribly revealing, but again, building on a bond, the kind you only created when you did know things. Or nothing. Just an interview, about a band and their lead singer. Another one. I could just disassociate myself completely from it all.

The cab was making the twists and turns through Kilburn and was heading down by Westbourne Park, over the railroad bridge and by the bus station. I'd once stood there, kissing a guy, both of us a bit drunk, not wanting to go anywhere, or take it any further, just enjoying kissing, late night, pubs shut. A few people heading towards the Tube had whistled at us, I remembered, and we just ignored them. Not that long ago. Of course I wasn't as pure as I thought—what the hell was I doing judging him and his conquests? Wasn't it just life? If you were ok looking and could get people to want you, didn't you carry through with it? He wasn't a saint—here I couldn't help smiling, thinking of him gesturing at the man in the car—and didn't I like that? A lot? I'd probably get further if I just opened my mind, and stopped being so fucking frightened and judgmental. I could do this. I was going to listen, and not be critical, and learn something, for once.

We pulled up in front of a small purple cottage, one of a multi-colored row, just ground floor and first floor, with white painted window frames and a climbing white rose reaching over the doorway to the upstairs. Showtime, indeed. I paid the cabbie, and steadying myself, walked up to the door. Open minded, right. Not purposeful, or sarcastic, or fearful. Open—to whatever she had to say. I was a journalist, right? That was supposed to be my job anyway. To transmit as truthfully as I could what I saw. With atmosphere. Yeah, but it's you seeing it. And you are compromised, way deep. So I am, and I thought back to our latest limo ride. And I like it, it's hot. Open mind, open mind, I kept repeating to myself, as I rang the white ceramic bell surrounded with enameled flowers. Pretty. Beautiful, even. Like she'd be. I knew it.

And I wasn't wrong. The woman who opened the door was lovely. Long, carefully highlighted blond hair, small sculpted nose and mouth, warm hazel eyes, lightly made up. A flowered dress, gauzy, boho, falling to mid-calf. She'd made an effort, but it was obvious that she probably looked like this all the time. She greeted me warmly. "Lily, so glad to meet you. Welcome. Come in. Can I get you some tea? A glass of wine? Come, follow me, we can sit in the kitchen, the doors are open to the garden, it's quite warm out really, isn't it? So glad you've gotten the good weather, we've been having nothing but rain."

I followed her in, faintly amused at her patter about the weather. I always forgot how the British really did talk about the weather to get social interactions going, and how you had to answer back with something, or else the conversation would die out, as though you had to say the magic words before you could step through to the next level.

"Yes, very lucky. I was just enjoying the sunshine, trying to get over my jet lag with some fresh air. Has it been a slow spring here, then?" We had reached the kitchen now, a big long room, with a skylight overhead, a long pine table, a red Aga stove against the wall and a big SMEG refrigerator. Ok, money Notting Hill. Although it might be old money. She seemed very relaxed. I looked around for the requisite dog, and found an empty padded dog basket. "What kind of dog do you have?"

"Oh, you saw the basket. Where is she, I wonder? She's lovely, an English Retriever, so loyal. Just a lovely dog. I'm sure she'll come down. Do you like dogs? What can I get you to drink?"

I really wanted a drink, but it was too dangerous. I'd relax. I'd fall asleep. Worse, I might talk too much. "Tea is fine, thank you. Yes, very fond of dogs. Keep meaning to get another one, but I travel too much." This was turning into a conversation. I was almost reluctant to get out the equipment, feeling it would change the mood. But I didn't trust myself to remember it clearly. I wanted to have the proof, as well, of whatever it was she was about to say. I watched her busy herself with the kettle on the stove, pulling out the brown teapot. This was real England, real London here—or at least the way it used to be. It felt more real to me, anyhow. She was tall, taller than me, I noticed unhappily, and cringed inwardly. No, I would not do this to myself. Open mind. Happy. I'd just read an article about a woman who had said all pretty women saw each other as competition. I would not be that shallow.

I might as well just dive in, I thought. "Do you mind if I record our conversation? It does make it easier for me to ensure everyone is quoted correctly."

"No, not at all," she trilled out. "Sugar?"

As I got out the equipment, I thought she sounded amazingly unperturbed by any of this. Perhaps it was an act. Perhaps it was her personality. We'd see.

Finally, everything was set up, the tea poured out, the dog, who was named Scone, patted and sleeping in the basket, a plate of biscuits arranged neatly, the radio turned off. She looked at me expectantly. Right. Questions. My turn. I took a deep breath. Did she look...amused? I felt instantly irritated, and tamped it down. Let the woman speak.

"Could you do a little introduction? You know, your name, what you do now, your connection to Devised? I'll just test the levels." I nodded to her to start.

"Hello, I'm Poppy Gough, I'm currently a PR consultant for various bands and fashion designers. I was the head of the fan club and I did PR for Devised in the UK and Europe."

"Great. Ok, so, how did you first meet the band?"

She laughed a little. "I was the booking assistant for the university pub bands. It was fun, I wanted to get into the business of promotion, and I liked music. So it was perfect. Most of the bands were your run of the mill pub bands, but every so often we'd get someone that was obviously on their way up. Coldplay, for example. I booked their first gig here. Chris was so nervous! But a lovely guy, really. Amazing eyes."

I nodded encouragingly. "And Devised?"

"I still remember it quite clearly." She was looking off into the distance, as though she were revisiting the entire time. "It was the end of the day, and I was in the little office off from the Student Union just getting things sorted out. It was a Tuesday, nothing on. Slow day. And the phone rang, and it was Working Class Records. The man himself, Trevor. Of course everyone knew his name, including me, so I was pretty surprised. But I asked him what I could do for him, on a rainy Tuesday." She looked up at me. "I had no idea that phone call was going to change my life."

Dramatic. Well, she knew the game. This one would write itself. "And what did he want?" I asked, even though I already knew the answer, of course.

She smiled, Cheshire cat like. A feline sleepy smile, with a hint of danger. There were claws behind this one. And suddenly, all my danger signals were on alert. I'd been lured in, and now I was trapped. I was going to have to hear it all. I tried to calm the panic I was beginning to feel, along with the impulse to run for the door.

"Of course, you know, he had a little band he had just signed. They hadn't played here yet, and they needed a gig to start up. Could we slot them in for tomorrow? Cancel what we had on? He'd send over some posters. Could I make some phone calls and talk it up? He was sure it was the start of something big, and if I could get some motion going on it, he'd make it worth my while." She paused. "Of course, I was intrigued. Naturally. But then he said something that surprised me."

"Really," I looked at her. "What was it? Why did it surprise you?"

She flipped her hair slightly, and smiled again. "He told me I sounded pretty. Asked me if that was true." She laughed. "When I told him I would do, he said 'good, you'll match my boys—and they like them pretty.' It was such a strange thing to say." She looked at me for confirmation.

"Yes, absolutely. Do you think that was part of the myth he was starting around the band, or the truth?"

She didn't hesitate. "A bit of both, I'd say. It was true, but he was already establishing their reputations as notorious womanizers. But they weren't, not really, not then, anyway. That came a bit later. Particularly for Tristan."

Ah, here we go, I thought. "And the concert?"

"Well, I spent the rest of the night and the next day making phone calls, putting up posters, handing out free tickets, calling in favors. It really was a forerunner of the job I was about to take on, but full time. I managed to create such a buzz, that there was a queue around the corner to get in, people lining up three hours early, just to make sure they got in. It was a fantastic success, and Trevor, who of course was there, gave me £500 and the offer to run the fan club and help do PR." She had a dreamy look on her face. "It wasn't as hard a decision to make as you might think. To give up uni—university. It didn't matter, not compared to what he was offering."

"Why was that? And the concert? What is your most vivid memory of the actual show?"

"They were brilliant. Just on it. So young, yet so organized, so innocent, yet so trashed." She laughed. "The music was fantastic. No one knew what to expect, but by the end, we were all rabid fans. That group formed the basis of the initial club. We were called the 'fast set,' and we got in everywhere first, so the scene at the front was always crazy. And the band was so good to us."

She stopped suddenly, and looked at me. "Have you ever been in it, at the beginning of something like that? Where you could just feel the energy, the buzz? We knew it, and it took over our lives." She stood suddenly, and I wondered if she was going to end the interview. But she gave me that catlike smile again, and I could almost see her grooming her whiskers. "It's nearly six, I'm having a glass of wine. Please join me?" I nodded, relieved that she wasn't stopping her memories, but enhancing them. Maybe the mental images of the band brought on the need for alcohol. I knew just how she felt.

I watched her uncork the bottle of Pouilly Fuisse, glad I hadn't poisoned myself with some cheap lager this afternoon. She handed me a large delicate glass, the buttery liquid inside looking like nectar. God I needed a drink. I would keep it together. This would help. Right? I thanked her. "So what was your impression of the band?" Liquid courage. I took another sip.

"Oh, everyone's first thought, darling, was exactly the same. Fucking gorgeous." We both laughed. She looked up under her lashes at me, almost seductively. "You think so too, of course."

I tried to deflect the question. "I haven't met all of them in person. But the photographs are always in huge contrast to most other bands, like the Pogues, say." I pretended to laugh at my own joke.

She waved her hands. "No, no. They were like models, supermodels. And sexy. And smart. When I said the decision to take on the job wasn't that hard to make, that was a huge part of it." She looked out towards the garden and back at me. "Does all of this have to be on the record? There are a few things I'd like to tell you, that will help you understand, that maybe don't need to be in the article? Or the book? Dave told me that there might be a book." She paused again, while I tried to catch my breath. Dave? I knew he had spoken to people, but telling her there might be a book? He knew she'd tell it around. Interesting. And back to me.

"Of course." I turned my head away, and switched off the tape recorder. Cool. Playing it cool. "Just let me know when I can put it back on. Do you might if I make some notes though? Jet lag." I shrugged, as though it were nothing.

"Yes, I suppose that would be all right." Poppy poured herself some more wine, and topped up my glass. I was trying to pace myself. I wondered if she wanted to get me drunk, and made a note not to count glasses, but pours. I thanked her, and drank some more. Perhaps she was all right. Perhaps the excellent wine was making it easier to open up, be trusting. Perhaps.

"So why off the record?"

"Ah that night. That first night. I want to tell you, so you understand. But I'm not sure it's just my story to tell."

"Ok, fair enough. Go ahead, I understand." I tried to look as though she were telling me something therapeutic, and I was the pair of ears she was pouring into. I put my simple and plain face on. I'm so dull, so harmless. It had worked before. I wondered how many people she had told this story to, anyway. Maybe it really was therapeutic.

"After the show, naturally I went backstage to meet the band. Trevor, the head, was very complimentary about the job I'd done with the promotion. So he wanted me to hang out with them. We sat in the bar, drinking champagne that Trevor had brought—none of that in the Uni bar—until the sun came up. They were so funny, such different personalities, all very amusing and attractive in their own ways." She sighed. "And then there was Tristan."

Ah, here we go. Showtime. Indeed. I nodded helpfully, trying to mash my features into a mask of concern and interested disinterest. Damn it. I was interested. But I couldn't show how much. Or why. But she had stopped. That meant I needed to prompt. I hoped my voice wouldn't give it all away.

"Tristan. The front man. What about him?"

She looked at me as though I was insane. "Tristan—let me put it this way. By the time they left the stage, he'd had several pieces of girls' underclothing thrown at him. Flowers. Phone numbers. One girl tried to climb up on the stage, topless. And he just laughed."

I could imagine it, all too well. I smiled, in what I hoped was a journalistic coup kind of way, instead of "I've heard that sexy laugh too" kind of way. "That's a great image. I'd love to use it."

She waved her hands at me, and picked up her wine glass. "Yes, yes, that's fine. That was part of it anyway. But not the part that's off the record."

"Great." It was all I could get out.

"No, that night the two of us wound up talking. When the sun came up, we went for a walk...alone, hand in hand. And that was the beginning."

I nodded, silently. Keep talking, keep talking, I thought. Give me a minute. Please. God.

"When the boss asked me to run things, and go on tour with them sometimes, we hadn't slept together yet." She looked at me to see the effect of her words. I was drinking wine. I lifted my glass to her, and drank again. Then put it down to make some notes. Look busy.

She was continuing. "After the shows, I'd hang out with the band. There were always so many girls around, and a few guys too. The bass player wasn't averse to both, well none of them were in theory, but he practiced it more than others." She laughed. I laughed. Safe territory. And interesting information.

"So what was going on with the band at this point?" I thought I'd make an effort to get us back to on record. I put my hand on the recorder.

"No, no, not yet. I haven't told you everything yet." She poured out the rest of wine into our glasses, and raised her glass. We clinked glasses.

"I do need more information for the actual piece."

"Yes, don't fret, darling, we'll get there." She had that strange English way of sounding friendlier the further away she was getting from actually being friendly, and I felt that sense of worry come over me again. I almost wanted to shake her. Just get on with it, I wanted to say. But I couldn't. So I drank some more, and tried to settle my mixture of unease and impatience.

She was enjoying this, you could tell. This was her moment in the spotlight. I wondered how much she would want out of this, and what, if anything, Dave had promised her.

"It was amusing. Thrilling, of course. The shows were getting more and more frenzied. As were the fans. The boys, as you know, were very careful of their private life. But I can tell you, a saint would have stumbled at the parade of flesh they were treated to every night. And there they would be, at the end of the night, sitting at a table, each of them surrounded by two or three lovelies. They'd developed a system..."

I interrupted her. "Can this go on the record? I think we can guarantee anonymity for any quotes you'd rather not have attributed." I hesitated, hoping I seemed like I was divulging a big secret. "I'm sure Dave mentioned it? The possibility of this being turned into a documentary? Film? And you'd have a large role, of course, particularly because of your special insights." Was that laying it on too thick? "If I can record it, then Dave will hear instantly how important your participation would be. Ok?"

She took the bait, and swallowed it whole. Along with another gulp of wine. Yes, that's right, who's in charge now, I thought, as I pressed the button, and made her repeat most of what she'd already said.

I had some ideas for where she wanted to go with this. I'd help her hurry it up. I felt a bit more sanguine about it all. I knew what she was going to say. The fact she wanted to build it up so much, actually made it a tiny bit depressing. This was her past. And it was amazing, naturally. No one would deny that. But it was the past. I felt this sudden need to call Tristan, throw my arms around him, touch his warm body, and be in his actual presence, instead of all these ghosts, however interesting.

I returned my focus back to the blond woman, looking at me quizzically from across her pine kitchen table. "You were talking about a system?" She looked surprised. Not that drunk yet, am I, Yoda says, I thought in my head. And giggled. Her face registered slight annoyance. She thought I wasn't taking her seriously, that's what that small frown at the corner of her mouth meant, I decided, thinking at the same time that she'd have to watch that, or it would be the prime place for her first Botox injection. I smiled at her. "I'm laughing because I can just imagine what they did. Did they let you in on the secret? Did you ever help?" Now for a little ego boosting. She needed to open up a little. This would do it. "They obviously trusted you, particularly Tristan."

She preened, and began playing with her hair, putting it up in a simple, artful bun. Taking a long black lacquered chopstick off the table, she placed it through her creation and secured it. She was aware of me watching her, and seemed pleased to again be the center of attention. Another one who liked having an audience, but her need seemed more selfish somehow, and more tiring. She was pretty, and what she was saying was interesting, but it felt like hard work. Keeping her happy. I wondered if Tristan had felt the same way, and before I knew it, a slow smile had spread across my face. I felt her eyes on me. More work to do.

"You're a beautiful woman. And they trusted you. How did this fit into the lifestyle they were developing around being the most in-demand group at the time?"

She patted her hair, moving one long tendril back into place behind her ear. "Tristan and I were friends. He didn't really want the follow through with the groupies. He liked the attention, naturally. But he was pretty indifferent to the constant sex on demand that the rest of the band were enjoying." She drained her glass. "It wasn't that he didn't like sex—or women! No. He was a fantastic lover. Fantastic. Extraordinarily gifted. In all ways, if you see what mean." She sniggered. "I'm not shocking you, am I?"

I smiled, politely. Focus. Focus. "No, not yet anyway," I replied, sweetly. "I'll be sure to let you know if you do."

"Would you like some more wine?" She smiled back. A dangerous game.

"Yes, that would be great. Thank you." I made a show of looking at the notes. "When did you become lovers?"

She stood and took another bottle from the refrigerator.

I stared at her haunches, slim, flexible, tried to imagine them wrapped around him. I closed my eyes. It was easy. Too easy.

I looked up again, and she was pouring out more wine into my glass. I scribbled something down. "And the system? You were going to mention that?"

"The system. Yes. The boys would pick out their favorites from the audience. I'd have to make a little map of where they were, with the colors of their clothes and hair, and send some of the roadies out to invite them to the after party. Of course they were happy to do it, they got the leftovers. If there were any!" She laughed. "They had a lot of stamina, the boys."

"Did you ever sleep with anyone else in the band?" It seemed a logical question. But her face was a study.

"You really don't know all the stories, do you? What a funny choice then to have you to do the book. Well, maybe they want someone who isn't contaminated by all the rumors that went about." She shook her head, as though she was disagreeing with something. "There were so many things said, the orgies, the whips and cuffs, the girls claiming that they'd been sex slaves." She drank more. "People don't realize how mainstream the whole BDSM thing had become in certain circles. It would have been like turning down cocaine. If it's offered to you, you don't say no, do you?" She answered her own question. "No, obviously not. Yes, I slept with AC. But that was after Tristan and I were over. It wasn't the same. Nothing was the same after that."

Her eyes were slightly creased now, and her cheeks were flushed. I raised my glass. Now maybe we could cut the bullshit. "To heartache," I said.

"To heartache," she answered, and we clinked glasses again.

"What happened?" I felt like I needed to ask.

"I don't know. The band was huge, of course. It was a moment that was over, the small clubs, the intimacy of it all, and the excitement. You can see it in the interviews they gave then. So much less guarded. Just a bunch of kids who had no idea what was about to hit them." She sounded sad. "I couldn't tour with them all the time. And it suddenly got to a point where it was either going to be serious, or it wasn't. And the time wasn't right." She sighed.

I suddenly felt very, very sorry for her. Was this going to be me? In a couple of months? Next year? I needed to know more. I'd never, might not ever, have this chance again. I needed to know this stuff. Now.

"Did he break it off with you gently?" I wanted to hear about the future.

She shook her head. "He didn't mean to be cruel. I flew out to meet him in LA for a show. As a surprise. He was sleeping with the drummer from the lead on band. I found her trussed up in the dressing room with his head between her legs. AC said he didn't realize they were in there, but I think he'd always been slightly jealous of how close we were. And he wanted a go at me himself. A way to get back at Tristan? Maybe. Or a way to get close to him. It was a pretty open secret that AC thought Tristan should explore the other side...with AC as the guide." She filled her glass up to the top. "Oops, a little too much there. Never mind." We both drank.

"And you and AC?"

"We were an item for nearly two years. Ironically, it lasted slightly longer than my time with Tristan. How funny is that? But it wasn't the same, never the same." She sighed. "Paul, the guitarist, you know, the one who AC punched?" I nodded.

"Good, at least you know that story. He always claimed that I was like their Yoko. That I started the split with the band. But that was bullshit, and everyone knew it. Everyone knew that he was hiding what his girlfriend had done. She was the one that brought the photos of Tristan and the drummer to the papers. We all knew it."

Well, this was interesting.

"Which photos?"

"Oh, of course they couldn't be published. One of the big mags wanted to buy one of the cleaner ones. Sheer porn."

"Did you see them?"

"Yeah, AC got a copy of some of them. I actually think he took them. Nothing that surprising to anyone in that circle. Tristan in leather. A collection of whips. Probably the most shocking one was the small brand on her hip, with his initials. But no one ever said whether he did it or not. The drummer, what was her name, Christina, that was it, chained and bound. His cock, with a cock ring. Pretty standard stuff, really."

Really. I laughed, I couldn't help it, but whether it was from nervousness, or the wine, or just the idiocy of the whole situation, I couldn't tell. "Maybe not to your average person."

"Yes, but who cares? No one. Anyone in the spotlight has to take it further. That's what they want!" She was becoming more animated. "That's what started all the stories. Those pictures. The rumors about what was really in them. And again, it all came up again later on, when his wife left him. Although no one was really sure why she had married him in the first place. Anyone who knew Tristan from the old days knew that he liked to drink, and party, but that he wasn't really about the party, he wanted to push the boundaries. She just wanted the money. To be the center of attention. Well, she's in Hollywood. Getting what she deserves, the bitch. I think she really hurt him. Hopefully someone even more shallow and concerned with appearances will dump her and her fake boobs." She pulled out the chopstick and her hair fell down around her face, and she energetically swept it back up again and rearranged it, again watching me watch her.

I couldn't resist. "Do you still have the pictures?"

Her hands slowly finished putting the chopstick in place. "Who said I had them in the first place?"

More flattery was needed. "I thought AC might have trusted you to keep them out of the wrong hands."

She pursed her lips. Her face grew more pointed, almost as if she were sniffing at me, like an animal. I gazed at her, levelly, or as much as I could, given how jetlagged I realized I was becoming. I wanted the information. This was what I needed to do to get it.

"You're not stupid, are you?" Poppy gazed at me.

"I try to avoid it," I answered. "I don't want the pictures, I'd just like to see them." Maybe I could make this a bonding moment. "I'd like to see what you experienced."

"He didn't really do that with me. Ah, simpler times." She smirked into her glass. "But yes, I've got them." I looked at her hopefully. "You probably want to see his cock. Most people do. Remember the 'plaster casters'? Now those were the days. When men were men, and women kept souvenirs of their favorite parts. I met one of the ladies once. She was fantastic. No point in living your life filled with regrets over what you haven't dared to do, that's what she said. I tend to agree."

I nodded. "I would love to see them." I tried to look grateful. Like I needed her to corrupt me.

"Yes, they're definitely erotic. Naturally not as impressive as he was in the flesh, but we take what we can get, don't we?" She looked me up and down. "All right. But this is off the record. You can only allude to how well-constructed he was...is. Some lucky girl. But once, that was me. Yes. I'll show you. Stay here, I'll be back in a moment. The loo is through there if you need it." And with that she swept away. I could hear her footsteps going up the staircase, and I wondered if they were in her bedroom.

That's where I'd keep them.

I went to the bathroom and I tried to straighten myself up a little. There were so many more questions I really wanted to ask, but I didn't want to give myself away. I couldn't decide what I felt about her. I liked her, even felt a bit like we had something in common besides the obvious, but it almost didn't seem real that she once had a relationship with Tristan, maybe even felt she was in love with him. That's what I would ask her, I thought. How she felt then. How she felt now. Maybe her answer would help make sense of my jumble of emotions. But I thought of his smile, his whispers in my hair, and I didn't want to compare it. I didn't want to think of our connection as some problem to be figured out, one more relationship on some long timeline that started and ended...when? I splashed some water on my face. The circles under my eyes were becoming darker. It had been a long day. It really was time to cut it, go home, stop feeding my irrational curiosity. I had enough material for now. But just a few more questions, couldn't hurt, right? I went out, and found Poppy sitting there, gazing at the photos, 8x10 glossies. She hadn't heard me, and I stood there for a moment and watched her. She was pretty, no question. Her long neck was gracefully curved, looking down at the pictures. She was smiling, but it was a smile so close to tears, that I immediately felt guilty for spying on her. I carefully backed up a few steps, over the large square red clay tiles in the hallway, and closed the bathroom door with a loud click, and advanced again into the room. Sure enough, she had mastered her emotions, and on her face was a bright, if pained smile.

"Oh, there you are," she called out, and we might have been at a garden party, discussing fabric patterns for the new curtains, instead of about to sit together and look at pornographic photos of her old boyfriend, my new one, except she didn't know that, having sex with yet another woman. Interesting. I sat down, and sipped at my wine. It hadn't escaped my notice that she had put the photos back into a folder. Maybe she had changed her mind. I waited. I had a feeling it would be better if I didn't show as much interest as I felt. I looked at her, and she held my gaze. Her eyes were strange, I thought. Soft and brown, but with darker spots. She didn't look friendly at the moment. She looked menacing. I shrugged my shoulders at her, and drank my wine. It really didn't matter. At least I wanted her to feel that way.

Finally she spoke. "I didn't know what to think about you at first."

"No?" I responded.

"No, I didn't know why you were doing this. And once you were here, I still couldn't make it out. What was your angle? You seem," here she tapped the side of her glass with a clear painted fingernail, "sound. But why? You don't give off the vibe of a high flyer, yet obviously you have the clearance, no offense meant."

"None taken. But where are you going with this?" I couldn't resist asking her. What was she going on about, and what did this have to do with the pictures?

"We still love him, you know. Those of us who remember the beginning. The band—was great—of course. I still see a lot of AC. He always comes and takes me out to dinner when he's passing through. He's a lovely guy. But Tristan," she moved her chair back from the table, so that she was facing me more directly, "Tristan had, still has, by all accounts, something special. But he's been through a lot. I really hope you aren't one of those hacks who get to the top by any means possible."

I started shaking my head. Even with the insult, and the vaguely backhanded compliment, I sensed the fear behind the pride. She was throwing out darts, seeing if one of them would hit its mark. I had no intention of giving her the satisfaction.

"Look, Poppy. I'm doing my job. And my job is to talk to you, and get your unique point of view on Tristan and the beginning of his career. It's been a long day, I landed here this morning, I'm jetlagged as hell, and you've been charming, really. Very gracious. But look, I'm not a vulture. I don't need to see the photographs, although obviously I want to. I'm not dead yet, right?" I laughed, and she echoed me, unwillingly. "Why don't we just call it a night? I know how much those photos mean to you. It's ok, really."

She sighed. "I'm sorry. I've tried to be helpful."

I rushed to reassure her. "And you have been. Really." I started packing up. Enough was enough. I wondered if she was coming to the show. Well, she deserved it. Maybe. Of course, then she might know exactly what my interest in all this was, but it couldn't be helped. If it was going to come out, it was. What the hell. "We can talk again. And, you're on the guest list for the day after tomorrow, of course."

"Guest list?"

Oh sweet Jesus, this was worse than I'd thought. She had no idea he was even here. Never mind. "Tristan and the band are doing a secret show day after tomorrow. At Dingwalls." I tried to make it seem legitimate that I knew and she didn't. "It's a press thing, a junket. And some fans. They're keeping it quiet until the very last minute. So you'll be down for yourself plus one."

She smiled, and she instantly looked years younger. There was a softness around her eyes that returned, and it lit up her entire face. I stood up, and held out my hand, but she pulled me to her for a hug. She was small and bony, and she felt wispy close up, as though she might blow away. We separated and stood apart for a minute. "I want to show you something," she said, and reaching into the folder, she pulled out a small square photo and handed it to me. It was the two of them, their arms around each other, smiling into the camera. Her head was on his shoulder, and she had a blissful expression on her face. He looked happy, but at the same time he was looking at something beyond the camera. It was a cute picture though.

"It's a sweet picture." I handed it back to her, carefully. "You looked good together."

She lit up. "Do you think so?" I nodded. "Maybe you could use this picture in the piece."

"I'll make a note of it. I won't ask for it to be copied until I'm sure there's a place for it. But I think so. It's part of the history."

She looked pained again, and I knew I'd said the wrong thing. I tried to backtrack. "Something so lovely should be shown off, so the fans can see you, understand your importance, your connection to Tristan." This seemed to cheer her up slightly, but there was a lingering shadow around her eyes.

"Here, I'll walk you to the door."

At the threshold, I thanked her for everything and told her I'd see her at Dingwalls.

"Oh, yes, of course, the concert. Yes, I'll look for you. Pleasure. Really. Safe journey."

I smiled and waved as I made my way down the slate path, and turned at the white fence to wave again. She was framed in the doorway, leaning slightly to one side, against the white painted frame, her flowered dress blowing slightly in the breeze. Her dog came up to see what was going on, and that's how I left her, crouching down in the doorway, patting the dog, and talking to it.

I walked along the small streets for a while, looking at the twilight, watching the sky change color, the shadows lengthen and merge, the yellow hued lights coming on in the houses. Through some of the windows, I watched people talk, eat dinner, watch TV, pour out wine, talk to their kids. A million different little rituals.

I walked until it was full darkness, then headed in the direction of Holland Park Avenue. I'd get a cab there. I didn't want to think anymore. About any of it.

Chapter 9

During the cab ride back to the hotel, I texted my friends. I'd already let them know in the afternoon that I wasn't sure when I'd be free. Now I didn't know if I was still up for meeting them. But they seemed enthusiastic, and at this point, I was overtired and wired, so sleep was out of the question. I was also feeling a bit depressed from the whole meeting with Poppy. Life was so strange, and it hurt; like the line from that David Bowie song, my stomach felt small. I closed my eyes, and just willed away the panic that was bubbling under the surface and threatening to ruin everything. If fear was the mind killer, I was centered in the sights.

We were due to meet up at a Greek place in Primrose Hill we all liked. Maybe some chilled Retsina and their conversation would at least put off the gloom, if not dispel it. The hotel seemed like a cavern, some open wound of loneliness that was looming ahead. I couldn't figure out why I had such a bad feeling about the place. But it struck me that if I went back, I'd tuck my head under the covers and never look up again. After a minute of imagining that, it took about a second to make up my mind. I rapped on the glass, telling the cab driver to take me to the restaurant instead, gave him the address when he didn't know it, and texted my friends to let them know I was on my way. Now. Perfect. They wouldn't have to wait for me at the bar, while I got ready, and I wouldn't have to face the emptiness of my hotel room. Anyway, I was as ready as I was ever going to be. I sprayed some perfume on, and checked my face quickly. A little bit of eye liner, applied carefully at the red lights, some lipstick. Nothing could be done about the huge circles under my eyes. I'd now been up for a long time. I couldn't even get my head around how long. The morning with Tristan? It seemed like another lifetime.

When I got out, the restaurant was busy and festive; people waiting outside, groups laughing and talking. The pretty green and white flowered tiles that decorated the floor and walls provided a sunny counterpart to the polished red stained wood and made the place seem both cozy and openly welcoming. I wondered idly if Tristan liked Greek food, and where he was right now. I had checked my phone when I got out of the taxi. No texts. That was ok by me—I wasn't ready to leave one for him yet either. I didn't know what the hell I was going to say to him. All the questions I had were piling up like a car crash in my head—nasty, bloody, and possibly fatal. Us. Together. That's what he had said. Maybe. A few questions could make neat work of that idea. I was still reeling from the interview, and the ride from the airport, and the jet lag, and I could not string my ideas together properly, no matter how I tried. So I couldn't even text him. Not yet. I wanted to be in control of what came out, not my dangerous emotions.

I pushed through the people waiting, and I spotted my two friends, Nick and Sarah, sitting in a corner table by the window, on the other side of the bar. Perfect. A little quieter, so we could hear each other speak. We all hugged, and it felt good, really good, to see them again, easy after all the drama. We had talked every so often on the phone, but it was mostly emailing, only the occasional call. I hadn't seen them close up in person for a couple of years. But they looked great, exactly the same. And there was the bottle of Retsina, chilling in the bucket and a bowl of olives. Some things never changed.

"Lily, you look fabulous!" Sarah said, kissing me on each cheek. "Exhausted, but fabulous." Sarah was her usual quirky social self. But when I told her how great it was to see her, and gave her a hug, something seemed off. In her eyes? Her hands behind her back? I couldn't make it out. Nick seemed ok. Still good looking and distantly cool in appearance, but easy to talk to once you broke through the surface. The two of them chattered to me, and I heard about half of what they said, trying to nod and smile at the right places. God, I was tired. But about halfway through my glass of cold resin flavored wine, I perked up a bit, and made an attempt to ask them some questions. This was in between the three of us reading the menu out loud, discussing the specials, and then, laughing, ordering what we always did.

"One day," I giggled, finally starting to enjoy my state of complete mental disequilibrium, "we've really got to order something else."

"You always say that. But you never do." Nick laughed at me, but with a wink and a quick squeeze of my hand.

"So tell me about what's been happening," I said, pouring them out more wine, filling up my glass, and waving the empty bottle at the waiter to show him he needed to bring us another bottle. I suddenly felt very expansive. None of it mattered anyway. It was all going to end up painfully, we might as well enjoy it. Enjoy this. I loved this place, and I hadn't been here for ages.

"No, we've got news for you!" Sarah said. Ah, now I'd see what was different. I knew it. I always could read people. It could be an annoying talent. Fuck it. More wine. The waiter came with the new bottle, and I drained my glass while I studied his hands quickly opening the bottle with an opener that he pulled out of his hip pocket. Nice hips. I shook my head, and put my glass down, watching his hands pour out more wine for all of us.

Once he left, I looked at Sarah. "Ok, spill. Make it quick. I want to know."

She opened her mouth to reply, and got as far as "you'll never guess what we..." when Nick suddenly interrupted her. He spoke more slowly, more deliberately than she did. He never just raced in, instead always weighing up the situation.

"Are you sure Lil? I promise you, you're going to be surprised," he said.

I looked up at him, exasperated. "Come on, just tell me. I'm a big girl."

He shook his head, and shrugged, turning to Sarah. "Well, darling?"

She burst out with it, so loudly some of the other tables turned to look. "We're engaged!" And then she did it, actually went ahead and thrust her hand out theatrically to show off the rock. Well, that explained the hands behind the back thing. Why did women always do that with the ring?

"Wow, that's a stunner. Well done Nick." I forced my smile to grow wider. A million uncharitable things to say flew through my mind. You broke it, you bought it, was the first that came to mind, and I swallowed it down before I said it out loud and acted like a total jealous bitch. "Sarah. Wow. Guys. Congratulations." I wanted to sound happy for them, I really did. I wanted to really be happy for them. And he hadn't knocked her up, she was drinking, I had checked, so this wasn't a shotgun sort of thing. That was good. And Nick. He looked really settled and happy, with her hand on his shoulder, sitting up a bit straighter. All sorts of thoughts were flying through my mind. Why them? Why hadn't he asked me, back in the day, although I thought I knew the answer to that already. What did I want? That was a bigger question. And I had no fucking idea on that one.

I asked more questions, heard about the wedding plans—an autumn wedding. They hated the idea of June weddings. That was something, anyway. And Sarah moaned happily about her in-laws to be, and the endless demands her own mother was putting on her, and their list at John Lewis. When I asked about children, they both giggled. It was kind of cute, even though in a really irritating sort of way.

"Soon," Sarah said, gazing at Nick devotedly.

He smiled, and held her hand. "Once we are a little more settled." I wasn't sure if he was telling me, or reassuring her. And then he told me about the architecture project he was involved with, another one of the buildings cluttering up the landscape, but it was a big deal, and meant more money, and Sarah gazed at him proudly.

And I just looked at both of them, and wondered why. Listening to them bicker over china patterns and their honeymoon plans—scuba diving in Pattaya—was sweet. Reassuring. But weird. A million miles away from my day. And maybe that was a good thing.

Then they remembered about what I was doing there in the first place, and wanted to hear all about the interviewing. I made them laugh describing "tits from Oz." I briefly mentioned Poppy. Tristan. The concert. They whooped when I said they would be on the guest list, and that we should meet up before the show.

"Damn," Sarah said, "Tristan Hunter. He always was such a pretty thing. And talented."

And Nick punched her arm. "Hey, it's in the contract that came with the ring, you can't say that anymore," he said mournfully, trying to kiss her as she dodged him, smiling.

"Sure I can, darling, because you know I only have eyes for you. But he's hot. Really hot. Like on fire. Don't you think so, Lil? Back me up on this." And Sarah looked over at me, and I could just feel the blush creeping up my neck. Damn tiredness. Damn wine. Did I just giggle? I met her eyes, and we both laughed out loud. "See Nick, look at her. She's a quivering mess. Knickers in a twist." He looked right at me, and I was embarrassed all of a sudden. If they only knew. And then just at that moment, in some kind of bizarre synchronicity, my phone started vibrating in my bag.

"Fuck," I said. "I can never get my phone when I need it." I tried to rummage through what suddenly seemed like an endless sea of papers and receipts to get to the phone before it shut off. Success. I pressed the button, trying to steady my voice and ignore the pointed stares Sarah and Nick were giving me. I knew who it was already though, thanks to Devised's first single as the ringtone. How inappropriate I was. I thought I'd better try and sound professional though.

"Lily Taylor here. Hello?"

"Lily." His warm voice melted through me, and suddenly, this morning swept over me in a rush and I was wet, wanting his arms around me, hiding the worst of the world.

"Hey there," I said, and I knew my voice had changed by Nick's open mouthed stare. "Hold on a sec, I'm just at dinner with my friends here, let me take this outside." And I nodded to them, and headed for the door. The fresh air, fresh as it could be here, felt good. "Hi." I suddenly felt really drunk, standing up, and I leaned against the building. "Wow."

"Hey doll, are you alright?" His buttery voice sounded calm and soothing, and I just wanted to be next to him, and have him make it all ok.

"Yeah, it's just been a really long and weird day." How much detail? Did he know where I'd been? He was a friend now. Right? Not just a lover. I didn't have to pretend I was endlessly perfect anymore. Right? Or not? Second guessing. God. Play it safe. "I'm sorry, don't mean to whine."

"No, darling. It's alright. I told you to call...," he hesitated. "I knew you'd been hurt by something when you didn't. You were bound to hear things you didn't like." His voice changed, grew harder. "Of course that was the idea. And now—you will judge me as well." He was silent for a moment. "You know, when I asked you to call, I meant it." The last line sounded distant, sad.

"Oh, Tristan, it's not like that." I sighed. "I didn't know what to say. What to tell you. What to ask." I stopped for a minute. The world was spinning again. "I needed to process it all."

He breathed. "So you're not leaving? Did she show you the pictures? She's a broken person, Lily. She was then too."

He knew already. Everything. "So it's not just because of you." Shit. That came out without thinking.

"I didn't help, no, I won't lie to you. But I couldn't stay with her, and she knew that." I heard him breathe in, and I could almost imagine him looking down at his hand, thinking. "Don't tell me you've never had anyone want you and you couldn't give them what they wanted."

I nodded in the dark. I knew what he was saying. It was true. But still. "It scared me. I don't know what the truth is yet. I don't know what I want. And I'm not even supposed to tell you what I want. You'll run, right? That's what we learn, right from the first primary school dance." I felt like crying all of sudden. A big gulp of air stuck in my throat, out of nowhere, and I swallowed, loudly, trying to get rid of it.

"Darling. Sweet Lily. No. That's not the way it's supposed to be. Let me look after you." His voice was soft, coaxing.

The tears started again. "I'm so tired, baby, so tired." I sniffled. "I can do this, but oh man, I'm so tired." I wiped my eyes. "My friends…" I broke off. I didn't even know what I was saying.

"I want to see you. No, rephrase that—I am going to see you." He was silent for a minute. "The hotel is crawling with photogs. I guess our little entrance this am wasn't as stealthy as it could have been." He laughed, and my heart lifted a little.

"No, guess not. I had the impression they were quizzing me at the front desk."

"Yeah," he muttered. "I think someone," he emphasized the one, ironically, "might have tipped off the press." He muttered something to himself that sounded like "and I know who."

"It's kind of depressing there anyway. Pink. Little baskets." I said it perfectly seriously, but he started laughing.

"Lily, you are divine. But listen. This is the question. Do you trust your friends? Are they the people you're bringing? I'm assuming they are coming to the show," he said, as though he were putting pieces together.

"Yeah, they're cool. I just found out they're engaged. Discussing patterns. I was going to ask if I could stay the night with them anyway." I leaned against the wall again. I had the feeling the ground kept sinking an inch, then coming back up. "I'm a bit trashed."

"Are they ok with that?"

"I think so. I'll have to ask to make sure, of course, but I don't see why not."

His voice took on that commanding quality again, sexy. At the moment, it was damned reassuring, because I felt like everything was coming apart. "Go inside now. With the phone. With me. Ask them."

I was walking in before he had stopped speaking. Sarah and Nick took me in as I sat down, the reddened eyes, the sort of smile, the unsteady sinking into my chair. "Ok, hold on." I held the phone away from my ear, and looked at them. "Guys, could you do me a big favor?"

"Sure, Lil, do you want to crash at ours?" Nick looked at me. "Is everything ok? Do you want me to beat him up?"

I heard the laughter through the phone, and I smiled. They both wrinkled their foreheads, quizzically, in exactly the same way. It was sort of endearing really. Maybe they'd make it. But I heard words coming out of the phone and I put it back to my ear.

"Let me talk to him. What's his name?"

"Nick."

I handed over the phone. "He wants to talk to you." Nick looked confused but shrugged again, and took the phone.

"All right mate? Who's this?"

I watched as his expression registered shock, then surprise, then his usual sardonic look became a wide grin. Then he started talking. "No, of course. I think you're right. Not a problem at all. Of course you don't have to pay for our dinner. We'd love to be able to help." He looked at me, and there was a flicker of memory that passed between us, what had been good, that wouldn't go away. "She's a great girl you know. Just so." He nodded. "Absolutely. I hear you. Well, good. Yeah. No." Nick looked up at me for confirmation and I mouthed "it's ok" to him. "Yeah, Lemonia, it's Greek, yeah. I'll text the address. No? Ok. See you in a few." He pressed the end call button, and handed me back the phone.

Sarah was punching him again. "What was all that about? Who was that? And what's going on?"

He raised an eyebrow. "Little Miss Retsina Jet Set here can explain in the cab. The short answer—we're having guests tonight and Lily here has pulled. Finally." He laughed as I protested.

Sarah was practically jumping in her seat. "What? Who? Is he coming over? And you, "she said, directing a fierce look at me, "why were you crying?"

"It's a long story." I glanced around. Some people turned away as I looked in their direction. "Definitely not for here." The waiter had appeared, and was patiently trying to explain to Nick that everything had been taken care of.

"When?" he spluttered.

"On the phone sir, just a moment ago. A friend." He smiled. "Obviously a good friend. Whenever you are ready, it's all been arranged, and a taxi is coming in fifteen minutes to collect you."

"Jesus, Lily," Sarah whispered. "What the hell is this?"

I was about to say something, but Nick threw me a look, and he turned quickly to Sarah, "Shit, darling, should have gotten another bottle of wine." And he helped her on with her coat, and planted a brief kiss on her cheek. "Come on ladies, let's go outside. I need a fag after all that."

Sarah was whispering into his ear, and he was nodding, smiling at the staff as we left, who were thanking us. They were always friendly, but were they just a little more obsequious than usual? I wondered how big a tip Tristan had put on, or if there were some fans among the staff. I shook my head, and sat down in one of the small garden chairs and tables outside, and took a deep breath. The last Greek coffee I had had woken me up a little, but I still felt woozy. Sarah and Nick had walked off a little ways together, a cloud of smoke coming out of Nick every so often. I watched as Sarah suddenly stopped and made a kind of squawking noise, and tried, unsuccessfully to cover it up, and looked over at me. I waved, and she looked away, back at Nick. I guess she knew now too. That made four people in the world— two drivers, and my two friends over here. And Alice, who knew for sure. Oh, and the handyman at his building. Probably. Six. Increasing rapidly.

A cab pulled up, and I waved at the two of them again. This must be us. I got up and went to the driver, about to ask him if he was here to pick us up, when I heard a low voice. No. Not possible.

"Hey darling," and his eyes were dark and intense even in the gloom of the taxi. "Surprised? Get your friends, and let's get out of here before someone spots us."

I felt my whole face go pink, as I stared at him, then quickly turned towards Nick and Sarah, trying to convey a sense of urgency without shouting "hurry the fuck up," which is what I really wanted to do. There were already people slowing down, just to see who was arriving in the cab. I didn't understand how he did it. Maybe he just gave off a certain energy that made people sense there was something going on they needed to see. But we didn't need any mobile phone photos out there tonight, not if we wanted to get to their house without being followed. I skipped right up to the two of them, and giving Nick a look, jerked my head in the direction of the cab.

Sarah, as always, was a bit slower on the uptake. But I hadn't slept with her. Nick and I had always been good at reading each other. She started to ask a question, and he stopped her. "Sarah, later, we need to hurry, and please be cool."

Her head swung around to stare at him, as we approached the taxi.

He was still there, waiting. I pulled the door open and dove in, restraining myself from flinging myself at him, sighing with pleasure when I felt his arm curve around me. Sarah got in next, too busy arranging herself to notice anything, and then Nick sat on one of the little fold down seats and slammed the door shut. We pulled away, and Nick gave the driver the address, their road in West Hampstead.

When we had turned the corner, and started heading down a quiet road, away from all the people on the main street, I felt his lips press against my head, his hand stroking my back. He mumbled into my hair, "introduce me to your friends." I pulled myself away from his hands, and sat up, out of the sensual languor I was quickly falling into, and I caught Nick's eye. He was shaking his head and beaming at us. Sarah was trying to see past me to get a clear view of who the stranger in the cab was.

"Nick, Sarah," I stumbled over what to say next, "um, I, can I, I'd like you to meet, my, um, friend, Tristan, uh, Tristan Hunter."

I moved aside, letting Tristan shift forward to the edge of the seat, as Nick held out his hand, always cool, nonplussed. I could still hear the nervousness in his voice though he was hiding it well. "Hey man, pleasure to meet you. I'm a huge fan. And so's Lily, obviously." He threw me a crooked grin, and I glared back at him but couldn't help smiling. I watched them shake hands, Tristan's huge hand covering his. It was strange to see the two of them together. Sarah had finally gotten a good view, and was now staring, open mouthed. Nick kicked her, gently, and she coughed, then recovered, extending her hand too.

"Wow, Tristan, wow. Pleasure. Amazing. Well. Our Lily. Wow. And thank you for dinner." She seemed to recover herself a bit. "You didn't have to. It's our pleasure to help the two of you out, we've plenty of space. Hot water. Not that you need it. I mean. Oh hell. Nick, help me out here!" And she dissolved into a torrent of giggles that only stopped when Nick glared at her.

Tristan smiled, charm on full. "No, the least I could do. I really appreciate you putting us up, especially at short notice. I hadn't realized the hotel had already been scoped out, surrounded by the paps, so you've really helped me with a serious problem." And he took her hand, and briefly kissed the top of it, giving her a blindingly seductive smile. She fluttered at him, and then looked over guiltily at Nick, who looked a bit green. Tristan saw it right away, and turned towards him like a beacon of dark light. "And I hear congratulations are in order. Nice one, man." He slapped the top of Nick's arm like they were on a team. "You must be doing it right, my friend. She's a prize." And then Nick glowed, and sat up a little straighter, nearly banging his head on the ceiling of the cab.

And I lay back with my head on his shoulder, curling into his arm, watching the half-lit streets go by, listening to them chatter. Amazing. I felt myself drifting off, but when I tried to sit up, I was rewarded by Tristan pulling me even closer to him. When I opened my eyes, Nick and Sarah were holding hands, Sarah having left the bench seat to perch on one of the stools next to Nick. They looked happy, talking quietly.

I turned and buried my head in Tristan's neck. God, the smell of him. I kissed him softly, and whispered into his skin. "You came."

His mouth was over my ear. "You needed me. I won't leave you alone, Lily." And I curled up against him, our heads nestled together, as the black cab rattled through the streets.

Chapter 10

The cab eventually pulled up outside their little house with the red tiled roof and the bow window on the ground floor. There was a tiny garden in front, and we all stumbled out and into the street, Sarah already heading towards the door. Tristan gave some money to the driver, pushing Nick away playfully, saying "I got this man, no arguments," while I stood there, staring at the two of them, taking in the quiet road, how surreal this all was and how utterly exhausted I was feeling. I started to stumble a bit, turning towards the house, and Tristan's arm was around me in a second, his mouth at my ear. "It's ok, we're almost there." Sarah finally got the door open, and we all filed into the narrow hall, Nick slamming and locking all the locks on the wooden door. Tristan and I followed her down through the small living room to the kitchen. It was much smaller than the one at Poppy's, but still had the obligatory AGA tucked into a chimney breast, and down two steps from the main kitchen, a round pine table with a purple hand blown glass bowl on the center, with four chairs, positioned in front of the white painted double doors leading to the garden. The stove and sink were on the other side of a tiled counter, which we all stood around, leaning on it, a little awkwardly now that the excitement of the getaway was over.

Sarah asked if we wanted a cup of tea. Tristan said of course, that would be great, and looked down at me, concern in his eyes. "I think tea would be good for this one, it's been a long day. Very long. Do you have any green tea? I think that would be best." And he kissed my forehead. I almost felt embarrassed. I could hear the small gasp Sarah let out. The famous Tristan, worried about me and deciding which tea I should drink. It was a lot to take in, I could imagine. It was a lot for me to take in. I wanted to say something, to smooth out the moment, make it more of a light jokey sort of thing, but I was too tired. And in the ensuing silence, I realized that I didn't want it to be a joke, I didn't want to pretend it away, I just wanted to revel in it, his presence, his attention, his control, the whole thing, down to my toes, and not act like it didn't matter. Not like before.

She gave us our cups of green tea, in the process throwing Nick a few meaningful glances, and started to chatter about the dinner, and how great it was to see me, and the concert to-morrow. Tristan listened politely for a couple of minutes, then stopped her. "Sarah, I'm sorry, you've been so kind to us, really, but I think Lily needs some rest. Could you show us where we can sleep?" Her eyes widened. People didn't usually have much success shutting her down. And he'd done it with just a few words. Sarah nodded silently, and looked at Nick again, an odd squint on her face. "Will you take them upstairs, darling? I'll just tidy up here, and I'll be up in a tick."

"Of course, buttercup." Nick was more relaxed than she was, and obviously handling it all a bit better, ironically enough. I wondered what the conversation would be about later, and if he noticed how strangely she was acting. "Come on peoples, let me give you the mini tour of the route to the spare bedroom." We followed him out of the kitchen, and into the small living room. "This is the living room, where the TV is. Left here, and up the stairs, goes, well, upstairs. Follow me." And we thumped up the small one and half person wide stairs to the first landing. "This is where our bedroom is, and the bathroom. There is a shower, it's on demand hot water, not one of those timer things, so Lily, Tristan, if you want a shower before bed, feel free. There's extra towels in the cupboard there." He waved his hand in the direction of a bleached pine chest at the end of the hall. "Your bedroom is up these stairs, now." And we went up one more little flight, to an even smaller landing with an attic door and a small door off to the right. Nick opened it, and led us into a little bedroom, under the eaves, with slanted walls, and a little French door that faced out onto a mini railing, towards the garden. It felt like we were in some enchanted room, high in the sky, away from everything. There was a little blue woven rug, and a small chest of drawers, again in pine, but other than a small light and the bed and the window, the room was plain. I thought I'd never seen anything as homey in my life.

I turned to Nick, and gave him a hug, and a kiss on the cheek. "Nick, sweetheart, thanks for all this. And being so cool with everything."

Nick smiled. "Lily, you know I'm devoted to you. I'm glad I could help." He looked up at Tristan. "Sounds like you're a bit hemmed in."

Tristan gave a brief, ironic laugh. "Nick, my friend, it's been pretty awful. I know publicity is good, but not for everything, if you know what I mean." He looked over at me. "I'm used to it, mostly. But Lily doesn't need this, not right away, anyhow. And it was supposed to be a secret visit, at least until the ticket give-away tomorrow. But someone didn't read the fine print, I guess." He sounded angry. "Anyway, Nick. Thank you man, so much. Do you mind if we take a shower? I'm wound up, and Lily just got here—be nice to wash off some of stresses of modern life." He laughed again, and Nick, who had been hanging on his words, like he'd been let into some great secret, seemed to remember where he was.

"Sure. Of course. Mi casa and all that. Don't stand on cere-mony." He held out his hand, and Tristan took it in both of his, and looked at him. "Look after Lily," Nick continued, "I think she's knackered."

Tristan smiled. "Got it covered."

Nick nodded to him. "Now I've got my own wifey to keep an eye on. Sleep well you two." He had just turned and was at the door, when he looked back at us. "Should I keep an eye out to-morrow for souvenir hunters, that kind of thing? Not opening the door?"

Tristan looked a bit guilty. "It couldn't hurt, man. I'm really sorry about all this. Are you sure you're up for it?"

Nick just looked at him. "Any friend of Lily's is our friend. Don't even think about it. Go get her, before she falls over." And he looked at me. "Nighty night, Lily. Get some sleep, tonight, ok?" And he winked and pulled the door nearly shut behind him.

The minute he left, Tristan pulled me into his arms and held me there, my head against his chest, his arms circling me, his mouth against my hair. "I missed you today, Lily. I couldn't play the star game properly today, I kept thinking of you, thinking of this morning. Nothing seemed that much fun." I held on to him tightly. I just wanted to stay like this, listening to his deep voice rumbling in his chest, feeling him breathing next to me. "I knew what you were doing all day, because Dave had given me your whole itinerary. But I couldn't warn you, or tell you what to expect. It wouldn't have helped anyway. You know? You believe me, right?" I nodded against him. "You're tired, darling. We can talk about all this tomorrow. I don't have to be anywhere until twelve—I've got to pop into a couple of radio shows for the give-away, and your first is with the famous Trevor, at twelve thirty. See, I know all these things. Not just a pretty face. I think your girlfriend thinks I am though." He stopped for a minute, and held my face between his hands. "What do you think?"

I was thinking a lot of things, but none of them seemed to make sense, and none of them were reaching my mouth. Instead I said the one thing I knew was true, the one thing I wanted. "Kiss me. Just kiss me."

His eyes glittered for a moment, and then he was kissing me, and all I could feel were his soft lips on mine, gentle, and warm, and it was though I'd been waiting for it my whole life. He was soft and sweet, and quiet, and he smelled good, and he tasted better and it was though the sun had come out, everywhere, all over. He pulled away finally, and dropped a kiss on my nose. "Lily. You let me in." He kissed me again, quickly. "Could this mean you trust me? A little? Imagine." He took off his jacket, and his boots, then looked at me. "Doll, let's go shower. I'm ex-hausted." He winked at me. "You're still surprised, aren't you?"

I reached out for his hand. "Wouldn't you be?"

He looked serious for a moment. "Maybe I would, at that. I don't know. Lily, it does no good to overthink things. We both do

it. But where does it get us? Come on. Hot water is calling me."
And he pulled at my hand and we walked back down the stairs
to the bathroom, hand in hand. Nick and Sarah were nowhere
to be seen, which was fine with me. I didn't want to be stared at
anymore.

We both managed to fit into the shower, if we changed places
under the water. The rounded lavender purple soap bar looked
good against his pale skin, my tired brain thought, as I rolled
it around his balls, and over his thighs and down to his muscular calves, and back up again. It was nice washing him, I
thought. He was beautiful. Washing just for washing. His body
was hard, but his eyes were velvet and deep, and they looked ob-
servant and thoughtful and tired, not intense. He soaped me
carefully, the way he had dried himself off that time in his bathroom. I thought of his apartment, sitting there silent, empty,
waiting for his return. Would we be in it again? I looked at his
dark head, down at his huge hands covering my breasts, sliding down over my hips, between my legs, where it was still sore.
I jumped a little. "It's ok, darling," he whispered, "gently now,"
and his fingers were soft and probing and it felt good, so good.
But he stopped, and carried on washing my legs, picking up each
foot and circling his fingers around each toe. All the tension in
my body was easing away under his touch. At last he rinsed us
off, and shut off the water. "Come on, I won't bite," and his low
voice was a fire, warming me, as I shut my eyes, feeling the towel
wrapped around my body, and his hands, rubbing briskly at my
skin. He tucked the dark blue towel in on itself around me, and
did the same for the lighter blue towel, which was wrapped at a
dangerous angle around his hips, and took my hand again, after
scooping up our clothes.

He led the way back up the stairs, my hand tight in his, and pushed open the door with his body, dropping the pile of clothes on the floor. "Later," he said, and led me over to the bed. He pulled down the comforter, and turned to me and peeled away my towel. "Beautiful," he murmured, "a beautiful woman, on a beautiful night." And his eyes traced over my nakedness, over all of me, and I was shocked to realize I didn't feel embarrassed, like I would usually. Like I had with Nick. This wasn't the same. His eyes were magic, making me feel special, glowing under his admiration.

I looked up at his face, and his expression was serious. "I wasn't lying when I said I didn't expect this." And he kissed me, slowly, his lips brushing against mine. He stopped and stared into me, through me. "But that doesn't make it less powerful. In fact, the opposite. I think." He pulled off his towel and let it drop to the floor. He was stunning, his milky skin shining in the half light from the moon that was all that lit the room now. I couldn't help it; I ran my hand over his torso, soft and hard, down to his thighs, up over his silken cock, and back up to his face, where I let my hand trace his nose, his fine cheekbones, his brows over those dark, intelligent eyes. He kissed my hand. "That's it. You see all of me, but you finish at my eyes. Like you know that's where what you're looking for will be." He opened my palm and placed his lips on the center of my palm. "It's so rare, darling, and that you don't even realize makes it even more so." He held me to him, his skin soft and lavender smelling, and I sighed. There was nothing to say, nothing that needed to be said. Words would only push it away. He bent down and kissed my neck. "Bed. Now. You need to be held, and that's why I'm here." He climbed into bed first, always on the left, I thought to myself, with a smile, and I clambered in after him, the sheets cool and smooth, his body warm and alive, and he pulled me into him, and we lay there, floating together. I finally spoke.

"Tristan?" I whispered.

"Yes?" His breath was warm on my skin.

"Thank you." My voice broke over the words.

"Oh love." He hugged me to him. "It's not just for you darling, but you're welcome. So welcome." He kissed me, soft and ticklish and gentle again. "Now sleep. I'm here."

And I curled up against him, and let the smell of his skin, lavender and dark, drift me to sleep.

Chapter 11

The next morning I woke early, the sun shining in through the sheer curtains, a grey yellow fog, but warm. I blinked away the sleep from my eyes until everything began to focus a little again, then looked over at the long curved back of Tristan, rolled away from me slightly, half-uncovered. I pulled the duvet back over the two of us, then wished I hadn't, so I could have admired the pale silky nakedness of his back, dotted here and there with moles. There was a tattoo at the line between his hip and back as well that I had wanted to examine a little more closely. But I wasn't going to uncover him. The need to protect him in some way was fierce; it was stronger than either my desire or my curiosity. He had come to my rescue last night, when I was sinking back into that abyss, the one that I wasn't going to tell him about, the same darkness that came to claim me on a regular basis, and always threatened the heart of anything I was doing. At this point in life, I was pretty sure I knew where it came from, and why, but as they said, the knowing didn't help. But he had seemed to get all this, without long explanations or questions.

I stared at the back of his head, his dark hair tangled, the whiteness of his scalp visible in places where the roots threw his hair up in different directions. All the things that went on in there. I wondered if it was hard for him, being an object, a pretty screen to project a million and one fantasies onto, few of them ever taking him in as a person. His words from last night came back to me—"stopping at my eyes." It had never occurred to me not to do it. His words, like his music, could make me cry. There was something like intelligent magic in what he did that ignored all the pretenses and broke through.

I watched his back rise and fall with his calm breathing for a while, then slipped out of bed as quietly as I could to use the bathroom. I didn't want to wake them up either. Nick and Sarah, no matter how nice they had been, would be awake soon enough with more questions. My head hurt, and I didn't feel like talking, or explaining. I managed to get downstairs and in the bathroom without hitting too many of the creaky wide wood floor boards. I drank some water from the tap and splashed my face, taking a bit of toothpaste to run around my mouth. When I turned off the water, I heard nothing. But when I opened the door, there was Nick, smiling at me, dressed in only a t-shirt and boxers. I jumped, but he raised a finger to his lips, smiling. "We always were the early risers, weren't we?" I nodded, reluctantly. He carried on. "Do you want a cup of tea?" I really didn't want to talk, but my head was on fire.

"Yeah, that'd be great. Have you got any aspirin?"

"Oh you Yanks and your aspirin. Hurting from last night? You looked like you'd been hitting it when we met up." His face was lit up, teasing. Just the tone of his voice was making it worse.

I grimaced. "No, look, never mind, I'm just going to crawl back up to bed. I'll come down later." I shook my head and started to move towards the stairs, towards sanctuary, but Nick reached out and stopped me.

"Hey no, don't go. I won't tease. There's some paracetamol in the bathroom, hang on, I'll get it." He stepped into the bathroom and opened the cupboard, more pine, I thought, it's everywhere, so domestic, and opened a bottle of max strength, placing two into my hand. "There you go."

"Thanks Nick, you guys have been great."

"Yeah yeah, no problem. It's not every day you find out your ex is shagging one of the most desirable, in demand rock stars in the world."

I smiled, shrugging. There was nothing to say.

Nick carried on. "He's really got you under his thumb, doesn't he? All that stuff with the green tea last night. Looking after you, or controlling you, Lily? Which is it?"

I bristled, and damped down the "oh go fuck yourself" I so wanted to launch at him. My tone was flat. "Thanks for caring, Nick. Glad to know you're still looking out for me as well. Now I'm going to lie down for bit, and kill this headache, and Sarah is probably awake and listening to you, wondering how long you're going to be out here showing off your boxers." I smiled, mask like. "We'll talk later, right?" And I turned and walked up the stairs, without really waiting for his answer. I really didn't need his concern right now. They weren't going to be ok with all this, were they? And I thought of something I'd read a while ago about someone who had become famous, and his old friends had claimed he had changed, and was a prima donna, when apparently all he had wanted to do was hang out with them like they always had, just be friends. He hadn't changed so much, as they had, in relation to his new status. And he had to stop seeing them mostly, because all their interactions were either snarky comments or requests, for tickets, contacts, stuff, money. I'd never really seen that from this side. I did know that you needed fucking nerves of steel to get anywhere and leave the circle you started in, I knew that, but now I was beginning to feel how much that might cost.

Oh my head, I thought, as a sharp pain cut through it. I blinked. Not going to think. Hurts. I tiptoed into the bedroom, and grabbed the water bottle, and threw down both tablets, and drank. I had a sudden moment of panic. Suppose they weren't what he said they were? Ridiculous paranoia. And angrily I pushed it aside, annoyed with myself for giving in to irrational fears and went to shake out the clothes. It looked like they were going to do double duty today. Or was I going to have to swing by the hotel? We needed to figure out the sleeping arrangements, because I had the feeling our stay here was a one night illusion.

I crawled back into bed, glad I'd run toothpaste around my mouth, and was careful not to touch him with my cold hands. I breathed in. He smelled warm, like sleep and skin and sex. Delicious. I closed my eyes, and tried to will my headache away, thinking calm open Zen thoughts.

I must have fallen back to sleep, because the next thing I knew, I was opening my eyes again, hearing movement, and a low voice, and looked over to see Tristan, shirtless, wearing dark jeans hanging on his hips, talking on his cell phone. I sat up, and he waved at me, smiling. He spoke a little louder now, nodding to me and pointing to the clothes on the floor and the phone. I looked at him quizzically, and he held up one long finger, and carried on talking. "Yes. That would be great. Anywhere, really, I was hoping to do this low key, but I think it has to be somewhere that knows how to keep their mouth shut. What about that one near Notting Hill? That's private. The designer one, whatever her name is. Anoosh something. Yes. Right. Sound them out. And Rick? Don't tell James. I'll explain later. Ok. And check her out. I don't want her going back down there. Message from Dave? Yeah, well give him a message. Say, I like my privacy. End of. Good. Ok. Let me know when it's done. And two cars. I'll text you the exact address. Somewhere in West Hampstead. Really? Ok. It seemed like fucking miles last night, I'll tell you. I thought we were driving back to the States. Ok Rick. Let me know." And with that he clicked off, and strode over to me. "Hello sleepy head." He sat on the bed and put his arm around me. I leaned my head on his bare shoulder, instantly feeling better and warmer. "Hurting much? I know there were extenuating circumstances last night, but love, you really shouldn't drink so much, you know?"

I smiled to hear that word, said so casually, like it was every day. I liked it. "I know. Believe me, I know. Just slipped a bit." I put my arms around him. "I felt like I wasn't visible, you know? That interview..." I stopped. I didn't want to go there.

He kissed my head. "Yeah, but it's different now." He turned my head to stare at me. "You know that, right? Our games aren't so...um, game-y anymore, you know? Serious play." I looked at him, confusion obviously evident on my face. "Lily. Pay attention. I don't do this. This is not what fuck and run looks like. Trust me on that one." And his smile broke out, a dazzling grin that made him look like a cross between a kid with an ice cream cone and a pin-up.

I couldn't help it, I grinned back at him. "Yeah. True dat."

"Word!" he flashed back. We both started laughing. The whole thing suddenly seemed so ridiculous, like we starring in some bad B movie drama. He kissed my ear. "You're a lot of fun, Lily, when your brain isn't smoking."

I giggled. "Pot, meet kettle." And I threw my arms around him and hugged him. He squeezed me.

"Ah it's a fair cop, I'll go quietly. Be gentle with me." He ran his teeth over my neck and I hissed.

"You don't play fair," I said.

"Why should I, Lily? Why should I?" He carried on biting at my skin, tiny bites that he'd then flick his tongue at, until I felt like if he didn't fuck me, I'd die. I didn't know what I was doing until his voice cut through my dazed state.

"Oh Lily, don't make that sound. I wasn't going to do this, not here."

I murmured incoherently into his shoulder, as his fingers found their way under the sheets. "Tristan, Tris..." His hand opened me up, and I clung on to him. "How do you...?"

"Shh, don't talk. You're going to come, very quietly, and very hard on my hand, and then I'm going to fuck you, very hard and very fast," Tristan spoke into me, his mouth over mine, his warm lips touching mine as he spoke. His fingers moved faster, in me, on me, and I was wet, falling apart as his fingers teased me, wet and sliding deep inside me. "That's it love. Let it go. Show me you want me." And his words pushed me over, as I thrust against his hand, biting down on his shoulder to stop from crying out as he pushed against me, then suddenly pulled his fingers out. He put them in his mouth and his long tongue licked off the wet, as his other hand unbuttoned his jeans, and they dropped to the floor. No underwear, was the last coherent thought I had, as he flipped the duvet on to the floor, and was on top of me at lightning speed, his cock finding me and sliding inside in one slick motion, I was so wet. Still shaking, I clutched onto him, wanting to feel him. But he was fucking me with abandon, holding my arms over my head, his eyes tightly closed, his hips angling into mine with fury. I shut my eyes. Nothing, ever, like this, ever, fuck, my ideas disintegrating under his body. I suddenly started coming again, and I tried to fight it, but it was too late. All I could do was wrap my legs around him, pulling him in closer as I writhed around his body.

"Fuck, love, now, now," he cried out, "mine, fucking mine." And he slammed against me, his warmth flooding me, so much I could feel it coming out between my legs. He collapsed on me for a moment, then moved slightly, his forehead against mine. We both lay there, semi-conscious, our breathing heavy and deep, somewhere else, not here.

After a few minutes, I tried to roll us over, as his large frame was becoming heavy. Tristan noticed, and pulled out of me, slowly, carefully, and lay on his back, breathing. He pulled me to him and held me tightly. "Lily. Love. It shouldn't mean so much but it does. The way you are."

I just held him, tighter, just wanting to feel his warmth, his skin, sweat, breath on my skin.

He whispered in my ear, "I didn't really think, but I wanted to...feel you. Is it ok? I'm good, I promise."

I whispered back. "It's ok. At least I think so. I liked it. You. Your... But we can talk about it later, yeah?"

"Anything, love, anything." He kissed me, and suddenly we were friends too. "Don't worry, though, yeah?"

I smiled over his mouth. "I don't think I'll ever worry again, after that."

He spanked me, and grinned at my howl. "So bad. That'll give your friends something to think about." He rubbed his hands over my ass. "There there. All better." He kissed me again, and rolled me over. "Come on doll, there's a city out there we need to take care of. World domination awaits us. And our limos." He laughed, and his face was joyful, impish. I'd never seen him like this. He pulled at the sheet, and wiped himself off, and me, then gestured to me to get up, as he tugged at the bed and took off both sheets, rolling them into a ball. "The perfect guest. No need to leave behind DNA traces, anyway," he smirked. Then he handed me my clothes, as he shrugged on his jeans, over his naked body. "Good thing they expect rock stars to be unwashed creatures of the night. It all works out."

I put on my clothes from the night before and ran a hand through my tangled hair.

"You look beautiful, Lily," he said. "No thinking. Enjoy their stares. Remember yesterday? They need it too." And he scooped up the bed linen, and took my hand. "Come, let's go meet our hosts. And Lily?"

"Tristan?" It felt different somehow, saying his name. I couldn't figure out why.

"Don't be surprised if your friends seem weird. It happens, you know? People don't always handle it all well. The way you didn't think about it, because it seemed natural to you, well, it might not to them. Just smile and get through it. They'll either come around or they won't."

I didn't tell him about meeting Nick earlier that morning. I just nodded, knowing what he meant already.

We went all the way down to the kitchen, and Tristan calmly stuffed the sheets in the washing machine. Nick and Sarah were sitting in the garden, in the milky London morning sunshine, drinking tea. I walked out through the open door and waved to them, glancing behind me. Tristan was already back on the phone.

"Hey Sarah, Nick. Good morning. How'd you sleep?" I called out, ignoring them looking me up and down and around me to Tristan, in the kitchen.

"Very well," said Sarah pointedly. "The question is, how did you sleep?"

"Beautifully," I answered. "A little hungover, but nothing unusual there. A very comfortable bed and room, Sarah. Thank you so much for letting us crash here."

Sarah looked at me. "Of course, Lily. We've got history." She paused. "Do you two want some tea? I guess you only drink green tea now. You probably don't eat regular breakfast food either, right? Macrobiotic sushi? Baby food diets?"

Tristan stuck his head out the door. "Good morning all. Could you tell me the exact address of your lovely home?"

Sarah looked at him, eyes widening as she took in his long legs and tousled mop of hair. He smiled at her, one of his smiles, and she stepped back a bit. She came to quickly though, and rushed to the kitchen like it was on fire. "I'll write it down for you so you can have it." She turned to me. "The two of you must come back. We'll do a barbeque out here, it'll be lovely." She skipped up to Tristan, who stepped back from the door just as it seemed she was going to launch herself at him. She put her hand on his arm. "Come, let me find some paper."

Tristan looked over her head to me and nodded. "I'll call you right back," he said down the phone, winked at me quickly, and turned to follow her. I could hear her strangely high pitched voice talking animatedly to him. She's really nervous, I thought. Well I can understand that.

Nick had been sitting there the whole time, drinking his tea. He picked up a piece of toast from the blue floral plate. "Want some toast Lily? Always used to work for you for hangovers."

"Yeah, I guess it did. No thanks. I don't eat bread so much in the morning anymore, though, thanks," I replied.

"How's the head?"

"Better." I tried to be light. "Thank god. Thanks for the pills earlier."

"No problem. So, big day today?"

"Yeah, interviewing Trevor—you know, the head of Working Class Records. All about the beginning of Devised. Should be interesting."

"He's still going? What a dinosaur." Nick laughed. "It's funny to see people sticking to the music even when they're all grown up." He looked up at me. "Of course it's a living, right? Give the punters what they want."

I looked back at him, about to argue, when Tristan's words came to mind. I took a deep breath. "No, it's not a job for everyone, or just anyone, should I say."

Nick chewed his toast, and I looked around at the well-tended garden. I could hear a plane flying overhead, birds tweeting in the trees.

"You've done a good job with the garden. Pretty selection of flowers."

Nick sighed. "It's all Sarah, she loves it. Makes me watch those garden shows where they redo someone's hideous back garden and turn it into some showpiece."

"Nice." I said. "Plants are, I guess, very, therapeutic. And it's a lovely space back here."

Nick put down his toast. "Lily, I've got to ask you. What are you doing with him? He's not serious. You're not a groupie. What's going on?"

I met his eyes. "Serious? I guess impending marriage means you're an expert."

Nick grimaced. "Maybe I am Lily. I've changed. There comes a time when you have to grow up, or it looks stupid. Maybe you need to think about that." He shook his head. "Look, it's just we're worried about you."

"Sarah seems quite concerned with me at the moment." Her voice was still trilling out to us from the kitchen. I knew Tristan could handle it, but I still felt for him. It sounded like he was getting the full on treatment. "I'm sorry you think I look stupid, but there's nothing to worry about."

Nick jerked his head up. "That's not what I meant. And you know it. It's just, none of us are getting any younger. It matters more for women, you know. I just don't want to see you on your own. Freddy still talks about you. He's doing very well, just started working full time as a consultant, cut ties with the fund after the crisis. Raking it in. Thinking about settling down. You should call him. I'll give him your number, actually. We could all meet up."

I thought of Tristan and his warning. This was a weird variation on the theme. "Does he? How nice. Well tell him hello from me. I might have some time this weekend."

"It's the best way, and you know it, Lily. Tristan? Devised? Come on, Lily, you're out of your league here, and you know that, too." Nick was frowning at me as he lectured. It all came back to me then, the nights we had spent together, while he told me that my ideas were too far out, that my job was going nowhere, that my pen portraits were too abstract, that my writing didn't follow the rules, that my lifestyle was not ideal. Yeah, it was all there. His pronouncements. My uncertainty. And how I'd sat there, and taken it.

Well no more.

"Nick, I know you think you're helping. It's ok. Really." I turned towards the kitchen to find Tristan. I needed to leave, now. Nick called out, but I didn't turn around.

I found Tristan and Sarah sitting at the table, while she showed him designs for her wedding dress. "Of course you have to come! Lily is coming, you can be her date! What do you think of this dress? I like the shape of it, it will show off my neck and shoulders, and cleavage!" She thrust forward. "The bride has to have cleavage."

Tristan looked at her breasts and back up to her face. "Yeah Sarah. Show 'em off. Why not? They're very fine. Are they real?"

I bit my tongue to stop from laughing, but the laugh died in my throat at her next words.

"All thoroughbred darling. High class and rubbed down. Would you like to check for yourself?" She thrust them out at him.

"Of course. You can tell. But Sarah, listen, maybe another time, right? I've got to get going today, or there won't be a concert. You and Nick," Tristan said, putting emphasis on Nick's name, "will be on the guest list." He pushed out his chair and stood up. I coughed and kicked the floor, pushing the door to the counter, as though I'd just walked in and tripped.

"Oh Lily, you can be so clumsy. I was just showing Tristan here my short list of wedding dresses. He's been very helpful."

"Great, Sarah, that's great. You always have such brilliant taste. Which ones does Nick like?" I paused for a moment. "Listen, we've got to run I'm afraid. I've got this interview and I need to make some phone calls."

"Lily, stay. You can use our phone. I was just going to make Tristan some tea." She smiled at him, then turned to me. "No rush."

I put my hand on Tristan's shoulder lightly, and looked at her. "Sarah, I'm so sorry. I really wanted to see your wedding dress choices as well. But duty calls."

Tristan picked up on my mood right away. "I'm just checking on where the cars are. I've got an interview at twelve. But thank you, Sarah, for everything. Let me just go say goodbye to Nick." And he walked out into the garden, leaving us alone.

"He's lovely, Lily." She seemed honest for a moment. I tried to forget what I'd seen, and tried to forgive her. She took a chance. I might have done the same once. Maybe.

"Yes, very easy to talk to," I replied, keeping my voice emotionless. "Very easy to be with."

"That's what I've heard." She clapped her hand over her mouth. "Oh Lily, that's not what I meant! I'm so sorry." She gazed up at me, innocently. "But all those rumors. And he's a rock star. You know what they're supposed to be like, goats in heat." She stood up. "But of course not anymore," she said loudly, walking over to the kettle and switching it on. "Not now that he's with you."

"Yes. Absolutely," I muttered. "Well, we'll see you tomorrow night. Thanks for everything, really. It was great of you to do it."

"Pleasure!" she sang out, and walked to the open door. "Tristan? Nick? Tea?"

Thank god, Tristan came bounding back in. "No Sarah, thanks so much though." And he gave her a quick hug and kiss, and released her before she could grab him back. "The cars are here."

I went up to Sarah and hugged and kissed her as well. A part of me was hoping to erase the scent of him on her—it was a sudden primitive reaction. "Thanks again darling. See you tomorrow." I poked my head out the door and waved at Nick, who waved back, but didn't move.

Tristan grabbed my hand. "Come on, love, time to go." I clutched it back and we walked single file, connected by our hands, followed by Sarah. Tristan got all the locks in record time and we were outside. "Bye for now, thanks again."

We walked out to the cars. There were two, exactly identical. I felt extremely conspicuous, and a little like I was in some mafia movie.

Tristan leant down and whispered in my ear. I had the impression Sarah was still there, watching. "There's always going to be that, Lily. You have no idea. Can you handle it? You're doing very well so far."

"As long as you think so."

Tristan kissed me. "You're you. Breasts are everywhere, trust me on this. I'll get another six offers today, of one kind or another."

"Lucky you."

"Now I am," he said, hugging me. "Call me, sweetheart. And good luck with Trevor. I'll see you later." With that he jumped in the first car, which started moving out even as I stood there watching.

I turned, and walked towards the other car, opening the door, and turning to give a royal wave to Sarah. I was the one walking away, going somewhere, while she watched. I felt like I was escaping.

The car was dark and cool and it suddenly was really good to be alone. "Hello Miss Lily," said the driver, "ready to head to your destination," and he gave the address. Nice. Tristan had thought of everything.

"Yes, thank you," I said, and the car moved off, almost silently, into the road. Back to the world.

Chapter 12

I leaned back against the seat, feeling oddly safe and protected in the small space. No wonder, I thought, all these people who are used to being chased down by the public have their cars and their limos and their drivers. It's a small bit of safety, quiet, privacy after all the weird shit they have to deal with in the world. I thought of Nick, lecturing me, telling me I was wrong and he was right, almost deliberately ignoring the idea that Tristan might be a real person. And Sarah—the image of her thrusting her boobs up like that at him. I closed my eyes. The car continued its measured pace through the traffic. It was like being a child again, just for a moment, without needing to worry or drive or even pay attention, calm in the knowledge that the plan was being put into action, all taken care of. The driver turned around corners, waited at lights, accelerated smoothly through the traffic. I imagined myself captive, held hostage and blindfolded, trying to remember the route without looking at it. I knew that even though I knew roughly where we were, I'd still be surprised when I opened my eyes to find the car was a little further on than I'd expected, or stopped at a completely different set of lights. A silly game that I'd used to play as a child after seeing some TV show where the super-alert hostage had turned the situation around in his favor, through his superior memory and ability to map out the terrain in his mind. I used to wonder how well I'd manage if it happened to me. But I wasn't being kidnapped, even if events were moving almost too quickly. Tristan and I were becoming increasingly public, which I hadn't planned on. And I'd not only agreed to see the entire project through, in theory I'd been looking forward to this interview in particular. In theory.

I shook myself out of the mind game, and opened my eyes to watch the streets going past, the people walking, doing errands, intent on their destinations. They'd all gotten up this morning, dressed, readied themselves for whatever their day was supposed to bring them. They wanted a minimum of surprise. And then there was me. I'd woken up, somewhat hungover and jetlagged, in a strange room, owned by strangers who apparently were my friends. And then I had sex with a rock star, was told off for being a groupie, and watched my friend fling herself at my...boyfriend? Madness. I started laughing. Even looking at what had happened from that angle, I wasn't bothered. In fact, I felt fucking brilliant. Happy, even. Strangely, oddly, unworriedly happy. It's the sex, said the miserable voice in my head, you'll be sorry. Risk taking. And telling the voice to shut the fuck up made me even more happy.

My phone buzzed. A text. Tristan. Already. I giggled.

> L no more pink basket horror. We are at the
> Hempel. Driver will wait for you. Good luck give
> Trevor my love. Don't take his shit.

Fuck. Tristan. The way he noticed things—dealt with them to his own satisfaction—and now I didn't have to go back to that horrible place. Only the "don't take his shit" set off alarm bells, and the happy excitement I'd felt a moment ago became a churning feeling in my stomach. Where was all my bravado now? I was about to go interview one of the heavy hitters in the business. Trevor was a legend, even if Nick thought he was some granddad with a Peter Pan complex. Nick was a tool though. His version of sensible was no longer required. No, no more negative thoughts. I took a deep breath and thought of Tristan. His vast quiet skills that had been arranging it all, thinking of us, thinking of me. Fuck. He did care, didn't he? I let out a squeal, which made the driver turn around. "Miss, you are ok? Did you forget something?"

"No," I hastened to reassure him, the giant smile spreading across my face. "No, just happy. Crazy, but happy." I sighed, then quickly threw in, "could you pull over at the next coffee place you see? I'm desperate for a coffee." He smiled and nodded, and turned back to the road. Fuck it was good being part of a world where the unpredictable was ok. Tristan. I had to text him back. Before I started overthinking it all.

> Tristan. You're a magician. I'll tell you what he
> tried to throw at me later. Make the radio people
> want you. Should be easy. Xx

I didn't want to say too much. Or too little. I pressed send before I started editing. A hotel. With him. Oh, Dave was going to have a field day. I hadn't wanted him to find out, not yet, but it looked like proceedings were moving right along. Well, I was going to enjoy the ride. But I couldn't ignore the question that was there in neon lights. What about my job, Dave being the boss and all? Yes, Tristan had requested me, and this was supposed to be the high point so far of my strange little career. But Dave could just fire me. Jealousy could kick in, especially after our dinner. Dave could tell me I'd gotten a little too close to my subject. That I was supposed to be a professional, not a groupie. Nick's insult came back to me. It wasn't like that, but it was easy to see how quickly our affair could be pulled apart, if someone had the notion to do it.

The car pulled over, and the driver looked back at me and pointed to the shop on the corner—one of the chain cafes in London. He was asking me if this was ok, I realized. I was surprised he was asking. Then I was surprised that I was surprised. Yet again my wishes were getting some airtime. Maybe this was the way it was going to be from now on. I gave him a thumbs up and got out to get my coffee. Time to ignore the fear and remember what I wanted, what I had to offer. Make them see my version of life. Whatever Dave would do, he would do. As I paid for the coffee, I realized that was the risk I'd run right from the start in trying to get ahead and get paid for doing what I wanted to do. I'd been committed from the start—and that was before any hope of fringe benefits. Ah, fuck it, I thought, as I grabbed one of the cup holders and a napkin and walked slowly back out to the waiting car. Waiting. For me. Yes, I'd rather have the upper hand with Dave, but I wasn't going to turn my back on this...whatever it was, between us. Me. Tristan. What we had was something else. Something I didn't have words for yet, something beyond what I'd thought were the limits of the real world.

I got in and thanked the driver, who looked pleasantly surprised, and leaned back, feeling the coffee work on my head, if
not my nerves. I shifted on the seat, and I pulled at my leggings,
remembering I was going commando today. Well, Tristan said
he was teaching me to be a star. Now I just had to learn my lesson
by heart. I thought of his teasing grin—the one that made his
eyes crinkle up and changed all that forbidding power into easy
charm—and I laughed. To no one. To the window. To my nerves.
And the feeling of lightness that came over me was almost ticklish, as though someone had brushed a feather against me from
the inside.

And the big interview. I was doing it, and in a few hours, for
better or worse, it'd be done. And I did wonder what Trevor
was like. I'd done my research. Unlike a lot of the music business people, he was educated—and resourceful. A bit like Dave,
I thought. A less wealthy, more from the streets, English version,
but someone that had gotten not only his Cambridge degree but
who had made it work for him in both directions—reassuring
the money and at the same time not alienating the range of tal-
ents and intellects that by all accounts, he enjoyed helping. Well,
we'd see. He didn't suffer fools gladly, that much I knew. And
he'd probably think that I was a fool, another music business
flunky that got paid too much and wrote shit that the tweens
couldn't stop swallowing, didn't understand and wouldn't remember. Like the article I saw the other day where the writer
had said that Prince had covered a Sinead O'Connor song—
"Nothing Compares to U." Incredible. How that ridiculous mistake had gotten past the editor made me wonder. But there was
a whole world of not-so-bright-but-very-loud people out there

winning the game. And trying to make Trevor like me would be the surest way to put him off. I'd just have to go in, take my chances, be bold and resourceful.

I tried to organize my questions for him in my head, but my mind kept wandering off. Not everything could be predicted or arranged, and that wasn't necessarily a bad thing. An image popped up in my mind of a person crying on Tristan's shoulder, in his office. Me—not so long ago—giving in to what I'd felt. Such a short time had passed since. But look where those emotions had brought me. What counted was turning up, just like they said in some koan, or t-shirt, or cocktail napkin. Or whatever the fuck it was. It didn't matter. Except it did, so I just gave up, and carried on looking out the window as we headed through the lights, and onto the Westway, the A40 heading towards West London and Oxford.

We sped up the elevated ramp, as I sat sipping my coffee, oddly pleased that we were coming this way. I'd always used to love driving down the Westway, whether I was driving, or being driven. Either way worked. It was good when you were driving west, heading towards a date, filled with the energy of an early evening of anticipation, watching the sun lowering red streaks over a grey London sky. And it was really good coming back at 3:00 a.m., free, wined and dined and touched, not having to make after-sex conversation in someone else's bed, awake from the cold and the strangeness, watching the super cars and motorbikes that would suddenly appear out of nowhere on the elevated two lane relic of the fifties, cascading past with a terminal roar doing over a ton, at least. Sometimes there'd be two of them, racing, and the one that came up behind you would veer off at the last minute, which would send your heart pounding with some kind of terrified excitement. Alone, no one knew you were there, driving through the lights of the city, everyone normal safely asleep. Possibility and danger. It seemed a good omen that the interview was in this direction, down this path. It was like a date—with curiosity— and the fear of the challenge.

Looking over the rooftops, I could see the famous— infamous—Trellick tower, the strange architectural council high rise with the elevator shaft as a separate part, connected to the main structure by little walkways towards the west. An architect's witty notion that became a watch word for the failure of government to look after the common people, like the Pulp song. Was it only yesterday morning that I was heading east, in the opposite direction, with Tristan from the airport, social engineering the last fucking thing on my mind? The way things jumped around. Time was speeding up, and nothing could be assumed or predicted anymore.

We got off the elevated highway, and came back down to earth in the twisting and curving streets of West London. Everything here was a mews or a road, or a crescent or a villa. We weren't that far from where Poppy lived. This had been the epicenter of cool for a long time, before things had shifted eastwards. You'd never know to look at the buildings now, but there was a time when the white or pastel stucco that covered them was cracked and blistering off with damp, and the windows were covered with hippie bedspreads and cracks filled in with newspaper. Now, gentrification had been going on for so long, it didn't seem possible that the neighborhood had ever been 'up and coming'. It had up, and come, and then some. Didn't a certain prime minister "live" here? Not so rock and roll anymore. And here I was, about to take another journey into Tristan's past. I felt like I was looking back for both of us, trying to figure out how the hell we got here. The trouble was, I didn't really care how anymore, I just wanted my present—with him.

Chapter 13

The car pulled up, and double parked in front of a tall stucco townhouse, painted clay red, that stood out in a Mediterranean way from the rest of its pastel compatriots on the street. The driver was repeating his instructions twice, as though he wanted to be absolutely sure that I wouldn't misunderstand him. I put his number into my phone in front of him, which seemed to reassure. "Take your time, Miss Lily. I will wait. Don't worry, we are looking after you." It was sort of sweet and endearing, and I was bathed in that warm feeling again. Was it all Tristan, and his instructions, or was some of it just about me? I waved at him, and he drove off, completely ignoring the car behind him who had started to hit the horn to get him to move on. I liked it. It was an omen, a good feeling to take in with me to the interview. It was all about not moving until I was ready.

I buzzed the intercom, and a sharply inflected, yet slightly louche female voice came through the little plastic speaker. Her accent wasn't London, but she'd picked up the streetwise drawl. I gave her my name, and the only answer was a buzz, and I pushed open the big door. It had crossed metal bars over the glass, which added to the sense of coldness I felt as I entered. The hall was narrow, and lit from high above with energy saving florescent lights, which gave off their usual colorless glow. There was a door immediately to my left, and I tried it. It opened on to a plain office, with a big ugly fake wood desk in the corner, surrounded above with shelves filled with box files. Strangely, the floor was covered in a kind of greenish carpet. It was soft, but had the allure of a lawyer's office that dealt solely in criminal cases. Cheap, functional, ugly. A very tall woman was standing behind the desk, on the phone. She wore shorts, very, very short shorts, a button down shirt that wasn't tucked in, and a plaid vest. I half expected there to be a trilby covering her long blond hair. She looked more like she was ready for a photo shoot or a festival rather than an office job. But this was a record label, and not just any record label, but one of the most cutting edge. So she was fine. Maybe what wasn't right was the carpet. Or the desk. I was trying to decide what wasn't working, when she got off the phone and barked out my name. I jumped, and instantly felt a complete idiot for doing it. Not moving until I was ready. I remained silent and stood where I was, about five feet from the desk, and I stared at her. Silence. An old trick, but a good one. And when I finally repeated who I was and what I was here to do, she nodded, still indifferent, but no longer rude. I imagined that's why she had the job. Meeting and greeting the famous, not changing her manner. She had the all the warmth of a drill sergeant, despite the shorts. For a moment, I wondered what she had been like as a little girl, before she decided to shut down and out, but it was a brief thought. I was only curious, not really interested.

"Trevor will be right down," she said, and now her accent did sound more noticeably foreign. I said thank you, and I went and stood by the window, thinking of Tristan's warning. Not the friendliest of places, and not for the first time I wondered why so many people in the music business wanted to be as off putting as possible. Strange, I thought. You'd imagine they were all happy people, hanging out, listening to music, going to concerts, doing a little work. But it's a business, the business of cool. Which means it's all a facade. I was just typing the idea into my phone, thinking it might come in handy some time, when the door swung open, almost like they did in those old vampire films, like the door was on strings, and in walked Trevor. I knew him instantly, from the pictures, but I was still taken aback. He moved very stiffly and precisely, and he was tall—maybe even taller than Tristan—and dressed in what appeared to be an expensive French suit. He wore glasses, designer grey metal, almost frameless, very severe, like his short grey hair, styled and coarse. He had the appearance of a gallery owner. Instead of the slick bouncer look—banker with ponytail on holiday via the mafia— that so many of the music folk affected, Trevor looked elegant, unconcerned, cold cool. One would notice him without knowing why. Nothing screamed out "I'm in the music industry! Can't you tell?" Instead he gave off a slightly intimidating aura. He turned towards me, and smiled. I was reminded of the Dracula movies again, but I found him oddly fascinating. His nose was from a statue of a Roman emperor, and his eyes were slightly empty, like a shark. He peered down at me from his height, and his eyes narrowed. I had the impression he had heard my thoughts, and his expression was hardly welcoming.

Then he spoke, with a voice that was both trained and polished. Another surprise. Sharks are silent. But this one had made sure that when he did break the silence, his voice was a weapon, a warning bell that sounded out before him, alerting you to the danger you were already in. I already felt like I was being swallowed up. But just as I figured I really was in too deep, water was over my head, I flashed on Tristan's text—don't take his shit—and suddenly I was breathing again. I didn't have to like it, but I could survive it. Maybe even better than that.

I stuck out my hand, half expecting his to be ice cold. It wasn't, just a little dry and dusty, a light covering of hair. His skin transmitted an odd feeling. "I'm Lily Taylor. Nice to meet you."

"Of course. I know who you are. Your reputation, in all things, precedes you." He looked at me quizzically. I should have had some witty comeback, but I had nothing. Perhaps that was better. He indicated the door at the back of the office. "Let's go upstairs, and we can talk." Said the spider to the fly, I thought. His voice cut through the atmosphere again, but he was speaking to short shorts woman. "Alina, bring us up some tea please." She responded curtly, and walked in front of him, heading off to what must be a kitchen. I wondered if he slept with her. Power was power.

He turned to me. "Come." And I followed him out of the green carpeted office, and up the stairs, which went up to an ugly landing, then turned. The spectacle that greeted me as we rounded the turn in the stairs was surprising. There were gold and platinum records in neat frames lining the perfectly painted bisque walls. The carpet was wool, and red, and plush, made to cradle your feet as you climbed. Once at the top, the sliding cream painted wooden doors were open, giving way to a large room, with three sets of windows that ran nearly floor to ceiling, and a chandelier dangling over a mahogany desk, whose curved legs sank slightly into an oriental rug. There were two yellow silk covered wing chairs, placed at an angle, facing the desk, and it was towards one of these that Trevor waved a long arm, the suit jacket moving up slightly to expose a fine, neat white cuff, and a miniature guitar cufflink, a small diamond where the volume control would be, a ruby at the head stock. A bit tacky, very revealing, and I felt myself relax a little as I sat down.

Trevor was looking at me, expectantly. Oh, ok, I was to begin. A chess match. Fine. And so the wary circling begins, I thought. "Do you mind if I record our conversation? It will help me fill in any gaps and check on my recollections of points we raise."

"Did your legal department give you that speech, or did you make it up all by yourself?" Trevor looked down at me. The first rocket launch. And the fight was on. I wondered if he would just go this route for a while to satisfy himself, or if the whole interview would be like this.

"I'm sure they'd agree. But I'm happy to write notes, if you're happy for me to rely on them."

"If you're competent," he snapped.

"You'll tell that from the article."

His voice became a silky threat. "No, I intend to decide that much sooner, Miss Taylor."

We glared at each other for a moment and then I smiled at him. He's a little too aggressive, I thought. Didn't really go with the suit. Must be part of the house of horrors act. So let's get him talking about himself. God knows everyone loves that.

"So, Trevor—may I call you Trevor? What in your background led you to the business?"

"I thought we were focusing on Devised here, not me. The

Guardian just did a piece on me a few years ago. You should have read it." He turned away slightly, almost inviting me to end the interview. But I wasn't letting this one go. Oh no. He'd have to try harder than that to get rid of me.

"I did read it. And I thought how neo-left wing of them to brush over your background. Perhaps that worked during a Labour government, some lovely notion of equality. Now that things have changed, perhaps your deprived past, given a lift by grammar schools, might be of more interest. A reminder, if you like, that all talent—and money—isn't just inherited."

He was silent for a moment, deciding which piece to move. "So you're going from the point of view that my sense of ambition helped me recognize that drive in Devised when I met them?"

"Did it?"

"Look, Miss Taylor, let's not play games. I don't need to be psychoanalyzed, and my point of view in terms of Devised is fairly well known. Why are you doing this piece? What's Dave's angle here?"

"I didn't realize you knew Dave well enough to be concerned about his motives."

"Everyone knows Dave, eventually. And questions his motives. So what does he want?"

"You're asking me a question now."

"Well spotted Miss T, or may I call you..."

"Lily. Don't bother with the Miss, we're obviously all feminists here." I couldn't resist the little jibe, but it was said more to amuse myself than score points.

He laughed. I smiled and pressed my advantage. "Trevor, listen. I have only a vague idea of what Dave is planning with all this. Movie, book, TV rights, who knows? World domination, as usual. A boost to Tristan's solo career. A boost to back catalogue sales, maybe he bought the publishing rights, and neglected to tell anyone."

"No, I own the publishing rights." This was surprising.

"You do? Still? How did that come about?" Now we were getting somewhere. I was holding my breath with excitement.

"I've had them right from the start. Before anything happened. You don't know the story then. Tristan, it was always Tristan who did the business, called me up from America. He'd managed to get my private number—to this day he refuses to tell me how. I think it was Alina's predecessor, Karolina—she always was a pushover. He said he had some songs he thought I'd like." Here his voice slipped into an odd mix of upper class huntin' and fishin' and cockney. It made for a strange, compelling mixture, one that betrayed the overwhelming self-confidence that was expected at both ends of the class system. "Didn't want to share them with 'just anyone,' he said. He'd chosen me, because I would understand. I agreed to listen. I don't know why. He always was a convincing cunt." Trevor looked to see if I flinched under the profanity. I was still scribbling notes, but I smiled up at him when he stopped. "And then?" I felt like repeating it over and over again, like the scene in that ridiculous movie, but I resisted the giddy temptation. Somehow, he was telling the story, and I was just going to smile and nod and get it all out of him, the bastard. "What songs did he play you?"

"No, he Fed Ex'd me two different formats of music— and photographs. The only musician in the history of the world who isn't allergic to doing the sensible thing. He understands so well all the tools at his disposal. Innate charm and intelligence. And when I heard the songs, three of which became the singles off the first and second albums, I knew there was something there. Naturally I held back on the first song until the second album. But you never sign someone on one song alone. You want to hear that longevity, a range. The last single we released was by far the heaviest and hardest of the lot. But it surprised people when it came out, as it was intended to. Timing."

Our tea came, and he waved Alina away when she tried to pour, following with his eyes the tight jean shorts disappearing into the curve of her ass at the tops of her thighs as she walked away. If he hadn't had her yet, he was planning it. He waited until she had left the room, and turned his attention back to the tea. "Milk?"

"Yes please." I didn't really like milk in tea, but it would do. I didn't want to waste time discussing preferences. Luckily he was efficient, and tea poured, sugar stirred, he took a long sip, then another and put down the cup. "Where were we? Ah yes, publishing. The package."

"How long did it take you to decide?"

"Yes, there's a question. Was it during the first chorus? I think so. I recognized instantly the light touch of a real genius. A songwriter of phenomenal talent. Rhythm, sex, and lyric. But I made myself wait until I'd heard all the songs, and even then I did nothing until the next day. But I knew right away. And the band—of course. The chemistry. Fantastic. And the photos. When I saw what they looked like, I saw all the pieces falling into place. But for the publishing, which is a big part of the business, and the money, as I am sure you know, I went on the songs alone. And that, like it or not, is Tristan, no one else."

Had he actually just complimented me, assumed that I knew

something? Between the pride I felt for his appraisal for Tristan's talent, and for myself for making some headway, I nearly started to like him. Stockholm syndrome. This would never do. I gazed at him warily, and felt protected by my caution. "The publishing really is everything. The average person has no idea it even exists. So you recognized talent and smarts in Tristan. When did you first meet the band, face to face?"

"I flew Tristan out the next week. Just him. He wanted all the boys to come, so they could play for me, but I told him that as he'd had the balls to contact me and send me the music, he could have the balls to meet me one on one, without his gang." Another sip of tea. "I remember him laughing. He knew I was right. In some ways, he was smarter then than he is now. Sharper. But success does that, it's unavoidable. You see it in everyone. Things get fuzzy. At least he didn't self-destruct, or should I say he stopped himself. Fantastic will power. But you don't get to the top by being just a pretty face."

I nodded. I really needed to record this. There was no way I was going to catch every inflection, every turn of phrase. And he was a fascinating speaker. I picked up my cup. "Wedgewood. Very old fashioned, old values. Craftsmanship." He looked at me to see where I was going with this. I'd thrown him at least. That was something. "Trevor, I would consider it a huge personal favor to both myself and Tristan if you would allow me to record this. You're very witty, you know—I'd like to be able to quote you verbatim and do credit to your descriptive powers."

Trevor was silent, and looked away, then turned back towards me. "You and Tristan, hmm? Interesting."

I started to protest and he raised his hand. "Don't bother,

Lily. I'm quite amused actually. Dave hinted that he had bagged you for himself. How pleasurable to see that his considerable ego has come unstuck." He studied me for a long moment, pressing his fingertips together. "But it's obvious there is more to it than that. He always was an inveterate liar. But he's so rich. Why argue with success? Yes, go ahead Miss Taylor. Why not?" He leaned back, and pulled open a drawer in the desk. "We'll make a deal. You record, and I'll fill the room with smoke." He then proceeded to chop the end of one of the largest cigars I'd ever seen, rolling it between his large thumb and forefinger, testing the moisture. "Havana. A beautiful place, which ships beautiful cigars. Have you been? Do you smoke?"

"No, never, sadly. But I've been known to indulge in the odd cigar."

"Nothing odd about these." He took an old fashioned ceramic match striker off the table and swiped a big wooden match down until it burst into flame. He lit the cigar slowly, carefully, warming the end and puffing out finally a large cloud of smoke, with a huge degree of satisfaction. Between his hawk-like nose, piercing eyes and now giant cigar, I almost felt as though he was a giant phallic symbol—all testosterone and repressed violence. It was sexy, I couldn't help thinking so. He noticed my change of expression, and gazed at me evenly, blowing out another cloud of smoke. "Are you ready for me, Lily?"

I stared back at him, more curious than afraid. There were no depths in his eyes, partially hidden behind the glasses—only the hard dark stare of the shark in his element. Yet he looked mildly amused, and I found his blatant symbolic display fascinating. The personal physical power of those who become a success on their own terms. Always electric.

Chapter 14

Although Trevor would obviously make a strange and unusual story all by himself, I wanted his power in service to the story of Devised, his experiences with the band that changed his life and theirs. Their phenomenal instant success had made him for life, and allowed him to continue the record company that not that long ago, he had seemed in danger of losing or forfeiting to some big company's control altogether. I tried to navigate carefully, hoping I could keep him talking.

"When did you finally meet the rest of the band?" Basic, but there were so many possible questions. I wanted to save the more contentious ones for closer to the end. Any wrong note could stop the interview, potentially. At the moment, that was the last thing I wanted.

"About a month later. It was the spring, April, as I recall. I had set up a few gigs for them, secret sort of show, although as hardly anyone had heard of them, they were fairly secret anyway." He blew out more smoke. "They came over, all very young and innocent really. I think Tristan was quite protective of them, at that point. And at that point as well, it was fairly obviously they were in awe of him. Naturally, that changed. Love turning to resentment. AC was in love with him I think, quite literally. He didn't mind, Tristan that is. I'd never met someone before who was so desperate to be loved, while being loved by almost everyone he met. Of course some people hated him on sight, and let him know it. Yet you usually see that kind of starved for love attitude in someone who no one likes. And everyone liked him. He was charming. But he worked like a demon. And he was terribly opinionated."

"Was that part of the problem the band had? Were they unable to deal with his personality?"

"Well, they weren't the first band to have problems dealing with success. They all do. Some of them get used to it—the sex and drugs on tap, the knowledge that pretty much anything you want, or anyone, is yours for the taking. Devised were no different. At first, they took—a lot. But Tristan insisted on the music. The stories of him throwing girls out at 3:00 a.m. to go wake up AC so he could play him an idea—well, it became legend. As did the naysayers who said Tristan couldn't have sex with a girl unless he finished it off with AC." Another few clouds of smoke followed this, as well as an awkward silence. "I probably shouldn't be retelling these old stories. I don't think they were true."

"Did they have a sexual relationship?"

Trevor looked at me strangely. "If you want to know for yourself, personally, you should ask Tristan. If your personal interest has made you phrase that question oddly, when what you really meant to ask was 'were they the keystone of the band,' then the answer is that their musical closeness and understanding were frequently misconstrued by those of lesser minds around them.

Did they use that to their advantage? Of course. It's as old as the hills. Think of Jagger and Richards, Bowie and Ronson, Page and Plant. The 'rock and roll dualism,' I believe Bowie called it."

I looked out the window for a moment, embarrassed. I would not be put off. I wasn't sure what he expected me to say or do. I crossed my legs and made some notes on the pad sitting virtually untouched on my lap.

"So they recorded the first album right after the shows they played over here?"

"Yes. The reception they got was incredible. They were ready to record—it was almost like recording live, back in the day. Tristan was obsessive about it, eager to learn. As I said, incredible will power. So it was finished very quickly, and they hit the road almost instantly. Of course, that's where the legend grew. They toured continually for nearly a year. By the end of it, everyone on the planet had heard of them. The sound bites, the pictures they'd pose for—they loved the attention..." Trevor became serious, suddenly, standing up, and walking to the window, and opening it slightly, releasing some of the smoke into the air. He turned back to me. "They were happy, on top of the world. It was a joy being anywhere near them." He sat down again, and waved his cigar towards the window, sending a bit of ash to the floor. He stared at the ground, and looked up quickly, at me. "But, Lily, they were driven. Tristan managed, but only just, to keep himself in check. By the time he was writing songs for the second album, he had noticed that the egos in the band had grown at the same time as his own. But while he was determined to explore his talent, some of the others were equally determined to exploit theirs."

"What happened next?" I didn't need to ask, but I wanted to

encourage him. He was almost angry now, and I wondered who he would blame for their break up.

"Tristan was struggling. He really was on the verge of being completely out of control. Some of it was that he wanted things a certain way, insisted upon it. He grew furious if the smallest thing went wrong. But he was trying not to take out his anger on his band mates, his friends." More smoke. "That was what he should have done, however. They needed a kick up the ass. But they suddenly resented the one person who made them who they were. It was odd. And the more he got them to work, the worse it was. The trouble was, they were so good. Even when they all hated each other, they played together so well. It was almost as if they couldn't help themselves." Trevor paused, and sipped his tea, coughing slightly. "One of the best bands ever. A tragedy that they split up. But they all do, eventually."

"So the rumors became more wild?"

"Well you had four very different individuals. Tristan could be very self-contained, as much as he loved the attention, loved the idolatry that followed him around. He seems to have understood that side of himself better in recent years, though. AC was a little bit of a lost soul. Organized, but potentially always one step away from disaster. Tristan looked after him. Yannick, a great drummer. Maybe a little more disinterested. Isolated almost. The last I heard he was recording indigenous tribal rhythms in Bolivia. Paul—well, Paul went hook, line and sinker for the cliché. Movie stars, the misguided attempt to write the soundtrack for a film—although it wasn't terrible—but it did take him away from the band, right at that crucial third album. His access to the Hollywood gossip circuit meant he could trade information on the band for a mention on his own work. Sadly, he did that frequently." Trevor paused here to suck on the cigar, reigniting the end with a red glow, finally letting out an enormous stream of smoke. He examined me, steadily, and began talking again. "And Tristan was more often than not the subject. When Paul introduced Tristan to Alixe, none of us could figure out why Tristan was so trusting about it. But he had, still has I imagine, a tendency to see the best in people." Trevor glared at me. "Watching him going through disappointment is a terrible thing. I'd advise you not to go there, Miss Taylor."

I shook my head. "I don't think that's on the cards. But it's good to know you look out for him." I looked him in the eye. "But as you said, this isn't about my personal life. Let's get back to the band. So two albums, one platinum, one gold, and then the third album needed to be finished. What happened there?"

"Tristan and Alixe were married, much to everyone's surprise. He started hanging out with Paul more in LA, doing the circuit. It was an endless party, and Tristan was falling into it. I think Alixe had hopes of being an actress, and every party she was seen at was a potential casting call." Trevor ground out his cigar, angrily. "Married to one of the most talented men on the face of the planet, and she's worried about her next role in some B film with explosions? Idiot. But Tristan encouraged her, helped her, coached her. Gave her money, lots of it. But the music—was getting further away. It got to the point where the big record company in the States was getting concerned about their investment. There had been rumors that the band was going to sue to be released from their contract. That they hadn't been given enough time to put out the albums. That they were losing creative control." Trevor pulled out the drawer containing the cigars. "Oh, one more I suppose. Why not?" He went through the ritual of cutting the end off and warming the tip again, before releasing more clouds of bittersweet smoke. "So they called me. Figured I had some influence with him. They wanted me to go out there, but I wanted him away. So I made him come here. I even bought the ticket, wouldn't take no for an answer. Said I would help him get out of the contract if I could—but that doesn't need to be in the article—capische?" I nodded. "Good. Anyway, he finally came over here, after many protesting calls. Alixe this, Paul that. AC was in France with some model. He was no help. And then Tristan got here. And do you know what I did when I saw him?" He looked at me, tense.

"No."

"I got on the phone, cancelled his hotel, cancelled all my appointments for the next week, not an easy thing to do, I can tell you, and brought him home with me. And then we tried to talk. I cried. I cried in his arms like a baby." He looked up. "Hard to imagine, isn't it? I'm not the emotional type, or so it seems. But when I saw him, and started talking to him, it was so obvious that everything was wrong. Wrong as in he was going to die. I've seen that look before—and since." Trevor looked away, clouds of smoke coming out at regular intervals. After a few minutes, he turned back to me. "They died."

I sat there in silence. Anything I could say seemed stupid, trite. I just watched him. Finally he began again, his tone steely. "I was not going to let him go. Let me describe it for you, in case you're missing something here. Tristan was not just thin, he was practically anorexic. A coke habit someone had forgotten to mention. A bottle of Jack a day to keep it all on a level keel. Anything else anyone brought to the party. At least he hadn't started injecting. But the light in his eyes, dead, buried, gone."

Trevor raised his voice. "Do you know what he told me? What he said? That he hadn't touched a guitar in six months. Nothing. Hadn't sung a note. Had thrown all his drafts and the demo tapes into a bonfire on the beach when he found Paul and Alixe fucking. He threatened divorce, and she went to the papers and said he was a sexual predator who engaged in S and M practices with unwilling girls. The DA's office was investigating him! He told me he couldn't even go anywhere without being followed by photographers, some of whom brought along teenage girls in the hopes that they would get the picture of their careers. He was a broken man, and that bitch, and I don't use the term lightly, Lily, so do forgive me, nearly fucking killed not only his music, but him as well."

I had stopped taking notes during this, and now sat absolutely still, staring at him.

"So you see, if you do have any intention of doing that to him, I will intervene. I had to watch him get off the drugs, the drink. He stayed with me for six months, and I hardly let him out of my sight. After that first week, when the coke was gone, and the nightly screaming calls from Alixe were getting old, then Paul started calling. Told him he was a failure and that there would never be a third album. That they could write their own songs. That he and Alixe were together now. They sent him a picture of his guitar, floating in the pool. Another, of the two of them fucking. I'm really not sure what drives people to be cruel, but it obviously gave them pleasure." He picked up his phone and pressed a button. "Alina. Tea. Thank you." He looked over at me. "Unless you'd like something else?"

"No, tea is fine. Thank you."

"Good. Anyway. I had my lawyers draw up a power of

attorney, as you say in the States, and I took over his affairs. Threw the bitch out, sold the house. Got the record company to threaten Paul with breach of contract. Begged some more time out of them, let them release the live album, which of course was huge, and brought in some more cash, which is always good. But during all this, Tristan would just sit there, in my garden. Staring into space. Sometimes he'd read, a little poetry, some Lorca, some philosophy. I got AC to come over finally, but he had his own drug problems to deal with, and it was an unhappy meeting."

Alina appeared with tea. There must have been something in his voice which made her hurry, as it seemed to have been only a few moments since he asked. This time, he let her do everything, but ignored her, puffing on his cigar, looking out the window. I watched her pour my tea, and picked up the cup almost immediately, staring into the milky reddish brown surface. I was in shock, a million conflicting emotions running through me. Did everyone know? No, of course they didn't. Who did? Was I supposed to report on this, these incredibly private details of a man's life? And then there was the weird recognition, the crazy similarity. And to think I hadn't wanted to tell him my story. Well, obviously, neither had he. And now I was hearing it from this strange, menacing man, who it turned out had saved Tristan's life. I couldn't take it in.

Trevor's voice broke through my reverie. "Have you ever watched someone sit, day after day, hour after hour, without speaking? Did you ever have to walk them to the bathroom, shower them, wash their hair, have to put them under the covers because if you left them lying on the bed, they'd be in the same place, shivering, the next morning? God, it was awful. Can you imagine it? This beautiful, vibrant creature, hollowed out, like a shell shock victim. There were times where I thought he was a drug casualty. That we'd never get him back. But I watched him. Gave him time. Fed him. Drove him to the countryside. No music. Never any music. He wouldn't listen to anything, didn't matter what it was. I finally made him one day. I played him their first album. And he started shaking. Before I could do anything, he was lying on the ground, sobbing. Crying. Sobbing fucking crying. I brought him tissues, a blanket, tried to hold him but he pushed me away. And when I went to turn off the album, he screamed. 'No!' he was screaming, 'No! Leave it on, I want to hear it, I need to hear it. It's all of me I've got left. It's all of me I've got left.' And he lay there, curled up, repeating those words over and over. Around three in the morning, I tiptoed downstairs, and he was sitting up, cross-legged on the floor, singing along, tears running down his face." Three clouds of smoke came and went before he spoke again. "I went back upstairs and broke down myself. Never, I tell you, never will I forget that night."

My eyes were tearing, and I was biting my lip. I didn't want to cry. Not here. Not in front of him. I quickly brushed something from the corner of my eye, but I was biting down on my lip so hard I could taste blood. I lifted up the cup to drink some tea, but my hands were shaking so badly I nearly spilled it in my lap. My throat was too tight anyway, I could barely swallow, but I managed to drink a little to wash away some of the blood. But going back down, the cup hit the saucer a little too hard, and it made me jump. And I took a deep swallowing breath, before dropping my head in my hands. I just needed a moment, I told myself, and then I wouldn't cry, and then I could carry on, and then I could pretend that I knew what to do. I didn't care if he was watching me; this was better than losing it in front of him. A tear started out and down my face. Shit. I wiped it away and raised my head. I'd have to try and talk.

"Trevor?" My voice came out a hoarse whisper. "I'm really not sure I can tell this story. I mean, it's not mine, I mean it is mine, but not his. Oh shit. I'm babbling. I guess what I mean is, I'm not sorry you told me, that's not it, no. But why? Why did you tell me? What am I supposed to do with this?"

He watched me wipe another tear away, still gaunt and slightly terrifying, but with a somewhat paternal air, as though he'd found me cleaning up something I'd spilled as a child. When he spoke, it seemed to come from a long way away. I hoped I wasn't going to faint. "So, Lily, you have a conscience? Perhaps even a soul? I suspected you might, actually. Now, are you going to be brave enough to tell the story the way it should have been told right from the start?"

My answer was immediate. "Not without Tristan's permission. Never."

"Even if he needs this story to be out there, and may not realize himself?"

I bristled, in spite of myself. How could this man, who had helped Tristan, saved him, be so cold? "As I said, never. I'm sorry."

"What if Dave told you to?" He put both his hands on the desk, leaving the cigar between his teeth. I felt like I was in the Army, in front of some deranged colonel.

"Dave will never hear this story from me. As far as I am concerned, this stays between us. And Tristan, of course."

"Then you'll tell him you know." The words were like a judgment.

"I don't really see how I can avoid it. For many reasons." I felt weak. There were more questions I had hoped to ask, but I didn't think I could carry on. Not like this.

Trevor blew out more smoke and put the cigar down in the ash tray. He looked thoughtful. "Lily, the music business has lost so many. The best, the genius performers and creatives, get chewed up and spit out. Or just chewed up. Maybe the way things are done now, it's a blessing. It's only the hardest, the least talented who generally get anywhere. Why? Because they can cope with the horrible cut throat nastiness of it all. Fortunately, the technology supports this. Talent? Skill? No longer a requirement. And then, from time to time, you get a real artist who decides he'll throw his luck in with the rest." He picked up the cigar and examined it closely before tapping some of the ash off, and sucking more smoke into his mouth. He blew a smoke ring and watched it float off. "Lily, good luck. Look after him—he's more fragile than either you or he realizes." He crushed out the cigar. "Let's all meet for lunch the day after tomorrow. I'll tell him I told you. That should make it easier. And you can get the rest of your story. We never did get to the saga of the third album. All right?" He stood up and held out his hand, which I grasped, more firmly than before. "I'll let you pack up, you can see yourself out." He released my hand gently and walked away, still with the odd almost limp, towards the stairs. I watched his slightly hunched shoulders, when he surprised me by turning around, his eyes bright and unnaturally shiny. It suddenly occurred to me that he was about to cry. "Lily?"

"Yes, Trevor?"

"People like Tristan attract vultures. It's the nature of the beast. I hope you've got a good right hook."

I felt the beginnings of a wry smile start across my face. It was all wrong, looking happy at a moment like this, but I couldn't help it. I stood up and went up to him and gave him an awkward hug. "I'm tougher than I look," I whispered to him, then released him and stood back.

"I don't doubt it, I don't doubt it," Trevor replied. "I will see you tomorrow night. I think that cunt Dave is planning on turning up. I'm looking forward to watching you shoot him down."

I laughed as he turned and walked down the stairs, raising one arm from behind to wave.

Chapter 15

I sat back down and packed up the recorder and my notes as quickly as I could, seeing as my hands were still shaking. The scent of cigar smoke was still heavy in the air, and I couldn't decide whether it was making me sick, or whether I was desperate for more smoke, like a cigarette, to calm myself down. I pulled out my phone and found the cab number in my contact list, and managed to press the button. The idea of the cab driver, and how kind he was and this morning, when I was so happy, so ignorant, made me start crying again, little tears that leaked out slowly and made my throat small. Trying to get my voice out, I managed to steady it, enough to tell him I was ready to be picked up. Hopefully he hadn't noticed. Slipping the phone back into my bag I felt like I was being dropped into some dark place, as though I was under a glass bell, and all the air was being sucked out, slowly.

So I grabbed all my stuff and ran to the stairs, not even looking around for one final summary glance, which I usually did, to fix the place in my mind, in case I wanted a description in the piece. It was though I had tunnel vision; the periphery was all black and I could just make out one clear path down the stairs, round the landing, down the rest of the stairs and there was the door, in front of me. I didn't stop to say goodbye or knock on the door of the office; instead I ran out like a kid cutting school. Opening and shutting the front door didn't make me feel any safer. I had the impression nothing would ever make me feel safe again. I wanted nothing more than to stand in the middle of the road, as far as from the building as I could. But I just stood there, on the pavement in front of the door where they could probably see me, the scary sweet man and his Russian moll, and spent long moments filling my lungs with air, trying not to think about how I would cope with lunch. Any part of tomorrow, or tonight, for that matter. How was I going to act in front of Tristan now that I knew all this? Somewhere, a rational part of my brain kept telling me that he must have known I would find all this out, but in another part, a lot closer to my heart, I knew he wasn't going to find this new knowledge of mine easy to take. Fucking people. It was as if they wanted to fuck everything all up, make it ugly, and maybe they'd get their wish. I felt sticky, like I'd escaped from something nasty and invisible, and I couldn't get it off, like gum on the pavement in front of a school. There was just too much of it.

Finally, the cab came, and the driver rushed out to open the door. I must have looked like crap, because he suddenly jumped into action. "Miss? You need coffee? Water?" I nodded weakly, and his face looked even more alarmed. After making sure I was comfortable in the back seat, he closed the door firmly, and got back behind the wheel. He drove rapidly to the high street nearby, and parked the car, still running, next to the wide white concrete sidewalk in front of a large corner store, next to a dry

cleaner, a vet and a pub. Except for the pub, the blinding whiteness of the concrete reminded me of Florida. "I stop at store.
You wait in car. Miss, do not move for me, thank you." I nodded
and closed my eyes. Everything had those black spots in front
again. I felt like my head was bursting. It was either a migraine,
or I was finally going to be locked up for losing touch with the
world, all control lost. The back of the car smelled like carpet
cleaner and leather, and for a minute, I thought I was going to
be sick. I quickly opened the window, and stuck my head out to
get some air, just in time to see the driver and a traffic warden
approaching at about the same pace. My driver sprinted to me
at the window, thrust the bottle of water into my hands, and
opened his door and slid in, pulling out as the door shut, leaving
the warden shaking her head. I closed my eyes again, and smiled.
Something good. I thought of the Bob Dylan song. He made it
sound so easy to break, like it happened all the time, and he just
picked up the pieces. I wished I felt more like a woman most of
the time instead of a confused kid.

I opened the water, and drank some, which helped. Maybe it
was just the overexcitement. Being hungover. But I couldn't go
back like this. Maybe just another ten minutes driving around. I
opened my eyes, and squinted painfully at the bright hazy afternoon light. "Sorry, I don't know your name."

"Tariq," the driver replied. "What can I do, Miss, for you?"

I sighed. Such a nice man. "Tariq, listen. I can't go back to the
hotel just yet. Could you drive around for another fifteen minutes, then we could go?"

"Oh, Miss Lily, I am supposed to take you straight there." He
was frowning at me in the rear view mirror.

"Tariq, it's ok. I'm feeling better. I just need a moment, ok?"

I hated to do it, because I thought of him as a sort of friendly protector, instead of an employee, but I couldn't let him follow someone else's orders right now, even if they were from Tristan. I pulled out a twenty pound note. "Look, Tariq, here, take this. It will pay for your extra time, ok?" We were passing by the canal near Maida Vale. "You can just pull up here somewhere, and park. We don't even need to drive. I just need a few minutes to rest. Ok? Please?" He looked uncertain, but he took the money, and pulled into an empty space by the canal boats and the water. It was very quiet here, all of a sudden, and I felt another burst of crying about to come on. I drank some more water to push down the impulse. No, I couldn't stay in the car, either. "Tariq? Mate? I'll be right back, ok? Just going to sit by the water. You'll be able to see me from here. Be right back, promise?" And before he could say anything, I leapt out of the car, and followed my strange tunnel vision down to the canal.

The glare from the sun and the hazy white sky reflected sharply and painfully on the water, and split through my blackness, exploding my entire vision with light. Fuck. Migraine. Brain freeze. Insanity finally claiming me, I thought, and I sat down on the edge, legs dangling over the water, wondering if I really needed rocks to drown myself, Virginia Woolf–like, or if I could just hold myself down with sheer will. The pain in my head was intense. Tristan couldn't see me like this. He'd know something was wrong. Maybe nothing was wrong. This morning. Oh fuck. Suppose Nick was right. I wasn't tough enough to play the game. Like Trevor said, getting chewed up and spat out. I lay down, elongating myself along the decorative red bricks along the edge of the tow path, and covered my eyes with one arm against the sun, crossing my ankles. My back cracked from stretching out on the hard ground, and I let out a deep breath. I could just stay here, forever. Someone would give me handouts, some cardboard. Maybe I could blag a ride or a bit of roof space on one of the canal boats. I could change my name. Would anyone look for me? Alice? Nick? Tristan would forget me, that was clear. The line to tell him that I was just another worthless bitch was already forming. By disappearing, I'd only speed up the process marginally. It didn't matter. It wasn't going to last. Eventually someone would tell him something he'd believe and that'd be it. Or he'd just get sick of me. Oh, right, the career. The articles. The movie deals. Yeah. I could recount to people how close I was, once. They'd throw me some more money, shaking their heads, pitifully. Another loser at life. They would have done it better.

I lay there for a while longer. It felt good, the warm bricks against my back. The pity party was nearly over, I could tell. The near compulsion to screw everything up before someone else could was subsiding. There'd be trouble, a dead cert. But it didn't need me to orchestrate it. I lay there a bit longer. Tariq would be worried. I didn't want to get him into trouble. Tristan—I'd have to tell him. After the concert. I didn't need to run off and confess and fuck him up. I was better than that. I just needed to keep myself together, alone, inside. I thought of all the people that would be there. Trevor wanting a showdown between me and Dave. Ah fuck. A million expectations. Someone was bound to be disappointed. For once, maybe it wouldn't only be me.

I sat up, taking it really slow, praying that the pounding in my head wouldn't begin again in earnest. I kept my eyes closed. Where were my sunglasses? Shit, I must have left them at Sarah's, I thought. I drank a little more water. I'd go to the store, get some proper English painkillers. Fantastic. That would help. Put a little distance between me and all the thoughts, too. I finished the bottle of water, and tried to get up, moving away from the canal, in case I fainted. If I was going to kill myself, I at least wanted to do it intentionally, not by accident. I was still too dizzy. I stayed on my knees in the rocky beige dirt of the tow path for a minute, to get my balance, wondering if I should be praying. I could hear the lapping water against the boats, the small creaks of the rope. The stillness was overpowering, the quiet movements of the boats in the still water, the small pebbles pressing into my knees. I made myself hold my breath, immobile, an object instead of a living breathing hurting person. Getting on my knees before the universe. When I could stand it no longer, I took a long gulp of air, and watched my chest rise and fall, my legs dark against the dusty towpath. And then I could hear traffic again, a door closing, some people talking. I stood up, very slowly, and dusted myself off before walking to the car. Tariq was sitting, reading the paper, and looked up at me as I approached the car. His face seemed calmer as his eyes took me in, and I was glad, because I knew it meant I looked better. Less crazed.

"Hi Tariq," I said. "Thanks for that. We just need to stop at a chemist, then you can drop me off at the hotel. Ok? Thanks again, I really appreciate it." He smiled, and I opened the door and got in. Here we go, I thought, as he pulled away, and I stopped myself from wrenching the door open and going back to kneel on the towpath, listening to the water and the boats, wishing everything would be all right.

Chapter 16

I persuaded Tariq that I was fine to go in on my own, hinting that it might be a woman thing, which made him blanch and wave me in hurriedly. I felt bad doing that, but I didn't want a chaperone. Maybe I needed one, but I wanted to ditch him temporarily. Besides, it wasn't like I was buying painkillers in every store. You could do that. There had been a time when I tried it, just to see if I could, test the waters. It was so easy. In fact, it got even easier after the fifth store. The first few, I must have had a furtive, guilty look on my face, which was ridiculous. People took this stuff all the time. Period pains, toothache. Come on. They couldn't tell what I was thinking.

So after a quick stop at Boots, where I was asked the usual question and gave the usual answer—"no, I am not taking any other medication"—we headed over to the Hempel. It was right in the heart of Notting Hill, nestled amongst the perfectly painted white townhouses and communal gardens belonging to the very wealthy. The city noises seemed to recede into the background, as though they had been asked to politely withdraw. The atmosphere was clandestine, by invitation only. We pulled in front of the five story townhouse, now hotel, the muted browns and greys and discrete engraved plaque the only sign, all inviting isolation and comfort. Tariq helped me out of the car, which accorded us some attention from the staff. A suited and booted man came over, simultaneously dismissive and solicitous. "May I be of some assistance, madam?"

Before I could say a word, Tariq had sprung into his role, pulling himself up, and continuing to walk me to the door, forcing the man to follow us. "Miss Lily is joining her party here, a Mr. Mustang. The room is of course ready?" I held on to his arm more tightly, intensely grateful for him running interference. I didn't feel up to proving my credentials, but I obviously no longer needed to, because the minute the flunky had heard the name "Mustang," he fell back, chastened. "Of course. Of course. Let me go ahead and get your key, Ms..." here he faltered, amusingly, "Miss, um, Mustang." I stopped myself from laughing both at him and the ridiculous name. People were such sheep, aching to know where they needed to line up for the barn, where they fit in. Never mind.

Tariq opened the door for me, and let me hold on to his arm as he walked me in, where the two staff on reception were trying not to look interested in the new arrival, behind their desk of marble and wood, their neat little outfits homogenizing their individual curiosity. I turned to Tariq. "Thank you so much," then more quietly, turning to face him, "you have no idea how much you have helped today. Do you have a card I can keep, in case I need you in the future?" He pulled out a card from his blue suit pocket and I slipped him another twenty. "You are very welcome miss. You take care now." And he turned and left, and I felt suddenly twenty degrees cooler, in the presence of the staff and the

muted carpets and colors of the hotel. I was about to say something, but realized a contained silence would be much more ef-
fective in getting me what I wanted as soon as possible without
a lot of explanation. I straightened my back and turned to the
man, and fixed him with a look. He understood instantly. "Let
me show you to your room." I nodded, and followed him up the
curved staircase, letting my hand slide over the beveled wood
rail. We reached what was called the first floor in the UK, and he
walked to the end of the short hall stopping in front of the end
door.

He opened it with a large old fashioned key, and we came
into a Japanese styled living room with long floor to ceiling windows that overlooked the green of the garden courtyard. There
was a low, glass covered table, framed in dark wood and metal,
topped with a bonsai plant and a vase of fresh flowers, obviously recently placed there. The table was surrounded by a low
L-shaped couch in brown leather, a few brown and black velvet
rounded bolsters left in the dips between the pillows. The windows had gauze curtains with an embossed cherry blossom pattern and at the end, there were heavier brown velvet drapes that
could be pulled across for more privacy. The other wall had two
long casement windows, rounded at the top, which were letting
in long stripes of sunlight across the wooden floor, whose brilliant polish was interrupted by two beige wool rugs that again
had a kind of cherry blossom pattern outlining the edges. There
were two black cabinets; one undoubtedly held the television
and copious mini bar. It was shady, and calm and quiet and I instantly wanted nothing more than to be left alone. The bellman
was about to show me the layout of the suite, when I raised my
hand to stop him. "That's fine, thank you—I'm sure I'll find my

way around." I slipped him another of my dwindling supply of twenty pound notes, and he backed out, handing me the keycard and wishing me a pleasant stay.

The door shut with a loud click. The room was undoubtedly beautiful, but it was a mere stage to my stronger need to organize my emotions and thoughts before Tristan turned up. I walked into the bedroom, a door leading off the short hallway that also allowed access to the bath. Tall windows again overlooking the leafy courtyard, the king size bed covered with a chocolate colored silk spread, a collection of coordinating pillows arranged artfully by the satin covered headboard. Overhead halogens that one could dim with a control left by the bed, on the polished wood end cabinet. More flowers. It was all luxurious and exotically simple.

The bathroom was the in the same color palette—thick deep brown towels and mats against a backdrop of pale marble shot through with brown and gold veins. This must have cost a fortune to install, I thought, and instantly felt guilty about how much this room must have cost Tristan to book, that he had done it for me, for us, and that I was simultaneously doubting him and fearing for our future together while being a party to some of his deepest secrets, secrets which I wasn't sure I had the right to know. Secrets which meant I was going to have to tell him some of my own. I sighed. There was no immediate way out of this one. I'd have a bath, and put it off, hopefully stop thinking. I spread out the bath mat, which seemed to have an impractical but beautiful silk border, and turned on the taps, pouring in some of the bath oil, instantly filling the room with the sweet and penetrating smell of sandalwood and rose. I peeled off all my clothes and left them in a pile, realizing I hadn't even looked around for our bags. Our bags. Our room. The enormity of it all came crashing down on me. What had been an idea was now the reality, and tonight, at the concert, how much of our relationship was on display was not going to be entirely under my control. I tested the water, and then sank into it, feeling the water curving over my shoulders as I submerged my head and listened to the water filling the bath, echoing against the sides, my pulse thundering in my head as I held my breath and tried to relax.

I popped my head out at the last moment and caught my breath, watching the glossy oil coat my skin as I sat up to turn off the taps. Tristan. This was all about him, wasn't it? And the revolution he had set off in my mind and body. My soul? God. I loved him. I adored him. He was everything I had ever wanted, more than I had ever even considered possible. It was though he was some long forgotten need that I must have known was there but was separated from. I lay in the bath, letting the water and the darkness soothe me. I was going to have to face up to this incredible need, desire, whatever it was, that I had for him, and try to remove myself from the insanity that was part of his world and the people that made it up. They would do their shit, and I would stand up for what I believed in, what I wanted. Hopefully I could manage to raise my voice above a whisper.

I was lying there, beginning to feel the effects of the warm water and the sweet-smelling bath oil, when I heard the key turn in the lock. Obviously I hadn't double locked the door as well as I thought, realizing I should have put the chain on if I had really wanted to keep everyone out. The water was cooling anyway— how long had I been there? Half an hour? An hour? It was time to face the music, literally, and I was going to have to do what I wanted, which was need him, look after him, be there to look into his eyes whenever I could. I wasn't even sure why I had panicked before, as I heard his voice call my name, and his rhythmic footsteps come closer. It wasn't like I had a choice. There was no way I could say no, not now.

I closed my eyes.

The bathroom door swung open, and I made myself look up. And there he was. Slightly sweaty, disheveled, hair partially in his eyes, his long legs heading up to his torso, which was now adorned with a tank top that announced "XMM presents..." And there, at the very top, was his brilliant smile, making it all ok. I smiled back at him, feeling that strange bubble of warmth come over me.

"Hey love." He bent down to kiss me like it was the most normal thing in the world, to come into a hotel suite and say hello to someone in the bath, when that someone was me, and I reached out a wet hand around his neck. We kissed, softly, friends saying hello, lovers reminiscing, the link completed. All that in a minute, his warm lips so much larger than mine, soothing rather than invading. How could this be the same person I'd been so frightened of just an hour before? It must be me, I thought. He's fine, everyone's fine, I'm the one who's a bit off. He broke off the kiss and squatted down, stirring the bath water with long fingers.

"Hi." I suddenly felt incredibly shy.

"Nice bath. I bet you thought you needed one. I hope you're washing off Trevor and not me." He laughed. "How'd you get on, anyway? He's weird, isn't he?"

I hoped Tristan would add something else, but he just waited for me to answer. I had to agree. "He is pretty strange. I guess it went well. A bit intense. But it was a two cigar interview, I hope that's a good sign."

"Two cigars, huh? Well, you must have gotten him talking." He squinted at me, as though he was looking for something. "He and I have a lot of history."

Oh god, here it was. Not yet. Deflect. "He's invited us to lunch Sunday. Said he'd finalize it with you tomorrow night." I tried to look as though that was fine.

"Did he now? Well he must like you—or he wants one more chance to scare you senseless." My expression must have changed to one of horror, because he reached into the bath to hug me. "No, no, sweetheart. It's fine. He did scare you, didn't he? Never mind. Whatever he did, we can undo. It's ok, shh." I'd started to cry again, grabbing on to his shirt.

"No, Tristan, I'm sorry. It's fine. I'm fine. I don't want to get all emotional. You've got the concert tomorrow..." I untangled my arms from around his neck and submerged my head under the water and came up, dripping.

Now he looked worried. "You're still coming, aren't you? I want you to be there."

I nodded. "Of course. I've got to be there to write it up anyway, or Dave will guillotine me."

Tristan grimaced. "Oh fuck Dave. And the article. I know you've got the job, and I'm after publicity..." and he paused. "I want you there. We've got a lot to talk about, I can tell, but it can wait. Just trust me, ok?"

I looked at him. How did he come up with these things? "Trevor wants to watch me blow off Dave."

"Ah, fuck both of them. Do what you want. I want you to

watch just me, so I can look out and see just you. Somebody real. Somebody who doesn't only want a piece of me."

Was I real? Shit, he needed me. I had to pull it together. "Ah babe, you're too much. Too much. I want all of you, not just pieces. I'm sorry I started crying. I guess I feel a little too real today."

"What did Trevor tell you?" His eyes bore into mine.

I hesitated. Shit. What was I going to do now? I couldn't lie, but I couldn't get into this. Not now. I dipped down under the water again. When I came back up, Tristan was frowning.

"Lily, it's ok. Really. I'll ask him myself."

"Don't ask him before the concert," I blurted out. "This is important to you. Deal with all the past shit after, ok? I'm fine. It's fine."

His smile became a little more dangerous. "Oh, we have ways of making you crack. Don't worry. I'll find out—all of it. But you're right. I've got to be there for sound check. We're doing a tape session tonight. I just wanted to make sure you were ok. Come down whenever you want. It won't start until late anyway. Just like tomorrow. Make 'em sweat." He smirked. "There's few desires that don't improve upon a little waiting time." He reached a hand between my legs and thrust up suddenly, making me gasp. "Even mine, love." He moved against me, smoothly, slowly, and withdrew his fingers and licked them off. "Nice." He leaned over and kissed me, laughing softly. "Shit, you're fun, darling." He stood up and went over to the sink and ran water over his face and ran his wet fingers through his hair. "There, I'm done. I'll see you in few. Don't be late or I'll send Trevor," he said over his shoulder as he walked out of the bathroom, humming.

I listened to the door open and close, and tried to ignore

the feeling that all the air had left with him. He needed me. He wanted someone real, right? Not some idiot that was going to cry at the slightest problem. He wanted me. And for whatever reason, that was going to be on display. I'd deal. I'd be the only person in the room for him, if that's what he was looking for. And he was right. Fuck 'em. Maybe with him there, beaming down at me from the stage, me making notes, tomorrow I would be able to play a little game with Dave. One that would satisfy Trevor and get us through to lunch. Tonight—maybe we could just leave, and be together. Not on display. Not really. I shivered as I got out and wrapped myself in one of the towels and walked out, partially draped, to see if my luggage was out there some-where. Yes, there it was. For a moment, I'd thought they had un-packed for us too, but fortunately, or not, that kind of luxury wasn't on offer. Good. I pulled out some lace covered underwear and a bra, and debated what to wear. The bondage dress. Yes, why not? Oh, but maybe that was too close to home—bringing back the rumors. On the other hand, it looked good. No. Too much. Jeans. Boots. See through top. Vest. Better. Festival girl with sex appeal. Easier to run in boots than high heels, too.

I went through the whole ritual of makeup and teeth, feel-ing a sense of unreality. I debated my drug choices—painkillers? Alcohol? There's always nothing, a voice in my head said. Yeah, right, I thought. Let's not push it. I decided to leave the pills in my bag, just in case, but I didn't take any. Keep it light. A beer, glass of champers when I got there. Simple. Easy. The star's girl-friend. Jesus. I thought of the car ride to the airport back in New York. The sedan had stopped at a light, and I had looked over at the sidewalk, but my view was blocked by a large grey plastic garbage bin. Yet somebody had scrawled on it in felt tip marker "become your dream." Maybe that was the scary part—you woke up in the middle of your dream and you'd put yourself there, in the lead. Then you had to make up the script as you went along.

Well, the curtain was about to go up, and there was no under-study and no cue cards. I hoped I'd like it once I was out there, in the spotlight. And then the door closed shut behind me. I didn't think the click of the lock sounded as definite as it had done for Tristan.

Chapter 17

I wanted to take my time, so I waved off the offer of a black cab from the doorman, and headed out. I needed to walk, needed to clear my head, and give my body another exercise than being willing and pliant under or over Tristan. The thought made me laugh, like I was becoming complacent about the idea of him and his talented body at my disposal. No, not even close. But I had the feeling we needed to spend a bit more time on the vertical plane if this was really going to work out. I crossed over the Bayswater Road, into Kensington Gardens, walking along the narrow paths under the huge oaks, still bare in the very early English spring. It was quieter here, the light fading, the shadows lengthening as people strolled, either taking in the last of the day, or heading homewards. The sounds were longer, more attenuated, making it easier to hear the light breeze in the branches, the sudden flight and movement of two wood pigeons. I breathed in the smell of wet dirt coming off the cold grass. I wasn't ready for a big talk about life, or what I learned from Trevor. In fact, I felt fairly calm now, the soothing bath and his relaxed attitude in the face of my anxiety resetting the levels.

I knew we'd get there, I knew it'd be weird. It was already. But it was time to accept where we were and what needed to happen. I didn't want to undo the magic, but magic has to be guarded and protected, and if we were going to have this, whatever the hell it was, we needed to make sure we were there for each other. Anyway, I had a plan for tonight. Me—calling the shots. Maybe Tristan was right. It was the air over here or something. But I couldn't do the sub thing happily unless I was sure that it was a choice, not a rut. Something we could pop in and out of when we wanted. When I needed it. When he needed it. Maybe I just didn't want to be a trendy lifestyle. I wanted that head space and going under control to mean something.

When I finally got to Selfridges, the huge and beautiful department store, where I intended on spending some of Dave's walking around money, it was already dark, and the lights were glittering on the windows, and the whole building was a big present, wrapped up brightly against the night sky and the street lights. It was the best place to shop in London. I wasn't a big fan of Harvey Nichols—too snooty, and Harrods was for tourists. I went straight to the men's department, and found what I wanted, with a little help from the salesman, who seemed to warm to my quest with a few dropped hints as to who it might be for. Paul Smith fit the bill, even if the price made me stutter. But I left as the store was closing, happily swinging one of the iconic yellow bags, and managed to find a cab with its light on. Heading down Oxford Street, with the driver teasing me about what I'd bought, and shouldn't I be thinking of spring now, and asking me where I was from and why I'd left, with Radio London a quiet murmur of news in the background, I didn't think I could ever be happier than I was right then.

We turned up past Euston Station, heading up to Camden. It was a street of B&B accommodations, council flats, a stripper bar. It hadn't been that long ago that I'd been living in a place not a lot better, and had come down here to visit a friend living in one of the bedsits. Against the backdrop of ugly green paint and a gas fire that took ten pence pieces far too often, we sat on cushions on the floor and fixed the world. We'd had beans on toast and a couple of cans of lager, and it wasn't paradise, but we were warm and safe. Now I was speeding up the road, having spent what used to be my rent on a present for my rock star— what? Boyfriend? I didn't know what he was. But I didn't want to forget what I'd been through to get here. What I'd rejected, what I'd chosen.

The cab pulled up by Camden Lock, and I got out, and paid the driver. He waved as he drove off, and screeched to a halt a hundred feet away to pick up another fare. I watched as five girls, all in amazingly short skirts and high heels squealed their way in. I laughed at both of us—their eagerness and mine. But maybe I'd finally figured out there was more than one way to live. I walked away from the road, stepping on the uneven cobblestones. The shops were either closed, or shutting up, but there were still a lot of people around. I tried to slip through them, invisibly, realizing that my bright yellow Selfridges bag didn't really fit in here, too much of a class marker, drawing attention to me. It was all right. I planned on losing the bag in a little while anyway.

I found the big wooden door, and showed the bouncer my pass. He let me in right away. My heartbeat sped up as I pushed through the inner door, and confirmed that the rumble of amplified voice speaking that I could hear as I came in was Tristan. He was being interviewed by a DJ for a show that was

going to go out when the album was released. I knew Tristan
had approved the guy in advance, one of the long-standing people at the station who had interviewed the band right
at the beginning, had always been a good person, not asking
asshole questions just to get a hot quote. I stood at the back
and watched. It wasn't full—just some people from the station,
some of the execs, some invites, and winners from the radio
station's competition to find the biggest fan. Christ, I thought,
I should really interview some of these people. Maybe I could
ask a few questions later. I didn't feel like interrupting the
whole thing with a lot of intrusive questions. And Tristan had
said he'd play and do the interview, but he wanted it to be intimate—just some fans, unlike the big show tomorrow, which
was going to be taped as well, but it was a proper concert—
electric guitar, lights, special guests, friends of the record company, the whole thing. This was a little different.

He was sitting on a little school chair, a mike on a bent stand
in front of him, an acoustic guitar sitting comfortably on his
thighs, his left hand wrapped around the neck with alarming
ease. It was only next to objects that you could really get a sense
of how big he was, otherwise he only looked perfectly propor-
tioned, maybe a bit taller. He was laughing now, answering a
question on how the recording had gone, and did he ever miss
Devised? Tristan fielded the question like the pro he was, making
a quick joke about never missing trouble, laughing darkly, his
hand going to the back of his neck, pulling at his shirt, exposing
more cream colored skin, then going into specs and the guitarist he had on board for one song, how lucky and grateful he was
to be able to work with people who really loved their craft. He
said so many of the tropes of the successful rock interview, but

he managed to make the answer sound new, like he'd really just thought of it, and what a good question it was.

I watched them go back and forth for a couple of minutes, the camera guy moving in front of them, trying for different angles. Then the interviewer asked him if he was ready to do a song. Tristan smiled, then looked around. I didn't know how I knew, but I felt like that was my cue to step up, be there for him. Except there was no way I could run to the front holding a big bourgeois shopping bag. So I grabbed the small tissue paper wrapped bundle inside, and stuffed it down my jacket and zipped it back up, kicking the bag back to the wall. And I started to make my way down front, trying to be polite, but moving people out of the way when I needed to get in front of them. And when I was about ten feet from the stage, I looked up. There he was, his eyes locked with mine, a small smile on his face. In about two seconds, people were going to notice the look on his face wasn't some distant appreciation of the crowd. So I wasn't prepared for Tristan giving me a wink, and running his hand through his messy dark hair, a small smile, like an invitation to crawl up there. I wanted to blow him a kiss. Anything involving blowing actually would do just fine. I made a half-hearted attempt to look somewhat less dazed, figuring anyone who was looking had already seen my giant ridiculous smile. But when Tristan raised his arm to the air, and brought it down hard for the first chord, I wasn't the only one who was holding their breath. He didn't usually do this, accompany himself while he sang. He had always said he wrote everything on guitar, but had never taken the time to really learn how to play properly. He wasn't an expert, but there was a certain raw quality to the chords and the way they fit into the rhythm he was building up with his voice, chopping along the beat, over it, next to it, on it suddenly with a feeling that you'd locked in and fit. Who could explain what made someone have something? But with his eyes squeezed shut, and his hands pulling out the notes, we were all watching a genius at work. He just knew where the notes should go, and he was so clearly getting off on the whole thing, his voice soft, then gritty, ripping through his throat. It was magic, and no one was breathing.

There was a beat of silence when he'd finished, like everyone was trying to figure out where they were and what they were supposed to do, and then the place erupted with shouts and applause. And Tristan sat there, on his chair, and waved, and looked so happy and pleased I understood why Trevor had committed himself to the task of saving him. And I made up my mind that I would do everything I could to make him happy, and when it ended, as it was bound to, I'd just feel fucking lucky that I'd had any part of him in my life. And when I decided that, I took my first deep breath in days, and everything slowed down—just a little, just enough. I was in love. And damn, I had chosen a fucking special person to lose it all over. Nothing was forever.

The interview was winding up and they were now standing, hugging. Tristan went around to all the sound engineers, the camera guy and thanked them, shook their hands, posed for some phone pictures. He was smiling, his hands gesturing in the air as he spoke to each person. Then to everyone's delight, he hopped off the stage, and signed autographs and posed for more pictures with fans. I stayed close, just enough to hear him talking to people, coaxing forward the shy ones, agreeing to pose for one more photo when the first one didn't come out right. He was calm, endlessly patient, very polite. It didn't seem like an act. Watching him sign over and over again, make a rock and roll face in between two fans, move on to the next one, never rushing anyone, never looking nervous despite the fact he was surrounded. I took a couple of pictures with my phone. This side of him needed to be written about—even if it didn't really jibe with the dark sex god. Maybe that was good. Or maybe people wouldn't be able to handle the complexity. Figuring out the public. Good to think about, but not for too long. Some of it had to be spontaneous, based on instinct, not design. Otherwise it felt too cold.

He spotted me, in the middle of one of my phone pictures, and waved. No one noticed—they were too busy thrusting things at him to sign. But it was winding down, the radio people were beginning to pack up, and a big man I hadn't ever seen before was coming forward, a light touch on Tristan's shoulder, which he acknowledged with a nod. "Thank you all so much for being here tonight!" Then he let the man put his arm around him, and guide him through the crowd, being a little more forceful than Tristan would have been on his own. I followed them, keeping my distance, but also keeping an eye on where they were headed. They went through a door to the back, and a minute or so later, I was there, showing my laminate to the guy by the door, who examined it minutely, looked me up and down, eyeing the bulge in my leather jacket, and finally letting me in. Tristan was standing by one of the metal pillars that were scattered through the room, drinking from a little bottle of water, chatting to the man who I supposed must be a bodyguard. I walked up, slowly, a little unsure of how I was supposed to act.

Tristan caught sight of me and waved me over. "Lily, there you are. Did you see the interview? I think it went well. Didn't you? Decent questions. Nice crowd. Guitar playing—hey!" His words came out in a rush, and he seemed incredibly wired. "Have you met Rick? No? Rick, Lily, Lily, meet Rick. He's my fixer—he does everything—really." He smiled and punched Rick in the arm with a big flourish. Tristan was taller than he was by a few inches, but Rick gave off a feeling of being grounded, the way trees are, and had a slightly dangerous air beneath his easy smile.

Rick said hello to me and we shook hands, mine disappearing in his. "Murderer's thumbs, I've got," he said amicably, "but don't worry Lily love! They look worse than they are." I examined his hand over mine for a moment, and tried to laugh.

Tristan spoke up, his voice still fast and jagged. "I've known Rick forever," he said. "Since the Devised days. You should talk to him. He'll tell you the truth. The real dirt. No. No, he won't." Tristan laughed. "He never says a word, that's why he's brilliant." He put his hand on both our shoulders for a moment, and then excused himself.

I was left alone in the makeshift green room with this man, who looked me up and down, then smiled. "So you're Lily Taylor, the writer," Rick said. "I've read some of your stuff. It's good." I thanked him, but he waved me off. "You're writing about Tristan now? He's a good man he is. Has always treated me right. Keeps his enemies close, but his friends closer, you know what I mean? His only trouble, is he tries to do things alone, when he needs help. I keep telling him to move over here, we'll look after him." I raised my eyebrows, and was about to say something, but he kept going. "California. No. He didn't know the right people out there. Come back, mate, I'd say. And he did for a while. Got himself straightened out, now look. Going to be a success again. But you never know what they're going to do. I've worked for a lot of people. You just never know."

I nodded. "It seems like he has had people who wanted to..." Here I stumbled. I didn't know what to say. What was I supposed to admit I knew? "He hasn't had an easy time of it."

Rick shrugged. "No. Sort out what I can. Some things...some things you can't tell the boss, you know what I mean?"

I thought I did know. "Rick, are you his bodyguard while he's here?"

"I'm everything! You heard the man." He laughed. "Why, have you got a problem?"

"I want to take him on a walk. Do you need to follow behind us, or something? Should I let you know where we are going?" I quickly tried to think of where I wanted us to go. Parliament Hill. Walking by the Thames past the Tate. Holland Park. Back to Primrose Hill. Victoria Park. No, we'd only get a chance at one. The Thames. Something about the water. Soothing. "I'd like to walk with him down by the Tate. Can we all go in a cab? I've got something..."

Tristan came out and interrupted. He still seemed wired, but a little bit calmer. "What's this? Sightseeing? A walk. What do you think Rick? Can we do this? With everything going on?"

I snapped my head around to look at him. "What's going on?"

Tristan shook his head. "Just the usual. Nothing to worry about." Hearing him say that made me worry more than before.

"Look!" I suddenly remembered. I unzipped my jacket, and pulled out the bundle of tissue paper wrapped items and held it out. It wasn't how I'd planned to give it to him, but needs must. "Remember we talked about sneaking out? Knowing London? Needing a hat? Here." I thrust it at him. "These are for you." I could see Rick examining me out of the corner of my eye. There was no point pretending. I looked at him, and smiled, and quickly returned to watch Tristan unwrapping his gift. He pulled them out. There was a long striped Paul Smith woolen scarf, and a simple grey hat, with a few stripes on them to match the scarf, but not too much. Before he could say anything, I jumped in. "You can wear them, cover your face, make it harder for people to tell who you are. Then we can go out by the Thames. Rick can come too." Tristan was wrapping the scarf around his neck, slowly. "Say you will."

His expression was hard to read. "By the Thames?" I nodded. He looked down at the scarf. "This is beautiful, Lily, thank you." And he threw a look at Rick, and crossed the space between us. He took an end of the scarf and wrapped it around my neck, and gave me a kiss. "You're always surprising me," he whispered. I pressed myself against his chest and felt his arms go around me. I wasn't sure what Rick knowing would mean, but I wasn't going to think about it. Not as long as Tristan was right here, warm and real and wanting me.

Tristan kissed my cheek and then my nose, and then I was sure Rick had no doubts that maybe we were more than friends. Maybe not. People kiss each other a lot. It doesn't have to mean anything. I looked up at him, and I wasn't trying to hide. Tristan smiled down at me. "Ok doll. Give us the orders. Rick, let's get a taxi. Can you take care of that? Lily, where are we going?"

I laughed. Give him orders. Well, you could try. "Tate Modern. We can walk towards Tower Bridge, on to Rotherhithe. See the river. "

Tristan laughed, low in his chest. "You heard the lady." Then more seriously. "We'll be out in a second." Rick moved fast for such a big guy, and then we were alone. "Put the hat on me, doll. Hide me." He laughed again, while I adjusted the hat. "Now show me you still know who I am." And his mouth was on mine, biting at my lower lip, hard enough that I gasped slightly. He covered my mouth with small bites, small flicks of his tongue, then pulled me tight against him, running his tongue along my neck. I could feel him, getting hard, the heat rising from his body. Tristan dropped his hands to the tops of my thighs and pulled me up and in against him until he was practically holding all my weight in his arms. He pressed my body against his cock, which was now a heavy, solid presence between us. Then he was kissing me, possessively, gently, his tongue teasing, exploring, pulling away and coming back, sucking on my tongue, over and over again. I would never get over how fast it had happened, from nice and familiar to hard and wanting, so fast. Then Tristan was breathing into my neck. "Don't forget Lily. You forget. And then I have to remind you." He grabbed a handful of my hair and pulled it back, hard, exposing my neck, then bit down, harder. I couldn't have stopped the sound that he pulled from my throat.

Tristan had his eyes shut tightly. "Lily...fuck...we've got to go. Just...a minute more...let me." And he turned me around and bent me over the table with the paper table cloth and bottles of water. He leant over me, his warm body pressing me down. I thrust up against him, the pull on the muscles in my legs as I felt his weight on me both making me tense and opening me up. I could feel the hollow want inside as I breathed out slowly. His hand ran over my ass, then pressed between my legs, holding me still. When he finally slapped the sensitive skin at the juncture of hip and thigh, it was like he had gone inside my body, my mind, he knew. Tristan murmured against my shoulder. "Say yes. I want you so much. I want to feel pain with wanting you." And his hips swept the air between us, rubbing up on me, quick and dirty, and then pulled away. It was suddenly cold and I waited, eyes shut. Anyone could walk in. I was sure anyone who was still here could hear me, needy, even if I was trying to be quiet. Tristan was lifting me up and spun me around, his mouth burning, taking my hands and pressing them both against the swell of his cock, moving them down over his balls, between his legs, pressing in. "So hard. You make me want to do everything with you. Want everything..." He raised my hand to his mouth and thrust in three fingers and sucked on them. His eyes met mine, as he licked up the length of my fingers. "You can take me too. You'd like it. I'll show you how..." Like a lightning strike right to the core, my skin was vibrating with want. My legs were shaking. He stopped and kissed each fingertip, biting on one hard enough that I shrieked. "Not too long an outing, doll. I think it's time to try something new between us. Tonight. That empty bed..."

"Short walk. Short walk," I mumbled, trying to make my mouth form words.

Tristan laughed again, that dark, dirty laugh that seemed to bubble up out of him, as he let me go, watching me stand up, trying to come back to earth. "Let's go find Rick." He kissed my hair. "Lily...you're so wonderful. Thank you for this—for thinking of it." He kissed me and stopped, pulling the scarf higher up. "Am I hidden?"

I tried to laugh, my voice still shaking with need. "As much as you can be."

We went out to the street, and found Rick with a cab. Tristan pulled him aside for a moment, and I watched them as Rick nodded, then pulled out his phone. Tristan told the cab driver we'd be just another minute, and he shrugged. The meter was on already, he didn't care. Rick was talking very fast, but I couldn't hear what he was saying, with Tristan standing between us. Then Rick whistled, softly, clearly, and Tristan turned around. Against the closed shop on the corner, the shadows cast by the overhead train bridge, and the old brick, dark with rain and dirt, they became silhouettes. Some signal was exchanged, and Rick spoke into the phone, pocketed it, then came over to us. We got in first, followed by Rick, who glanced around as he shut the door. Then Rick said, "Tate Modern" to the driver, and we were off.

Chapter 18

We were approaching the Tate and Rick told the driver to drop us at the main entrance on Holland Street. I raised my head and looked quizzically at Tristan, but he put his finger to my lips. "You'll see," was all he said. We all climbed out of the cab, and Rick paid the driver, Tristan watching and looking around. They were both so edgy. Something had to be up. But I wasn't going to ask or point it out. Rick tucked his wallet back in his pocket, and we all began walking down the grey slope to the revamped power station. Just as a monument, it was incredible. The sheer size of the turbine room was a spectacle in itself. But this wasn't walking along the Thames.

"Where are we going?" I asked. They both had a very similar smile. It was somewhat unnerving. The row of glass doors seemed shut and the interior looked completely dark, except for the lights on in the bookshop, but then I saw there was a man at the corner, opening a side door for us. Tristan waved, and Rick gave him a quick hug.

The man turned to us. "I'm Julian Cross-Ashby. A pleasure to meet you. On behalf of the Tate, welcome." We all shook hands.

"Let me take you up to the members' dining room. We won't be doing our final shut down for another hour or so, but certainly you are very welcome. Some of the staff will be at your service."

Tristan was efficiently polite. "Good to meet you, Julian. I appreciate your help in this. It won't be forgotten. Thank you. Rick will make all the arrangements, right?"

Julian nodded, and Tristan and I followed behind the two of them, Rick and Julian. I watched them talk. They didn't say a lot, but they obviously knew each other. At the lifts, Julian stepped aside, as did Rick, then Tristan did as well. All three of them. So polite. I smiled and said thank you, and walked to the back of the very small elevator. I had no idea what was going on, but if Tristan had thought of it, then I was curious. We went up to the sixth floor, where the woman at the desk gave us all a quick smile, before turning her full attention to Tristan. She was more formally dressed, in a white suit, with her name tag, and beautiful, her thick dark hair tied up in a neat bun. Tristan gazed at her appreciatively, shook her hand, and watched as she held open the white door for us, before striding into the long corridor-like section of the room.

Here, at the back, you had a view of the neighboring office buildings, their lights on in scattered patterns. We turned the corner, and there was the bar, and beyond that, the first glimpse of the view—a full-on panorama of St. Paul's, the Thames below, the office buildings of the city, the metal lines of the cranes and their intersecting planes, the mix of old and new, glowing against the low level grey clouds, reflecting the light back, a hazy orange glow from the streetlights. The sky barely showed the outline of a few wisps that stood out from the black grey mass of heavy cloud cover. With the illuminated dome of the cathedral mounting heroically to the skies, there was an epic quality to the picture just outside the clear plate glass windows. The interior was barely lit, candles on low tables, the bottles behind the bar sparkling in the halogens, the mirror behind them casting a flickering mix of colors over the bar. Tristan stepped up to the stainless steel counter, and shook hands with both the bartenders, inviting them to the show tomorrow, thanking them for their generosity. I was sure he was paying for it as well, but it was a gesture of good will and they responded in kind. He glanced at the menu, ordered a good bottle of Spanish wine, and some olives and cheese, and then wrapped his arm around me, and steered me towards the deep maroon velvet couches directly facing St. Paul's.

He pulled me to him, and kissed me, familiar and comfortable. "Surprise?" He grinned. I looked back at him. He shrugged. "It probably wasn't a good idea to walk out tonight. Maybe I'm paranoid." I shook my head, about to speak. "I'd love to see it all. Rotherhithe. The water. But I got them to open the Tate for us. Good trade?" He squeezed my hand. "I've always liked it up here. There's something epic about it."

I was about to say something, although I wasn't entirely sure what, when our wine arrived. The bartender cut off the metal covering, quickly twisting in the corkscrew, and pulling it out with a satisfying pop. I looked over at Tristan. He had been watching as well, and was now looking down as his wineglass was filled with a small amount. "Let Lily taste as well," he directed, and the bartender did as he was asked, pouring a small amount in my glass. I swirled it around, gently, as Tristan watched me. "Taste first, and tell me what you think."

I took in the scent of the wine. It needed to breathe, but it had a deep earthy quality that was part of how the wine had been made, not added on with extra oaked barrels and additives. I drank a bit, breathing in. The wine had different notes, different levels, developing on my tongue as I swallowed, slowly. It was really good, and I said so, forgetting for a moment that he was the one in charge, the one with the plan and the money and the fame. Tristan smiled and nodded the bartender away. "If I can coax out your experience, your mind..." He crossed a leather covered leg over one knee and leaned back and shut his eyes. "This is good." He looked tired again, and there was a line between his brows that wouldn't smooth out, but his body was relaxed, his hand wrapped around the wine glass. The little bowl of mixed olives arrived, with the two white china dishes for pits, the cheese plate, the crisp linen napkins with a knife and fork. The delight, the anxiety, the familiarity of things done correctly, elegantly. I let out a long sigh, and drank more of the wine. It was getting even better as it aired out. I reached for Tristan's hand, and he examined me, smiling, linking his long fingers with mine. We sat there, side by side, watching the clouds move past in the wind, past the bright white stone of the church. There was nothing to say, nothing that really needed to be said. His hand was strong, fleshy around the thumb, and I stroked the inside of his palm. It was soothing, his warm skin around me, his quiet reflection.

• • •

The next morning, I woke up late, the sound of birds from the gardens directly outside, the big bed already empty. I could hear the water running in the bath, but I didn't rush over to see him, but stretched out across the mattress, the sheets smooth and cool, but warm where the indent of his body had been. So he hadn't been up that long then. I closed my eyes, and wriggled under the covers. We'd stayed at the Tate until we had to leave, then did actually walk to Tower Bridge, holding hands as we finally went by the river. Late at night, it was fairly quiet, groups of friends heading home after a night out, some couples, a few lone souls heading somewhere. Rick trailed at a distance—I turned around once to catch sight of him—but he was a distant presence, stopped at the corner of a building to light a cigarette. I felt his annoyance when he saw me looking.

Tristan and I hadn't really talked much. Little kisses, and his hand wrapped in mine, and the cold damp air sinking into my skin, his warm skin a ball of warmth that kept me going. We walked under the bridge, and down past the sculptures, over the little bridge by the old warehouses that were now flats. "I like it here," Tristan said suddenly, and stopped and kissed me, right in the middle of the tiny bridge. The tide was coming in, and the lapping of the water was soothing, slow. We stood there, listening, holding each other. Tristan kissed the top of my head, and held me a little closer, and neither of us moved. Then a group of guys came along, laughing and swearing, and we moved aside to let them pass, looking out at the river, any couple of lovebirds out too late at night, maybe with nowhere to go. After the sound of their voices faded out, we carried on for a while longer, but it was late, and Rick was edgy. So we headed up to the main road, and a cab came just as Rick was about to call a service.

We didn't get back until nearly three in the morning, and Tristan threw his clothes off in a straight line as he headed to the bedroom. "Bed, doll. Come on. I'm completely done." By the time I'd brushed my teeth, he was already asleep, that line in his forehead still there, the circles under his eyes huge and dark. I turned off the lights, and opened the window slightly. It would be dawn soon enough. I got in next to him, and straightened the covers. He murmured something, and rolled up against my back, the long warmth of him like a protection. And I hadn't moved again, until I woke up to find him already up the next morning.

Tristan came out of the bathroom, and fell on the bed, pulling the covers down, tickling me with cold hands. I shrieked, and swatted him away. "Cold!" He laughed, and crawled under the covers. I rolled over towards him. "Hi," I said. I suddenly felt shy.

Tristan kissed me. "Hi yourself." He rolled over on his back, and bent one arm behind his head. "Did you have fun last night?"

"It was wonderful."

"Even the surprise?"

"Absolutely the surprise."

Tristan was quiet for a moment. "I'm sorry I crashed out last night. That wasn't...," he pulled me closer to him, then continued, "...what I had in mind. Sometimes I just lose it though. It's taken a lot out of me, all this. It's been more than I thought it would be, the concerts, the shows, everything coming up. I should know by now...know what it's like. The stress. Switching back and forth between music and media. But it still surprises me."

I hugged him. "It's ok, you know. I fell asleep right after you. It's all good, sleep, you, the whole thing."

Tristan lay quiet for a moment, his hand running up and down my back, tracing patterns that only meant something to him. Then he spoke. "I don't want to disappoint you." I started to protest, and he stopped me. "You say this now, but people sign up for the whole dream. Sometimes they aren't too happy to wake up."

I leaned over his face, and looked at him. "I'm awake." And I crawled on top of him, and put my head on his chest. "I don't want to pressure you. But I'm here, ok? I think I get it."

He breathed out. "There's a lot going on. It gets to me. Not all the time. Still." He closed his eyes. "Still." I watched him as he squeezed his eyes shut. Without any warning, he flipped me on my back, and he was hovering neatly above me. "Still." He laughed without any warmth. "It pays the bills, and gives us the nice room, and the respect of our peers." He leaned down and kissed me, quickly. "I've ordered some room service, I'll grab a piece on the way out. The label set up another interview—a little TV time. The next time you see me, I'll be covered in pancake." He sat up, cross-legged. It was a little distracting. He saw me looking, and pulled the covers over him, then just as quickly threw them off again. "Hell, doll, look all you want."

I blushed. "You're awfully attractive. Sorry."

"Don't be. If I had more time, you'd be doing more than looking, I promise." He leaned over and kissed me. "I promise."

I kissed him back, gently. I did want him. But I didn't want him to think I was just there for the incredible sex. I wasn't.

Suddenly he held me tighter, and I grabbed back with all my strength. He buried his face in the corner of my neck, and there was something desperate in his touch. I held him as tightly as I could, until he finally, slowly let go. He looked at me, a world of emotion in his eyes, now light, a mix of colors, the circles underneath still dark. He kissed me again. "I've got to get going, Lily. You've got everything you need, right?" I nodded.

I watched him grab a new pair of black and white boxer briefs from his leather duffle, and dress himself, following the trail of clothes he left behind last night. When he got to the shirt, he looked at it skeptically, and tossed it over a chair, coming back to the duffle for a soft black v-neck that seemed to meet his standards. He ducked down and kissed me again. "Lily, I..." he started. I looked up at him. He shook his head. "No, it's ok. Now's not the time. I'll call you after this." He ran his fingers through his hair. "TV! They'll do it for me." He made a face, stuffed his wallet and his phone into the pockets of his leather jacket, and undid the lock, waving as he left.

I lay back on the pillows. I could hear a bird in the garden, just over the rapid beat of my heart.

Chapter 19

The Roundhouse, in Chalk Farm, had been a building site for years—used for neither trains nor anything else—until the funding finally started coming in, as well as the political will to do something with it. It was a fairly large venue, but it was split up into different areas. After the Barfly was ruled out, Tristan's concert was going to be in the studio theatre—about 200 seats. He didn't like it there because of the fixed seating, but it was a great place otherwise, and very central. But he had insisted, and threatened to pull out altogether, telling the radio station XMM and his management he'd do a late night radio concert instead, that he didn't play where he didn't want to be.

So the place that had finally been chosen for the show actually wasn't that far from the small bar where Devised had had their first gig. It was small, and a bit of a dive, but central to all the action. Tristan had told me that all the tickets were going to be released either to friends of people in the business, which he wasn't that happy about, but recognized that it was part of the whole thing, always had been, always would be, or through XMM, where he'd spent the afternoon playing records and taking calls, announcing to the lucky fans that they were going to see him. I had wanted to hear what he sounded like on the radio, one distance removed from reality, his voice going out on the airwaves to belong to everyone, while I listened, knowing him that much better.

But I was listening to Trevor's revelations instead. I wondered if I would have rather heard screaming fans or the truth. Put that way, it actually made it all a little more complicated. What did I want to know? I had to share him with the world, but in some ways, the difference between me and the fans was the level of trust he had in me. I hoped that wouldn't change once he knew the full extent of what Trevor had revealed. I had the impression that there had been some kind of unwritten agreement between them, that Tristan had thought unbreakable, and Trevor hadn't. Or hadn't for the right person. Oh fuck. I really had to stop over thinking it.

The staff at the hotel called me a taxi. They were efficient and distant, which I supposed was part of the price that was being paid for the room. No photographers here. And it was restful, if a little cold, the way so many places that cater for the rich and famous can be. No rough edges.

I had the cab drop me off by the Tube, and I walked up the high street, past the shops selling pins and t-shirts, the usual Union Jacks and "my friend went to London" sorts of things. Now they were joined by more crass displays, like the one that said "I love sushi" and had a graphic of a stick figure man with his head between the legs of a stick figure woman. Lovely. There were still a few punks around, enjoying it secretly when they let the tourists take their pictures for a little beer money. The rest were mostly tourists and kids roaming in packs, feeling they were free and somewhere important, outside of the familiar safe influence of home. I looked around to see if there were any likely early arrivals for the show, but all the people just seemed one mass of moving, pulsing humanity. It was still early though, not even 7:00 p.m., and while the hardcore fans would be outside, either waiting, or hoping they could blag a ticket, or catch a glimpse of their hero, the people on the guest list wouldn't show up until the very last minute, hoping to evidence their cool, and show how little this kind of thing really meant to them, seeing as they had basically an open invite to anything they wanted. And the guest list—I didn't want to think about how they'd all be there. I'd checked my phone for messages before I left the hotel, but there hadn't been any updates from Dave, and Tristan didn't need to contact me—I knew where he was. I had a vague wish for how it was before, when everything seemed kind of new. Now I felt in it so thick.

I turned left, and walked along the canal, up over the bridge. There was a group, cheering on two guys who were standing on the railing of the walkway that went over the canal, poised to jump in. I stood for a minute and watched, wondering if they would really do it. The bridge was about twenty feet above the murky canal, and it was warmer out than the day before, but not enough to make the deep green water appealing. But after a steady round of cheering from the crowd, and the two guys realizing that they had a pretty large audience at this point, they nodded to each other, and then jumped, disappearing behind the mass of the crowd, and splashing into the water to even louder cheers. Everyone watching clapped, including me. They swam over to the edge, where their friends were waiting to help pull them out. They were lucky, I thought, that there were no cops around. Surely that would have gotten them some anti-social behavior order or at least an evening with the filth. I'd had a friend who got in a fight with her boyfriend and was totally pissed out of her mind, so she jumped in the canal, attention seeking. Except she had nearly drowned. They had to call 999, stomach pumped, nasty. But watching these guys climb out and shake themselves off, a little like happy dogs on an outing, it struck me that not every crazy action had to be the result of some deep depression. It could just be fun. Fun for fun's sake. And maybe you could remember how to have fun again.

I turned away from the canal, and threaded my way through the stalls of food and jewelry, past the people drinking at the little tables in front of the waterfront pub, and headed over to the entrance to the club. Sure enough, there was already a group of people watching from different vantage points, and a line of people who were ticket holders waiting to get in. Lots of indie boys with tight skinny pants, and a range of Devised t-shirts that marked out the long-standing fans. There were a couple of Tristan t-shirts as well, his logo and a nice little line drawing. They were worn mostly by girls, but there were a couple of male fans proclaiming their allegiance as well. Crossover appeal—that was one of the reasons he was so famous. One woman was walking up and down, holding up a sign that said "will pay £100 for a ticket—help me out, please!!"

I stood and watched them for a while, feeling the buzz increasing with each new arrival, as they saw the already long line and all the people hoping they would get in. I spotted James Max, gesturing wildly to one of the bouncers, who was trying to keep the people who wanted tickets away from the people who already had them. The bouncer was huge, but Max pushed right past him. I saw who he was trying to get past the line—a tall blonde wearing a skin tight dress, who towered over him in her heels, but she didn't seem to care and neither did he. She finally got through, the rope cord separating the inside from the outside was unhooked, and then she was bending down, the curve of her ass more pronounced as she leaned over seductively, and kissed the balding man on both cheeks. I laughed, and turned my head away, moving behind the very tall boy with the curly brown hair who was lighting a cigarette and talking to his friend, who had the same curls but blonde, in Spanish. I didn't want to be spotted anyway, not yet. I was enjoying taking in the whole build-up. And it would go well in the article. I took out my phone and took a few pictures. Backup. The magazine might use one or two. Rough fan shots. The assortment of people who were either slowing down to watch or hanging around in the hope of getting in, somehow, was astonishing. There were the usual Eurotrash bunch, the indie kids complete with straw trilby or grey pork pie hat, super tight black jeans that seemed to only hold on to the last curve of their ass through sheer willpower, the girls in short shorts and ruffled tops. But there were also some old school rockers, jeans and band shirts, grizzled by experience and perhaps a few too many drugs. There were some lovely women, chatting while on line, obviously very happy to have scored tickets, definitely not concerned about what people thought. There was an older man in a wheelchair, with his partner, who had pushed him over the cobblestones and was now waiting to talk to one of the bouncers, probably to get a better place inside, maybe one where he could actually see. It occurred to me that it was a testament to Tristan's intelligence that although aspects of his music had all of the simple straightforward appeal of the pop song, his lyrics as well as his complicated chord structures and syncopated rhythms were something you could go back to again and again and find more. Complicated ideas that seemed simple on the surface. It was pretty fascinating to see all these different people with different lives, different ideas—but the one thing that held them together was an intense appreciation of Tristan's music. It made me hope that there was almost something here like a tribe, a group of people held together by an ideal, a stronger bond that could overcome the stupid little petty fights that tore most things down.

Of course, that hadn't worked in the case of James Max, Tristan's manager, whose jealousy, if that's what it was, or meanness had almost derailed us from the start. And there he was over there. What had happened to the blonde? Or had he spotted me right away? The tall boys with the dark and light hair had moved while I was observing the crowd, and here he was, coming right for me. The smirk on his face, all thick eyebrows and balding skull, didn't fill me with much hope that he was feeling the love.

He started speaking before he even reached me, making very sure everyone around us could hear him. "Lily. Lily Taylor. How are you? I thought I spotted you over here—you look different in a crowd. Didn't you get an All Access? Did Tristan forget? Shame. That's what he's like with the female talent. But I'm sure I can do something for you."

"You're an asshole." I had no time to think of some smart reply, just the first thing that came into my head. I turned away. There were already people looking and although I really wanted nothing more than to punch his face in, some smarter part of me really wanted to avoid a public scene. I started walking back to the canal, away from the venue. I guess I'd be later than I thought. But he was still following me.

"Now, Lily, honey, that's no way to talk. I saw this coming. Dropped by Dave and Tristan. But I can get you in if you still want to lust over him. As long as you promise to let me taste what he left behind." He ran a thick hand down my arm, while I stared at him, frozen to the spot with rage. I pulled my hand out of his grasp, feeling slightly sick.

"Listen motherfucker, isn't there some bald dwarf convention that you're late for? Fuck right off." I started to walk away, but he grabbed my arm, hard, and spun me around as I cried out. I still wanted to avoid a scene, but he was making it all but impossible. Before I could even think what I was doing, I pulled back and slapped him, hard, with the back of my hand. My rings hit his eyebrow, and I could feel the skin break before the blood started, spattering his face and my arm. I didn't know which one of us was more shocked, but I went for it, while he released me to hold his hand over the cut. "I told you to fuck off. Touch me again and I'll scream for the police." I started to walk away again, shaking with rage.

But he had recovered as well. "You sad aging bitch. You don't know, do you? You were watching, weren't you? The tall blonde? The one with the gorgeous bod? Some reporter. You didn't even recognize Tristan's ex, did you? And you didn't know he asked her to be here, did you?" I could hear him starting to laugh and I could hear his voice following me. "You thought you were in his league, what a joke."

I just kept walking. I could feel the eyes of curious people on me, on us, how many people had heard him? Ten? Fifty? It hardly mattered. My fingernails were digging into my clenched palms, resisting the effort to go back and smash his face in, fighting against the effect his words had had on me, despite the raging argument now commencing in my brain. It couldn't be true. It couldn't be. We had the hotel room. Smart move, Lily, I thought to myself. Good way to leave yourself wide open. But what about Trevor? The story? And he was so trustworthy. James has always disliked you. A smart girl would have tried to flirt him up, keep him on side. But no. You had to show him your true colors. And now? He was going in there. Covered in blood at least, I thought. Stupid motherfucker. Shit.

I kept walking along the canal, away from the lock, until I was nearly at Regents Park. It wasn't far, but the distance felt good. A part of me never wanted to go back to the club. Another part wanted to go back, right away—and smash a bottle on his stupid head. Shit. I sat down on the thankfully empty bench at the corner, where the canal opened up and turned, and stared at the garish Chinese restaurant houseboat, moored in the little harbor. Fuck. I'd have to call Tristan. I didn't think I could go right up there, alone. I thought about waiting for Nick and Sarah, but the fact that both James and Nick had pretty much said the same thing, didn't make me feel like their support would be exactly what was on offer. Dave? No. Before I could think anymore, I brought up Tristan's number and pressed call. Just hearing his voice would make it ok. Like it always did. I held the phone up to my ear, waiting through the rings. Then his voice came through.

"Tristan, it's me..." But it was a recording. It had sounded just like his voice, live, but all he said was "hello," then "if you need immediate assistance, call James Max on..." Fuck. Fuck. Fuck.

I nearly threw my phone in the water. And I didn't have Rick's number, the fixer, the one that had booked the room, arranged our getaway, away from James's prying eyes. He must have found out. That would explain the vindictive rage. But it meant I was on my own. And now another pair of eyes would be on me, sizing me up, looking for weak points and failings. Ready to laugh. Fuck. I crossed my legs up on the bench and leaned my head over and closed my eyes. Just a little moment of calm, and then I'd have to be up there fighting. Fuck.

Ok. I'd said this was showtime, and here it was. The moment everybody knows is coming, where everything you do is going to be scrutinized, and it may change everything, and if it fucks up, you're going to know, deep in your soul, that it was your doing. Yes, lessons to be learned, karma, endless wheel. Yes. But on some kind of existential level, you'd blame yourself. And it would be pretty difficult to walk around spouting "life lessons" if you'd lost everything you'd ever wanted. Wanted. Needed? Maybe.

I really hoped it didn't come to that. I stayed there for another minute, curled up, asking the universe for strength, trying to find some kind of energy and determination. Then I felt a light rain drop on the back of my neck, then another, then a few all at once. That was my signal. I uncurled myself, trying to believe that I probably had some wiggle room, that perfection was overrated and arrogant, and hoisted myself onto the tow path, along with the other revelers heading either into the bars of Camden or out of the rain.

I reached the lock in what seemed like record time, and thought briefly about going to get a beer. No. I had a mission now, and I wasn't going to be shy or frightened. Or at least I was going to try really fucking hard not to show it. The line was still there and had gotten longer, as people placed themselves behind the diehards at the front who were hoping to be right on top of the stage, in the mosh pit, if there was one, singing along with and idolizing their hero. The light rain wasn't diminishing the party atmosphere, although some of the hopefuls who were watching, just to see what happened, had drifted off. I saw a girl talking to another woman, who had been there before, shrugging, before she went off to unlock her bike. The woman gazed after her, possibly wondering if that was the right course of action, before advancing closer to the barrier that was protecting the little courtyard that they had created around the entrance. Slow and steady. I felt for her. It wasn't easy to go to these things alone, keeping the hope and energy going. At least she didn't have someone telling her she wasn't in their league, I thought. And she wasn't leaving, and neither was I. We were advancing on the bouncers and gate keepers with the invite list. Forget it.

I walked up to the two guys on the door, one white, one black. The black guy wasn't as tall, but he looked like a boxer, solid and immobile if you tried to move him, fast if he wanted to move you. The white guy was having a cigarette and talking to a man who looked like he was the manager of the venue. He had the clipboard, so I headed towards them. Instantly, the first guy, the boxer, was in front of me. "Can I help you, Miss?" At least he was polite. And that was his job, to stop me. Now I just had to speak. Of course my voice came out in a croak.

"Hi." I paused. "I'm on the guest list." There, that wasn't so hard. Hopefully James wouldn't come out.

"Your name?" I told him, and he grabbed the clip board and

flipped through a couple of pages of print out. Shit, they couldn't have given away that many tickets—the whole place was going to be filled with record company liggers. Oh well. That's the way it went. As long as my name was on there, and no one had done a little magic with the delete key, James.

The sound of his voice brought me out of my thoughts. "Lily...?"

"Taylor, yes, that's right."

"And you're a guest of...?"

Hmm, that was a question. For the ticket? Tristan? Dave? I figured I'd try both. "Probably Tristan, but it could be under Dave Fanning and *The Core* magazine."

"Yeah, got it. Lily Taylor. Right here." He clipped a wrist band around my left wrist. He fished around in a bag sitting on the bar stool just behind him. "And your laminate," he muttered, looking at me more closely. "AAA. Better put this one on now."

"Great, thank you." I put the nylon cord over my head and tucked the card inside my shirt. No need to advertise it right now. I nodded to him, and started walking towards the two big wooden doors, one of which was slightly ajar. It was already nearly eight, but I remembered what Tristan had said about keeping them waiting. He was right. If anything, the energy outside was growing, fed by each new person that was admitted early from the guest list. Now, that was me. I admired my silver colored wrist band with his logo on it and "VIP guest" in little bold letters. Nice. I waved my wrist at the bouncer on the door, and passed through the doorway. In. At last. My eyes had to adjust to the fast absence of light. Shit it was dark in here. I couldn't see a thing. I left the thin strip of light that was coming in from the outside and walked further into the dimness of the small entry hall, towards the next set of wooden doors. These were closed, and I reached out to touch the metal handle and curled my fingers around what felt like twisted wrought iron and pulled. Hard. The heavy door opened slowly and instantly the buzz of conversations hit me. I stepped aside and let the door close behind me. I reasoned with myself that I wasn't being overly cautious; that instead it made good sense to check out the lay of the land before I launched myself, unprotected and unprepared.

The stage dominated the center of the far wall. It wasn't very big, and was only raised about four feet, so your most rabid fans would get a good look at shoes, legs, and depending how tall they were or weren't, a pretty straight-on eyeful of what lay at the top of the tight trousers. But they'd all be looking up? Right? I smiled. Maybe not. The sexual buzz of the musician. Despite all my anxiety, I still felt the potential energy. What had some band said in an interview? That they felt they had done their job if people danced around and were happy, and went home together to fuck. Something like that. I had to focus on the happy of it all, or I'd be the wallflower at the party. And that wasn't how I wanted to come across.

There were roadies finishing the set-up—there was no break down and move forward, because Tristan was the only person playing tonight—no lead-on band. There were two massive stacks of speakers on either side of the stage, which also effectively blocked the audience's view of backstage, which had to hurt to stand next to. Well, I'd be finding out if my ears would start bleeding. That is, unless I took the journalist way out, and perched myself up in the private balcony over at the other end of the room. I'd still get a decent view, and no moshing, I thought.

I thought of his face, the strange expression as he kissed me goodbye, when he had left this morning to do interviews. But he wants you there. Right? The argument continued in my head as I did my sweep of the room. Somebody was already up in the press balcony, maybe I'd go up there and talk to them, buy some time. And over there, near the stage, with a small group of fans watching her laugh and snap her hair over her shoulder was the tall blonde. So that was the ex. I'd seen pictures, of course, but she'd always looked kind of wasted, grabbing on to Tristan, not the platinum Hollywood goddess she appeared to be now. I wondered if he really knows she's here, I thought. I hadn't seen him around. No. Must be backstage. I wondered if it would be breaking some kind of protocol to go back there and find him, and decided to wait and see before I ran to him, all needy.

I was watching her chat animatedly to some record company people, when there was suddenly a tap on my shoulder. I jumped and let out a strangled scream as I twisted around, fists up.

"Commando training, Lily?" Trevor's laconic clipped voice was sarcastic, but his eyes were bright with amusement. Maybe he'd be an ally after all, in this fucking mess.

"I thought you were James. Or Dave. Lucky for you I'm so controlled." I turned back to the growing crowd. If anyone had noticed, they'd looked away.

Trevor laughed. "So it won't just be Tristan giving the show."

I snorted. "No, probably not. And while we are on the subject of violence, do you know James Max?"

Trevor closed his eyes briefly. "Nasty little man. But tenacious, like a terrier. I'm afraid I'm to blame for his presence in Tristan's life. Why?"

I felt oddly uncaring about putting sensible limits on what

I wanted to say. "One, he dislikes me. Or he does now, after I slapped him when he tried to come on to me. Drew blood. Don't think 'sorry' will fix that."

Trevor threw a dark smile in my direction. "When will I learn to not do the washing up before I come out?" He paused. "Is there a two, or was the one for effect only?"

Clever motherfucker. I found myself almost liking him again. "There might even be a three. So impatient. And you might know something about number two." I sighed. "I am pretty sure that James invited the ex-wife."

Trevor raised his eyebrows. "Really? And what gave you that impression? Did he tell you before or after you tortured him?"

"Oh, he'd know if I tortured him." I really wasn't in the mood for endless chat. "But I saw him greet her at the line and invite her in. Then he told me who she was, and that Tristan wanted her here."

Trevor's face was unreadable. "Strange. Very strange. But I can't pretend to know what goes on his mind anymore, if I ever did. I suppose the two of us will just have to wait for further updates from the front." He must have seen the expression on my face, because he slid a protective arm around my waist. "Come my dear. Generally these events have a free bar for the likes of us. I'm sure a strengthener won't hurt your lethal right hook either."

I let him lead me through the crowd that seemed to have increased exponentially while we were talking. They must be letting in the line, I thought, and hoped Nick and Sarah would fend for themselves if they turned up. Or when they turned up, Sarah no doubt arrayed in something vaguely obscene. Suddenly I felt very underdressed. I'd gone with the leather trousers. I should have worn the dress. Men like tight dresses. Maybe I should go blonde.

Trevor tightened his grip slightly as he felt me grow distracted. "Oh no, Lily. A drink with me before you go off to your duties. Did you get a chance to mention lunch to the star?"

We were at the bar now. We showed our wristbands and the bartender nodded. "A gin and tonic for me, Hendricks if you have it, Tanqueray if you don't. Lily?"

"Scotch," I muttered, "single malt if they have it, anything if it's just the regular stuff."

"And a good scotch with water on the side for the lady." Trevor turned to me. "Would you prefer something else?"

I shook my head. "No, that sounds fine. I could use something stronger, thank you. And I did mention it to him. He seemed ok with it."

Trevor watched the bartender pour the drinks. "Make them doubles, please." The bartender turned around, and nodded, then added another shot to each glass. "Always the driven star. Nothing matters except the music. And maybe you?" He raised his glass to mine. "Take a big drink, my dear, we're about to go over and say hello to his ex-wife."

I choked on the sip I was taking and tried to cover up my coughing fit by trying to drink more while holding my breath. Trevor looked down at me, concerned. I managed to stop coughing, then raised my glass to him, and took a long swallow. The classic burning warmth, moved through me, both comforting and igniting. "Trevor. I'm your girl. Let's go."

He smiled, but placed a pale restraining hand on my arm. "We need to pick our moment, dear. Talk to me about, I don't know, thread count, while I watch."

Obediently, I blathered on about hotels, and sheets, and decor, hardly listening to what I was saying, as we both watched the crowd. She was behind me, so I also watched his face. I had a feeling that when he decided it was time to move, we'd have to be quick. His eyes were darting around the crowd. Occasionally someone would approach him, timidly, and he would smile, that oddly vampiric smile, and pull out his iPhone and made a few taps on the screen. For all anyone knew, he could be ordering groceries. He probably was. The person would then withdraw, practically moving backwards, out of the presence. It was fairly incredible to watch.

By now the place was nearly filled. It had to be almost show-time. Whatever we were going to do was going to have to happen soon. I tried to look around for Sarah and Nick, but there were so many people, individuals were hard to pick out. Poppy was bound to be here somewhere as well. I was surprised none of them had found us. I glanced back up at Trevor. There was a certain tension in his expression, and I felt sure our moment, whatever that meant, was about to come. I added some water, swirled the scotch around in my glass, and drank off what was left. Just as I swallowed, Trevor tapped my arm. "Let's go. Let me do the talking."

I gave his arm a little squeeze. I don't know why. But I didn't look up at him. I felt we both were going through mental preparations of some kind. What was he going to say? Would he introduce me? He'd have to, really, it'd be weird if he didn't. We might not even get that far. I schooled my expression into some kind of blank, benign carelessness, or at least I hoped that's what it looked like, and wished I could get away with wearing sunglasses all the time. We were only a few steps away from her, and although she was talking animatedly to a man in a pinstriped shirt and vest with a tight salt and pepper ponytail, who looked vaguely like the guy from Status Quo, she began turning towards us as we approached. Maybe she could feel the waves of tension like some force field coming off me, at least. Trevor always seemed to part the crowd as he moved, a little like Tristan, so maybe it was that. Was I wrong, or did I catch a slight nervous hesitation as she spotted Trevor, only noticeable because of the sudden change to blinding smile? She hadn't even really looked at me, but that was normal—women like that never really looked at other women unless they were sizing up the competition. I wasn't blonde, or in high heels, or carefully made up or really any of the things that might make her feel threatened. But I was here, and I was with Trevor, and I didn't really give a fuck anymore, especially after the inhaled double whisky, and not caring was the most dangerous pose of all. So she might have to notice me anyway, I thought.

Trevor spoke first. "Alixe, what a surprise. How delightful to see you after all this time. I thought you hated London." He smiled, she smiled. It was obvious they despised each other. Trevor turned to me. "Have you met Lily Taylor? She's writing a piece on Tristan for *The Core* magazine. She's been interviewing everyone who had something to do with Devised. Perhaps you'd deign to give her a brief run-down of your...involvement with the different members of the band?" He smiled again, artlessly, like someone who's hoping to hide the fact they just made a really good move in chess that won't pan out for another few turns.

I stuck out my hand, the innocent abroad. As if. "Pleasure to meet you, Alixe. I've heard so much about you." Trevor snorted. She stared at my hand as though it were covered in blood, which actually, not that long ago, it was. I wondered if James had told her how he'd come by his little accident.

"Trevor, darling. Lovely to see you." She nodded at me as though I weren't there. "Lily. Hello. Don't think I've read any of your work. Sorry." She turned her body towards Trevor, so I could now admire the backs of her arms. Had she had lipo? Surely one couldn't have army grade triceps and giant boobs at the same time. The magic of Hollywood. Her voice suddenly went up an octave for absolutely no reason. "But Trevor! Hanging around with journalists? How the mighty have fallen. You must be scripting the story." She turned her high-wattage smile on me. "So lucky to have a little help."

I knew Trevor had told me to let him talk, but I wasn't going to stand there. "I am very lucky. But as Humphrey Bogart said, I make my own luck. And as you've been able to watch lots of movies in Hollywood, if nothing else, I'm sure you know that one." I smiled at her.

She looked momentarily irritated, but it was gone in a nanosecond. I pressed my advantage. "I'd love to interview you for the article as well. Naturally, you and Tristan would have final approval on whatever I wrote before it went to press, unless you'd rather make a statement off the record. Any lingering regrets?" I felt, rather than saw Trevor's warning look, and I stopped. That was enough anyway.

"Oh talking shop. At a concert. Boring. I'll have someone contact you." She dismissed me, turning her head back towards

Trevor and running her long nails through her hair. "But Trevor, a real treat to see you." She turned to go.

Trevor coughed. "Alixe—why are you here? I'm sure I recall telling you to avoid anywhere within 1000 miles of Tristan. Or have you forgotten about the cellulite showing in that very exposed picture you sent of your frolics with his best friend, in the love nest you no longer own? Your ass does look magnificent now. And it will look even better in your first-class seat heading west back over the Atlantic." He smiled again.

She shook her hair so that it fell over her shoulders. "Oh Trevor, that's all old history. Old. Paul wanted to see Tristan. And Tristan said to bring me. He's obviously forgotten all about it. We're all just very very good friends now."

Trevor snapped at her. "Who told you Tristan wanted you here? Have you spoken to him yet?"

She waved her hand towards the stage. "Oh dear, does it matter? No, I haven't seen him yet. Paul's backstage now."

Trevor raised an eyebrow. "Vultures at feeding time? No, my mistake. Vultures wait for things to die first. Maybe you ran out of money? I hear plastic surgery is so expensive these days."

"That must be why you haven't had any, Trevor."

He laughed. "Alixe, so happy to know that your values are still as sterling as ever. What does Paul want with Tristan?"

"He's one of his oldest friends, Trevor." She waited for his acknowledgment, but nothing came. He just stood there, still like a stone. It was intimidating, and I had the impression she was beginning to feel the chill. "We'll watch the concert, Tristan will clear all this misunderstanding up afterwards." She turned away, and then looked over her shoulder at Trevor for one last missile.

"You're getting too sensitive these days. Must be the lousy company you're keeping."

I started towards her, but Trevor's arm went around me. "Your limited understanding, Alixe, was always what made sure you remained strictly a horizontal extra. But we'll see," he said, turned away, with his hand spread firmly across my rib cage, both an odd comfort and a warning. We headed back to the bar, where once again, he managed to find a place for us almost immediately, and he ordered us another round. I'd walked with him placidly enough to the bar, but as soon as his hand released me, I started to turn and head back to the stage.

Trevor grabbed my hand and tugged me back towards him. "Don't do it love. Tristan won't like it. She'll love it. She's obviously heard rumours. Lose this battle gracefully, win the war effortlessly. A little more confidence, my dear. She's trash. You should know that by now." I was staring at the bar, tracing an indent in the varnish covering the wood. He handed me my drink, and put his hand on my shoulder, which made me look up at him. His eyes looked sad, and I felt like an idiot. Foolish. But an angry fool. I raised my glass to him, and took a sip.

"Why should I trust you? Why?"

Trevor chuckled, which was the last thing I was expecting. My fist clenched up. I could just walk out of here, I thought, and leave all these monsters to their ball. "Lily, trust no one. That's my best advice. But in this, I am thoroughly on your side, for reasons that elude my complete understanding as well."

I glanced towards the stage. Tristan. The concert was going to start. He had wanted me here.

Trevor followed my look. "I'll say please if it will make you reconsider. Please. Don't walk out."

I said nothing, and drank more of the whisky. My head felt heavy. The party atmosphere around me seemed miles away. I tried to speak. "Trevor…"

"He needs you, darling. He needs someone. If there's a void, you'll have just paved the way for Sindy doll over there."

I couldn't help smiling. "Sindy doll?"

"Oh, I keep forgetting you're a Yank. That's quite a compliment to you. Barbie, dear."

I tried to laugh. The place was packed, and the temperature had gone up noticeably. Maybe it was the drink. "He told me he wanted me here."

"Then believe him. Finish your drink, we'll go down the front. Two pairs of friendly, watchful eyes."

I chugged the rest.

"Easy, girl. Let's stay upright. Come on." We left the bar and tried to navigate a path through the crowd. The roadies were finishing up the last minute adjustments to the guitars, taping the setlist down, checking the levels. Tristan would be backstage, getting ready. I hoped he was getting a minute alone, he told me he liked having a quiet moment before it all "cracked open" during the interview. I looked around for Alixe—Sindy doll. She was still out front, that was both good and bad. No sign of Paul, though I wasn't entirely sure I'd recognize him in his current configuration. We managed to get right to the front, thanks to a few people moving aside, evidently out of respect for Trevor. I was glad to see they didn't give up their places entirely; we were all just jammed in a little bit closer. The old excitement was bubbling up, the thrill of knowing your heroes were going to be on stage in a moment, the animal pressure of the crowd making everything sweaty and immediate. I looked away from the stage, up

at Trevor, and followed his gaze. He was watching the side door
to the stage. It swung open, and out came a guy who looked like
he must be Paul. And Dave. Now that was interesting. What the
hell was he up to? They shrunk into the corner. And then, almost
on cue, the lights went down. Instantly the crowd began screaming, whistling. It was total blackness, except for the little red
lights on the amps, and the eerie glow that was the stage light for
the performers. The clouds of dry ice started, and then I really
couldn't see, drums disappearing then re-emerging as the cur-
rents of air, rising on the heat of all the bodies, moved it around.
The cheering grew even louder, and a guy yelled out, "Tristan,
man, I love you!" Then the steady clapping started, speeding up,
like some kind of football match. I could just make out the band
coming on stage, strapping on the instruments, readying themselves. Then the guitarist playing a note progression, just six
notes, but more and more rapidly until the entire thing was like
a screaming blur. Then Tristan loped onto the stage, waving to
the crowd, and the entire mass of people surged forward. I was
pressed against the barrier, and I pushed back a little so I could
breathe. It was insanity.

Tristan twisted the mike out of the stand, and murmured
"hello London...you motherfuckers!" Everyone yelled back. And
then crowd swept forward again, just to be even closer, and the
whistling was deafening. I could see him smile, just a little. And
he turned and nodded to the band, and raised his hand. "All
right boys and girls! Let's do this!" His arm sliced through the
air, and slapped his jean covered thigh just as the rapid fire drum
opening of "Broken Window" started. Nothing mattered anymore except the perfection of the beat, the howling guitar, the
sultry smile on Tristan's face that made you feel he was into it

as much as you were. Then he started singing, every nuance of every word, every meaning you could get out of it, the smartness, the consciousness behind it slapping up against the intense beat. It was amazing, fantastic—I didn't even have to pretend that I thinking about anything but this. Nothing fucking mattered. I had the impression that Trevor was watching me, studying the expressions on my face, seeing me dancing around, but I didn't care. Let him think I was a groupie. Maybe that's really all I was.

Chapter 20

I wanted to catch his eye, and I wanted to remain invisible. It wasn't really him, and yet it was. I was having the dilemma of every serious fan, except I wasn't your average fan. And—it had been a long time since I'd really thought the people on the stage were different. But there was that one little thing— they did have this strange ability and charisma that set them apart. That deserved respect, even if nothing else about them did. I didn't want the performers to show all their workings— I liked the mystery. So this section of his life and mine met in one way: I was the swooning, greedy spectator; Tristan was the visual object and the magician, the creator of these brilliant songs, conjuring music out of the ether. And for him, this was his element, where he connected with the solidity of the crowd, without singling out any particular individual or moment. That, at least, I could understand—the need to perform, the strange, very personal yet very distant emotional bond you created with the people watching you. The way you responded to their shifts in mood, subtly, while remaining true to what you intended to do, altering it all, your face, body, voice, just slightly, to try and coax the reaction you wanted out of the mass. Or maybe on a different day you simply refused to fuck with anything, insisting they follow you. It was a dance in another dimension. Any one individual could influence the whole, but the role of the person on stage was to be bigger than life. And the power and energy that was required to do that well was enormous. I didn't want to distract him. I'd be there when and if he was ready to look.

The next few songs were thunderous, as was the reaction. The crowd was going literally insane. The band was tight, his voice was spot on, the energy they were building up was dangerous. I wiped away the sweat that was dripping into my eyes, the place was boiling. I didn't care about anything anymore. Music had saved me before. Suddenly it was doing it again. The fact that I had fucked the guy on stage, that I was falling in love with him, even if I no longer really understood what love meant, was distant and irrelevant. All I cared about was the count in, the chorus, the timing, the way the drums and the bass worked together and moved apart, the way his voice mimicked the guitar then fell back into an almost whispery, conversational tone, like someone telling you their darkest secrets in the back booth of the bar.

The song ended, and we all clapped and shouted. Some people in the audience yelled out requests, and Tristan began responding to them. "Oh that one. Yeah. Well, it's a Devised song, but hey, you never know. Not right now though." He turned and made some gesture to the band. "This one," he drawled out, and he looked right down at me, like he had known just where I was all along, "is for those who don't sleep." He shot me a quick smile, before looking back out to the crowd. "How many of you fuckers don't sleep? We're going to keep you up all fucking night!" he

yelled out to the room. The audience screamed back their appreciation. And he began the song, the song that had made me cry,
the one that started it all. It was a dreamier, more introspective
ballad than what had come before, but it felt right after all the
bombast and pulsing thrust of the last few songs. The audience
had a chance to take a breath, to feel, to light a metaphorical cigarette after being thoroughly fucked by the band. I kept thinking
how lucky I was, and how that scared the hell out of me. There
was more to all this than just my crazy past and my fears. A door
had been opened, like the gates of perception, and through it I
could see everything I'd always known, whether I'd consciously
realized it or not.

I gazed up at him, his eyes tightly shut, his dark eyelashes
dusting the high cheekbones. Singing as though it were the
last song he'd ever be allowed to do. Stunning. Beautiful.
Unbelievably, undeniably beautiful. I felt embarrassed to be staring at him so openly, but at the same time I didn't care. If all my
feelings were written on my face, so were his. And he had smiled
at me. I didn't need it broadcast—I'd seen his look and it was for
me, no one else. I knew, and that was enough. Something deep
inside me settled and was calm, at last. I shut my eyes. I wanted
to keep this moment inside, the fading last chorus of the song,
this sense of rightness apart from all the nonsense in the world,
as though I'd seen into the heart of the universe and knew which
way to go. I couldn't explain it. I opened my eyes again to watch
him, and felt that same shock all over again, like the click of a
lock opening.

The song ended, and the audience, including me, went
crazy, waving hands in the air and whooping, hollering. Trevor
nudged me. "He's good, our boy, isn't he?" He smiled, and even

if he looked a bit like some kind of ghostly hawk, I could see the magic of it all had hit him as well. So, another lost soul who felt the music, hard. I grinned back at him. There was nothing to say. Words would just fuck it up, like always. Luckily, the drummer started right in again, slamming the drums with such force you felt he was going to either break or break something, and they began a series of three songs, each one becoming louder and more furious, until they started the opening notes of the new single and the entire room started singing along. I couldn't even tell Tristan's voice out of the massed crowd, who knew every word. Usually I didn't like listening to people sing along, out of time and tune, but there was such devotion here, like everyone really wanted Tristan to know that they were still there, that they'd follow him, that maybe Devised didn't really matter so much anymore, as long as they had him.

When the song ended, Tristan waved to the crowd and bowed, and the drummer got up and threw the usual sticks into the crowd, and the guitarist and bassist took off their instruments and handed them off to the roadies. They all bowed together, then pushed Tristan forward. He bent his head in acknowledgement of the crowd's applause, his dark hair partially covering his face. Then he dropped to his knees and bent over into the crowd, the drummer instantly coming up behind him to get his back, as the crowd went into a frenzy to try and touch him. A couple of girls piled in first, and touched him, screaming. One of them was pulling at his shirt, like she wanted to tear it right off. She probably did. He laughed, and got up, and moved to the other side of the stage from me, brushing against as many of the outstretched hands as he could, before dropping to his knees again and letting some of the screaming girls throw their arms around him. One of them managed to place her hand on his ass. He didn't seem to mind, if he even noticed at all, but the drummer was watching her grope him, and he was cracking up. But when her hand snuck around the front to try for a grab at something else, Tristan jumped up like he'd been stung, and leapt to his feet, waving and smiling at the crowd before he walked off.

The audience kept clapping, whistling. The lights hadn't gone up yet, so there was a still a chance. The red lights remained on, then one of the roadies came out to adjust something. Oh, so they were definitely coming back. They just wanted to make us sweat a bit more. Work for it. Someone started a slow clap, and then there was a stamping, that got louder and louder, until I thought the ceiling was going to fall in. The whole building was shaking. I looked over at Trevor, and he seemed pleased, although he wasn't clapping himself. I couldn't see anyone else, but I was still crushed up against the barrier. I was glad Trevor was there. His presence was definitely helping to prevent people from trying to nick my spot and push me aside. The stamping grew faster and louder, and then there they were, coming out again, and the screaming and yelling started again, and the foot stamping gave way to clapping, and people calling out song titles.

Tristan's voice cut through the cacophony, and the crowd immediately settled. "Well, fuck yeah," he drawled. "London! Thank you so much. I don't think we'll have a better group than you guys this whole tour. London!" he said. The audience began hooting again, happy that their devotion had been noticed. "Well, we've got a little surprise for you." More screaming. "Some of you wanted a Devised song." Here he was interrupted by actual shrieks of joy. "I'm not sure why," he laughed, "but we've got someone here to help us do this fucker." The surge of the crowd forward felt dangerous, and I braced myself against the heavy weight of the crowd leaning on my back. I pushed out with my arms from the barrier, and tried to give myself a little room, as people pressed forward, wanting to get as close as they possibly could. One guy climbed up on the stage, and ran to Tristan, getting his arms around him and nearly kissing him on the mouth, before the two big bouncers from outside rushed out from backstage and grabbed him, carrying him out, one holding his legs, the other clutching him under the arms, and headed offstage with him, like some giant quarry. Everyone yelled even louder. Somebody called out, "Tristan, why didn't you kiss him?" Tristan laughed. "Thanks man for the instructions." "Kiss me!" one of the girls at the front shouted. "Ok, darling, but later," he murmured into the mike. She screamed so loud I felt my eardrum vibrate. It was funny, but I felt for her. Wanting it, that much. I wondered if he would meet her, and actually give her a kiss. Probably. Looking at all the pictures from the past, he seemed to like being touched, touching his fans—as long as they kept behind a certain line, which the girl grabbing for the goods before had obviously crossed. He hushed the crowd. "All right, all right, let me introduce an old friend of mine."

My heart stopped. Had Paul managed to convince him? Was it going to be a big happy reunion, and my services would no longer be needed? I looked over at Trevor, but he was frowning, squinting into the wings, trying to see who was coming out. He was waiting to see, just like I was. Fucking Dave. It suddenly occurred to me that's why he'd wanted the book. I felt like I knew everything that was going to happen next.

"We haven't played together too much for a while, so cut us some slack, ok?" The crowd yelled their approval. "Can you show some appreciation for..." I held my breath. "Your friend and mine—AC Clark!" The crowd screamed, and out came the other guitarist, the one who had punched Paul in the famous restaurant fight, the one who was related to Dave—how? I couldn't remember. But it wasn't Paul, and the breath I'd been holding came out. I was sure I heard Trevor mutter "thank god" but I couldn't be sure. Then AC skipped out, giving a shy quick smile to the hyper-excited crowd, and waving at them, before walking up to Tristan. The two of them hugged, tightly, holding each other close for a minute before Tristan pounded AC on the back with his fist, and they pulled apart, grinning at each other. It looked like Tristan was really happy he was there, like he'd thrown a party, and the one person he was hoping would show up, did. AC walked downstage and strapped on the guitar a roadie was holding out to him, playing a couple of notes of sheer feedback that rattled through the dark walls of the club. Suddenly everything seemed a little better, a little more serious, and Tristan clutched his mike stand tightly and nodded his head to count off the song. "I think you guys might know this one." And the first notes of their very first hit, "Nobody Gets It" rang out. I thought my ribs were going to be crushed. I tried to fill my lungs with air, but it was a madhouse. Everyone around me was pumping their fists, jumping up and down. Trevor looked down at me and shrugged, as if to say, "what do you expect?" and stood there, swaying gently to the music, while everyone around burst into spasms of delight. I started jumping up and down with the crowd, I couldn't fight it, it was though they were picking me up with their bodies, and we all pogoed together, in one joyful wild mass. I managed to slip my hand up to my face to swipe away some of the sweat from my eyes. It was fucking insane.

Tristan screamed into the microphone like a banshee, while AC knocked into him, leaning against him finally, his back against Tristan's chest, their heads almost together. Tristan was dripping sweat, and AC's shirt was wet where he touched him. Tristan threw the mike into his right hand, and slid his left down AC's side, letting his hand rest on the top of his low-slung jeans, his fingers pointing inwards. I drew in a breath. There was something so intimate about it, the casual possession of AC's body. The music got louder, and AC's guitar wailed more intensely every time Tristan pulled him closer. It almost looked like he was rubbing up against him, ever so slightly, his dark hair shadowing his face as he bent over AC's shoulder, finishing up the last two lines of the song as the audience banged and whistled and shouted their approval. The two of them turned to each other and hugged again, AC's guitar neck sticking out from between their dripping torsos. Tristan was beaming, and AC's cautious smile was adorable. They were whispering to each other now, oblivious of the turmoil they were causing. "Kiss him, man! We love you!" someone yelled out, and Tristan waved his hand at the audience, before planting a big kiss on AC's mouth, making a giant smacking noise into the mike. "I love this man!" said Tristan, as the crowd screamed. "But you guys always want me to kiss people." Everyone cheered. "I think you're a sexy bunch of motherfuckers!" More cheering. "AC and I never leave anyone unsatisfied, so…" He left his sentence unfinished as the crowd began clapping again. "So…we're going to do one more for you before we call it a night. If you haven't felt it yet, this could be the one!" The sweaty, shouting mass of the crowd writhed behind me. I wondered for a moment if we were all going to come from this alone, if anyone out there was taking advantage of the crush to make sure they did. I felt like if anyone touched me, I'd explode. I imagined the sweaty man on stage under me as I straddled his hips, and I closed my eyes. Tristan's voice broke through. "Not yet!" I looked up to see him gazing at me, amused. I started to laugh. He grinned and pointed the mike stand at me. He nodded his head at AC. "Come on dude," and he groaned into the mike, "let's make them lose their fucking minds!" He shouted the last words, and the crowd heaved forward, singing along to the first line of "Fucking Mind," the Devised song that was banned for airplay. "I saw you, I wanted you, couldn't have you, had to ask for help." Tristan's face became contorted in an orgasmic scowl as he screamed out the lyrics. AC's guitar playing was burning up the song. He'd obviously been practicing. He sounded tighter than ever, working in syncopation with the bass. The song shrieked to the end, the drummer slamming out the last beats with angry precision and the crowd roared. Tristan and AC gave little bows to each other "Thanks man, for helping me out," here Tristan paused, "like you've done so many times before!" They hugged again, and as the other band members stepped forward, they lined up, the drummer giving AC a big hug. They all looked really happy. "Thanks so much everybody for coming out tonight. We love you, really, even if you're all fucking crazy. See you soon." And he put the mike on the stage, and they all headed offstage, Tristan waving his arm in the air as he left. The crowd still yelled and clapped, hoping for one more, but we all knew it was done, and for once, I had the impression everyone was leaving satisfied. The press behind me had eased up a little, and I could look around again. Everyone's hair was lank and wet with sweat, their clothes stuck to them, shirts see-through, necks and chests and arms shining. It looked like we'd all been in some giant orgy, and we were going to crawl out of the warm bed, dripping wet and dazed.

I looked around, but Trevor had vanished. Strange. I figured he would turn up again, or not. He'd stayed with me for the concert. I really couldn't ask for any more. I wasn't sure if I should head backstage, or wait until the crowd had thinned out a little. There was going to be an after-party, upstairs in the roof bar. The people invited knew who they were, but there were bound to be a few people, girls generally, who stuck around, knowing if they looked good enough, they'd possibly snag an invite, and that was all they needed. I scanned the room for Sarah and Nick, or Poppy, or even Dave. I couldn't see any one, and the corner where Dave and Paul had been was empty. I had the sudden panic that everyone else was somewhere I needed to be, and I pushed my way through the remaining punters to the door where they had been standing. I ran my fingers through my wet hair, hoping I looked vaguely presentable. Time to go backstage and see what would happen.

Chapter 21

I was scared, but I wanted to see him. And I needed to be there, meet and greet, talk to Dave. I wondered where all the courage of the two drinks had gone. I opened the door to the backstage area and I was instantly on guard, listening out for the laughter and where everyone was. There was Trevor, the tallest of the group, tall like Tristan, who still was nowhere to been seen. He was chatting to the drummer. I was scanning the room when suddenly someone was next to me, squealing my name. Sarah. How the hell did she get back here before I did? I must have really been in some rock music induced fog, standing bewildered in front of the stage. Never mind. Act as if. I threw my arms around her, and we exchanged some air kisses.

"Sarah! How are you?" We started walking, arm in arm towards the group where Trevor was. "How did you like the show?"

"Oh, it was awesome! We came backstage before it started and said hello to Tristan." She beamed as I stared at her, oddly jealous of her initiative. "He was so nice! I got a big hug and kiss. He's promised to come to the wedding. But where were you? We looked for you, but didn't see you. It was crazy out there, wasn't it? That last song! I love that one."

I nodded and mumbled some platitudes while I scanned the crowd. There was Dave. No sign of Paul. I'd have to go up and talk to him. No choice there. I gave Sarah a big hug, and said I'd be right back, that there was someone I needed to see. She squeezed my shoulder, and winked at me, as though I had just admitted some secret assignation, and went off to the table laden with beers and a few bottles of wine, where I could make out the top of Nick's head amongst the people getting beers. Still no Tristan. Where the hell was he? I quelled a moment of panic and real fear. Stop. No point borrowing trouble. I walked right up to Dave, who was talking to the bassist. I tapped him on the shoulder, while giving a big smile to the blond, curly haired bass player, who didn't seem to mind too much, fortunately, that I'd walked right in and interrupted their conversation. Act as if. I'm important, I'm important. It wasn't exactly Om Mani Padme Hum, but it would do for the minute.

"Dave, how are you? How did you enjoy the concert? I wasn't sure if I was going to see you here." Casually friendly, that was the way.

Dave bent down, paternal, a hand on each of my shoulders, as he kissed me on each cheek, with surprising gentleness and finesse. I could feel the texture of his lips against my heated cheeks. He smelled good. I bet he hadn't even broken a sweat. He didn't need to. He paid the bills.

"Lily, darling, how are you? Oh, have you been introduced? Jack, this is Lily, Lily Taylor. Lily is writing the article on Tristan. She's our newest literary star." I smiled and tried hard to feel the words as a compliment rather than a reminder. To me, "newest" meant there had been others before and there would be others afterwards. Never mind. He had said star too. That was fine.

"Jack, what a pleasure. Great show, I really loved it. Terrific lines. You really got the crowd going."

He looked pleased. "Thanks Lily." He took the opportunity to give me a kiss on each cheek as well. Maybe sweaty was a good look after all. "It's nice to meet you." He had that hopeful look on, the one that men get when they're wondering if something has legs, or they're planning the rest of the evening.

I thought I'd take advantage of the attraction, however misguided or temporary. "Jack. I'd love to talk with you about being in the band, what it's like to play with Tristan. Bass players shouldn't be overlooked." I avoided saying are always. "Maybe tomorrow sometime, before you fly back?" He agreed, readily. A little too readily, I thought, but I took his number as Dave watched. I turned back to my boss, who was playing with one of his cufflinks, immaculate under the buttery cuff of his leather jacket. He obviously needed more attention than I was giving him.

"So, Dave. Would you like an update on the story? Any instructions?" I couldn't resist. "Maybe there are some other Devised...connections you'd like me to talk to?" I met his eyes. Yes, he did know exactly what I was talking about. Of course.

He was unfazed though by my very broad hints. "Sure. Paul is here. He said he'd give a quote for the interview. So is Alixe, Tristan's ex."

His words triggered a reaction before I could even stop myself. "Yes. She is. How handy they've come together. I spoke to her earlier. She seemed, how shall I put it? I think she said she was bored with the topic. Indifferent. But you've spoken to Paul already." It came out as more of an accusation than I had intended. "Have you sweetened the pot enough for him to share some words?" I made myself stand still, legs slightly apart. The fighting stance.

Dave frowned, but kept his words neutral and his voice steady. But I could tell I'd annoyed him. "Paul's a great guy. I'm sure he'd be more than happy to tell some stories for the article." He pushed his jacket aside, and placed his hands on his hips. Crisp.

I pretended nothing had just transpired. "Terrific. Maybe I can meet up with him tomorrow. After my lunch with Trevor." Bull's-eye. This time the frown deepened, and the bassist, Jack, with the unerring instincts of the musician, sensed the waters getting deeper and said he was looking forward to talking to me, but needed to get a beer. I gave him a hug, and watched him retreat to the table. Still no Tristan. What the hell.

Dave squeezed the top of my arm, very gently. "Lily, what's up? You're a bit tense. You seemed happier when we were out to dinner." He smiled a little crooked grin. "Maybe I need to take you out again." His hand on my arm felt possessive and controlling. Fuck needing to pay bills. I moved away from his hand, pretending to turn to see something.

"I'm fine, Dave. Been busy, that's all, very busy, collecting some very interesting stories for the article. Or the book. Or whatever it is. Trevor's been super helpful."

The crease in the middle of his high forehead returned. He was thinking of which tack to take with me, that much was obvious. He wanted to know what I knew. That wasn't going to happen though. I carried on talking.

"I spoke to Poppy, that was illuminating. The early days. Got some good stuff there." I paused. "Tristan's been great as well. Really kind."

The frown deepened. "Yes, I heard about the hotel." He lowered his voice, so we couldn't be overheard. "Did you really think you'd keep it a secret? I'm going to assume you're having a moment of curiosity, but that you know what side the bread is buttered on." His eyes were serious. "I need you to finish the article. We do have a contract." He rubbed his eyes with his thumb and forefinger, and looked down at me again. "I thought we had more. Maybe I was wrong." I opened my mouth to say something, and he placed a finger over it. "Don't make excuses. I don't really mind your wild side. I know what you're like. And fundamentally, you're like me. You want security. You like clean and comfortable. I'll wait."

His words made me feel like I was a kid being told off for playing in the mud. I was annoyed, but a part of me worried that he was right. Was he? Was this just a blip? Jesus, what was wrong with me? I wanted to change the subject. "What were you and Paul talking about, by the way? And where is he? Where's Tristan?"

Dave smiled, and I saw immediately I'd given him just the opening he was waiting for. "Tristan's upstairs already." I jerked, involuntarily, like I'd been stung. Dave put his hand out again, to stop me moving off. "He and Paul and AC are talking about a reunion. They just need a little time alone, then we'll all go up and join them."

"You knew this all along. That's why the article, that's why the book, the film—whatever it was supposed to be."

"Of course I knew." He hesitated. "I can't make them decide

in that direction, but I can help move it along." He looked at me. "I flew out Paul and Alixe last night."

"Then you don't know..." I blurted it out before I could stop myself.

Dave looked amused at my blunder. "Know what, Lily? All the rumors? Sure. I started a few of them myself, so yes. Of course. Do I know the truth of what went on? Not really. Or perhaps I do." He lowered his voice again. "We're in the business, Lily, of selling jealousy. If a little of it spills over on to us," he shrugged, "we're adults. We move on. I can't stop people self-destructing if that's how they're made. Sad, shame, loss, boo hoo." I glared at him. "Oh Lily, come on. You've met enough of the idiots in this game to know what I mean. Someone gives them the key to the candy store, and no one ever taught them how to say no. So they burn out. Now, our boys, they might have a second shot at glory."

"With you sweeping up some of the rewards right behind them."

"Yes, of course. You liked our dinner. You like the luxe. I hear you're staying at the Hempel. Lovely place. Silk costs, though, right?" He threw his arm around my shoulder. "Now let's go get a rock and roll beer, and enjoy ourselves. That's why we're here, correct?"

I walked a few paces with him towards the table, then delicately removed his arm from my shoulder. It really wouldn't do for him to be displaying possession, certainly not of me. "Look Dave, I have a couple of friends here I need to touch base with. And Poppy." I'd just seen her, standing off by the door, looking a bit lost. "I promised her I'd check in if she turned up."

"Don't go upstairs." He threw it over his shoulder, casually, like it meant nothing, but the timbre of his voice changed completely. Menacing, quietly, like a dog rumbling at you before it jumped. It was an order, clear and simple. He was drawing a line in the sand. It would change everything if I crossed it. And I knew that. But if I was going to play spy, I wasn't going to do it so openly. And, oddly, part of me was relieved that at least Tristan wasn't alone with the ex. I didn't like it though.

I kept my voice light. I laughed. "Don't you trust me, Dave? Good relationships are built on trust. I'll come get that beer in a minute. Save me one."

He turned briefly, examined me, gave me a thumbs up, and continued to the table, where he was quickly accosted by one of the other record company people who was there. I turned away, and looked for Trevor. I needed to talk to him. I didn't really want Dave to see me, but it couldn't be helped. Wait. There was Sarah. And Nick. I could enlist them. I walked up behind Nick and threw my arms around his waist and squeezed. He yelped.

"What the fuck!" He wiped the beer away from his mouth as I laughed. "Lily? Crazy woman. You startled me." He turned around and gave me a hug. "Where's your boyfriend?" he said, eyeing the room.

I shushed him. "Nick, you're the only man for me. Sorry Sarah. You know how much I love you, but Nick's tighty whities fill me with lust."

She laughed. "I knew it. But he is irresistible." She bounced up to him on her toes, and kissed his cheek.

"Did you guys enjoy the show?" I tried to stay calm, while keeping an eye on Trevor. I didn't want him disappearing again.

"Oh, Lil, it was fantastic. I love Tristan. But when the old guitarist from Devised came on, I thought I was going to die!

Even Nick here was shouting." She poked his belly button, and he caught her hand, rubbing it with his own over his stomach, which would start pushing out from his t-shirt soon enough.

"Nick, you old rocker. I thought you were done with the hijinks of youth." I swatted his arm. Out of the corner of my eye I saw Trevor ending his conversation. Now. "Guys, how would you like to meet Trevor Sears? From Working Class Records?"

Sarah squealed again. "Oh, Lil, you mean it? Come on!" She pulled my hand, even though she didn't know where to go.

I pulled back. "This way. Yeah, I mean it." I dragged her along, skipping in her heels and white low-cut dress with a pattern of big tea roses. She looked like something out of a Southern plantation, with her full breasts dipping out of the top and her dark hair. Like a doll. "Come on." Nick followed along behind, dutifully, taking pulls of his beer.

I intercepted Trevor as he was about to head in the direction of the drinks table. He was near a darkened corner, so I led Sarah towards it. "Trevor, I'd like you to meet some old friends of mine here. This is Sarah." Trevor smiled at her, then his eyes fell to her breasts, and he smiled some more. Like someone had just laid the table for supper. "And this is Nick, her fiancé." Trevor gave him a quick cold smile, and nodded, as though he'd just signaled for the hangman. Nick stepped back, involuntarily. I spotted his reaction and felt oddly pleased. Payback's a bitch, honey.

Trevor turned to Sarah. "My lovely, where have you been hiding in London? You must come and see the record company sometime. You like music, of course you do, you wouldn't be here otherwise." Nick was giving me dirty looks. I ignored him. It wasn't my fault if the rock business attracted guys with testosterone.

"Trevor," I interrupted, trying to make it seem like I was saying nothing terribly exciting. "Did you know that Tristan was upstairs with Paul and AC? That they were discussing a possible reunion? That Dave flew out Paul and Alixe last night to assist?" I tried to keep my voice down and make it look like we were just doing introductions, just in case Dave was watching. Trevor shook his head. I tried to control my voice. "What are we going to do?"

"I will investigate. And you and Tristan are meeting me for lunch, yes? One p.m. The usual Japanese place. Tristan will know." I must have looked at him doubtfully. I still wasn't sure if I was going to be sleeping alone tonight. "Kinwa. Soho. The driver will know it."

"I'll be there."

"Don't worry, darling. Things will work out." He gave me a hawkish smile, then took one of Sarah's hands in both of his. I was forcefully reminded of all the vampire movies where the virgin suddenly realizes that the party was going to have a bloody ending, in both ways, top and bottom. Sarah had paled slightly, but she had a game face on. He was still admiring her breasts, and she couldn't resist that. "Come, my dear." He called out to the room. "This charming lady and her friends are gasping for champagne. Which, apparently, is only to be found upstairs! We are horrified, and intend to remedy the situation immediately." His mouth widened into a terrifying, toothy smile. "Who's in?" A little cheer went up from the group. Trevor headed to the door, Nick following closely behind, with me bringing up the rear, immediately followed by the rest of the group, following Trevor like some kind of Pied Piper of alcohol. I glanced over in Dave's direction, obliquely. He was furious. But I would swear that all I

had done was introduce my friends, which was true. He probably didn't think I'd reveal anything in front of them. I'd certainly
never admit it.

We all filed through the door, and in to the club, which was
now empty. As we walked through, the door to the ladies' burst
open, and two blonde girls tumbled out, drunk, pink-faced and
very excited, wearing some of the shortest skirts I had ever seen.
One of them went up to Nick, as he was alone. "Darling, we just
want to party. We'll be good. Really good." His face was a study.
I laughed.

Trevor looked over his shoulder, seeing his opportunity to
keep Sarah for himself. "Of course you may stay, young ladies."
They squealed. "I'm sure we have some entertainment somewhere for you, isn't that right, Nick is it? Yes, Nick here will
escort you upstairs. Tell him all your problems. He's very understanding." Nick looked bemused, but the first girl had already clung on to his arm, her hip nearly up to his waist and her
breasts pouring out of her light blue crinkled spandex top. His
eyes widened, and he swallowed. I saw him shift his hips slightly.
Adjusting already. Maybe there wouldn't be a wedding, after all.

Chapter 22

Trevor led us up the stairs, obviously knowing exactly where he was going. Of course, the trick was, we didn't know what we would find. I knew he was as curious as I was, although probably not as anxious. Would Tristan be wrapped around the ex? Snorting coke off a newly signed contract, Paul looking on? I felt vaguely irritated again at all of it, the intrigue, the things I didn't know, wasn't a party to knowing. Tristan must have known about all this. And the idea that she was up there, and I wasn't, enraged me on some level. My jealousy made the whole thing even more ridiculous. I watched Nick in front of me, completely overwhelmed by the attentions of the two girls, who still weren't sure how important he was, and therefore how much of themselves they needed to give away. It was funny, really. He wasn't saying anything about practicality and age now, was he?

We had reached the point where the staircase branched out left and right from a landing, and Trevor nimbly turned left and strode up the five last remaining steps. He disappeared briefly from view, and I could hear him cackle, sarcastically. I followed as quickly as I could, willing Nick to hurry up. Nick finally managed to get up there and was dragged over to a sofa by the girls, leaving me with a clear view of what had precipitated Trevor's hollow laugh. There, on one of the red velvet sofas, was Tristan, flanked on either side by the ex and Paul, several lines of coke on a little tray on the ex's lap. As I watched, he bent his head over her thighs and snorted up a couple of the lines, neatly, expertly. He inhaled, his finger just making sure there was nothing left on his nose, and as he looked up, he suddenly realized that they were no longer alone, as more and more of the party from downstairs filled the room, noisily clustering at the bar, the sound of glasses clinking and corks popping disturbing what must have been relative calm. Trevor put his hand out to stop me, as I was about to march forward and confront him. He must have felt my bristling anger, as his hand went from my shoulder, to my waist. "Not now," he whispered.

I ignored him.

I walked up to the sofa, feeling slightly sick to my stomach. The three of them looked up at me. Tristan looked completely stoned. The ex looked me up and down and looked away. Paul had a questioning expression. I tried to keep it light.

"Hello Tristan," I said, "Thanks for the invite. I told you I'd make it."

His voice, which had been so strong on stage, seemed to come from a different place. "Lily. Good. Yeah. I'm glad." He started to get up, then reconsidered. "Have you met Alixe? And Paul?"

I held out my hand to Paul first. "No."

"Guys, this is Lily. She's writing an article on us."

Paul finally held his hand out. "Nice to meet you. Say good shit, ok?"

I nodded and turned to the ex. She just stared at me. I held out my hand, which she took by the fingertips, limply, then dropped her hand like she'd been injured. I looked back at Tristan. He looked strange, uncomfortable. Not the super human in-control rock god I'd just been watching an hour ago. I didn't really know what to say anymore. And oddly, horribly, it looked like he didn't either.

I straightened up. "Well, pleasure to finally meet you." I couldn't bring myself to say their names, the bile rising in the back of my throat already. "Tristan, don't forget the lunch at one with Trevor tomorrow—the usual Japanese place, apparently. I want to wrap up the article as soon as possible. I know Dave wants to see it put to bed." I smiled, a stiff little smile that barely reached my cheeks, let alone my eyes. He was about to speak, but I turned away. And walked to the bar. I didn't want to hear it, see it. Any of it. I bumped into Sarah, who was holding a bottle of champagne, and looking a bit flushed. I snarled at her. "Where's Trevor?"

She waved the bottle over to a corner sofa by the window. "Oh Lily, this is so much fun! Thank you!!" She was squealing. I hoped it was too loud in there for her voice to reach Tristan. It was obviously too loud for her to notice anything wrong. "Come on, I'm just bringing this to Trevor." She grabbed my hand, and we walked over. "He's so nice, Lily. I mean he looks so scary," she giggled, "but he's very smart. Sweet. Shh. He'll hear us." She was obviously getting legless. But at least she was happy. I turned briefly, but I couldn't see the sofa clearly, there was a crowd around it.

Trevor was watching us approach, calmly. "Lily, dear. How is Tristan?" His eyes raked over me. "Come sit down and join us."

I suddenly noticed I was having trouble getting the words

out. "He's fine, Trevor." My voice sounded strained, even to my ears. "I reminded him about lunch tomorrow." I coughed briefly to try and shift the lump in my throat.

Trevor rose and stood over me, towering. His voice was a whisper. "Have a glass of champagne. Don't leave yet."

I nodded, and he went to retrieve another glass from the bar. I stared out the window. Sarah was bleating on about something. I wondered if she knew where Nick was, and if she did, why she didn't care. I looked out, down towards the canal, where the crowds had thinned slightly. You could see the rooftops from up here, the window just slightly higher than the surrounding buildings. Not enough for a full on view of the area.

Trevor tapped me on the shoulder, and handed me the glass of champagne. I downed it in one, and handed it back, as he looked on, astonished. The lump in my throat was still there. Maybe if I never spoke again, never sang again. I could join some Buddhist monastery, like that one in Nova Scotia, or somewhere. Never see anyone again. No one would care. Trevor was waving the refilled glass of champagne in front of me. "Lily. Lily. Pay attention. It will be fine. Trust me."

"How can you know that?" Now I felt the tears right behind my voice.

"Of course, you're right. There are no certainties in life. I just know the man I used to know." He clinked glasses with both of us, as Sarah looked on, realization slowly dawning on her face.

"Oh Lily! No! That's terrible. You were only just with him yesterday, we could hear..." Trevor shushed her by kissing her, which made me laugh, in spite of the sick feeling that had come over me with her words. True. And it was only just this morning we'd woken up together.

I looked around at the crowd, away from the two of them. It was really bizarre to see Trevor kissing anyone, his physical demeanor so far from being tender. But he was kissing Sarah with what could only be described as a gentle passion.

I looked away. That would figure. Engaged, and now Trevor. I slid out of the chair and walked away from them, back into the crowd. I walked by the sofa. It was occupied by three other people now. There was no sign of Tristan.

I spotted Dave across the room, and walked up to him. "Lily!" he said. "All alone?"

"Yes," I replied tersely. "And I have a favor to ask you."

His chiding expression changed, and he looked serious. I must really look bad, I thought, if I am having this impression on people.

"Of course. I wouldn't deny my star writer anything."

"I want to finish up the piece."

"Naturally. And you will."

"No. I want to finish it this week. I'll interview whoever else you want me to. But I want to complete the writing back in the States."

He looked bemused for a moment, and opened and closed his mouth, ever so slightly, as though he had been about to speak but then changed his mind. "Sure. I want you to meet with the engineer who was at Electric Ladyland, where they did the last album."

"Where is he now?"

Dave laughed, softly. "Why? Do you want to interview him right now?"

"Sure. Is he in London?"

"No. He's still in New York. Why? What's going on?"

I shook my head. "Nothing. Just want to get back. Can the mag book me on the first flight out tomorrow?"

Now he really did look astonished. "Yes. Of course. If that's what you want. Just call my assistant. Here." He held out his phone. "Do it now, or save the number, and do it when you leave."

"I'm leaving now." My voice was trembling. I couldn't stop it. "I'll just take the number."

Dave looked at me. I met his eyes. Then I looked down at the phones, transferring the number. I handed him back the phone. "Thanks. Sorry. I'll see you in New York."

I walked away, glancing over at Trevor. It couldn't be helped. He'd understand. And then, making sure no one was really paying attention, I walked over to the stairs and walked down them, speeding up as I got further away. There was no one in the club. Everyone was upstairs, celebrating the return, the solo tour, the whatever. I didn't fucking care anymore.

I went through the doors to the outside, breathing in the damp, fresh air that smelled faintly of the canal, wet and green and like old brick. I'd miss London. I missed it already. Then I did two things: I called the assistant, and had her book me a seat on the first BA flight that left. Just before 9:00 a.m. It would have to do.

Then I called Tariq. Funnily enough, it seemed he'd given me his direct line. I recognized his voice. "Tariq? It's Miss Lily. Are you busy? Can you come get me? Or send someone?"

We arranged it all and I dragged myself over to the high street. Had I been hoping in the back of my mind, that if I stood out here long enough, Tristan would rush out, find me, grab me, kiss me, and march me back to the party, swearing love and proclaiming me in public as his girlfriend? Yes. Of course. But as I stood under the railroad bridge, watching the headlights of the cars go past, I knew it wasn't going to happen. I didn't know why. I just knew.

And when Tariq's car pulled up, I didn't even wait for him to jump out. I pulled the door open and taking one last deep breath of the wet air, I slid into the dark warm cocoon of the car.

"Miss? You ok, Miss?"

"I'm fine Tariq, mate, thank you. Better than I was." I sighed.

"We're going to hotel, yes Miss?" He turned to look at me.

I tried to smile at him. "Yes. Then we're going to a new hotel, out by Heathrow."

He looked at me oddly. "You sure, Miss?"

No, I wasn't sure. But I wasn't going to ask for help, or advice. It was done. "Yes. If you could wait, it won't take me long to get what I need. Ok?"

He nodded, and turned back to the front. The car pulled out, and we glided in the traffic. I leaned back, wanting to watch it all disappearing, and not. I closed my eyes.

And cursed my luggage.

Chapter 23

We drove along the streets. A light rain started to fall, and the traffic lights shone back from the wet tarmac. There was still a fair amount of traffic, and we waited at a couple of lights before we could make our way across Swiss Cottage roundabout and down over in the direction of Notting Hill. I felt strangely calm. Like I'd hit the edge and was surveying the damage. It reminded me of the time I'd broken my ankle, and everyone was running around, very solicitous, but I just lay there, wondering what all the excitement was about. It didn't hurt then, not yet. But it hurt like a bitch a little while later, I thought. I shut my eyes again.

"Tariq?" I had decided talking was the best way to drown out my thoughts.

"Yes? Is anything wrong?" He sounded worried. I wondered what I sounded like to everybody. I couldn't tell.

"No, thank you. Everything is fine. Just fine. You drive very well."

"Thank you, Miss Lily. Of course, I have much practice. But London drivers, they are bad. The worst. They don't look. Too many people now, too many people don't take their test here. Very bad."

So he was chatty. Good. "Yes, I've noticed it's gotten worse here. I used to drive quite a bit when I lived...was here before."

He nodded, but said nothing, as he overtook a bus that was apparently waiting for the police to show up. It happened. Someone got in a fight, or refused to pay and then refused to get off. But now the bus was in our way. And it was late. I felt extremely fortunate to be in a car, out of the rain, away from the fights.

"Tariq, are you married?"

He sounded startled, but answered, gamely. "Yes. Yes, ten years now. Good wife. She puts up with me." He laughed.

I nodded. Of course. "Any kids?"

This time he rustled around on the seat next to him and came up with two pictures in a little red leather frame, embossed with gold. "Here miss. Two. One boy, one girl. She is very naughty." He handed me the frame, and I looked at them. One dark haired boy, with smooth skin and clear eyes, staring right into the camera. He appeared to be about ten, with a very serious air. About to leave childhood behind. The little girl had her hair in two long braids and was frowning. She was very pretty, with delicate features, but the expression on her face gave the impression she didn't like it when things did not go her way. She was probably only four, I thought. How can she do that? So soon?

I gave him back the photos. "They're lovely. You're very lucky."

He laughed. "Sometimes, very hard work. But good, good to have family. You think of marrying? Your friend, he very handsome. Make him marry you." He laughed again.

I had to laugh with him, even as his words twisted my insides. I couldn't make Tristan do anything. I wasn't even sure if I'd ever see him again. I wasn't sure I wanted to see him again.

After another few minutes, both of us with our own thoughts, he pulled in front of the hotel. I suddenly felt terrified. Embarrassed. Was I about to walk into a hotel lobby, the last to know, behind the staff, that Tristan had already gone upstairs with someone else? I wished I could just leave my luggage. Just run, like I'd wanted to do. Follow the initial impulse. But all my notes were there. My clothes. I was tempted to send someone up for them. But I couldn't. I needed to do this myself.

"I won't be long. Ok?"

"I will stay here if I can. Otherwise, you call me. I will be parking."

I nodded and got out, straightening my shoulders and trying to look, once more, like I didn't care. I walked up the stairs, and went in. It was quiet, aside from the sounds of conversation coming from the bar. I avoided looking to see who was in there. I leaned on the marble countertop. The icy coldness of the stone came as a shock. I dropped my arms by my sides, and tried to smile at the blonde woman, who had her hair pulled back severely. With the uniform, she looked like a dom. I wondered if she ever got any after hour work. I was tempted to ask, and book her for Tristan. On his bill.

My voice came out in a croak. "Could I have the key for suite three, please?"

"Your name?" She checked a list. Of course. The hotel needed to be careful. Probably for their protection too. Some drunk rock star starts announcing his room number at the bar, then regrets it, blames them. I gave her my name. She smiled. I hoped that was good.

"Yes, Ms. Mustang. Here is your key." She looked somewhat confused. "Mr. Mustang authorized another party, they've already gone ahead. Would you like anything sent up?"

I swallowed. Ok. So that was that then. She was warning me. "Of course. No, not right now. Thank you."

"We have room service available all night, should you need anything." I thanked her. And wished there was a back door so I could sneak out, unheeded, with my suitcase and notes and slapped face.

I went upstairs. What I really wanted to do was to go back in time, to when I was in the tub, and Tristan was making it all better. When everything smelled good and felt soft. The silk on the towels. The soft blue water of the bath. His hands. No. Fuck it. This was no good. I needed my wits about me now. I was about to fight, though whether it was going to be against or for, I wasn't certain.

I walked down the corridor, the white door coming closer and closer, almost as if it were advancing towards me, instead of the other way around. Did I just use the key? Knock? What was the protocol when you walked in on your lover and his ex-wife fucking? I made a mental note to write a modern-day book of etiquette and let my forehead drop softly on the door. Fuck.

Almost instantly, a voice called out from inside. I guess my head had hit the door harder than I'd thought.

"Tris? Is that you?"

Now I was confused. But the footsteps were approaching the door, and the locks turned, and I still stood there, silently. I didn't know what to say anyway.

The door opened, and there, wearing a bathrobe, was AC. We both stared at each other, shocked.

Chapter 24

He spoke first. "Uh, hi? Are you Lily? Where's Tristan?" He looked around the hall anxiously. "Shit. Come on. We can't talk out here." He stepped away and opened the door further, and I walked in. He shut the door, and did all the locks up. He looked nervous. "Hi, sorry. Where are my manners? Come sit down. You probably weren't expecting to see me. You were here first. But where's Tristan? Oh, I'm AC. But you knew that. Nice to meet you. How did you get here?" He was firing off questions at me, as he sat back down on the sofa and started flipping through channels again, tapping his foot. "Is he coming up now?"

I turned to him. "Hi. AC. Listen. I thought he'd be here. With..." I still couldn't say the name, "the other guitarist, um, and..." I stopped and tried to make what I was saying make sense. "The last time I saw him was at the party and he was sitting with them."

AC snorted. "Yeah, the cozy little trio. So what did you do?" He stopped switching channels and poured himself some more wine. "Want some? I hate drinking alone, but I'm so used to it by now, so don't worry if you don't. There's glasses over there."

He pointed to the mini bar behind the teak cabinet. The door was open, revealing a small fridge and a collection of plates and glasses on top.

I sighed. I knew I should just be getting out and forgetting it all, but I couldn't resist. Talking to AC. I might never get another chance. I looked at the door to the suite. Exit or entrance. I wished I could stop hoping. "Yeah, I'll have one. Just need to make a quick call to my driver. Hang on." I walked over to the bar, putting the code in my phone. AC actually turned around to watch me talking as I came back holding the glass, telling Tariq I'd been delayed and would let him know when to get me. His face registered some disbelief.

"Apologizing to the driver, huh?" he said. "That's a new one." I shrugged. "Have some wine." AC poured out some of the Barolo into my glass.

"The good stuff?" I asked him as he carefully wiped the lip of the bottle.

He laughed. "Hey, why not. I came out to see Tristan. Now I'm haunting hotel rooms."

I took a sip. God, divine. It almost stopped the bleeding. Almost. I stared into my wine. Velvet red. All the things that could have been. That were. I drank some more to keep myself from jumping up from the sofa.

"So why aren't you at the party?" AC asked, switching off the TV.

His question startled me. There was a relentlessness to him that put me on edge. "I could ask you the same question. With more reason." I pointed at his guitar, in its case, leaning on the window. "You were on stage with him." I drank some more. "It was a great show, by the way. I like the way the two of you are on stage." Liked, I thought. Over. Done.

"Were you there?" He peered at me more closely. "Yes. You were the one in the front row. Next to Trevor. The one Tristan was flirting with."

I tried to be flippant. It wasn't really coming from the right place. "Yeah, that was me. Having fun."

AC looked like he was trying to remember something. "You. Lily. You're writing the piece." He glanced around. "More importantly, you're shagging him. That's your stuff here. You're the girl Tristan said would be here."

"Was that before he started snorting coke off his ex-wife's thighs, or afterwards?" I snapped.

AC let out a low whistle. "Oh man, is he doing drugs with them now? Fuck, man. I told him I wasn't into it. I just got out of rehab. Shit. Fucking parties, Lily." We drank some more. "It's always the same. I ducked out. A bottle of this costs half of what I used to spend in an hour—and apparently red wine keeps you alive. Makes a nice change." He raised the bottle. "More?"

"Yeah, why not?" I waited until he'd finished and took another sip. If I kept focused on him, I wouldn't see the door to the bathroom. Wouldn't remember. Wouldn't see his hands. His face in the mirror. I leaned back. I didn't feel like chatting. I didn't feel like anything. And now I was planning on heading to some generic hotel out by the airport. Or I could sit here, drinking Barolo with another rock star. Either way, I still felt like shit. But I could feel like shit and have just a little pride. "Listen, you'll have the room to yourself tonight anyway. I'm leaving."

"Isn't Tristan coming back?" AC looked genuinely surprised. "He said we were going to have lunch with Trevor tomorrow."

I stared at him. What the fuck. "Yes. That was all arranged. For the article. I think Trevor wanted to speak with him too." I was trying to make my words sound precise. To my ears, I was starting to slide them all together. "I was due to be there as well. Trevor." I stopped suddenly. What was I saying? I wanted to trust this guy. Would he even remember this conversation tomorrow? No idea. "Listen. I'm leaving. Would you..."

AC interrupted me. "Tell Tristan you left?"

Suddenly all the upset became anger. "No. I don't give a fuck what you tell him. But Trevor. Tell him I'm sorry."

AC's face became fixed on a point somewhere above the TV. For a moment, I thought he was going to turn it on again, and stop talking. But he just sat there for a moment, then turned to me, and oddly, took the glass out of my hand, and held my hand. He didn't say anything for a minute, but seemed to be examining my hand. "Nice ring," he finally said, looking at the antique silver art nouveau ring I always wore. "Lily. It's none of my business. But he's hurt me too. Look, I flew out from LA just to be here with him. I thought maybe we were going to tour." He paused. "We probably still are. Business is business."

I pulled my hand away. "Business is business? What the fuck does that mean?" AC sat back and stared at me. I covered my face with my hands. "Shit. Look. I should go. This isn't your fault." I started to get up.

"No. It's ok. He's an asshole, sometimes. Stay. Finish your wine, anyway." He stood up and grabbed a packet of pretzels from the mini bar, then flopped back down on the couch.

We sat there. It was very quiet. My ears were still ringing

from the concert. I ran my hand over the fabric. Nice. Wool. Little luxuries. Like Dave had said. It all cost. I was finding it cost a little too much, that's all.

AC cleared his throat. "It's none of my business."

"No," I said.

"But," he started.

"But you're going to give me advice," I laughed bitterly. "Go ahead. The whole world seems to be clocking in with advice for me lately. Let's hear it from his side. Forgive him, right? He's a rock star. Parties. The fast life. Etc. Etc. Go ahead. Tell me."

AC listened to my tirade with surprising patience. Then he put his hand on my knee. I jerked. He laughed. "Tris talked about you, you know."

I smirked. "Yeah, I bet he did."

He moved a little closer. "That's not what I meant. Though he did mention you guys were very...um...compatible." AC smiled.

"Nice. True love. Please spare me. And your advice is to keep on with a good thing?"

He took his hand away. "I think you're getting the wrong idea."

"I usually do. So make it clearer for me, so even I can understand it." Suddenly the polyester green bedspread that awaited me didn't seem that bad.

"I think you should dump his sorry ass." He put down his glass as he said this, and went over to the phone.

"Are you calling him?"

"No, I'm calling for another bottle of wine."

I suddenly wanted to cut to the chase. "Is there subtext here? Because I'm tired. And perhaps every other girl he's fucked has just dropped down the scale from one of you to the other, but you know, other than your taste in wine, I know nothing about you." I got up. "Aside from which. I don't do that. Were you supposed to be my consolation prize?"

He put down the phone. "Shit. No. Sorry. Though I'm flattered you at least put me on the scale, even though you're not my type," he said sarcastically.

"You're welcome."

"What I was going to say," he continued, picking the phone back up, and holding it to his ear, "was that you...oh wait." He ordered another bottle to be sent up right away. "Yes, put it on Mr. Mustang's bill." He hung up and came back to the sofa, where he re-established himself in very nearly the same position. "I think Mr. Funtimes owes us, don't you?"

"I'm not sure, but yeah, he owes you. You came over to play."

"And not you?" He looked at my glass. "Drink. Heartbreak's such a good excuse to get wasted. Why miss out?"

I could feel the lump in my throat coming back. I couldn't play this game of "I don't fucking care" anymore. "Yeah. Great advice. Was that it?" I got up. "I'm going to get my bags, ok?"

"You're really not going to wait for him?"

"What, so I can sniff out another woman all over his face? Yeah, brilliant. No. No." I was angry, very angry, I realized.

"Good. Because that was my advice. Leave him. He's so fucking used to getting whatever he wants. Hot and cold cunt running on tap, and always somebody to clean up the mess after him." He caught my eye. "Sorry. Didn't mean it like that."

I bit my tongue. No more crying. "I guess that means you think he's moved on too."

AC got up and walked over to me, quickly. I was suddenly wrapped in his arms. He smelled of expensive fragrance, not unlike Dave. It was a strange juxtaposition, with his skinny body. He kissed my neck, and ran his fingers through my hair, then all the way down to the small of my back, stopping just above my ass. "You're the real deal, aren't you?"

I removed his arms, gently. "AC. I'm going, ok? This isn't my scene."

He squinted at me, and shook his head. "It's ok. I'm sorry. I should have...forget it." The doorbell rang, and he jumped away, apparently grateful for the interruption. I watched him take the bottle from the guy at the door, but careful not to let him in. That'll be the source of gossip downstairs, I thought. He came back towards me, holding the bottle. "Lily. Another bottle? I'll behave, I promise. You just have to understand...most women... once you're at a certain point, you know." He stopped speaking just long enough to pull the cork out. "They usually don't say no. I forget sometimes." He poured both of us a glass. "Come on. One more glass. Maybe Tristan will turn up, begging forgiveness."

"Maybe you won't finish that bottle and watch porn on TV."

He laughed. "Yeah. I guess you're right."

I took the glass he offered me, and inhaled. "Ah the beautiful things in life. Weren't they supposed to come to you when you appreciated them? I guess they did." I drank half the glass.

"Whoa girl, you're not appreciating that."

"No, I'm doing the quick thing. Good, but it won't last." I drank some more. "AC. Is there a way out that isn't through the front?"

He thought for a minute. "Yeah, there's the service entrance. You can get to it from the basement."

"I've got to go." I walked to the bedroom to get my bag. There was the bed, still perfectly made. The scent of the flowers was stronger now at night. It would have been a beautiful place to make love, I thought. And almost as I thought it, the bed looked frozen, like a big glass wall had just come down between us. Over. Untouchable. I wanted to run my hands over the bed, imagine him behind me, naked, ready to mess up all the perfection with me. Instead, I took one last look around and picked up my two bags. Turning away slowly, I stumbled back into the living room area. AC was back on the sofa. I put the bags down again and picked up my glass to finish it.

"AC, it's been a pleasure." I leaned over to him and gave him a kiss on the cheek. Then I picked up his glass and drained it as well, while he squawked and put his hand on my ass.

"You sure, Lily?" he said conspiratorially. "Come on. We're both here. Why waste this room? This bottle of wine?" He lowered his voice an octave. "I know a few tricks too, darling. Carpe diem." He looked up at me, trying to look sexy. But he couldn't hide the look of lonely hopefulness in his eyes. I almost felt bad for leaving him.

I gave him another kiss on the cheek, which he tried to turn and catch on his mouth. "AC. I get the carpe. In my next life, I promise I'll fuck around more. And you'll be first. Maybe." I laughed. "Don't get up; just tell me how to get out. Oh never mind, I'll just go out the front. I won't be the first whore they've seen leaving in the middle of the night. Just maybe just the first one with a computer. Could be a trend."

AC gave me another hug.

"Now piss off and watch porn. Maybe if you're lucky, Tristan will come back."

He shook his head. "Don't tease me."

I really looked at him then. "So it's true." He paled, but said nothing, looking even more frail than he had before. "Shit. Well, that's both of us screwed then." I leaned my head on his shoulder. "Look me up in New York. We can reminisce. About the good times we never had."

A spasm of worry crossed his face. "You won't write about this." It was almost a question.

I patted him on the back. "You really don't get it, do you? But why would you? Why would anyone?" I opened the door. "Take it easy, ok? Dave will know how to get in touch." I walked a step out, then turned back and pushed the door back open. "I really won't write about you," I whispered, "as long as you won't laugh about all this." I kissed him on the cheek. "Take care. Ciao."

I walked through the lobby with surprisingly good balance and dignity, I thought. I was tempted to order another bottle on the way out, to keep me company in my polyester haven out by Heathrow. Tariq was still in the car, dozing. I suddenly felt bad for keeping him up, away from wife and kids, while I got drunker with some famous people. Famous. For what? My head hurt.

Tariq shook himself awake, and started the car without a word. We pulled off into the night, heading for the M4 out to Heathrow. I watched the darkened houses go past, people sleeping, hopefully peacefully. Nothing mattered. That was their world. Not mine. I got to do the overview.

Chapter 25

I was finally alone. Alone on the plane, as much as I could be alone with 300 odd other people around me. Most of them just looked resigned to spending the next seven or eight hours crammed into their seats. I thought about when plane travel used to be more like a voyage, an adventure rather than an ordeal, and people were excited about the newness, the speed of it all. Now plane rides, even transatlantic ones, felt more like bus rides. "Familiarity breeds contempt" popped into my head, and with it, the painful reality of trying to guess where Tristan was at this very moment. I didn't figure it was that hard—passed out across the silk bedspread that was supposed to be ours, a blond head, or two next to his. Had he even noticed I was missing? Or was he just grateful I hadn't caused a scene?

When Tariq had dropped me at the hotel, both of us were too tired to really say anything, but his "good luck miss" seemed both sad and genuine. Maybe he had been hoping too that he'd get a call while we were driving, instructing him to turn around. But nothing came. No texts, no phone messages, nothing waiting for me at the check-in desk. Just the bland smile of the uniformed man assigning my seat and handing me back my passport, wishing me a good flight.

And now, as I looked across the person next to me, to watch the plane make its turn into the runway, feeling the thrust of the engine rumbling through the metal into the seats, the hotels and buildings starting to rush past, the bumps on the runway juddering the plane as we went faster and faster, beyond that point of no return—what was it called again?—and then the nose lifted up, and we had left the ground, racing into the sky and banking, quickly, horribly, to keep the flow of planes taking off going. I watched the green and grey of England sinking away from me. Had I just made the biggest mistake of my life? I could have stayed there, stayed with Sarah, written the article, headed back—or not. I could have stayed there. Now that Tristan was obviously a memory, I didn't know whether I'd get more jobs or not. Would it help me or hurt me, that fleeting connection? I listened to the hum of my thoughts, rattling on about practicalities as though they were considering someone else entirely. I barely noticed the tears starting to flow, one after the other, until one dripped off the end of my nose. I wiped them away, hurriedly. Great. Crying on the plane. Add it to my list of clichés, like sleeping with the star and flirting with the boss. What next? Rehab? Botox? Adoption? But all the words meant nothing. They just served to drown out the endless hum that was filling up more and more of my head.

He's gone. You won't have him. You tried and you failed. He's gone.

The memory of waking up with him at Sarah's, my head nestled into his muscled, pale shoulder, rushed up at me like a car crash, and I found myself gasping for air as I grabbed at my seat belt and made for the bathroom. A stewardess tried to stop me, but I made the gesture as if I were about to throw up and she let me go. Less to clean up, she probably thought. And I did feel sick. The pain in my side was sharp and unclean, like a rusty knife wound. I locked the door and counted how long I probably had to stay in here before they started banging on the door. This was nice, sitting on the toilet seat, my head on my knees, breathing in the strange deodorized smell of the blue chemical that they flush with, trying to not think. Stopping thinking. Stopping feeling. That's all I needed to do. But write the article. Make some money. Go out with Dave. Keep alive.

I wondered, for a moment, if it was really worth it. If this was it...was all the effort really worthwhile, seeing as it all led to nothingness anyway? Through the blackness of my thoughts, I felt like I could see Tristan's eyes, looking at me. He looked disappointed. I had to stop this. He had cared. Maybe he just couldn't care. He wouldn't be the first guy who found it easier to walk away than figure things out. Or woman. He may have been a no-show, but I was the one who skipped out. Somehow, oddly enough, that made me feel better. I was still in control. Right?

I got up, and washed my hands and wiped the towel over my face, and went back to my seat. The stewardess looked at me quizzically, and I nodded what I hoped looked like thanks for her bending of the rules. I felt like some kind of out of place animal in the midst of all these people that apparently knew where they were going and exactly which kind of pretense they were willing to live by. Maybe that was the problem. For a little while, all their rules seemed all right—as long as Tristan had chosen to be with me. Or maybe his attention made me feel like I could break any rule and it wouldn't matter. But you couldn't live like that, could you, depending on someone's love to feel like that? Or could you? Love, that feeling of completion, did it make you weaker, or stronger? Could life contain "curtains hanging in the window," "I'll light the fire"—all those combinations of domestic bliss, made even stronger by the fact a man was singing about them? Did women even sing about domestic bliss? I couldn't think of a song. The only thing that popped into my head was Joni Mitchell waiting for a car "climbing, climbing the hill." That was betrayal and suspicion. No curtains and warm fires there.

Moot point, I told myself, accepting a glass of champagne from the stewardess. Thank god for business class and for drinking mimosas without the juice and only raising the smallest of eyebrow twitches. It didn't matter. Time for hard honesty. I loved him. He was beautiful, sculptured, intelligent perfection. Cooler than you. A fantastic lover. Smart, witty, sexy. Fine. With just the one little flaw—he was like every other man in the universe and he wanted his woman to be airbrushed and flattering, distant, cold and pretty like a china doll. My canvas was a little too rough. I cared a little too much. "Try not giving a fuck" worked really well. Too bad I could only pull it off intermittently. Why did I have to do that? I thought, but I knew the reason. Cool to be cold. Of course.

I tried not to down the whole glass of medium-quality business class airline champagne all at once, figuring I needed at least fifteen minutes before I could ask for a refill. I turned on one of the TV shows on offer, *Lie to Me*, and tried to become involved in the constructed story line. He would have known, right? Whatever his name was on the show. The guy. He would have looked at Tristan's face in the club, as he looked up at me, and he would have known exactly what that expression meant.

There would have been none of Trevor's uncertainty. Or mine. Coke on, then off, the lap. Now there was a seduction strategy with merit. I giggled out loud, and my seat mate looked at me, dismissively, and curled up further towards the window. What a prize I was. A crying, rushing out of her seat, drinking at 9:45 a.m., cackling witch-like creature. No fucking wonder, then.

I looked like hell. I hadn't slept all night, lying on the sheets staring around at the plump rectangle of the airport hotel room, with its bank of fake mahogany veneered drawers that no one ever used, and the grey square of the TV. The windows went from dark to grey to a white mist and it was time to go. I left the room virtually as I found it. So why wasn't I tired?

I'd lain there, thinking of all the times we had been together. Tristan. The poet. The artist. But masculine, proud, taking his place, a strutting peacock. I thought there was a heart under there, He'd made me feel beautiful. Intense. Super-charged. I could deny it all I liked. Pretend. And I'd always know that I was lying, lying, lying to myself. The lies we tell ourselves, just to get by. Passing, just enough not to be questioned. I stared into my glass. No answers.

But the TV show was almost over, which meant the waiting period was over as well. I touched the steward on the sleeve as he passed by. In my best possible "you're here to respond, but I'm indifferent to the reality of that and what it means, as well as what asking for a refill at 10:15 a.m. implies" voice, I inquired about the possibility of more. "Of course, madam," he said pompously in his best "I may be the steward and a floating waiter but I get free travel and the chance to sleep with my boyfriend in Singapore regularly so fuck you" voice.

And it was all back to normal. The games. The unreality of

reality. Oh fuck, I missed him. I wondered if it was too late to text Sarah when we landed and ask her to send me the sheets. Had she run the wash already? Probably. Did I have anything of his? Nothing. He had been, as promised, very careful.

I settled in to watch another episode about the ambiguity of truth. No more tears.

Chapter 26

New York. Again. It was busy, loud, bright, brighter than London. People walking fast past me as I climbed out of the cab. It made me feel dizzy, like I was about to be struck and whirled around, like a character in some farce. Big trucks clattering over potholes, making noises like mini-explosions, honking, sirens. I felt like the kid in the Stevie Wonder song, and I almost looked around for somebody sidling up to me with some drugs to deliver. But I'd made the decision, and here I was. Forget that I had no idea what I was supposed to do now that I'd made my grand gesture. Well, there was work. I had the notes. Obviously, I knew how to use them. The question was, could I think about him for hours, professionally marginalizing my sidebar comments, pretending I didn't give a fuck, beyond some hipster admiration? And as I pulled my suitcase down my street, grateful that it was somewhat quieter here than on the avenue, I wasn't even sure I could pull it off.

As I turned the key in the lock, I listened out for any sounds that would reveal the presence of my lovely roommate, Alice. I was not in the mood. The last thing I wanted to do was have to give some superficial blow by blow, when I knew just looking at me would give the game away. So I opened the door slowly, trying not to make the floorboards creak or bang the brass knob against the wall, and hoped that the silence meant she was out. Then I could reintroduce myself to the world on this side of the pond, post-jealous meltdown, without having to give a running commentary. I tiptoed in. So far nothing. Thank fuck for that. I left my bag at the door, and headed towards the kitchen, thinking that a cup of tea, before the usual bath and attempt at a nap, would be just the thing. I turned the corner and my breath caught in my throat.

There, on the table, was a large, no, huge, bouquet of roses. They had some paper and ribbon wrapped around them from the delivery, and the large vase was a cut above the usual utilitarian florist pot. I inhaled, and their scent was delicate but strong, swirling towards me on the breeze from the slightly open window. I just stood there and stared. The petals were an intense color, a deep, shadowy shade of damask red. I still hadn't moved. Was there a card? Was this the peace offering I'd been dreaming of every minute since I'd run out on the whole thing? I almost didn't want to look. It was better to live in the possibility. For this moment, it was like gambling. Your lotto ticket could win, the ball could fall on black, that next card would be the one. I wanted it to be right, so much. Come on. Let me dream, just for now.

No point in dragging it out. I thrust my hand blindly into the stems, perversely satisfied when I was badly scratched by one of the long thorns in the center. There. A card. A ribbon. I pulled my hand out, walked to the other side of the table so I could read what it said. I didn't want to untie it in case it was for Alice, while all the time I could hear myself saying, please, don't let them be for her, don't let them be for her.

And there, in someone's neat florist script:

> *We missed you at lunch. He's sorry, you know. So*
> *am I. Don't give up, my dear. In New York end of*
> *week. Will call. Love Trevor*

I sank into the chair. All I could think of was the line from *Persuasion*:

> "Such a letter was not to be soon recovered from.
> Half an hour's solitude and reflection might have
> tranquilized her...It was an overpowering happi-
> ness."

Overpowering. They had met. He had said something. Trevor had said something. My absence had been noticed. With that unheard, unseen conversation, I existed again, like a shadow that had life breathed back into its form. I pulled the vase closer to me, and I buried my nose into one of the roses. Soft, delicate, velvet like skin, like his skin. I'd see him again, maybe. I read the card again. Trevor. The unholiest of guardian angels. How had he managed to be conscious enough after the party, and his se-duction, however brief, of Sarah? I measured the softness of the flowers again my cheek. Tristan. My god. All this desire was ter-rifying. His eyes, piercing me.

I sat there for a while, holding one of the long stems I had freed from the vase, and stared out the window. The fragility and strength of happiness, as though everything broken within me was being knit back together. Success, achievement—all the thinking aspects were good—amazing, even—but this petal touch of want and need and desire was something else, big and as out of control as the sea during a January storm.

I untied the card from the flowers, and brought it and the one rose I had picked out from the rest. I stretched out on my bed, and fumbled around in my bag for my phone. I found Trevor's number and sent him a text. Just two little words. Two words that would hopefully make up for my inability to stay there and fight my corner, and let him know that the roses had made all the difference. I pressed send, and lay my head down on the pillows, the image of Tristan's sea and earth-colored eyes looking at me thoughtfully like a mirage in my head. Nothing but everything.

Chapter 27

I had fallen asleep, finally completely overcome by the events of the past few days, but I woke up a few hours later, clammy and cold. I waited until the room stopped turning, and tried to remember where my body was, which room I was in, which side of the globe I was on, what lay outside for me. It was still quiet in the apartment, the light giving off the longer streaks of approaching evening. I rolled over and looked at the rose. Such a cliché. Fine, I'd roll with it.

But I knew there was no time to lose. There was no more of the easy drop into first love dreaminess. I had to make use of my knit-together nerves before someone or something stronger came around to break them again, and this time for good. I swung my legs out of the bed, avoiding glancing at the wreck I knew I'd see in the mirror, and went to make some coffee. Twenty minutes later, I was at my small white desk, setting up the computer, plugging in the drive, getting out my headphones and notes. I couldn't let this derail me. This was what I did, what I was good at. While I could, I would. More than usual, the ugly tyranny of the blank computer sheet spooked me. What idiot had decided that they would reproduce that depressing reality in the virtual world? More coffee. Free association, that's what would work. So for a while, I just wrote down everything that stood out for me. Meeting him in the office. His casual control of things. Playing the songs. Crying, again, for the first time. His idiot manager. Slapping him. Blood. I idly wondered if I could put that in. Too bad there weren't pictures to prove my nervy heroics. Perhaps I could say someone else had done the deed. Or that it was a rumor. There had to be a way to slide it in—what it meant was too tempting to leave out.

Trevor? No, keeping that light. The quotes. Not the story of Tristan at 3:00 a.m. losing it. Or him doing coke with the ex. That wouldn't be there, no matter what, even if some picture surfaced of him with his head between her legs instead of just on them. Some things were beyond pain and jealousy. Poppy. A kind portrait. A fan, a moment in time. The guitarist, AC. He needed a light hand as well. Or did he? Was there a bigger future market for the rock journalist who told tales, or the one who kept some stories under wraps? That was a judgment call. No, I decided. Allusions, rather than concrete details. Everyone knew already that he had been in rehab. Why hammer it home? That just sounded petty. His love for Barolo and dislike of rock parties made the cut. I needed to call him and get his viewpoint on Poppy. God, why had I been so wrapped up in Tristan? It had put me off asking all the questions I really needed the answers to. Never mind. Maybe in a few days. After the engineer interview.

Shit. What time was it? Nearly 11:00 p.m. I'd been writing for five hours, steadily, fuelled by coffee and a sense of desperation. I needed to call Dave. Oh, why not? No time like the present. I needed a break anyway. Maybe there'd be another dinner in my future. And would you be up to it, whatever it was, the veiled offer on the table? I had no fucking idea, I realized, as his cell phone rang. A very good question. The phone went to voice mail, and I left what I hoped sounded like a more together message, more together than my plea to get on a plane, asked about the engineer, and how soon could we do it, and that I wanted to meet with him with the article—by—what day was it? Monday now. Ok. Tuesday. Short deadlines meant less time to fuck around. Good. Limits.

My mind was whirling with everything that had happened in the past few days. I noticed that I was not thinking of the Greek restaurant or my old friends and their reaction to the arrival of the man in the cab. The bittersweet memory of those tucked-away hours in the attic room. Shit. I would not think about it. There were no guarantees. Flowers from Trevor did not equal flowers from Tristan. It could be a sort of warped apology for seducing my friend.

I felt the light-headedness of too much coffee and not enough sleep, but I had to continue. Who knew when the hammer would come crashing down? I kept typing, looking through the notes. But I knew I was putting off the inevitable. With a long sigh and a new cup of coffee, I finally reached for the headset. I flicked on the switch with a sense of fatalism. His voice, murmuring to me over the wires. 2:00 a.m. The perfect time to confront ghosts. Papers being shuffled. Mumbled numbers, sound check. And then. The soft tones of his honey stung voice came though the headphones. Fuck. I listened without hearing anything, just letting the feeling of it run through me. God. A voice. Just a voice. Why that effect? I threw down the headset and walked out of the room. The kitchen—neutral territory—away from the atmosphere I'd created in there—a shot of the single malt, a glass of water. This was going to be an all-nighter—one of the many all-nighters I should have pulled right from the start instead of following him around like a lovesick puppy.

No more listening. Writing up the notes. Describing the gig that Poppy had seen. That needed to go in there. Tricky, balancing her account with her bitterness. Guiltily, I wondered what she had done after the show. We had all abandoned her. I hoped one of the band had seen her, and given her some love. The innocence and excitement of university parties. Pretending you were super cool, when really you were super lonely, or super terrified. But the sweet moments too. That picture with Tristan. Would Poppy find something to take her out of herself again? It was harsh to think there was only one moment that counted in life. Or maybe not. Maybe that was love. Maybe that was what I had been missing out on, always hedging my bets, riding on the next thing to come along to take me away from the disappointments of the last mad rush. True love had a different feel to it, whether it was requited or not, whether or not it worked out. Time taught you that. Some things you didn't just move on from. Sometimes you never really moved on.

Four am. Good. And there was still more to say. Maybe if I made more coffee? I was already buzzed. Maybe lying down. Just for a minute. The light in the room looked fuzzy around the edges, too bright. I turned off the light and lay down on the bed. One, two, three. Sheep? Rock stars? I opened my eyes again. This was never going to work. I could still see the screen against the dark ceiling. Where the hell was Alice, anyway? The garbage truck stopped outside, rolling its metallic gears over the plastic bags. I sat up, too quickly, and had to squeeze my eyes shut, the sheet bunched in my fists, to stop from falling over. I remembered the last time I had sheets clutched in my fingers. Couldn't I just stop thinking? Faint gracefully, and be rescued? For now, all I cared about was saving the recordings to my phone. I'd go for a walk, listen to the voice outside through my headphones. Have breakfast somewhere. Assimilate. Pretend. Just like everyone else.

Chapter 28

It was just getting light when I made it out the front door, earphones in place, hat to keep my head warm and protected against the chill early morning air, and to give me some anonymity. I walked down to the park, and stood at the corner where his limo had picked me up, that very first time, and I shuddered with the memory of straddling his hips, his hands tracing endless patterns over my body. I could still remember what it felt like, his lips on mine, god that taste of him, sweet, soft, hard, finally. I closed my eyes, and hit play, and let his voice pour over me, as I stood there, under the street lamp, alone. No one to watch me leaning against the cold, ridged metal of the lamppost. I wished I could cling on, stay there, invisible. This was where I was stuck in time. I slid down to the pavement, and sat there, my back against the metal. His melodic voice hummed on in my ears. All about his plans, his creativity. What the fuck had happened then? Something inside me cried out. And I had no answer.

The pebbles in the pavement were starting to press into my skin. The self-preservation side of me told me to get up, before all that weakness was noted by someone out on the prowl. Reluctantly, I raised myself up and leaned against the lamp again, until the feeling of lightheadedness left me. I had what I needed. This was just torture. Sweet, agonizing torture, but pain just the same. "You do it to yourself," I sang out, into the trees and the apartment buildings of the Upper West Side. No one answered. My voice died on the wind. This was New York, after all; no one would notice one more lunatic singing to herself at 5:00 a.m. I felt my face twist up into a half-smile. His voice was my new drug, my new best friend, and I could come out to be crazy with it when I wanted. Nobody would notice.

I switched it off, putting the phone back in my bag, and started walking uptown, north. After crossing the next street, I decided to walk along the park. I stood at the corner, and waited for the light to change over the nearly empty avenue. I waited for the next set of headlights to pass, thinking I'd run across once they'd gone. One dark car was headed for me. They wanted to pull up where I was standing. I backed up, irritated that my bit of space had been invaded. It was a town car, not a limo, but you couldn't see inside. I was curious to see who would get out, and then I felt scared. I turned and started walking uptown again. I didn't really want to see anyone anyway. I heard the door slam. I didn't turn around. It didn't matter. Curiosity killed the cat.

There were footsteps behind me, then I heard the voice. "Lily? Don't walk away, please?" No, now I was hallucinating. I needed breakfast and sleep, obviously. The voice started again. "If you don't want to see me, I understand, but let me say one thing, ok?" I took three more steps, then I stopped. If it was a total disconnect, at least I wanted to enjoy it. Maybe there would be visual too.

The hand on my shoulder made me jump. Without even thinking, I reached up and put my hand over it. Soft. His long fingers. Where had they been?

I felt Tristan gently swing me around to face him. He looked sad, and faraway. There were inches between us. It was him. For real.

"You. Are. Here." I whispered. "Why?"

"You ran off," he answered. "I didn't..." He stopped. "I wasn't expecting that."

I stepped back, like I'd been slapped. Had he thought I'd just stick around? Watch? A big part of me didn't care if that was what he had thought. Fuck he was beautiful. "Tristan?" I asked, trying to keep my voice steady. "What the fuck were you expecting?"

He laughed, that same sexy throaty laugh as before. Like nothing had happened. I winced, and he stopped instantly. He picked up my hand, and looked at it, small against his large palm and pale skin. "Honestly?"

"You're here. You must have a reason." I felt the urge to negotiate. I tried to quash it. Heroines kept their mouths shut. This was my turn to shut the fuck up and let him talk. I didn't want him to say anything I had prompted.

"I thought you'd sleep with AC." He looked sheepish.

My brain was having trouble processing his words. So it had been a set up. "Did you want me to? Or were you setting up a future threesome? Games, right?" Shit shit shit. I needed to calm down.

He licked his lips, and took a deep breath before he answered. "I'm not proud of it, ok?" I stared at him. "Not the threesome, no. That's not what I meant. Even if it could be fun." His smile faded as quickly as it had come. I shrugged.

"Lily. Please. Listen. This isn't coming out right. It's simple, really. Maybe you don't understand exactly what it's like." His words came out in a rush now. "How many people just want a piece of you? For their own aims. How many times have you been betrayed? Once? Twice? A hundred times? It's not sweet, is it, to have someone you relied on let you down." He ran his hands through his hair. It looked unwashed, like he hadn't been home since London. Maybe he hadn't.

"Yes, I've been feeling that. Quite recently in fact." I stared at him. Why did his eyes change color like that? They were a kind of maple syrup color with flecks of green at the moment. It was mesmerizing. "If you've come to apologize for going back to your ex, thank you. But it happens all the time. I get it."

"No, you fucking don't." The flash of anger from those eyes jolted me awake, and I was suddenly on guard. "You don't. I get played all the time. All the time. Do you want to hear about the most recent event? My intention was to come here, and find you, and tell you. Then it's up to you. Do you get it?" I wanted to ask what was going to be up to me, but silence felt better. He tugged on my hand. "Come on. Walk with me." I followed him, holding his hand, half delighting in his touch, the muscles in his fingers, the taut veins beneath the soft skin, half trying not to feel, not to think. He went up to the driver of the car and told him to wait for his call, then whirled me around as he looked up and down the avenue and ran with me across the street to the park. He pulled the hood of his sweatshirt over his head. "Better like this," was all he said, and we went through the low brown stone wall and on to the curving grey paths of Central Park.

We walked silently for about five minutes, towards the reservoir, and began circling it. I thought it was a risky place for a quiet conversation, but maybe he was right. Hiding in plain sight. I said nothing.

"Lily. I owe you an apology. I treated you very badly. It wasn't my intention...for things to go like that."

I tried to keep quiet. I failed. "What was your intention, then? What the hell happened? I know we had a free and easy thing going on, but..." I stopped. Ranting never worked.

Tristan looked pained. "Let me just tell you. Ok? I wasn't expecting them to turn up. And I'd been told that you and Dave were..."

I couldn't help interrupting him. "Dave arranged for them to come over. To see you. To restart the band, for his greater fame and financial glory. Did you know that?"

He pinched his nose, and dropped my hand to run his over his face. "Yeah. I mean, now I do. Or I did. Before you just told me, I mean."

"So...," I started, then stopped.

"So," Tristan continued. "So. So. Look, there's no easy way to say this. The ex. She told me she'd heard rumors. From friends in NY. That you and Dave went way back. Partners in crime. Partners in bed. That you were in it for the prestige, climbing the ladder. That sex with any rock star would work for you. That I needed to see it. James had said the same thing." He pulled his leather jacket around him, and wrapped his arms around his waist to hold it closed. "She told me I'd missed all the signs. Again."

I stared at him. He looked at me, then looked away. He nodded his head towards the path leading away from the reservoir back into the park. I followed him, glad to be away from the early morning joggers coming up behind us. This needed to be private. Alone. We couldn't both break down, not here, not in the open like this. I wished Trevor was here, some master of ceremonies to fix our messed up selves. We walked some more. I kicked a few pebbles. If this was to be our last time together, I wanted to drag it out at least. I didn't want to be angry at him. I was angry at him. My mind was in pieces. Any rock star? Any?

I turned to him. "So she convinced you I was a groupie on the make, only worried about my career?"

He darted his tongue quickly between his lips and sucked in his cheeks, before frowning. "Um, yeah, something like that. Yes. Basically."

The blood was rushing in my head. "And it was that easy? Did she do this before or after you snorted coke off her...?" I stopped. No. Wrong thing to say.

He seemed to be getting angry too. "Before. Of course. Fuck. I'm not proud of this. Don't make it hard for me."

I felt like slapping him. "Don't make it hard for you? Why the fuck not? Why shouldn't I?" I could feel the pulse behind my eyes. I was too tired for this chess game. "And AC? Did he back her up?"

Tristan looked away again. "No."

"Did he tell you he hit on me? Or had you already told him to do it?" What a fool I was. All of them conspiring together, with their little games. What an idiot. The image did not match what was within, obviously.

"No one needs to tell AC to hit on anyone. He'll do it automatically."

"So what did he tell you?"

"He told me I was a 'complete fucking cunt,' I think those were his words."

"Was this at 5:00 a.m., when you turned up completely wasted with the ex and Paul?"

"No, actually. It was at 4:00 a.m., when he came to get me from the club. Sharing the rehab love." He smirked.

"So I have AC to thank for you not sleeping with them? Thank you AC, I guess. Were you horribly disappointed? Or did AC help out? Who was on top? Do you fuck him every time he does you a favor?"

Tristan stopped, and put his hands on my shoulders. I flinched and he took them off. I couldn't tell whether I was sorry or not. I stood rock still. Whatever he said next—that would decide everything.

"You know, you're being a bitch. But, fair enough. Yeah, I was disappointed. In myself. For being such an easily led fool."

I snorted. "Yeah, I know the feeling."

Then his arms were around me, and my face was crushed against his chest, while he buried his head in my shoulder. I wanted him to hold me like this forever. I wanted the earth to swallow us both up so all this could stop. I wanted to get away from him before he was like a drug I couldn't say no to. "Partir quand meme," like the song. I didn't want to be played. Again. Not again. His low voice rumbled through me. "I'm sorry, Lily. I'm really sorry."

I just held him. I didn't know what I wanted to say. He smelled so fantastic, like leather, and water, and sky, and airports, and cigarettes, and sweat, and him, over all of it, the sweet heady scent of his skin. It was like all the cells in my body had been starving.

Tristan kissed my head, and straightened up. "I don't trust people. My faith in human nature…um…fragile. At best." He looked at me. "I'm not sure why I choose the wrong people to believe. Trevor asked me if it was because that way I wouldn't be disappointed, my twisted world view could carry on as before."

I smiled, in spite of myself. Trevor. "That sounds like something he'd say."

"He likes you, you know."

"So on the recommendations of your friends, you've come back?" It burst out before I had time to pull it back. I knew it was the wrong thing to say as it was hitting the air. His face crumpled, and his mouth became a line, his jaw clenched.

"Yes. Ok. I deserve that. And what you're going to say next."

"Which is what? Enlighten me."

"That it's not enough."

I turned away from him, to look at a tree. Funny, how the bark had little lines in it. I wondered what it meant. I reached my hand out. I couldn't look at him.

"Are you offering to come back? While saying that you wouldn't take you back if you were me? That's not very convincing," I said towards the tree.

"Ah, shit...yes...no?" He came up to face me. I kept examining the tree. "I've been playing games for so long. I...Lily, don't do this for me."

"Don't do what?"

"Walk away. Don't walk away to teach me a lesson. Please." He picked up my hands in his.

I stared at his wrists, then at each finger in turn. My throat was tight with the effort not to scream or cry. I felt like I was running out of air. One of his songs was repeating in my head. I couldn't figure out which one it was. I looked up at his eyes; now they were dark, a burnt sugar and tree color. I noticed the circles under his eyes for the first time, the faint shadow on his cheeks. His mole. We stood there, staring at each other.

His voice, when it came, was like a groan. "Ok. Go."

And I did.

Chapter 29

I retraced our steps. I was dead. Numb. He was right. If I stayed, he wouldn't respect me. It would be over before it began. I'd have nothing. Now I had his apology. And the cold comfort of dignity.

I made it to the reservoir, and I stood and stared at the ducks for a while. Then I headed back towards the apartment. I stopped when I saw a bench with a view of a nice tree and the entrance to the park, where we had come in. I sat down, very calmly. I wasn't crying. I was proud of that. No tears. I'd made my decision. My life had shifted. He had offered the choice—integrity or obsession. No matter than the two of them were tangled up in my head beyond belief. But if Tristan saw it that way—thought that there was only one choice—I had to agree.

I sat there, and the sun warmed the back of my neck, and I watched the nannies wheeling the toddlers to the playground. And a few people came and sat down with coffee. A group of teenagers turned up one of their phones really loud to play some song. One girl had a high pitched squeal, like an electro-cuted mouse. They moved on towards the tennis courts and it was relatively quiet again. I watched the people come and go. In pairs. Chatting. Alone. I could hear the buses on the street. More kids came out, threw their knapsacks in a pile and started a game of Frisbee.

The sun filtered the light down through the branches onto my face. It felt nice, I thought. Warm. But soft. I took a deep, gasping breath. Good. Still no tears. I looked at my hands. They seemed very far away. The fingernails were slightly blue. I thought I could hear a voice telling me to go inside. But that seemed very far away as well.

I noted how well my hands fitted over my knees. Strange. Yes, they were mine. I had legs. And then I realized I needed to leave. And I got up, slowly, all pins and needles and walked out of the park. Through the brown stone wall again. Across Central Park West. Down the street. Through the doors. All just like normal.

Just before I walked into my building, I thought about my phone. Did I have it? Right. I walked a bit past my door, and leaned against the building. The bricks rubbed cold and rough against my back. I turned on the phone, and it lit up like a Christmas tree. Four voice mail messages. An uncountable number of emails. Two texts.

I went to the texts first, like a drunk to a tallboy. The first one was from Alice.

> I let in flowers had to go Sis broke wrist. Squash bitch. Back Thurs. U gd? Luv u babez

I laughed. Street Alice, with the minted family. Too funny.

I opened the second one without looking at the phone. I wasn't sure if I wanted to see it.

I miss you.

Chapter 30

Inside, I'd calmed down enough to decide two things. One, I needed to organize my life. Two, I needed some time away. Some retreat somewhere. Trees. Water. Rice. Yoga mats. For now, at least the organizing part. I sat down on the floor next to the bed, looking up at the sky through the window. It was almost like being a child again, little against the big furniture, the big sky. I let out a long, tight breath. The pain in my throat was back, tight and dry, like a rope made of sand. I swallowed hard. It hurt. Fuck, it hurt.

I reached up for the phone, which was resting innocently on the bed. And there the message was, staring at me. "I miss you." I miss you. I hadn't been gone that long. Or was he the one who was gone? Organization. I pressed one for the voice messages, and listened, not without a certain feeling of dread, that fortunately lessened as I deleted each message in turn. One telemarketer, one from Alice, two from Dave. And it was him calling personally, not his secretary. I must still be in his good books, despite my runner from the UK. Or maybe the story of you walking away from Tristan has already made the rounds, intoned the annoying voice in my head, and he wants to hear it personally. I leaned back against the wall and just sat there for a little while, fighting the urge to close my eyes and sleep. Every part of my body felt heavy and thick.

Finally, I dialed Dave's direct line. It was time. I had used up all my hibernation points, unless I really did intend on walking away from everything—and the shitstorm that would provoke. I listened to the rings, once, twice, then a third time, preparing another message in my head. Something about accounting for my time today. My deep sense of responsibility. I was contemplating how thickly I could lay it on, when the rings suddenly stopped. I was surprised when his clipped, slightly nasal voice came through the phone. "Dave Fanning here."

"Dave?" I asked stupidly. "It's Lily."

"Lily. Good. How are you? Better?" His voice softened from his initial official greeting, but there was still a certain insistence there. Like he knew he'd get his way. I wondered how much he had heard already. How up to date he was. If he'd heard the latest, that would mean that everyone else in the world had too. Well, the line of girls waiting for a chance at Tristan could reform. It probably already had. It probably never had unformed. I shook off the image.

"Oh, I'm fine. A little tired," I lied. "I tend to feel jet lag more in this direction. Usually means I stay up late, then crash hard." Well that part was true enough. "How are you?"

"Perfectly well. Your flight, I mean. You said you needed to get back. Have things improved since then?"

I felt like we were talking in code. Not for the first time, I wasn't sure if we were tapping out the messages from the same book. He'd hear about it all anyway—that was his job. It just didn't have to be from me. I tried to be evasive without seeming so. "Things are the same. But things are always the same. I suppose you want to know about your piece."

"By necessity. But I called to inquire about you as well. What do you say to early cocktails tomorrow evening? Send me your draft, we can talk it through then. As well as everything else."

My throat hurt again. So this was it. My future. Twenty-four hours to decide which way it was going to go. I couldn't call it my destiny. I was pretty sure I'd missed out on that. "That sounds lovely, Dave. I appreciate you looking after me. Thanks for flying me out. You're a great boss." Distance.

"I'm more than that." He paused. "I think friends should look after each other, don't you? Benefits. Part of the package deal."

I laughed, and so did he. I didn't think it was for the same reason though. "Ok. Well then. Brilliant. Where should we meet?" Which watering hole would he suggest for the shakedown?

"Oh, why not Verlaine? No view, but they have some lovely ginger and sake cocktails. Tuesday's acceptable there. Take your mind off..." He paused again. "Can't be all work and no play. Then maybe some Italian food. You looked a bit off in London, we can't have that. Hold on a sec." I heard him give some muffled command to someone. "No, need you ready and on form. Especially when you're about to go out on the road."

That woke me up. "What?" I said the next part, very slowly, as though I was learning a new language. "Out on the road? When? What about the piece? With who?"

He seemed to find my confusion funny. "Had you forgotten? The second part. Part two. The tour. Devised reunion on hold, but AC has graciously agreed to join Tristan on the tour.

Big news. And you will be covering it." It sounded slightly like a threat. I couldn't figure out why.

"Still?" It was the closest I could let myself get to mentioning what had happened.

"Still? Always. Consider it a homeopathic cure. We'll talk more tomorrow evening. Rest up. Finish the piece. You're probably going to be the cover. If it's good enough." He chuckled. "No pressure. A demain, chérie."

I closed the phone and held it to my chest. Bloody fucking hell. This was what I'd wanted, right? A shot at the big time, drinks at the right places, air kisses, my name in lights? Right? Damn. Not for the first time, I wondered why so frequently you got something just at the moment you didn't really care anymore. I saw my zafu cushion and bowl of brown rice disappearing in a puff of smoke. On the road? With Tristan. Watching him. Every night. I tried to remember how long the tour was supposed to be. A month? Longer? Tristan on show for me every night. His face, those hands, his long legs. Was Dave right? Would proximity cure me? Or would I simply lose what was left of my mind?

On the other hand, could I really say no? It's all torture, I muttered to myself. Fuck it.

And then, almost on cue, my phone vibrated. Another text. Tristan.

I want you there. If you hate me, we can fight.

Again. His unseen hands, pulling the strings. I put my head between my knees, trying to rest my aching brain. And Tristan obviously wasn't going to make this easy for me. Fuck. If I went out with Dave, then it would get back to Tristan. What the fuck was I supposed to do? Tristan. Fuck. I closed my eyes again. I still wanted him, so badly, I could feel it thrumming through me like the sound next to a high-tension wire. But I couldn't give in. It couldn't be that simple. And he couldn't think I was with Dave. That would be worse than anything.

Exhaustion was starting to get the better of me. Dave was right about one thing at least—I needed to rest if I was going to be up for all this. I needed a shaman, some kind of fairy god-mother with a magic wand and a big lantern to light the way. I dragged myself up and threw myself, fully clothed, on to the bed, and wrapped the quilt around me. I was nearly asleep again when I thought of Trevor. Trevor. Of course. He would know what to do. I reached for my phone, double checking that there were no more texts. I typed quickly on the tiny keys. Honesty was going to have to take the place of wit on this one.

> Trevor. Rose King. What to do? I'm lost.
> Love Sleeping Beauty

I pressed send, and turned off the phone. I'd mixed, now it needed to bake. And I needed sleep.

Chapter 31

I woke up, twisted in the covers. It had been a fitful night's sleep, filled with dreams half remembered that seemed vaguely important. It was no wonder I was dazed. I lay back on the pillows, willing myself to have the strength of mind to not just grab for my phone and turn it on. I padded out of the room, still feeling disorientated, my hand reaching out against the cold blank wall to steady my progress. I made it as far as the kitchen, wrapped in a sweater and managed to make a cup of tea before I succumbed to the inevitable and skipped back to the bedroom for my phone.

I pressed the button that would turn the phone on, and looked away from the start-up screen, slightly embarrassed. Very nervous. I didn't want this, didn't want these feelings. And Trevor? What the hell was he going to tell me? Nothing, probably.

I opened the text message icon. And there they were. Two from Trevor, one from Tristan. I held my breath and went for

Tristan's first. Maybe Trevor's words of wisdom would make sense of whatever Tristan was going to say and my response, which I knew was bound to be irrationally emotional.

> Lily. I'm not perfect. But Dave? Where are you
> meeting him for dinner? Give me a chance to fight.

Bloody hell. I let out my breath with a long hiss and chucked the phone on the bed. My head hurt. I lay back and closed my eyes. And if I had pushed Tristan away for good? There was no way of telling what Dave had told him. The idea that he thought I had given myself to Dave... I clenched my fists. No, I would fix this. On to Trevor. I clicked on his text. He was good, coming back with something right away. I hoped it would be useful.

> Wake up then, love. Thorns all metaphor no
> substance. Arriving Thursday. We will go out and
> drink and discuss. But I think you know.

Then, the next text.

> No money-back guarantees on this one. BTW,
> what's your friend Sarah's number? I feel a bout
> of pre-flight homewrecking coming on.

I laughed. And then bit my lip. And then swallowed some more tea. Had I really expected he would tell me what to do? Or had he? I sat there for a while, watching the blinking red light on the phone remind me that I still had unread emails. I texted back.

> Thursday then. If you know and I know, does he
> know? Sarah 0207 434 2967. I used to go out with
> her fiancé. I don't want him back.

It really was all down to me then. Drink and discuss—by then it might be a post-mortem.

Well, on to the emails. The usual this and that, and there it was—the confirmation email from Dave about dinner that Tristan had alluded to.

> Lily. Tonight. Let's skip cocktails and go further
> east than Italy. 7. Pylos. Expect to sign contract
> on whole deal over an expensive bottle of red
> wine. I know your weaknesses.

Ah. So it really was party time. Dave, cleverly, would never come out and say anything "unprofessional" especially not in an email. But he knew what he meant. And so did I.

Chapter 32

I was right on time. Early even. I peeked in the window. I'd never been here before. What was it with Dave and womb-like spaces? The room was long and oddly low ceilinged and over-decorated in a way that was obviously supposed to evoke the faux peasant earthiness of your last holiday spent at your Greek villa, and the tavern where you finally hooked up with 1) your ex, 2) the bartender, 3) your sailing instructor, or 4) your Sapphic yoga/creative writing teacher. Whatever. I walked up the street and looked at the people in the wine bar, looked up at the windows of the old apartment buildings. I still hadn't completely made up my mind. The last time I had seen Tristan, I'd been so angry. But he had seemed so broken, yet so distant. The words of his cryptic little texts swirled around in my mind, but nothing stuck, it was all so fragmented, like words of a sentence in a foreign language that you hadn't quite memorized.

And then there was Dave. Who would be here any minute. I was looking out for his usual dark town car. And soon after his arrival, he would make me an offer I wasn't supposed to be able to refuse. He had me; he had the twin threat of the career and my shameful flight from the sight of my lover's deceit. Cut the crap, I thought. He knows how to win and that's by either stepping on the losers or tying them to you with a lifeline. "Oh everybody plays the game"—the beginning of the lyric, as said by The Strokes, my pragmatic grandmother, and a million other people. And the end of the line in the song—"if you don't you're called insane." Fuck. At least the song was ironic. I hoped. I imagined Trevor looking at me sorrowfully. Why Thursday? Why not now? I could use some backup.

And just as I was about to stumble back up the street in my heels, I saw the car. Showtime. I stopped short and looked around. Funny how no one noticed, no one cared. It was just the massed assemblage in my head, all catcalls and advice, who were paying attention. I tried to tune it down to a low buzz as I prevented myself from going to the car. Let him come to you. Act as though you just arrived. Slowly. Fuck, who taught me this shit, I wondered? And why has it been of so little assistance? A retro punk rocker pushed past me, all piercings and Mohawk. If you don't you're called insane. Easy to say.

Dave had exited the car and caught sight of me once the green spike of hair had gone past, and smiled as he strolled up. Christ alive, was he taking even more time with his walk than usual? It was a peacock pigeon mating strut. I half expected him to turn around and fluff out his feathers. And of course, I had to wait and watch. I smiled, hoping it looked genuine. Laughing at the strutting peacock was never a good survival strategy. I breathed in and tried to feel super feminine. Needy. Dangerous. Seductive.

"Dave! So good to see you on this side." We stopped for the usual French air kisses. His seemed to be landing dangerously close to my mouth. Possession, already. I tried to swallow down the sudden bile in my throat. This wasn't me. This was me. Act as if.

"Lily. You look lovely. That's a beautiful dress." He ran a slow finger down my neck towards the deep neckline and stopped. I shuddered, but it wasn't with desire. His eyes flashed slightly anyway. "You clean up so well." He took my hand and raised it to his lips. His eyes spoke a question that he had already answered. I tried to look blank. It had worked for Garbo. Let him project. I forced out a tense smile, and hoped he read my nervous swallow as desire. He took my arm. "Come my dear. Let's go have a lovely dinner and talk about our future plans."

He opened the door to the restaurant and as usual, was greeted by the maître d' like a long-lost friend. I nodded and smiled some more, watched myself being appraised, watched Dave slip him some bills as he took our coats, watched us being watched as we paraded to our table, felt Dave's arm slink about my shoulders, protectively, possessively, in full view of the other diners, who were memorizing our posture in our chairs at one of the best tables. Predictable, choreographed, exciting—except I felt hollow, like some kind of defective Christmas cracker—and I wished I could feel I warranted the jealousy and curiosity that was hanging in the air. I looked up to see a blonde with superb highlights purse her lips and turn back to her companion with a shrug. Whatever. I faced Dave again, and tried to gaze at him, winningly. He glanced at me as if to say, see? See all the good things that come from being with me? And then he gestured towards the waiter and ordered a bottle of wine, in Greek. Show off. I forgot to even consider that I knew enough Greek to know what he was saying. But it would have been obvious anyway. The waiter bowed and scraped, and Dave twisted slightly in each direction, just long enough to weigh up who was on either side, and let them know that he was there.

We sat there for a few minutes, like any other awkward date couple, and talked about the weather, the news, another band that the magazine was running a story on. Tits from Oz came up—apparently there had been a big fight after the gig, and now she was staying with some producer, who had punched one of the guys in the band who tried to interrupt his tale of how to make her a star. I laughed. It was bound to happen. She would be easily convinced of her own star potential and follow anyone who promised to make it come alive. I felt bad for the other guys, briefly, imagining them back on their Qantas flight, their big break broken, and a lot of nights gigging to drunks ahead of them, no tits in sight. My effort was running as a kind of last interview could-you-see-it-coming type of piece. A by-line. That was good, although I felt superstitiously reluctant to let my name get linked up with their failure. Then the wine came, and their tragedy evaporated as the bottle was uncorked and delicately poured, artfully swirled, apportioned to me for my pleasure. Dave winked at me over the rim of the glass as we toasted to our future. In business, in business, I murmured in my head.

I breathed in the scent of the wine, being sure to tip my head forward, letting my hair brush my cheek, the curve of my back revealing cleavage. I heard him breathe in. A dance, that's all it was, a dance. First one way, then the other. A formula. And for all my seeming expertise, I was really such a novice at this. I liked to go on feelings. Most people relied on the ritual, relieved there were steps to follow. Ideally, I supposed, it was a bit of both. And luck. So I listened and responded. And drank. One

thing I couldn't argue with was the quality of the wine. Fuck, it
was hard to have high rent tastes on a spiritual budget. It was
a lovely golden ruby color, dark and warm all at once—and it
tasted that way too. The waiter came and poured more, which
reminded me I needed to slow down. It was only fun for men to
get women drunk if they saw it as a challenge, not if they were
racing after them breathlessly to catch up, glass still full.

Dave, on the other hand, was puffed up like a winner. He
beckoned to the waiter, pointed expansively at dishes, asking for
slight variations. When the plates came, he tasted the herbs and
oil on the organic feta shipped in that morning from Greece, ap-
plauding the choices of the chef. I tasted everything and nothing. It was easy to admire his knowledge, his command of the
situation, his willingness to display his sensual enjoyment of
the food. I tried, anyway. Could I do this, for the rest of my life?
Nibbling at tiny plates, discussing which bands we would make
and break, or that he would, returning home to have artistically
mechanical sex on fancy sheets, worrying about my thighs with
my friends at Soulcycle the next day?

Sure I could. Yes, I'd seen it break my grandmother, but it was
hard to know whether she would have wound up the same if she
hadn't hooked on to my grandfather. Canny. Clever. His needs
paramount. Play the game or be insane. By the time we were on
Greek brandy and coffee, I had erased all my doubts—along with
my credit card balance. I would still write, of course. Of course.

Then I noticed his hand on my arm. How long had it been
there? I'd answered mechanically, yet attractively to everything,
I was certain of it. Hadn't I been playing nicely? But he was now
staring at me with an unwelcome intensity. This was it then, was
it? Yes, there was his expensively shaved upper lip, starting to

move. I waited, with an audience-like expectation of a show to come. My role in it was already blotted out by the brandy, of which I took yet another sip. Slowly. Slowly. I looked over at him, and put on my best blank smile of appreciation. I was a little more drunk than I needed to be. Damn.

He raised his glass to me. "Lily, I'm proud of you." His hand caressed mine, in what was supposed to be a soothing way. Instead, it felt like I was being pinned down. Manicured flesh.

I took another taste of the brandy, and found myself holding on to the glass tightly. "Are you? Why? The article? I think it turned out very well, really."

He smiled at me, indulgently. "No, my dear. Because you succumbed to the appeal of the mass market, but then you came to your senses." He picked up my hand and kissed it. I wanted to look to my right, I was sure that we were being watched. Dave continued. "You're thinking about your happiness long term. Now, of course, you can play whatever game you want. But in your forties? Fifties? Look at Courtney Love. So much work. So little time. And for what?" He sat back and folded his hands together. I felt like I was being lectured. "Women need protecting." I raised my glass to protest. "No, Lily, it's not a bad thing. Not at all. You're talented. Independent. All those qualities should be nurtured, not extinguished."

I nodded. Dutifully. The horrible thing was that on some level, I agreed with him. It was like sitting on one of those oceanside marinas in the TV shows from the 80s where the boat pulls the piers away. It was all tumbling down around me. Stupid.

I started to say something, but he raised his hand for silence, and I felt my lips pinch together. Fine. I didn't really know what I was going to say anyway. His hand was on mine again. "Lily, I want to look after you. I know how independent you are. I like that. Yet, perhaps there are limits to freedom, right?" He paused, and his face took on a serious air. "I have a proposal for you. I own a beautiful place I don't use. I want you to see it." He looked proud. "Let's take our time. You can stay there—you don't have to move in with me. Not yet, anyway."

Now it was my turn to be astonished. "You...you want me to live with you? Go out with you?" I grimaced. Even to my ears that sounded lame. "I mean, us, together? Seriously?"

He gave that low chuckle that he had, and pointed to our glasses and nodded to the waiter, who seemed to arrive instantly with the bottle. I started to say something, and he tilted his head towards the waiter, indicating that I should wait until he had left us. I couldn't see how anything we were saying wasn't going to be public knowledge anyway, seeing as our table was close enough to be eavesdropped upon by at least half a dozen tables, but I waited.

The waiter left, and I started up again. "Dave..."

He interrupted. "I don't know why you're surprised. We talked about this before." He held my hand in his. "You came to me for help in London. You wanted to leave. I'm the one you asked for help."

It was true. But... "You had sent me there. I felt you were the best person to talk to."

"And I was. I am. Lily, listen. I've cared about you for a while now. You're such a diamond in the rough. I am the perfect person to polish you, show off your highlights. Look at Tristan. What did he do? Use you. He saw what you had, and he was willing to go back to that D list actress despite it all." I listened, unable to speak. It was like a train crash, everything happening in slow motion. "And, let's be honest, you're not a teenager, Lily. I can't really see you as a hanger-on. You're an elegant, intelligent woman. And you deserve better."

"It wasn't like that...," I began, but I trailed off. What was it like? Nothing I could discuss with him. Maybe I'd better buy time, a voice in my head muttered. Yes. "What about the piece? If I say no, or maybe, or not yet, then what happens?"

He looked at me, crestfallen. "Is that the only thing I have that is worth anything to you?"

I realized that I'd actually hurt him. Kicked the preening pigeon. Made my own desires a little too clear. Idiot. "No, no. No. Of course not." I shook my head. I would have to touch him. It couldn't be that bad. He looked very clean. I stared at his hand. All the hairs on it were in a row, as though they had been combed. I could smell the slightest tang of citrus and wood cologne. There was nothing not to like. But I couldn't get my hand to rest on top of his. It felt like the air was thicker near him, a force field. "Dave. You're a very attractive, successful man. I would have thought you would want to be sure I was choosing you for you. You as a person. A mentor." Ok, maybe that was a bit thick. No, he looked completely mesmerized again. "I don't want you to think that I've..." Sold out? Given up? "...done, decided this to get a piece on the cover." Or anywhere, I thought. Fuck.

His smile was slow, and victorious. "Naturally not. That's why I wanted to enumerate all the, let's call them qualities, I think you find attractive. That answer your...needs. Aside from the writing job." He bent closer, and his voice dropped to a whisper. "It's only made you more interesting, you know, this whole thing with Tristan. If you could please him..." He moved slightly in his chair. "I know you. I know you'll be good, we'll be good." His voice was so low, I could barely make out the words, whispered across the table. "Let's go look at the apartment. You don't have to stay, or say yes right away. But come. Come with me. It's beautiful, like you." He stared at me, as though willing me to do what he asked. It was all possible. All I had to do was reach out my hand.

He was leaning in closer now, drawing me in, but the candle flickered and blew out as a gust of wind from the open door blew through the restaurant. A waiter rushed over to relight it, and I took the chance to lean back, and retreat slightly. I looked over towards the door. A group of people had come in, but through them, one person had pushed through and was heading our way. A few people nudged each other. All I could do was stare. Leather jacket over tight black jeans and a multi-colored shirt that practically shouted "look at me" followed by "don't try this at home." His hair was its usual artful mess and he was smiling at me, having spotted us. Dave looked at me, then turned his head in the same direction just in time for Tristan to slap him on the shoulder and slide into the seat next to his.

"Dave! Lily. What a pleasure. Your secretary told me I'd find you here. Brandy? Great idea." He turned to the waiter who seemed to be either hovering or invisible. "Same, please. And a coffee. Medium sweet." His eyes raked over me, exploratory. He seemed to make his mind up. "Greek food really is one of your things, isn't it? That restaurant in London was just fantastic. We have to go back."

Dave, jolted out of his pre-coital striking position, was taking some time to adjust to the new situation. Tristan was sitting back, one leg crossed over the other, having shrugged off his jacket to reveal the rest of his shirt, sleeves rolled up, his wrists crisscrossed with bracelets. The waiter looked delighted when Tristan twisted around to help him with the coffee and told him to pour himself a brandy. "Night's almost over, right? You can relax a little. Everyone gets a chance to chill out eventually, right, Dave?"

I wondered if they were going to come to blows. Dave looked rigid in his seat, ready to kill, while Tristan was all expansion and energy. One cold, one fire. Tristan raised the glass to his lips. "Chin chin." His throat muscles moved under his skin, and I found I was staring at him, as he lowered the glass and ran his tongue over his lips for a second, his eyes burning into me. The warmth that flooded between my legs was as instantaneous as it was surprising, and I looked down, almost expecting it to be obvious, as I moved my legs together slightly. Tristan was smiling at me, like he knew a secret. Dave was even angrier. He tapped the table and Tristan and I both looked at him.

"Lily and I were just discussing her future."

Tristan's body was instantly a little more taut. I felt sick. "Were you? And is it as bright as it should be?" He winked at me. I tried to smile back.

"I've got a nice apartment she can use. I'll be getting it ready while she's on tour with you." His hands rested on the table, as though he'd just put down the pen on the contract.

Tristan considered this for a moment. "Well, that's quite an offer." He studied me. "Lily, have you seen your gilded cage yet?"

I gritted my teeth. "No, I haven't. And it's an offer, not an acceptance."

Dave laughed. "Really, Lily? I thought we were about to...seal the agreement, as it were, just before Tristan dropped by to say hello. I enjoy this business so much..." he said, a slight metallic tang to his words, "...the stars come to me."

Tristan bristled. "Yes they do. Because you need something to write about. Lovely suit, by the way. Dior? You must really want to impress Lily here."

"Obviously," he said slowly, looking at Tristan's clothes, "not your style. But she's worth impressing, naturally we agree."

"No, I prefer Dolce. But impressing Lily? Of course. Maybe we just differ on what to do to get her attention." He glanced at me, as if for confirmation, and continued. "But you don't want to force the issue, I don't think she likes it."

Dave shot back. "Meaning?"

Tristan leaned back and drank some coffee, placing the cup carefully back in the saucer and turning the handle to four o'clock. His fingers tapped on the china for a moment. "I didn't blackmail her."

"No, having sex with your ex was appeal enough, apparently." Dave looked grim.

Tristan's fist was clenched on the table. "Nothing happened."

"Really? Well whatever Lily here saw, it was enough to make her mind up."

Tristan looked at me. "Did it? And have you decided in favor of the tasteful condo?" He was suddenly silent. Contempt was written all over his face. Dave looked smug and distant.

At that moment, I hated both of them. I bit back what I was about to say. I raised my head to look at them. They were both waiting, waiting for an answer, both anticipating success. I started to speak, and stopped. No, I thought. Time. Take your time. Whose life is this that they're discussing? I drank the rest of my brandy down and rose to my feet, unsteadily. "Yes, I've decided."

They both looked up at me, the same uncertainty written across both their faces. I almost laughed. I waved for the waiter to bring my coat. Then I looked at back at them. "Yeah. I've decided. To leave. Fuck both of you."

Tristan looked at me sharply. "Haven't you already done that?"

The blood rushed to my face. And the words tumbled out before I could stop them. "No, I fucking haven't. And you know it. Or you should." I pushed my chair in and looked around. People turned away.

I steered myself through the tables, and out the door into the cool night air. I just kept moving, one foot in front of the other, furious. I'd nearly gotten to Second and A, before I looked around me. Jesus fucking Christ. What had I just done?

I heard footsteps and someone calling my name. I couldn't tell who it was over the traffic and I didn't turn around. Instead, I ran all the way up to Houston where a couple was getting out of a cab. I leapt in and slammed the door.

"Where to, sister?"

"Uptown. No. Rivington Street. No. Shit." My voice was starting to crack. "I'm sorry. Can you just go around the block, a couple of blocks actually, please, thanks?" He put his foot down on the accelerator about the same time that I felt the first bursting sob break out of my throat.

Chapter 33

We drove around a little, circled Tompkins Square Park, while I sat in the dark and tried to get myself under control. Every so often, the cabbie would look in his rear view mirror and say, "all right girlie?" in the kind of accent I thought didn't exist anymore. The last time I'd taken a cab, late at night, drunk, I managed to snap out of my delirious state long enough to be surprised that the driver was a Muslim woman wearing a head scarf. She literally rolled her eyes when she asked me how much change I wanted back and I burbled out, I don't know. She looked a bit disgusted. I felt bad. She was probably a math professor, doing this because she had to, and some drunken fool couldn't even add up a tip.

But this guy, with his growly voice and sad brown eyes, reminded me of a cab driver from a movie. Which one? Which one? I couldn't believe I was thinking about it. My life was in shreds, and I was trying to work out which fictional character he reminded me of. I laughed, a little too loudly. He looked back at me, startled.

"Look, lady, I could drive you around all night and use up your money, but it's the end of my shift and I need a beer. You should go home. Or," he hesitated, "can I buy you a beer?" He tried to meet my eyes as often as he could in the mirror. "No funny business, I promise. Look, I know a decent bar right near here. One beer. Then you can get someone else to drive you around, ok?"

I was torn. Don't go out with strangers. Especially not ones who have been watching you cry in their cracked vinyl backseat. But all the alarm bells going off were irrational, and a bit late, I thought. Where were you when I was busy storming out of the restaurant and ruining my life? Ringing off the wall, but I had been too intent on destruction to listen. I opened the window all the way and let in some cool night air. The light changed. Deadlines. 3, 2, 1, green. I forced myself to speak, stabbing at the switch to close the window at the same time. "Ok. Yeah. Why not? Near here?"

"Yeah, right near here. One of the last decent places left." He drove more energetically now, and pulled into a loading zone that had passed its hours of limit. "Nice. Come on."

I got out, a little unsteady. I looked around, nervously. We were still in the neighborhood of my outburst. I scanned the street. No vivid shirts. No dark cars. No one I knew. Good.

The driver looked at me oddly, as he locked the doors. "Are you on the run from somebody? Did someone hurt you?"

I glanced at him. I wasn't sure I was in the mood for sharing. "Yeah, well, sort of. And no, I'm fine. I just don't want to see... someone."

"Ok, that's your deal. No fights though, right? I just want a drink. And you look like you could use one." He laughed. "Or another one, maybe, huh?" He seemed to find this very funny, and we walked along the street, with him laughing to himself. I tried to surreptitiously wipe away the tears and smudged makeup from my eyes, I hoped I didn't look too bad. It was one thing to curl up in on yourself in the back of a car, another to go out on the street with pain and suffering etched all over you. Loser, sad case drunk. No.

He held the door open for me, and we went into the long darkened room, simple and straightforward. Some stools. Some red sofas towards the back. The centerpiece—a big old fashioned wooden bar facing the oversized clear glass windows. They were unexpectedly clean. The bartender looked up when we came in, and finished what he was doing and came over. The two shook hands across the bar. "Frank my man. What's new? The usual? And who's this?"

"Steve, this is my new friend. I'm buying her a drink. What do you want, sweetheart?"

I hesitated. "What are you having?"

Steve answered for him. "A Brooklyn, and a shot of Jack. Right, Frank?"

"You know it."

Frank looked at me. "Anything you want. Glass of wine?"

I shook my head. "No, same for me if that's ok. Thanks. Really."

Steve adjusted the plastic strap on his trucker hat meaningfully—some garish white and yellow thing proclaiming 24/7 happiness in New Jersey—and went over to grab glasses for the beer. I hoisted myself up on one of the stools, took off my jacket and scrunched it up on my lap, not really wanting to talk. At least I didn't have to pretend anything. Whether they liked me or not, it didn't matter. I breathed a sigh of relief, and mumbled "fuck it all anyway."

The beers arrived and I was about to pick up my glass, when the cab driver stopped me. "Hey. You gotta do things right. First, the shot. And before that first, first I don't drink with people I haven't been properly introduced to yet. I'm Frank." He stuck out his hand. I grabbed it, and shook it. Not sweaty, not polished. Just a hand. Good.

"I'm Lily. Pleased to meet you."

"Likewise. Now isn't this better than driving around?" We raised our shot glasses and cheered. I chucked the burning stuff down my throat and put the glass down, grabbing for the beer. His eyes widened a little. "Huh, done that before, yeah? I guess you needed one."

I didn't say anything. We sat there for a while, not speaking, listening to the weird mix of music on Steve's iPod. He came over finally and stood in front of us. "You two are sure quiet. You want another beer? On the house. It's late. Frank here, I'm sure the bar owes him a beer. And you're here with him."

I laughed. "Yeah, sure. Why not? Thanks, thanks a lot. I mean it."

Frank looked more relaxed when he heard me speak. "Yeah Steve. You owe me one. That's right. You got that right, for once." They both laughed, a kind of matching ridiculous half snort that made me laugh. "What's so funny Lily? You cheering up now?"

We clinked glasses again. "Yeah, I guess."

He put down his glass after a long slug of beer and frowned at me. "So what happened, Lily? Was he chasing you? Did you turn him down? Prick. I'm sure he deserved it."

I swallowed another gulp of beer. God this felt so normal. Yes. Fuck them. "Yeah, they were both acting like jerks."

"Both of them?" Frank put down his beer abruptly on the

wooden bar. "I can't fight off two of them, girlie, and Steve here, well, Steve, he doesn't fight anymore. You get my drift? Are they both after you? Do you owe them anything...?" Steve gave him a look that cut him off. His tone was light, but there was a slight worried look in his eye, like he hadn't been expecting to hear complications. And didn't want to, either. He had played Good Samaritan up to a point. And this was the point.

"No, no. Don't worry," I said, expansively. "One's my boss. He just wants to run my life. And sleep with me. The other one, well..." I trailed off. My throat had closed up again.

"Oh, now I get it. The other one, huh? You love him? Is he good looking? No, don't answer that.' Steve had come over now, and was resting his elbows on the bar, listening. "They're all good looking, aren't they? You've seen a couple of fights in here over the ladies, haven't you Steven?"

The bartender groaned affirmatively. "Oh yeah. Oh yeah. I keep out of it. I pour. I don't pour. That's it."

Frank was warming to his subject. "Remember the time those two guys started slapping each other, and then the girl threw down and punched one of them in the face? Shit that was funny."

"You didn't have to clear it up," said Steve, mournfully. "Idiots. I don't want 'em in here."

Frank turned to me. "You sure no one is chasing you?"

They'd probably never be chasing me again. Wasn't I at the age I'd been warned about? I suddenly realized they were both staring at me, waiting for an answer. "No." They didn't look convinced, so I repeated myself, a little more loudly. "No. No. Really. I think I blew it. No job either. Turned down the boss. And the boyfriend. Who wasn't a boyfriend. I know. I know. I thought I loved him..." I stopped. I didn't want to say it out loud. It sounded too true, too dangerous. I was just drunk enough to start talking. And not stop. Or texting. Texting. That was an idea. Trevor. Yes. No.

Frank cleared his throat. "Well, at least you're not crying. Anymore." He glanced up at Steve. "She was upset, Steve. In the cab."

He rolled his eyes. I thought I saw him mouth "sucker" in Frank's direction. Damn. Was this going to be one more someone else who wanted something else from me? They're just being nice. Play nice. I tried to smile. "No, I'm ok. Now. It's fine. Really. The beer's great. I like this place. I just need to think, that's all. I'm sorry I'm not very good company."

"Sweetheart, when you look the way you do, talk is optional. You're decorating the place just sitting there. Here." He turned his back on us, and took down the bottle of Jack. "Come on, the good stuff. On me. One for each of us. Life's hard enough."

He poured, and I tried out a small smile, quickly wiping away another tear. Drunk, sentimental fool. They just want something in their lives, a bit of fun. Can't I even do that? Sit here and drink their liquor. Make some small talk. So generous. I thanked them both, and tried to think of something to say. But I had nothing. There was nothing. Everything I'd thought I was, I wasn't. Anymore.

So I turned towards the window and looked out at the street while they discussed the basketball season and the upcoming games while Steve, the bartender, went off every so often to serve the few remaining customers. I drifted away a bit, letting the rhythm of their sentences stuffed with unfamiliar names wash over me as I watched the people on the street walking by. It was a constantly changing view, still moving, but we were heading down the slope to where being out late became another cold, empty night turning into another grey morning. I was past being upset. I wasn't even angry anymore. They—Dave and Tristan— they hadn't done anything out of character. I'd just wanted my freedom. And fucking piece of luck, I had it. So I sat there and watched more people go by. Hell, it was a Tuesday. Didn't these people have jobs? So what was I doing there? I didn't have a job anymore. Perfect. Or I'd be demoted. And then I'd leave on my own. That's probably what would happen.

Frank said something and I nodded. What? Yes, I'd go home soon. No, not yet. Yes, he could call me a cab. But not yet. Not yet. I kept repeating it, as if it meant something. It was all kicking in now, the stress, the tears, the various forms of alcohol. Dave wasn't wrong; I did need someone to look after me. But they wouldn't. Not without conditions, conditions that I seemed to be unable to accept. So I would go it alone. For as long as I could.

The iPod switched songs, like it'd been doing the whole time, but I hadn't been listening. But this one made me notice. I tried to tune out all the other noise in the bar, staring half-focused at my beer glass clutched in my hand. This song was going right through me. Who was it? Bowie. I knew it, of course I did, one of those classics in your blood. But my brain wasn't working. "And she's hooked to the silver screen…" The line kept repeating itself over the others in my

head. That song. All the operatic suffering. I was in an opera, and this was the soundtrack. And I had been told to go, and I had seen it before. Now which stock role was I playing? The foolish girl who couldn't make up my mind? Or the tormented lover who wanted it all, or nothing? I shut my eyes to stop the prickling. No more tears. I couldn't cry anymore. Fuck it all, I loved him. I did love him. I wanted to understand, and I couldn't, couldn't even figure out why I wanted it to make sense or if it should. My head started to spin again when Bowie's voice cut through the haze, and the keyboards spiraled downwards. I quickly put down my glass and grabbed the edge of the bar to keep myself upright on the stool.

I loved him. It was all crazy. I was crazy. I shut my eyes tightly and wished, just wished I could explain it really, and Tristan would know, would understand. Maybe he really would listen to me. I could text him. We could meet up. Even as I thought it, I knew it was one of those moments you get when you're drunk, one of those great ideas that keep you running, but that crumble like your smudged soul the next morning. But maybe...maybe this time it would remain intact. I opened my eyes very slowly, and continued watching the street; all these people had their own problems and lives. We weren't alone. Right? There was some kind of reason to all of it.

I watched people go past, pairs and groups and loners, without really paying attention. Every so often one group was so loud you could hear them through the window. But it was a mostly muted show, black and blue and red and green, the lights changing with indifferent repetition. A very tall, dark haired man in a leather jacket caught my eye, as he stood at the corner, waiting for the light to cross the avenue. I stared at him through the window, and he turned, the way people do when they feel someone looking at them, and glanced in my direction. It took him the same amount of time as it did for me to understand who we were watching. And with the recognition, he walked very slowly, across the street and up to the window and simply stared at me through the glass. Neither one of us moved. His face was half in shadow and half lit by the orange haze of the street light. His eyes had their own energy, and they were burning into me. Everything I'd feared was there. I was mesmerized by his stare. Everything else fell away. But then he shook his head, a bit of dark hair falling across his eyes, and he began to move away.

All the blood drained from my face. He was leaving. He couldn't go. I threw myself off the stool, and stumbled towards the door as fast as I could but he was faster. And when I got to the door, he had vanished. I wrenched open the door, ready to run, but I tripped on the short step to the pavement, and landed on the sidewalk, my hands and knees on the concrete, stinging. I cried out his name, no longer caring, sure that I'd lost him and my one chance to make it right.

Then a shadow fell across my hands spread out on the pavement. I looked up, and there he was, in front of me, a half-smile on his full mouth, but a serious expression in his eyes. I looked up at him, and he looked down at me for a moment, before he stretched out his hand to me and I took it. He pulled me up. Then he walked me backwards into the bar with one hand under my arm holding me up and the other flat against my shoulder. We went right into the middle of the room, and Tristan dropped his hands, so he was no longer touching me, but blocking my exit. He looked even taller than usual. I half expected him to give me an order. But his face was cold, observing me. Maybe he thought I had been running away. The two of us were standing there, face to face, silent. I wanted him to touch me. Smile at me and tell me it was all right. But I couldn't move or speak before his vast silence.

His voice, when it came, was the same pleasing rumble. But he wasn't talking to me. "Hello Steve. How are you?"

"Tristan, my man. Long time no see. How goes it? A drink?" Both of them were acting perfectly normal. I was sure my knee was still bleeding from the fall. Had they not noticed what had just happened? Or that we were still facing off, inches apart?

Tristan said nothing else. And I was still staring at him. He looked like he was thinking. I couldn't think. He was beautiful. And then he did it. He closed the distance between us with a swift motion, and put his arms around me and held me tightly to him.

"Yeah, Steve, a beer. In a minute. Have some business here with…"

Frank interrupted him. "With our Lily? You know her?" Then to me—"This is him?" He turned to Steve. "That's him." He stood up and tapped Tristan on the shoulder. Tristan turned his head slightly, still holding me. Frank's words came out in a jumble, a kind of drunken threat. "I'm looking after her. I found her and I'm the one who brought her here." Frank stopped and looked him up and down, looked at his arms still around me. He continued, a little softer. "She was crying, buddy, you know, in my cab. Lucky it was me. Treat her right, or you're gonna lose her. And just so you know, I think she loves you, not the other guy. Just so you know. Sorry, Lily, but somebody had to tell him."

Tristan removed one of his arms from behind my back and reached over and shook Frank's hand in one of those dude clutching handshakes. "I understand, my friend. Thank you for looking after her." He turned back to me and whispered in my hair. "She's a bit feisty, this one."

I wanted to laugh, but I could barely breathe. The music

started up again. Perfect. What was it with Steve and the love songs? A romantic under the trucker hat.

Tristan was talking into my hair again. "You scared me, Lily. But I was proud of you. You did the right thing, you know. I was an idiot. I'm sorry."

"Me too." I mumbled into his chest.

"I thought you wanted him. That life. What you'd worked for."

"No."

Tristan hugged me tighter. "You're not what I expected, you know?"

"No."

"You find it hard to trust anyone."

"Yes...no..."

He interrupted me. "Do you trust me?"

I was silent.

Tristan stopped and put a hand on each one of my shoulders, and moved back, an arm's length away, intent. "I'm going to ask again. Do you trust me?"

I let out a long sigh. It was the sort of question there was only a one word answer for. "Yes."

Then he moved us, his arm circling swiftly around me, away from everyone. He made me look at him, my face in his hands as he sat us down on the window ledge. His voice was a low murmur. "Then if I tell you something important, you'll believe me?"

I just looked at him. I felt like I was falling into his eyes, as though there was a long tunnel. And through him, there was the rest of the universe. The silent part, where explanation was unnecessary, where everything did make sense, where it was all wordless, the way it was meant to be. Then his mouth was on mine, and his lips were soft and his nose pressed into my cheek, and all I knew was the taste and feel of him.

I sensed, rather than heard him, say "I need you" in me, against my mouth. Then he said it again, a little louder, and I felt his voice rumble through me. He pulled away from me, and gave me another one of his searching looks. "I think we belong together, not apart. Ok?"

And all the desire that I'd been trying to hide, all the need and pain I'd been trying to fight against was right there. I touched my lips to his and he was kissing me. He clasped me tighter to him, and I knew he could feel it, that maybe it had been the same for him, that he'd been fighting the same things in the same way.

He cradled his long arms around me and I could feel his hands, each fingertip insistent against my skin. I rested my head on his shoulder. Tristan started talking to me, quietly, so only I could hear him. "I want to do all the stupid things, you know? Except they won't be stupid. They'll be the way they're supposed to be." He sat up a little and choosing carefully, unclasped one of the chains around his neck. Moving my hair to one side, he placed it around my neck and reclosed the clasp. He placed a small kiss on the chain and my neck and moved my hair back in place. I started to speak, but he quickly placed one of his long fingers softly against my lips and shook his head. "Not everything needs to be said, love." He smiled. "Look at me, really look at me. Is it what you want? Do you believe me?"

I looked at him, his deep eyes holding me. And I did. Want him, more than I could admit, trust him, more than I'd ever let myself before. For once, there was no second guessing. There was just him, and his dark eyes, and his severe look, his sweet smell, and his happy smile and the feeling that it was right, that it was all meant to be. I came closer to him, practically sitting in his lap, and for an answer, kissed his mouth, very softly, and rested my head against his chest. I was suddenly exhausted. But it didn't matter. He was there, and he had found me.

Epilogue

Was I actually going to do this? Go on tour? Go public with Tristan?

Tristan had smoothed out my little outburst in the restaurant. He also handled the ego slap I'd delivered to Dave when he realized that I'd chosen Tristan over him. It had taken some delicate negotiations, which included a photographer coming along on tour, an opening slot on a couple of dates for the newly solo singer from what I would always think of as "Tits from Oz," and an exclusive download, but in the end they had both gotten what they wanted. Which for Tristan, even though I could scarcely believe it, was me, on tour, with him, and writing the article, job intact.

What had Tristan said to me? Something like, "don't ever believe the people who said they never did anything for money or power or position, when they are in positions with money and power." He had laughed at the interview I had read to him where a famous artist had claimed she had never given an inch and had remained true to her art. "Yes—she's right about that, trying to stay true to your vision of art," he had said, arm around me as we were tucked up in bed, me reading the papers online, as he was going through a new paperback biography of Beethoven. "But the rest of the sanctimonious shit. 'I was never tempted, I'm not interested in money, only what's right.' Yeah, right. Everyone's tempted. That's the whole point. And she made her name doing what was the wrong thing. Simplistic crap. She's not sleeping on a park bench now, is she?"

It was a Sunday morning, early. He had climbed out of bed after saying that, and his long torso pale, muscular, smooth, curving down to his strong legs, was still a shocking nakedness that made my mind go blank. But then he threw on a robe, and came over to give me a kiss. "I'm going to make some of that matcha green tea we bought the other day," he said, "do you want some?" And he added, as he went towards the kitchen, "we live in a world of negotiation. You just have to remember what you really wanted in the first place." He smiled, his serious face suddenly lit up with amusement. "That's how I got you."

And that was how I had gotten here. About to go on a very public tour, trying to mix work and pleasure, and on the verge of giving up all my privacy, to spend six weeks on a bus. With him. Wouldn't that kill it all? Could I stand that much scrutiny? All my personality flaws now on tour! And if I were honest with myself, I was scared. Scared of what came next. Tristan had told me he wanted me to come live with him after the tour. "Well, during the tour we will be living together. Although you will have your very own bunk. So why not? Come on, Lily. Stop fighting me. I want you."

Yes, but. Could I do it? The things I wanted the most scared me the most. That was the problem, always had been. And here was the universe, conspiring to give me what I wanted. But a bunk? On a bus? Moving in with him? Having to be scrutinized by the band? The wanna-be groupies? The other journalists? Suppose he decided to go off and do coke again on some girl's warm and willing freshly waxed thighs, and there I'd be. No Dave to call. No, that safety net was very done. Alice didn't really care, never had. Sarah—but London was a long way to run, to hide in the attic guest room. Running away. It had been my favorite pastime. But it really wasn't an option anymore.

Then I remembered the vulnerability in his face. The traces of all the doubts, all the struggles. The mistakes. And I wanted tell him it was ok. Tell him that I'd fucked up too. That not everyone sucked, was mean and thoughtless and selfish and grasping. Maybe we could be each other's reason to carry on.

And this...feeling. It was more than that. It was like a knowing, one that I couldn't explain, and couldn't tell anyone about, and couldn't even understand myself. It wasn't want, and it wasn't desire. That would be like saying I wanted blood in my body. It was like we had connected, somewhere, and it couldn't be broken. It existed in a place beyond all that.

I dialed Trevor, wanting a bit of reassurance. And hung up before he answered. What the hell was I doing? This was between Tristan and me. No one else. When the phone buzzed, I dropped it in shock. I picked it up gingerly, as though it were about to go off, and looked at the text.

> Why are both of you calling me and hanging up?
> Call each other. Shouldn't you be on tour by now?

Trevor. Of course. So why was Tristan calling him?

A moment later, the phone buzzed again.

Meet me. Don't say no. The usual place. 20
minutes. I'm getting in the car now.

I got up very slowly, and looked at myself in the mirror. Whoever came back to this room, would never be the same. I'd linked myself to the future, and now it was here. I ran my hands through my hair, and calmly sprayed myself with perfume. The suitcase was packed and waiting by the front door. It was though I'd already left; I was already standing on that curb, I'd done it a million times before, and here it had come around again, and I knew every step on the way.

The air outside was cold, but I barely felt anything. I patted myself to check I was actually dressed, and wearing my jacket. One foot in front of the other. And then there I was. On the same windy corner, watching the taxis go by, listening to the branches sweep past each other and tangle and separate. The lights changed and changed back. I stood there. People walked past, words floated towards me and off again. More cars went past. Buses. Strollers. People hurrying by. And I leaned on the lamppost, as though to anchor myself to something. And then the car pulled up, slowly, like always. And stopped. And the door swung open.

And I stood there, still and cold next to the street light. Waiting.

A leather covered leg emerged from the car, followed slowly by the other, as his boots met together on the pavement. Then his long body emerged, a pale hand on the door to support himself as he rose out of the darkness of the interior. And there he was, towering over me, his smile slightly amused, his eyes shining.

"So we're going to do this out here, are we?" he whispered, his arms already beginning to circle me.

I couldn't help smiling. "Yeah, I guess so," I murmured, letting him draw me against his chest, listening to his breathing, wrapped in the smell of his skin.

"Are you sure?" he said into my hair. "I'm a pain in the ass."

"That's why we get on."

"We do though, don't we?" He lifted my face up to look at him. Again, that strange feeling came over me when I met his eyes. "Oh, yes, we do. That's…"

"Don't talk."

And he brought his lips to mine. And they were soft and smooth, and hot and suddenly we were kissing in the middle of the street, his tongue against mine, his arms clutching me to him furiously. His body was hard and a shiver went through me, and he held me tighter. He whispered into my mouth "I need you, now, I'm sick with waiting. Say yes. Please fucking say you'll have me."

I was about to answer, when we were both startled by the flash of a camera. He turned towards it, a protective arm around me. It was two teenage girls with a cell phone. I looked up at him, but he was smiling.

One of the girls burst out. "Tristan! I knew it was you! See, Sophie." She gave her friend a look. "We love you! Will you sign us?" She pulled out a Sharpie pen and pulled down the neckline of her shirt, exposing a bit of flimsy blue lace and a curve of fresh white skin. Tristan looked at me and shrugged. I laughed.

The irony of it all wasn't lost on either of us. Without losing his grip on me, he took the pen and signed a quick flourish across the flush of her breast, dipping low enough to make her squeal, while her friend took pictures. Then he signed the friend's cd cover, and waved to the few people who had stopped to watch, before kissing me again. A few more flashes went off.

He leaned down and spoke quietly. "I've staked my claim, Lily. I hope you're ready to be staken." He laughed.

"That's not English." I protested as he marched me to the car.

"I'll show you all the languages I know. All the tongues." He smirked at he opened the door to the car. The driver was closing the trunk on my suitcase.

"Promises."

"Threats. Now get in."

"Make me," I laughed.

"Oh, I'll do more than that, sweet one. But if you want me to beg first, I will. Listen. I love you, now please let me fuck you senseless. There." And he pulled me into the car, briskly shut the door. He pressed the button for the intercom to the driver. "Drive around the park. Thanks mate." Then to me, "We'll go to the bus later, we're a little early anyway."

I threw my arms around his neck. "Just like old times."

Tristan smiled, his eyes darkening. "Oh no, Lily love. These times are all new. Now show me how much you need me. Then— we go on tour."

ABOUT THE AUTHOR

Alice Severin thought she was on to something when her professor, a noted poet and translator, told her that her writing was "considerably above the average." Sadly, there was no time to pursue it as she became possibly the only person ever asked to leave that school. So she headed to London, where she quickly found like-minded people backstage and behind the scenes in the music business. Ms. Severin has been a delivery driver, a baker, a teacher, a copywriter, and a performance artist, among other things. She even went back to college.

www.ingramcontent.com/pod-product-compliance
Lightning Source LLC
Chambersburg PA
CBHW032142190626
46814CB00005BA/1795